...WITH A WOMAN
WHOSE SCANDALOUS
DEATH STILL
HAUNTED HIM...AND
ALL WHO KNEW HER.

THE
IMPERSONATOR
DIANA HAMMOND

ISLAND BOOKS
Published by
Dell Publishing
a division of
Bantam Doubleday Dell Publishing Group, Inc.
666 Fifth Avenue
New York, New York 10103

This book is a novel of fiction. Names, characters, places, and incidents are either the product of the author's imagination or are used fictitiously. Any resemblance to actual persons, living or dead, events, or locales is entirely coincidental.

ISBN: 0-440-21416-5

Reprinted by arrangement with Doubleday

Printed in the United States of America

Published simultaneously in Canada

April 1993

10 9 8 7 6 5 4 3 2 1

OPM

THE
IMPERSONATOR

At dawn we leave White King,
    its clouds all colored,
For passage to Kiang-ling
    in one sun's circuit:

While both banks' gibbons cry
    calls still unceasing,
Our light boat has gone by
    many fold mountains.

—*Early Departure from White King
City*, Li T'ai Po

PART

1

1

Theo had been more beautiful than Jane, more celebrated than Jane, more desired than Jane. But Theo was dead.

A perhaps overly consecrated kind of dead, Jane couldn't help thinking as she and Robert emerged from the musty room with its dark, official furniture, where they had just been married, only to find a cluster of reporters and photographers waiting for them outside in the finicky light of a Paris afternoon. Not one of the journalists was so brash as to ask her, "How does it feel to be the bride of the man who was once married to one of the most exquisite creatures on earth?"

But the question hung—ever so politely—in the air.

Their interest in Jane, even in Robert, was peripheral. They had come because of Theo, the dead Theo, whose face, whose history, could still sell newspapers. Jane's wedding day was evidently to be rearranged by the press into yet another chapter in the silvery myth of Theo. Jane smiled graciously for the photographers and reviewed with mild dread the tasteless position in which she had been placed.

By the following morning she would have become a figure of idle curiosity to millions. Tried in absentia. Second best. How could a man who had had Theo Buckley for his very own ever hope to scale such heady heights again with a mere mortal? And so on.

Not that Jane Donovan was just anybody. The Donovans had been producing responsible public servants, prosperous eccentrics, philanthropists, and generally upright citizens along the eastern seaboard for almost two hundred years. Coming from a good family no longer meant much, but it did to Jane. It was ground under one's feet. It was continuity. It was backbone. Jane, who had come down on the artistic—thought by some to be flighty—side of the Donovans, was a travel writer whose quirky eye, passion for history, and willingness to take on dubious modes of transportation and unfashionable journeys had begun to bring her recognition for her seriousness and for her flair.

She was exceptionally well proportioned, she had striking off-center good looks, and she had always wanted, more than anything, to be wise. "A Jane Austen girl," her first husband, Tyler, would instantly, if a bit wryly, describe her when asked by *Vanity Fair* on the day after her wedding to Robert what she was like. From which one could only suppose he meant that she was True.

Being married to someone who was True had had its consequences. Nine months after Tyler's own wedding to Jane, they had been at a cocktail party in a rambling West Side penthouse overlooking Central Park and Jane, who had gone in search of a safety pin and a full-length mirror in order to do up a section of hem in her plum-colored silk skirt, which had unaccountably begun to unravel, walked into one of the bedrooms and found Tyler with his trousers down around his ankles, enjoying the passionate ministrations of one of the female guests, a young film executive from Los Angeles to whom they had been introduced only one half-hour earlier.

Jane had stared—with apparent composure—at the unlovely little tableau, and looking Tyler in the eye had quietly remarked, "You idiot."

She had turned and left the room. She had told her hosts she had a headache, and departed in a taxi. When Tyler arrived home some ten minutes later, she had had a large brandy in one hand and her wedding ring in the other. The fact that she was in love with Tyler evidently did not deter a Jane Austen girl from holding to her standards. She had thrown the glass of brandy at his head, the wedding ring in his face, and filed for a divorce.

In the days, months, and years that followed, Jane would from time to time find herself reviewing this decision, generally coinciding with her birthday, Christmas, and almost always when strapped inside an airplane roaring down a runway for takeoff. These little reviews brought with them their fair share of anguish but had not once included a wish to reverse her drastic action on the night of the party. She had only two regrets. The first was that Tyler had not been, after all, a man of character. The second was her secret shame that she could not be more like other people. In a decade abandoned to sexual license (it was 1979 when she divorced Tyler) her fastidious position was noticed.

Jane could neither tolerate infidelity nor inflict it. Could not. What was it that had made her so primly exacting, so uncharitable? She did not know. She only knew that for her, a promise was, simply, something one kept. Her implacability on the subject was, as she was well aware, a handicap with poignant and even comical implications, including the personal and social embarrassment of having to defend what was generally considered obsolete thinking.

At the time of her divorce from Tyler, friends had tried to get her to change her mind. "Tyler is still out of his head in love with you," they said. "If you were really in love with him, you'd put aside your own ego." "Can't you forgive one incredibly stupid moment at a party with someone who meant nothing to him?"

"I can't," Jane had replied over and over, adding privately to herself, "How can I explain what I've never been able to explain to myself? That I can forgive with my intelligence ten times over. But I cannot ever lie down with him again."

It was a choice based neither on religion nor on any criticism of or deficiency in understanding how the rest of the world accommodated its disappointments and nasty surprises. She had as much passion for Anna Karenina and Emma Bovary as anyone else. She envied her women friends for being more pragmatic than herself and was intermittently taken with those bloodless word separators, the English playwrights of the day who constituted a collective sensibility in which faithlessness was brilliance. This dramaturgical tradition was of course far older than any of them, but the Restoration playwrights, for instance, had at least exercised the wit and even the taste (thought Jane, whenever she was arguing with herself) to present The Subject mainly as farce. The current lot, elegantly louche, were up to something else.

Never having committed an infidelity herself, she was forced to accept her lesser status. Perhaps that is why she wrote about temples and large bodies of water —and never about betrayal.

2

Roberto Elias de Peña (called Robert since his Harvard days), trendy scholar, dilettante, author of two slim but popular books on philosophy for the layman, and former husband of Theo Buckley, had met Jane on a stifling afternoon in 1983 in the fly-infested waiting room of the airport at Abu Simbel. A sandstorm had grounded all air traffic. As was usual in Egypt, no announcements or explanations had been made. It sufficed to note the sudden appearance of soldiers in green cotton uniforms to guard the doors, letting no one out, letting no one in.

There was not much to do except read one's guidebook if one had brought one, order sticky, lukewarm coffee, examine a dusty collection of cheap necklaces, or stare through the walls of pocked glass at the whirling pink Nubian sand. Those who had not found seats walked up and down or leaned against the walls. Most were members of tour groups who had flown up from Aswan that morning to view the famous rock tem-

ples, had duly examined them, and were now anxious
to get back to Aswan for a civilized drink.

Robert, who had chartered his own plane from Aswan, now sat on a hard wooden bench, waiting, like
the others. He held on his lap the head of the young
woman he had brought with him to Egypt. He had been
invited to join a Nile party of twelve and had been
encouraged to bring along a companion if he wished.
He had chosen Susan because Susan was agreeable (at
least she was willing to converse on topics other than
herself, and had the confidence to dress like a lady, not
a circus pony). Nor was she tied down to a regular job
that might have prevented her from being available.

True to form, she had not complained about the delay. At the onset of the flying sand and the green cotton
soldiers, Susan had sipped daintily at her coffee, not
liked any of the necklaces, and was now fitfully asleep.

On a facing wooden bench sat Jane.

Robert examined the attractive, tanned ankles above
the laced-up espadrilles, the neat khaki shorts, the plain
white T-shirt, the hefty paperback copy of *The Book of
the Dead*.

And the face. Not a girl's face. Thirty, possibly more.
Evidently not restless. Evidently not bored.

Jane turned a page, raised her head, saw him staring
at her. Over the body of his sleeping girlfriend, they
began a conversation.

"Heavy reading, that." He smiled, indicating her
book. "I vote you the most serious person in this airport."

"The plot's a bit thick" was all she allowed him. But
she smiled back and ran her strong, ringless fingers
through her short hair.

Bookish. Modest. Sensational legs. Likes men. "I
gather," he said next, "*The Book of the Dead* makes
Christianity look like the senior play."

She in turn had been examining him. "The early Egyptians are quite provocative, yes."

"Better jewels? Better sex?"

She laughed. "Better journeys, maybe." She paused. "I'm in love with rivers. I don't know why."

"What part are you on just now?"

"The Ka."

Having meanwhile been appreciating the graceful way her bones were arranged, he dutifully inquired, "Which is?"

"The Ka was an abstract personality endowed with all the characteristic attributes of the individual person it was a part of. But the Ka also had an independent existence. It could go from place to place, separating itself from the body when it wished."

"So technically the Ka is a double?"

"Technically it's not anything we have a word for." She frowned. "It's not the soul, it's not character. For instance, whenever it separated itself from the body, it had to be fed."

"And when the person died? The Ka died with it?" He was totally uninterested in the Ka. Spirits were neither his field nor his taste. But her absorption was charming. Mentally he undressed her.

"On the contrary." Jane noticed the quick discreet downward flicker of his gaze and felt an equally quick stirring of pleasure. "In fact, offerings of food continued to be made to the Ka. With nourishment, it was believed, the Ka would survive."

She had, after a few minutes, realized who he was. The faintest trace of a South American accent. Blurred photographic memories of his aristocratic profile taken with Theo Buckley. In black tie, arriving at a gala. And after Theo Buckley. In mourning, walking in front of the catafalque. He was older. He would know things she didn't. She liked that. She liked the set of his shoulders. She found herself eyeing the maleness of the way his flat black watch lay against his wrist, and the tiny, fine hairs there.

She wondered if she had been staring too long and hastily continued with the first thing that came into her head. "I suppose what endears the ancient Egyptians most to me is not the panoply of their showpieces— which I find embarrassingly large and cumbersome— but their belief that when we leave this life for the next, we get to take our things." With a grin she added, "It beats all hell out of ashes to ashes and dust to dust, doesn't it?"

He seemed to be considering his answer. He was frowning.

Had she offended him? Was it possible he was religious? Had he thought the sphinx just dandy? She wished he would take off his dark glasses. She wished she had not been *quite* so chatty.

He regarded her gravely. Very quietly he asked, "Where are you staying in Aswan?"

The Book of the Dead slid off her lap. He could not pick it up for her because he was holding Susan. Quickly Jane retrieved it and replied as evenly as she could, "I'm not. If we ever get out of here, I'm on a tourist boat to Luxor that leaves at nine o'clock tonight."

In his lap, Susan was beginning to stir. "You'll be making the usual stops? Kôm Ombo? Edfu?" Robert asked Jane quickly. "What is the name of your boat?"

And it was done.

Legend has it that when Napoleon's army first came upon Karnak, the legions fell strangely silent, slowed to a complete halt there in the white-hot desert, and—to a man—presented arms. Five days after meeting Jane,

Robert had his first look at Karnak and less than an hour later asked Jane to marry him.

His proposal did not seem all that impetuous to either of them. Since Abu Simbel, each was fairly certain that something momentous in their lives had happened. To Robert, Jane had appeared in the form of fresh deliverance. Jane was exactly the sort of woman he wanted in his life. The Susans of this world were pleasant, practiced, and they knew the score. Robert had sensed instantly that Jane did not know there was a score, or if she did, had never deigned to subscribe. This unwitting purity sharpened his desire. He loved the way she looked. He loved the generosity of her spirit, her intelligence. Her very presence at his side promised to unmuddle the muddles of the past. Every moment they had stolen on their way down the Nile—from Susan, from Jane's rigid itinerary—had increased his determination to have her for his own. He would have a wife again. He would be happy.

They sat at sunset under the bleached, striped awning of a wispy café on the riverbank, looking across to the other side, where the Valley of the Kings lay.

"Marry?" Jane gave him a cautious but good-humored stare. "Why not sort of live together. And see."

"I've already seen." Discreetly, under the plastic tablecloth, he slid his hand under her wide cotton skirt. They exchanged a look of congratulatory lust, each thinking of the narrow bunk in her single stateroom on the vile tourist boat where two days earlier they had had exactly twenty-five minutes to exchange their initial carnal vows.

Robert caught his breath like a boy. "What is your answer?"

The watery melon disc that had hung slightly out of focus over Luxor all afternoon sank out of view. Behind them, the lone waiter smoked, dreamed, rattled little cups and little saucers on the baby-blue plastic bar. Three stern blasts came from Jane's boat. She picked up her purse, her sunglasses, a few parcels.

"I must go, or the chief purser will shoot my foot off. Unlike your tony yacht, we on the Sheraton boat must obey the small print on the backs of our tickets."

He also rose, put some money on the table, glanced at her, but said nothing more.

"I'm vamping," she said contritely. "For time."

"I know." He took her arm.

They walked along the little croisette, poignant with its dusty historical litter of abandoned dreams. Baked for centuries, peeling, corrupted, done for, rosy Luxor remained a stubborn romantic. A mangy horse and carriage clip-clopped by. A spindly, flowering tree bent in the hot breeze. At their backs was the knowing stillness of Karnak, which had gone—for the moment—the color of saffron. The great stones of the temples that held the city's blood secrets were still, in the early evening, warm to the touch and would remain so long into the darkness.

"Why not in Paris, on the way home? I have friends with the embassy," Robert was saying. "I could telephone them from Cairo. Ask them to make the wedding arrangements." He smiled at her. "You remain the only obstacle."

She smiled back. Men. They were never so alive, so absolutely clear as when they were determined to have you. Cavemen cartoons did not lie. Really, it was charming. What had her life been like five minutes before meeting Robert? She could scarcely remember.

She had come to Egypt to write about the Nile. Conscientiously steeped in its history, she had not counted on its wiliness. "Just here," she had written in her notebook a few days earlier, "the west bank is parrot green with fake-looking palm trees as artfully arranged as in

those overcolored nineteenth-century paintings that are
suddenly going for so much money. The sky is tipsy on
fruit punch. At the water's edge, a dry, biblical bush
casts the only smudge of shadow to be seen anywhere
on the landscape. As we round a bend there is another
river still life. A woman gowned in black stands on the
bank, eyeing her buffalo. She does not look up as we
glide by. She doesn't believe in me, I don't believe in
her. The only real thing is the hot swish of the river."

Yes, there was only this. There was only the tourma-
line water, and the flat yellow barge that was going by,
and, buried centuries beneath the sands, wall paintings
and jeweled chariots. There was only Robert, who was
now saying, "What will you do tonight? So I can imagine you doing it?"

Jane, looking at the river, felt the inevitability, the
excitement. She tried to speak casually.

"Have a drink in the bar with the couple from Ve-
rona. Take a walk on the deck. Go below and make
notes." She paused. "Think of you. Think endlessly of
you."

She had made up her mind. There was a healthy
amount of child in Jane, enough for her to want to
claim as her due this golden favor from the gods. She
had always liked to entertain questions of destiny.
Newly minted lover that she now was, she embraced
the happenstance of their meeting at Abu Simbel as
having been designed by an unseen hand.

Time for a passionate, mature love *bien fait*. The
wayward, enchanting Tyler had been chosen by a
breathless girl. A wiser, glowing Jane would now have
the seasoned Robert, man of the world, with the handsome brows.

At the foot of the gangplank, quickly, with only a
few minutes to spare, they made plans. In Cairo, Robert's companion would be packed off. He would book a

suite high above the city. They would have a princely
bed under a silk canopy, a veranda enclosed in white
scrollwork. They would be a couple. They would walk
in the bazaar. The muezzin would cry out the hours.

At Kennedy Airport, the grimy glass door to the outside
stuck, shuddered, finally slid open. Jane and Robert
walked out into the stench of another great city. They
sank into the coolness of the car Robert had ordered.
The driver piled the luggage into the trunk, came
around to the front, and started the motor. Robert
leaned back, reached for Jane's hand, closed his eyes.

Jane was looking through the window at a young
couple standing on the curb. Rumpled T-shirts,
backpacks, and a small dirty baby. They looked stoned
and poor, and Jane wondered where they had come
from and what it would be like to be them. As the car
pulled away she continued to stare back at them with a
sick heart. She had always been so lucky. What, she
began to castigate herself, did she contribute to society?

Robert, perhaps sensing something, lifted her hand
to his lips, kissed it, murmured "home." His eyes remained closed.

After their wedding they had gone to Normandy to a
little half-timbered farmhouse Robert and Theo had
bought in the early days. The woman who had always
looked after the place had scoured every corner, polished every tabletop, and filled the rooms with sprays of
lavender and bowls of apples, but Theo's presence was
still warm; the wall of amusing and interesting photographs of herself and her friends, a raffia hat with a
long tangerine-colored scarf wound about it, a pair of
yellow wooden clogs by the door to the garden, a dressing table with silver jars filled with makeup brushes and
tortoiseshell hair combs.

Robert, horrified and penitent, stared bleakly at Jane. "I am an asshole."

Evidently he had a word with the housekeeper, for when they came back from a walk after lunch, all traces of Theo had vanished. While Jane thought it baroque that a dead woman's things should still be lying about several years later, as if she had merely stepped into the garden for a moment—why hadn't all this stuff gone into boxes, to heirs? to charity?—she forgave Robert because it was plain he was not keeping a shrine, he had simply forgotten about the things.

In his high corner apartment on Riverside Drive, a welcome breeze blew in off the Hudson through open windows with long, fluttering white curtains. There were thousands of books and not a whisper of Theo. Everything spoke of Robert, her husband, her love.

He went straight into the bathroom for a shower. Jane had a look around, liking the open views and the spaciousness. She went into the slick, faddish bachelor's kitchen, found a sleek white kettle, put it on to boil, and experienced a sharp pang of homesickness for her own apartment across town. Her own answering machine and all the messages that had to do with her own life. Her Chinese rug. Her blue and white teacups that Great-Gran had bought as a bride in Macao. She would go there first thing tomorrow to sort out what was to be packed, what was to be stored, what was to come here, and to make arrangements for subletting the place.

Steam rose from the kettle. The lid rattled noisily. As she began to look for cups and saucers, the smart, glossy kitchen seemed very large and she very small. Shrill car honks from the street floated up through the windows, mixed with the sporadic, more muted sounds of river traffic. Overhead, airplane engines whined. She looked out the window. Across the water, smoke belched into the colorless sky. All of New Jersey appeared to be on fire.

The little phone on the wall rang. She picked up the receiver, said hello. There was a pause, then a click.

Unnerved, displaced, she reviewed the single life she had led since her divorce from Tyler. She had liked that life. She had been in charge of it. Now her self-image wore two heads. Mated. Joined. We.

And then a geometrically shaped cup she would never have chosen had she been doing the buying slipped from her fingers, hit the floor, and broke into two pricey pieces. Damn. Was she going to cry?

Robert walked in, a thick white towel wrapped around his waist, his strong legs bare and tanned, his hair wet and slick as a boy's. His eyes searched hers. Without comment, he took her in his arms.

Those who had known Robert during his years with Theo looked on with approval at his new marriage. Theo had been captivating, but really she had been too much, too much for any man, and it had become clear toward the end that Robert was unhappy. He had not talked about it but he had turned morose and reclusive, and this had worried his associates and friends, who were now ever so delighted with Jane.

Between Robert and Jane, Theo was never mentioned except when absolutely necessary. There remained leftover bits of business having to do with her estate, intermittent inquiries from journalists, and the occasional crank—or poignant—letter from a fan, and these continued to be handled for the most part by Theo's former secretary and assistant, Una, who lived in Los Angeles and whom Robert had kept on retainer all these years so that he could call on her whenever it was necessary.

Jane, who had been merely an anonymous member of Theo's vast public and who knew her only from her records, concert and cabaret appearances, and films and interviews, regretted from time to time that she had not in the beginning asked Robert the questions she might have, had Theo been merely a dead wife instead of a household word. Now whenever Jane felt a sudden petty heat rising in her to Know—ordinary things, humdrum information that might pry Theo from her legend and place her in the more factual context of Robert's past—she was prevented from asking by the precedent based on pride and good manners that she had so fastidiously established at the start.

Robert volunteered nothing. But then, rather more quickly than she might have expected, time got in the way of her curiosity. Time, and the fullness of their lives.

They had been married three months when some old friends of Robert's passed through the city and hosted a dinner party at a new Italian restaurant downtown to which Robert and Jane and six other people were invited. It was a convivial gathering and everyone was having such a good time that no one wanted to go home when the restaurant closed, so the group departed on a late-night crawl around the neighborhood in search of music, dancing, and more fun.

The first place was unacceptably dreary. They looked in and left. The second, called The Touch Me Club, looked slightly more amusing. Red gels had been placed over the spotlights that crisscrossed the smoky darkness of the small, crowded room. There was a three-piece jazz group and a tiny dance floor. The party settled in.

Drinks arrived and there was yet another toast to the newly married couple. Jane and Robert, flushed with wine and the triumph of their union, looked across the table at each other with the sweet smugness of certified lust. Later, each would privately speculate, attempting to recall who in the party might have deliberately led them into The Touch Me Club, or if anyone had; whether in fact it had been sheer coincidence as opposed to mischief on anybody's part.

Suddenly all the lights went out. There was a roll of drums. A spot hit the little dance floor. The figure who stepped into it needed no introduction.

Theo Buckley—it couldn't be, but it was—her straight, silky red hair swinging, her simple linen trousers and silk shirt impeccably pressed, walked to the center of the dance floor with her inimitable leggy stride. In the startled hush there were a couple of enthusiastic whistles and then loud applause.

"Good evening," came the throaty, golden, one-of-a-kind voice. The apparition stood quite still. The room quieted, as if knowing what to expect. And they got it; the heartbreakingly familiar long, candid look at the audience with which Theo had always begun her stage performances. Then came the equally familiar quick intake of breath, the controlled exhale, the incandescent smile.

At Robert and Jane's table the group sat like stone figures in a moonless garden. Jane tried to make out Robert's face. What she could see of it wore an expression entirely unknown to her. His gaze did not leave the stage.

The performance went by in a flash. The brilliance of it lay in its absolute, chilling naturalness. It was easy to believe that it *was* Theo. First there was a nostalgic old standard from her repertoire. Then a spiky monologue, "delivered" by Theo's famous alter ego, Fanny Lou, exploring the notion that the two most famous male characters created in literature by women writers had been Frankenstein's monster and Peter Rabbit. The monologue crackled with wit and was impeccably up to Theo's standards. This was followed by another song, a quick bow, then the spotlight went out. There were calls for an encore, but the apparition that was Theo did not return.

The red gels glowed again. Handsome young waiters in long white aprons circulated. At Robert and Jane's table everyone was ready with a sympathetically considered remark. "The songs must have been lip synced." "Uncanny mimicry if you happen to like impersonations—and I don't." "It's the parasitic aspect that offends."

Robert met Jane's troubled gaze. He returned it with a gallant look that seemed to say "I'm so sorry, my dear." But his reassuring smile belied his eyes, which seemed to be warning her off.

In the taxi going home he and the driver discussed baseball for seventy-three blocks. For a while Jane passed the time by laying out in her head an article she might write on the various forms of passive male abuse. This led her—somewhat understandably—back to the impersonator's monologue. She decided to challenge it. What other equally famous male characters had been created by women? Heathcliff. Much less known. She racked her brain. There really wasn't anyone else. You couldn't count the Wharton men as world-class characters, or George Eliot's. Or Austen's. Wait. What about Rhett Butler? She pondered for a moment. No. Rhett Butler was glittery enough in the context of popular fiction but paled in comparison with the vividness, the timeless authenticity of Peter Rabbit and Frankenstein's monster.

She forced herself to admit that the impersonator had been quite amusing. Men, the audience had been reminded, had dreamed up Ophelia, Camille, Helen of Troy, Lady Brett Ashley, Madame Butterfly. Glamorous heartbreakers all. By comparison, the two most notable contributions made by women writers to immortalizing the male gender seemed skimpy if not downright insulting.

A monster and a rodent.

Jane looked at Robert, at the driver, absorbed in the discussion of balls, bats, and runs. Another twenty blocks to go.

As they undressed for bed, Jane said with some heat, "Could we clear the air? Could we talk about it?"

"Would you mind? I'd rather not," he said nicely enough. He got out of his trousers, opened the closet, reached for a hanger. He rolled up his belt, put it away in a drawer. He contemplated his folded handkerchief and refolded it. She noted this unusual tidiness. He was trying to put away the evening as well.

She tried another tack. "Nothing can be done to stop this person, I suppose? From progressing to uptown, to television, to *People* magazine?"

"Darling, there's no copyright on memory." An abstracted smile accompanied this. He got into bed, picked up his book.

Shut out. She stood there, not moving. After a moment he looked up.

She said coolly, "I draw the line at getting into bed with strangers."

He put down his book, looked at her kindly. "I don't know what to say. In that first flash I thought it *was* Theo. I was disoriented. Someone you've said good-bye to forever and suddenly—" He paused, didn't go on.

She waited.

He spoke as if to himself. "There wasn't the slightest exaggeration to the performance. That's what fooled me at the start. She's fantastically talented."

"Or, he is."

"I think it's a woman." He frowned. "There was

none of that campiness with which men usually impersonate Dietrich, Davis, Monroe. Essentially what those fellows do is caricature. As gifted as they are, the most they can give us is a patina, a succession of brilliant flashes. Back of that, there's only a shell and a codpiece. Their memories are rooted in the wrong gender. It's why they can never reproduce the sensuality, the sheer pull of the original."

"And you think this impersonator did?"

In some surprise, he asked with the incautious naïveté of someone who has forgotten the subtext of the conversation, "Didn't you?"

She turned away to undress and he saw how quiet she was. When she came to bed, he turned out his lamp and gently pulled her to him.

"I'm really tired," she said. She kissed him lightly, then turned her body away from him and closed her eyes.

He knew only that he was being punished. She knew only that she was in danger.

The doorman rang on the intercom to say that the man from the dry cleaners was on his way up to the tenth floor. Jane put down her pencil and went down the hall. From a hamper she took out two blouses and a dress. She looked into the bedroom. Robert, who had left in a hurry for an early dentist appointment, had thrown a jacket and a pair of trousers across the bed, which presumably meant he had remembered it was dry-cleaning day.

Jane went through the pockets of the trousers first. Robert had a habit of jotting down notes for his lectures on anything at hand—receipts, cocktail napkins, the back of theater tickets. Early on, Jane had attended one of his lectures and had been impressed by the ease of his scholarly glamour. He came on to his students with the dazzle of a tennis star, perfect serve after perfect serve, the information delivered with unerring form and the congenial charm of his bloodline, backed up by a faultless education and, she suspected, a mind far better ordered than her own—if less elastic. She was beginning to understand the limitations this imposed. Robert served the fortress of what he knew was known. Jane, eyeing this worthy structure with respect, nevertheless experienced intermittent impatience with it and was grateful for the more comforting vantage point of her own cheerful daily house of cards. On occasion, when he truly irritated her with a devoted homage to a subject he had not readdressed for twenty years, she wished she had a husband with more imagination.

And would immediately feel guilty. Surely on the same point she exasperated *him* with the untidy leaps of her mind? Or did she? Did he mind her hastily thought-out exuberances? Did he study them? Did he notice? Did men notice?

At the auction of a painting they didn't buy (questionable provenance, insisted Robert) she had touched him on the wrist and whispered, "Who cares? Are we dealers, or are we lovers of beauty?"

"Shh."

"I *want* it."

He had given her an indulgent look. "That's an insolent reason for buying a work of art or, for that matter, anything of value. I'll get you an ice cream on the way home."

"I'm not going home." She had turned her face away.

"Okay, an emerald." His gaze had lingered on her face, on her mouth, traveled down to the hollow in her throat. "There." He touched the hollow with his index finger. "You'll wear it just there." It was style, it was power, it was seduction, and it was all right with her, except sometimes it wasn't. But it was still new. For Jane, uncharted territory was irresistible.

"An emerald is the last thing I want," she had announced.

"What, then?"

"An ice cream."

He had been enchanted and she had been enchanted with him being enchanted, and it was only later that she became cross again at what he would have described as good sense and she, timidity.

She had now finished going through his clothes. He had left nothing in them this time except a book of matches in the right-hand pocket of the navy jacket. Robert did not smoke.

Jane stared at the matchbook cover, which announced in red and silver: *The Touch Me Club.*

The doorbell gave three short jaunty blasts. Jane stood where she was, holding the jacket. Robert had worn it the previous evening. He had gone to have dinner with an old school friend who was this year's chairman of their class reunion. She herself had gone with friends to a performance of *Nabucco* and then to a late supper. She had returned quite late, to find Robert already asleep.

With the matchbook still in one hand, she went to the front door, gave the man the clothes, chatted briefly with him about his two favorite subjects—nutrition and teenage prostitution—and then closed the door.

It had been three weeks since the night of the impersonator and her own—admittedly—overwrought reaction to the experience. By the evening of the next day she had apologized to Robert and he to her, and they had agreed that they had overreacted to the incident and life had returned to normal. Since then, Jane had been immersed in research, preparing for her trip to the

Amazon, and Robert had been equally busy getting his new manuscript ready to deliver to his publisher. In addition, they were redoing the dining room and had been spending weekends at auction houses looking for the perfect eight chairs. Really, time had just flown by.

But Jane remained standing in the hall by the front door, one hand still on the knob, the other holding the red-and-silver book of matches. Robert had bought the navy jacket on sale at Saks only ten days earlier.

While the possibility that he had gone back to see the impersonator for a second time seemed to be the only explanation, she knew she could not ask him if he had. A question like that was beneath her. She walked toward the kitchen, intending to throw the matches away. Actually, he could have picked them up on the first night. Phyllis Barkham had sat next to him, and Phyllis smoked. Robert, always courteous, would have lighted her cigarettes. The next day he might have absently transferred the entire contents of his pockets to a clean pair of trousers and then in turn eventually to the navy jacket and . . .

Standing over the trash bin, she opened the matchbook. The matches lay flat and close. Undisturbed. On the inside flap a phone number had been written in ink. The handwriting was spiky, unfamiliar.

Late that afternoon she said to Robert, "There was the most awful stain on your new navy jacket. Could it have been curry? Where did you and Jobo have dinner?"

"Where was the stain? I don't remember dropping anything."

"In the front. I tried to get it out with that stuff they advertise on television. It's called Cry or Yell or something."

"It's called Shout." He smiled at her.

She smiled back. "*Was* it curry? How dare you go to an Indian restaurant without me?"

"If you feel like Indian food, we could go to that place up the street tonight. Drink daiquiris. Hold hands." He smiled at her again, then looked at his watch. "Should I book a table for eight, eight-thirty?"

Jane, whose life had thus far been untainted by jealous obsession, did not yet dream of its bottomless depths. Already uneasy at her own duplicity, she felt her heart skip as she brightly inquired, "Is that where you and Jobo went? What did you have? Go on, torture me."

He got up, scanned the bookshelves. "I only saw Jobo for a drink, actually. Didn't I tell you?" He took out a book on Cathar history and began flipping through it, looking for a particular piece of information he needed for a chapter in his book that he was devoting to secret societies. "He and his wife were going to see that German dance company at the Brooklyn Academy, and he'd forgotten."

"Oh, yes. I saw a performance when they were here several years ago. Quite striking, but like everything German, it was just that little bit too striking. One less spot of rouge, one more inch of hair, might have improved things." Jane's hands were gripping the chair. This was exhausting work. In her mind she was shouting to herself, *Ask him, ask him what he did after the drink with Jobo.* But she could not. She would not insult him. All indications were that he was undisturbed by the conversation and innocent as to its investigative aspect. If she pressed the point, she would be discovered. Her suspicions would be revealed as paranoic imaginings and she would end up a fool. A jealous fool.

She would have to trust him. It was what she wanted most. And as a reward for her trust, the gods in turn would provide—soon, she prayed—a simple explanation. Meanwhile she would go to the Amazon. She would do her work. She would love her husband.

On the afternoon of her departure for Brazil she sat in the Pan American Clipper Club, reading *Tristes Tropiques* and eating peanuts, waiting for her flight to be called. When the announcement came she stood up, picked up her purse, her carry-on bag, and started for the doors. Suddenly flooded by negative resolve, she went back to where she had been sitting, put down the carry-on bag, opened her purse, took out the red-and-silver matchbook, lifted a telephone receiver, and called the number that had been written in ink on the inside cover.

On the second ring a youngish-sounding woman with an arch, actressy voice breathily inquired, "Hello?"

Her heart pounding, Jane hung up. So the impersonator *was* a woman. Or the voice could have belonged to the impersonator's girlfriend, or wife, or—

She tore the matchbook into two pieces, put them in an ashtray, and went off—like a good girl—to the Amazon.

Hearing the click of Jane's hangup, Marly put the phone down and called across to the supine figure in the bed who lay under a fur blanket, "It was no one."

She crossed to the squat refrigerator under the compact stove top and took out a carton of eggnog and a wedge of plastic-encased cherry pie.

The figure in the bed, who was, in fact, the Impersonator, spoke, asking her for a nectarine.

"You ate them all yesterday." Marly sat down at a small table on the other side of the large room that, except for an airless, chipped bathroom, comprised the entire apartment. The curtains at the high windows were green velvet, second-hand, chosen by the Impersonator, who had also chosen all the other furniture. But had not paid for any of it. Marly had.

She began to eat the pie and drink the eggnog, but the chance word "nectarine" had touched off a wistful memory. In the first week she had known him he had taken a fresh, dewy nectarine and, gazing at her gravely, had commenced to take slow, considered bites from it, his (perhaps too generous) mouth seeming to caress the plump globe of fleshy fruit each time he sank his teeth into it. He had kept his smoky eyes on her the entire time, while she, mesmerized, understood with a gasp that he was instructing her as to how he would take her when he took her. That it was a studied performance—something from his little bag of tricks—did not lessen the sexual thrill but in fact pleased the actress in her as well as the woman. She had become in that moment the nectarine. Happy to be that nectarine. Wanting only to be that nectarine.

From the bed there was a sulky sigh.

She reached for a plate holding a desiccated spray of pale green grapes and walked it over to him. He took the plate without looking at her, his eyes riveted on a tiny black-and-white image playing at the foot of the bed. The picture tube was almost done for and there was no sound at all. In the center of the screen there was only a minute boxy space of light no more than a few inches square in which a minuscule John Wayne had been riding, fighting, and loving under the rapt, attentive eye of the Impersonator for the last hour and a half.

Marly stood looking down at him as he began to put the grapes in his mouth. No erotic performance here—only a driftless boy-man. He had been in that bed for days, watching the television set, playing with himself, eating fruit, taking little sips of Chivas Regal from a small crystal decanter he had found in a thrift shop. He had gone back to behaving exactly as he had before his brief gig at The Touch Me Club, which he had said he walked out on, but she did not believe him. Something had happened and they had let him go.

With a moody sigh she lightly ruffled his hair, but still he did not look at her. His gaze did not leave the television screen. He was naked, she knew, under the luxurious black and silver pelts of the fur blanket. She felt a familiar contraction—the sexual hangover of her love for him, which she prayed was finally behind her.

Until recently she herself had gone around naked most of the time—a habit she had picked up from him early on. He was quite female in the way he luxuriated in his pale, thin body and liked it to be looked at. She had found this titillating as well as liberating. But these days when he looked at her he had ceased to see her, just as he had ceased to eat fruit for her in that special way.

The doorbell rang. Marly put on her flowered kimono and opened the door, already knowing from the sound of the voices who it would be—Rick and Patti and Keith and Sandy and whoever else they might have picked up on the way. They came in with their canvas shoulder bags filled with telephone beepers, appointment books, résumés, gym clothes, photo composites, and nuts and raisins from the health food store. They had brought someone new, hoping as always to entertain the regal figure in the bed, who now greeted them with a sad, mildly condescending smile. The Stray they had brought was a wispy girl with a silk flower in her hair who wanted to be a dancer. The Impersonator was rumored to favor dancers because they had small breasts and large rib cages on which he liked to nibble; however, no one had actually ever seen him with anyone but Marly.

They grouped themselves around the bed and said things like "Yo" and "What's happening." The Stray whispered to one of them, "Is he sick?"

"No, my dear," the Impersonator intoned in the accents of an English lord. "Just cozy." He eyed her with what appeared to be scant interest.

The Stray thought she had never met anyone so classy. The fur blanket covered him to his shoulders, which she saw were bare, with the patina of polished bone. Jesus. Naked and silky-voiced under fur at four o'clock in the afternoon. She wondered what the rest of him looked like.

Marly went into the bathroom and closed the door. She took off her kimono and let it fall to the floor. She had once been beautiful. Black black hair, porcelain skin, softly rounded here, rounded there—he had likened her to a Rubens, from which she had supposed him to be better educated in subjects like art than herself. And for the most part he was, though not nearly to the degree she had originally thought him to be. His gift, she had come to understand, lay in the presentation of what little he knew.

Marly looked down at herself. No longer a Rubens. A fat girl. A reject. At twenty-nine. More than anything, she was bewildered by what she had somehow allowed to befall her, she with all the potential to become one of the greatest actresses of the theater. She shut her eyes and prayed not for revenge but deliverance.

Through the door she heard laughter. He was entertaining his court. She herself was due—in forty minutes —at the restaurant where she worked six nights a week to keep the two of them afloat. She stepped into the shower now, glancing over her shoulder at the mirror above the sink, and was only slightly consoled by the sight of her very pretty heart-shaped face. Her spirit remained heavy with the dark, amorphous unease that came with having eaten herself up to one hundred and seventy pounds.

She turned on the shower and began to sing. Her bell-like voice ricocheted off the chipped tiles and floated on steam through the open, old-fashioned glass transom over the bathroom door. The group around the bed ceased their chatter, listened to the sweet, true sound of Marly singing.

The Impersonator sighed. "Poor Marly," he said with a charitable smile.

They called themselves actors, but life had so far denied them their credentials. With the exception of the Impersonator they worked as waiters and waitresses, as demonstrators in department stores, as messengers, and as operators at telephone answering services. They talked knowingly and ceaselessly about what was going on in the theater—and to a slightly lesser extent Los Angeles—as if they were seasoned veterans, whereas their actual experience so far had been limited to acting school and community theater. They went to open auditions for everything, including commercials, tried to get appointments with agents, money from their parents, introductions to anyone Who Knew People. They lived in a communal limbo of fervid fantasy and disappointment.

The Impersonator stirred voluptuously under the fur rug, rearranging his perfect slender limbs. He ate the last grape. Of all of them, he would be spared the struggle. This he knew must be. This he had always understood must be.

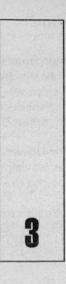

3

The intense stillness in a landscape already made up of odd silences presaged a late afternoon downpour.

Jane fanned herself with a limp page of yellowed hotel stationery. With the other hand she dialed a number on the clunky black telephone. Beyond the balcony the light was a prison gray. The Rio Negro, which a few miles to the east would converge with the yellow Amazon, bubbled past her eyes, black and oily, vaguely troubling.

Robert, looking out at the battleship-colored Hudson and the firestorm of New Jersey, gladdened to the sound of Jane's voice on the telephone.

"Where are you tonight?" he asked.

"In civilization. Manaus. The hotel has armed guards at the gates. All the guests have to carry identification cards. It's like a German theme camp. The decor is part Jacobean, part Iron Cross."

"What do you think of the place so far?" Robert asked.

Painted cherubs and glossy jungle fronds. The ebony
shine of a vulture posed on the decapitated top of a
blackened tree. A city as whim. A third world dreaming
and dying under a cottony nineteenth-century sky.
"Quite operatic. How's the work coming?"

"Inching along. I miss you."

She drew in her breath, about to answer, but he continued. "You just caught me. I was leaving to have dinner with the Thompsons. What are you doing? So I can
imagine it."

"I met a Swiss couple on the way into town. He's an
engineer. Profoundly boring type, but she's special.
They may come to New York later and you'll meet her.
I'm going to have a drink with them and then spend the
evening writing up notes."

The minute she hung up it began to rain. She went
out to the balcony to watch the wide sheets of silver
water fall straight down, precise as guillotines, from a
low ocher sky.

She had been in Brazil a week, and she had worked it
out, bit by bit. Robert *had* gone back to The Touch Me
Club. Perfectly understandable. She could forgive his
curiosity. It was only human that he would have
wanted to know how and why the impersonator was
able to duplicate Theo so brilliantly. During the conversation the impersonator had no doubt pressed her/his
phone number on Robert. Robert had put the book of
matches in his navy jacket and, having no intention of
following up on the acquaintance, had forgotten about
it.

When Jane walked into the icy hotel bar she saw
Hanna Spengler sitting at a table in a corner. She was
the only occupant of the room except for a young barman who was crushing limes with a glass pestle.

"Albert's waiting for a call to come through from

Zurich," Hanna said. "You'll have one of these?" she asked, indicating her drink.

"Thanks." Jane sat down. Hanna held up two fingers to the young barman, who nodded and wrapped some ice cubes in a clean, starchy white napkin, then picked up a little brass hammer.

It had grown too dark now to see anything but blackness through the slick glass walls of the bar. They sat for a moment in companionable silence. Jane thought of the river and the jungle outside, of the faces in many colors of the people on the hot, rickety bus that went into town, of the children chasing chickens through the muck on the banks. "I love this country. Don't ask me why. It's such a mess."

"I feel the same. Every year when Albert makes his trip here he suggests I might spend the time in New York and he'd meet me there later, but I always end up coming. It mystifies him."

"I suppose," Jane suggested after a moment, "we make the same irrational claim to a particular piece of geography as we do to someone we fall in love with. A logical reason is not required."

"Precisely. It's all in the wanting."

"So if I wish to believe that this ground is blessed with ancient magic, this population with insight and wisdom—this very air with heartbreaking sweetness—I can make it so. It needs only an act of the imagination."

"Desire as deceit," Hanna responded with a smile. "Meanwhile Brazil remains unaware of our infatuation, even of our presence. It goes its own way in high humor and corruption."

Jane examined Hanna. Compact and elegant. At fifty, she had the aura of someone who had managed to live a great deal of her life on her own terms. Given the overbearing Albert, Jane admired this. "Are you really what you told me?" she asked now. "The fulfilled mother of five children and nothing more?"

Hanna gave her a humble look. "I couldn't remember whether I told you that one or the one about my being president of the Montreux garden club. I'm a psychoanalyst. I never admit it when I'm on holiday, for obvious reasons." She looked up. "Here's Albert."

Hanna's husband settled his rangy frame into a chair and addressed his wife. "I have to fly back to Santarem tomorrow and won't be back until late." He now included Jane in his glance. "Perhaps you two can find something to do together."

Hanna gave him a gently reproving look. "Jane is here to work."

"An article, is it?" Albert asked politely.

Jane, who disliked talking to strangers about her work, smiled agreeably. "A book. About rivers."

"A travel book?"

"Not in the sense that it will tell you where the four-star restaurants are on the Ganges, but—"

"It's one of those picture books?"

"There will be photographs, yes, but—"

"Which rivers?"

"It's planned as a series of three books. For the first one I'm doing the Nile, the Amazon, and the Mississippi."

"You have a publisher?"

"It was the publisher's idea. Travel books of this sort are very much in vogue these days. I suppose it has to do with all the money that's around."

"What precisely do you mean by that?"

Trying to conceal her irritation, Jane realized she had begun to be irritated by something else. A young man with thick, curly black hair and dusty black shoes had come in, turned on a microphone, sat on a stool, and begun to sing, accompanying himself on a beribboned guitar.

His voice was pleasant enough. But the recorded music coming from the speakers in the ceiling had not been turned off. Against the young man's husky rendition of a Brazilian folk song came the voice of Michael Jackson with a barrage of electronic backup. No one in the bar —which had begun to fill up with American engineers, Scandinavian tourists, and arms dealers from everywhere—appeared to have noticed that two pieces of music were playing simultaneously.

Jane glanced at the singer. Why didn't he stop, ask for the speakers to be turned off? But he sang on, seemingly impervious. Jane looked over at the barman, hoping to catch his attention. He was crushing more ice, and whistling to Jackson's piece.

Albert, still waiting for Jane's answer to his question, noticed her impatient glance at the barman. "Can I get you something?" Albert asked her.

"It's the music," Hanna said. "Ask them to turn it off." Seeing that he did not understand, she explained. "The hotel music, Albert. It's still playing."

Albert took a minute to work this out. "Ah," he said finally. "How incredibly stupid these people are." He left the table and strode to the bar.

Jane and Hanna exchanged a look. "How is it," Jane asked in frustration, "that nobody notices?"

"Desensitization is now universal." Hanna rattled the ice in her drink. "You want to live where someone might notice, go to the Gobi. Go to the bottom of the sea. Go to heaven."

At the bar, Albert waited impatiently to speak to the barman, who was now busy at the other end, attending to two handsome-eyed Varig pilots in crisp white shortsleeved shirts with shiny gold epaulettes who had just flown in from Miami.

Abruptly Jane asked Hanna, "When you come to New York, could I see you?"

Hanna met her gaze. "If you want to know about love, I probably can't help you."

The young guitar player finished his plaintive folk song, strummed the last chords, and smiled humbly in the direction of his cheap, dusty shoes, while a few people applauded and Michael Jackson sang on.

Robert *was* to have dinner with the Thompsons that evening, but first he had another appointment. After his conversation with Jane he took the elevator to the street and hailed a taxi. He got in and asked the driver to take him to the East Side. Then he leaned back and closed his eyes.

The brief biography that appeared on the jackets of Robert's books stated that he had been born in Santiago of Chilean parents, educated in Paris and, later, Harvard, and had been living and teaching in America since the seventies. His flawless, slightly accented English, his large, graceful frame, his handsome, scholarly look, and a slightly patrician manner made him an attractive figure as well as an acceptably learned one, and he had parlayed all this in his understated—and very shrewd—way into a modest notoriety of his own some time before he met the internationally famous Theo.

It was a decade in America that permitted, even encouraged, one to have a single bright but simple idea and to write a book around it and then to do a national tour of radio and television talk shows and become overnight a vetted expert. So Robert had become after the publication of his first book, which was a largely unashamed, wildly lay approach to how the underlying belief theories of the Gnostics could bring personal happiness in the twentieth century. He had done it for the money. Everyone was doing it for the money.

While Robert was known—and firmly lodged—mainly in academic and New York social circles, Theo came with the razzle-dazzle of her own group—film and theater people, media stars, royalty. Robert, trained early by his very social parents, got along with everyone. As a couple they held court wherever they went, were much photographed, and were rarely really alone. Theo had in almost constant attendance her writer, Emma, and her secretary, Una.

Because Robert had not known Theo before she was famous, he had scant understanding of the changes she might have undergone since earlier days, of what circumstances might have formed her. Theo's personality was so vivid, so seemingly fixed in her own glittering cosmology, he tended to assume she had always been thus. She wasn't a subject for study, she was his famous wife. It was only after her death, exposed to the millions of words written about her, that he began to realize with some uneasiness that he had bought—and lost —a package he had not struggled very hard to open.

The taxi had stopped. Silently, the back of the driver's head waited for the fare. Robert paid him, got out, and walked several leafy, well-kept blocks to a neat brownstone with a large brass doorknob. He pressed the bell for 4F. There was an immediate answering buzz. Robert entered, climbed the narrow carpeted staircase to the second floor.

Amos Miller opened the door. He was in his shirt-sleeves and had a can of Diet Coke in one hand. He ushered Robert through the tiny one-person waiting room into his spacious office, which held a discreet, unshowy collection of very good pieces, both furniture and art. "You want a drink?"

"No. Thanks for seeing me."

Amos sat behind his desk. "I've been staying late on Tuesdays for a patient who can't make it during the day." He looked at his watch. "We've got half an hour." He smiled at Robert. "How's Jane?"

Outside the high, barred windows, there had been a subtle change in the sound of the traffic. Night was falling. Absently Robert answered, "She's in Brazil."

"You said there was a problem?"

"It's not Jane I'm here about."

"What's up?"

Robert began his story with the night he and Jane had seen the impersonator, and went on from there. He got up and began to walk back and forth. Amos listened, took sips from his drink. Robert finished. He sat down again, stared quizzically at Amos.

For a moment Amos was silent. "When is Jane coming back?"

"Why?" Robert said with an uncomfortable look. "This isn't a case of infidelity."

"It's an incipient one."

"Goddammit, Amos, this is a guy."

"You just told me you've never seen him as a guy."

The meeting had taken place in a dark, narrow space backstage at The Touch Me Club. The impersonator had sat with one long linen-trousered leg slung over the other and one braceleted arm flung over the back of a kitchen chair. Robert had stood.

He had expected that up close all the artifice would be revealed. But even now there was that eerie authenticity. Even now the breathing came and went like Theo's. If anything was off, it was off only by an indiscernible fraction, very much like looking in a mirror that had been so deftly repaired that only by knowing it had once been cracked did one notice it was not perfect.

The red hair was clean and shiny and even the freckles across the bridge of the nose looked real. The eyes, deep set, were smoky like Theo's and had natural-looking thick long lashes. And the fragrance that wafted toward him was the spiky freshness of Vent Vert. Theo's scent. Not sold in America.

Amos was asking a question. "Tell me what you talked about."

"It's hard to recall exactly." Robert was remembering the sound of his own heartbeat, and his excitement at being so close to the living impersonation of Theo.

"Take your time. It'll come back. You told me you started to get an erection. Seems to me it would take slightly more than a queen in a red wig to produce that. He must have said *something*."

"He's not a queen."

"Strike 'queen.'" Amos threw Robert a good-humored glance. "Did he come on to you?"

Robert, crawling out of the warm cocoon of memory, looked up, wondering if he was flushing. "He's not what you think. There's nothing remotely cheap about him."

With a patient look Amos asked, "How the fuck do you know that, Robert?"

"What are you accusing him of? He didn't come looking for me—I went looking for him." He had known even that first night that he would return to stand alone at the back of the room and wait for the radiant ghost. He had thought of nothing else. Theo, warm and fleshy and clear-eyed, flaring in his brain, had become a suboccupation while he prepared his chapters, his lectures, went to dinners, the movies, and made love to Jane.

He looked across at Amos and found himself being casually examined.

"So you want to tell me why we're gathered here?" Amos asked dryly. "I mean, it would help."

After a thoughtful silence Robert suddenly chuckled. "I've got to hand it to you, Amos. Your sword is swift."

"It is? Is that good?" Amos raised his eyebrows.

"A couple of chops and you've restored my perspective." This was a lie, but Robert, offended by Amos's cynical dismissal of the impersonator's integrity, needed an acceptable way to quit the subject and be gone.

"I'm glad." Amos's look was bland. "In what way?"

Robert's expression was wry, very Latin. "You've known me since Harvard. And that I can get a hard-on from reading a girl's name in the telephone book. So what's so bizarre about being turned on by a flesh-and-blood reincarnation of a woman who was, damn her, the love of my life?"

"Indeed," Amos said, and scribbled a note on a little pad in front of him: "Handing me so much crap I can't believe it." He looked across at Robert. "How did you leave it with him?"

Robert hesitated. "I said I'd like to help him. Starving artist, that kind of thing."

"So he must have told you something about himself? I thought you said he kept to the Theo persona the whole time."

"It happened when I was saying good-bye. I thanked him for his excellent and respectful impersonation. I wished him luck. He was clearly very touched. He tried to hide it by turning away and pretending to cough, but I saw that tears had come to his eyes."

Robert realized he had fallen into the trap of pleading his case again but, plunging on, he felt sweet relief in it. "Then he told me how much it meant to him that I had come to see him again. His existence is pretty much hand to mouth. His career as a dramatic actor is going nowhere and he's trapped in a painful relationship. He'd been having thoughts of suicide."

"He spoke in his own voice—not Theo's—when he told you about himself?" Amos now asked.

"Yes."

"What's his real voice like?"

"Attractively male. Not uneducated but not studied either—that is, there were no acting school pretensions. A slight regional cadence, southern I think."

"Theo's accent also had a southern ring."

"Right."

"And did he return to the Theo persona before you left?"

"It was amazing. He closed his eyes for maybe one second. When he opened them, he'd disappeared, he was Theo again, not a trace of the private bit of himself he had shown me. For a moment I thought I'd imagined it. He's incredibly gifted."

Amos, practiced at concealing irony, remarked with a sincere look, "Evidently."

Robert's smile grew expansive. "And witty. When he became Theo again, he said, 'That painted loser. He tries that suicide story on everyone. He wants you to feel sorry for him. He's not worth the trouble, believe me. He's rotten through and through.'"

In the outer office there was the sound of the door opening, then closing. Amos glanced at the little clock on his desk, and under the cover of this scribbled another quick note. Then he stood up. "Sorry, we have to stop."

Robert glanced affectionately at Amos. "Thanks. Really."

"Anytime."

"You want to go to the tennis matches next week?" Robert asked as he walked to the door.

"Sure."

"I'll call you."

"Right. Oh, by the way. How much did you give him?" Amos asked.

"Fifty." Robert went through the door without looking back.

It had been five hundred.

4

Sweetly but firmly, Marly demanded half the money for herself. She reminded the Impersonator that over the period of their nine years together his chief contribution to their shared household had generally been limited to the consistent presence of his ever-interesting self, and that now that they were living in New York and trying to live like grown-ups instead of hippies, she, Marly, was beginning to find this state of affairs unacceptable.

Their income came partly from her waitress's salary and partly from a check that arrived monthly from her parents in Vermont, who had no idea that this allowance—which was supposed to be used for dancing and voice lessons, tickets to cultural events, splurges, and little emergencies that would come up in the city—had been used for many years to support the Impersonator.

It wasn't that he never earned anything at all, but he was picky as to the kinds of work he would accept. Not for him the kinds of jobs their would-be-actor friends suffered. He had told Marly on their second day in

New York that before stultifying his spirit by having to
become a waiter or a demonstrator at Bloomingdale's,
he would do away with himself. Marly, who bounced
back and forth in rubber shoes six nights a week asking
people what kind of dressing they wanted and if everything was all right, could not help but admire—in theory—the uncompromising light in which he continued
to regard himself.

From time to time he served as a nude model at an
art school nearby, and on occasion—if the money was
right and the neighborhood was acceptable—he painted
someone's apartment. He had never planned to tell
Marly about Robert's money, but she had found it
while rummaging through his underwear drawer, looking for some socks to wear with her rubber shoes that
evening.

When called upon to explain, he told Marly that the
five hundred dollars was an advance for one of his intermittent painting jobs. Then, in order to support this
fiction, he realized, he would have to spend several
eight-hour days away from home. He walked the city in
loathing, wearing a hat and black sunglasses, following
attractive, prosperous-looking people into jewelry and
fur stores, luggage and shoe shops, observing their
purchases, their speech patterns, their manners. When
he wearied of this he sat in Central Park smoking and
dreaming.

In the end he spent the entire sum on her. It was to
be her birthday the following week and she had seen a
pair of boots for two hundred and fifty dollars that she
began to hint about, adding (again tactfully) that he
had never given her anything for her birthday, not really, that is, with his own money. And in fact he hadn't.
Her parents would send money and with that he would
treat her to a splendid day of his own devising. Champagne, flowers, a lobster dinner that he would prepare

himself, and especially romantic lovemaking. He was highly gifted at pleasing.

He was also good at reading her mind. Even before she had acknowledged it to herself, he had smelled the case she was—yet again—beginning to build against him. The point was that he had nowhere else to go. It was not the moment to cross her. What was five hundred dollars if it bought him another few hundred days under the fur rug with his television and his fruit and Marly's family to bail them out at the end of every month?

So he decided it would be prudent to buy her the boots, even though it was painful for him to give up the money. He had planned to spend it on a racy-looking raincoat with epaulettes. He wished Marly was capable of understanding the extent of his gnawing emptiness and spiritual paralysis and how much the raincoat might have helped him feel better about himself. She was a decent girl, perhaps the most decent he had ever known, and he had admired—and envied—her plucky, straightforward character from the beginning. But her very lack of complexity was at the same time her major flaw. Her all too easy—and all too often offered—solutions to his problems, to his life, indicated an absence of depth that he found, at times, really annoying.

When Jane came back from the Amazon, Robert held her tightly against him, closed his eyes, kissed her hair, brought almost to tears by the physical reassurance of her existence. He loved the look of Jane, the quickness of her, the laughter, the honesty. Theo had been honest too, but her truths had often contained a careless brutality that had hit the bull's-eye of him over and over until he had felt skinned, owned, possessed—strung out beneath her brilliant glare.

When she died he was so occupied with his role as the bereaved husband of a world-famous woman now lost so tragically that he didn't think much about how it had really been between them, because the press's version of her, her life, and their life together was so much more palatable and reassuring. The memorial services in four cities, the Sunday feature stories, the requests for photographs, the interviews by documentary makers, the inquiries from would-be biographers, and the thousands of fan letters all served to obscure memory.

The advent of the impersonator had brought— among other things—remembrance.

Holding Jane in his arms, kissing her, trying to get her underpants off, he decided not to visit the impersonator again.

And anyway, Theo had not loved him. She had said quite candidly that she could not. "One reaches a point." She had looked off into the distance. "I want us just to be dear, passionate friends."

Robert had not really believed her. She mixed up her own fictions with reality, depending on the time of day. "Adorably wacky," he described her to his parents, a cheerful euphemism by which he meant that the inconsistencies in Theo's moods—and, of course, her favors —constituted her power over him, and therefore her profound allure.

At the same time, he fully understood that she had chosen to be married principally for practical reasons. A famous woman without a mate was vulnerable, prey to invasion wherever she went. A husband was buffer, excuse, security. Someone to have dinner with on the train, as it were. Theo wore Robert. At first he didn't mind. She could have had so many other men, but she had chosen him. That he would eventually win her heart, he had no doubt, no doubt at all.

In bed Theo had been graceful, relentless, oddly silent. Was she possibly fantasizing about someone else? After a time he asked her. Was she summoning up another face, another body?

Two beautiful eyes bored into his. "I've never had that kind of fantasy in my life."

"Everybody does."

"Me, I'm always right where I am." She put out one arm in the direction of the bedside table, picked up a pencil, made a note. "Thanks. I should think about that." And he knew the conversation had been dismissed.

A month later she and Emma had polished up a screamingly funny monologue on the subject of sexual fantasy and incorporated it into her act. After that it would have been futile to bring up the subject again because Theo's thoughts had now been fused into those of Fanny Lou, the fictional character she had created and used with much success in her cabaret and one-woman performances.

Robert had hated Fanny Lou. Intellectually he had tried to adopt a certain detachment toward his wife's professional alter ego, but he was rarely successful. He even discussed it once, in the early days, over a drink with Amos.

"Theo never 'does' Fanny except onstage, so theoretically I don't have to contend with her around the house, but she exists nevertheless. She hangs around the fringes of the day. Of the night."

"Fanny's the character who's never been out of Georgia and who has a very big mouth when it comes to social and topical comment?"

Robert nodded.

Amos smiled. "My recollection is that she's very amusing."

"Oh, she's funny all right." Robert stared bleakly at Amos.

"What's the problem?"

"To start with, she doesn't give a shit what she says. She doesn't go for the jugular, she goes for the balls."

"She's the one who hates men? Who was jilted?"

"At the altar."

"So maybe she has cause."

Robert stared at Amos. "Listen to us, talking about her as if she were real."

"She obviously is, to you."

"She makes fun of things that shouldn't be made fun of."

"Like what?"

"Like me. Right now she's shooting off her mouth at the Winter Garden every night. You know what I'd like to do? I'd like to kill her."

5

The Impersonator—as Theo—sat on a plain wooden chair in a pool of dusty light that filtered through the high window with its green velvet curtains. He regarded Robert through violet-tinted glasses.

Robert sat some four feet away, as instructed, on the edge of the bed that was covered by the fur rug with black and silver pelts. It was his second visit to the apartment and the first since Jane's return from the Amazon. Of course he had not planned, really, to come again, but here he was.

The initial visit had been suffused with uncertainty, as strained a rite of passage as the telephone conversation that had preceded it. Even given the degree of Robert's heat for the adventure, how did one choose the words to ask a stranger to dress up as one's dead wife and be available for an hour's respectable entertainment? In the end it had been his relentless assumption that his wish would be gratified that had carried the idea forward; that, and to a much lesser extent, the grave, somewhat monosyllabic acquiescence of the impersonator, who set a time limit of thirty minutes.

It had begun on a long silence. Two figures, stuffed with straw, propped up inside their self-devised tableau for two.

In some agony Robert had said at last, "Talk to me."

The Theo apparition studied her long red fingernails. "I suppose you want me to pull your dingdong."

Christ, it was Fanny Lou.

"I mean, isn't that all you guys ever think about?" The myopic Georgia shrew peered at him. *"Big babies* is what you are."

"Shut up." Robert was on his feet. One more rush of blood through his arteries to his neck and his head would blow off. He stared down at her, tasting already the release that violence would bring.

"Bob?"

That wasn't Fanny Lou. It was Theo.

"Bob? Sit down. I'm sorry. It's the full moon tonight. You know how I get." There was a jokey pause. "And this nerd who's impersonating me isn't really sure what you want."

Robert sat down, crossed his legs. "Neither am I," he said affably. The relief, the relief of Theo flooded him. "Just don't bring that woman anywhere near me."

"I used to use her to say things I knew I couldn't get away with saying myself, you know, things I'd figured out were true but that would make men not like me. So if Fanny Lou told the truths, expressed the hurts, asked the unaskable questions, guys could always say, well, she's just this load-of-bananas kook who nobody's ever wanted and who's really dying for it." His dead wife paused, gave him a candid look. "There was a lot of responsibility to doing what I did. People never thought about that."

Watching the rhythmically swinging, linen-trousered

leg and the hint of pale, polished ankle in the high-heeled red shoe, Robert speculated as to the unseen portions of the man's body. An inhalation moved his fancy to the back of the knee. And up. She had had a thing about her legs. Her coming had always had to do in part with the loving of her legs. That first time, she had showed him how.

He looked up, wondering how long the silence had lasted. His dazzling partner was studying him, taking his measure, Robert knew with rising excitement.

Had Robert taken the time to *really* wonder how the Impersonator was able to "get" Theo to such a brilliant extent? Curiously—and at the same time understandably—the answer was no. Had he had any personal experience with the rigors of acting and impersonation he might have been rendered speechless by the Impersonator's skill and demanded to know more of his tale, but to Robert, after all, the situation was a provocative, highly personal experience. To Robert it was all so familiar, it was the faithful reproduction of his late wife, and the really compelling aspect for him lay in what might be ahead.

As for the Impersonator's startling expertise, Robert knew that pirated tape recordings of Theo's live monologues had existed and there was also quite a bit of film and he assumed television networks kept archives just as newspapers did. And he *had* asked an initial question about it at the first meeting.

The Impersonator had replied in a Theo drawl, "Don't flatter him with compliments. He's basically an amateur who got lucky. Our tonal levels are identical."

The already beguiled Robert was soon stuck fast in the beguilement itself, unable, unwilling to entertain anything that might threaten his new pleasure. Some weeks before he had had occasion to telephone Theo's former assistant in Los Angeles and he had mentioned

the performance he had seen at The Touch Me Club.
He instantly regretted this when the devoted, humorless
young woman, whom he remembered always in beiges
—expensive beige blouses, beige makeup, beige hair—
doggedly adopted the same tack as Jane, i.e., couldn't
this person be stopped?

"That's loyal of you, Una," Robert had said, "but
this guy's so good, all I can do is wish him well." He
had changed the subject and firmly declined to discuss it
when she brought it up again at the end of the conversation.

For his second visit to the apartment, Robert wore a
new shirt. Five-hundred-threads-an-inch cotton, navy
and white stripes with a pure white collar. On arriving,
he took off his jacket and loosened his new dark red tie.

His costumed host had also dressed especially for the
occasion. Robert caught his breath when he saw what
had been added—a visored woodsman's cap with
floppy ear flaps. The flaps hung loosely, swinging jauntily.

Generally unknown to the public (though Robert recalled that it might have been mentioned in a *New
Yorker* profile), Theo worried obsessively about her
voice and was convinced that if she kept her ears pro-
tected from the cold, and especially from drafts, there
would be less chance of any respiratory ailments.

On a freezing, snowy night in Boston as she was
leaving the theater after her show, one of her musicians
had offered her his homely-looking cap. Enchanted by
its shape and the flaps, she had asked the next day if she
could buy it from him. She didn't want one from L.L.
Bean; she wanted that one, and it became a kind of
mascot, something she would always have with her. It
was perfect when she didn't want to be recognized—the
visor, the flaps, and a pair of sunglasses had disguised
her completely. Even in warm climates she would have

it around, to plunk on her head for inspiration, she said. Robert had memories of the cap, sometimes cock-eyed, sometimes backward, sitting on Theo's head while she sat by the pool reading, or dozing in an airplane, or dashing from the stage door to a waiting car. In winter she had worn it every day, always whipping it off at the last moment, handing it to the driver to keep as she stepped—always glamorously—across the threshold of a restaurant.

The Impersonator was making the flaps swing by moving his head this way, that way, in play. "I know," he said saucily, "you think it makes me look like Snoopy. But this hat is *me*."

Robert felt the tightness of remembrance inside his chest. He sensed they were crossing an invisible line. The wearing of the cap was a brilliant stroke of intimacy.

In addition, there were certain austere glances that seemed to propose more complicity than before, that acknowledged the heat of Robert's perplexed desire, that hinted that a reciprocal passion did perhaps exist and was being held, fastidiously, in check. Was the comely Theo/boy, scrupulously monkish up to now, preparing them for physical pleasures?

What would they be?

Across the four feet that separated them, Robert sat in consternation and rapture. The entertainment continued chastely enough, fronting for what Robert hoped might be a hidden agenda soon to be revealed. He declined to name to himself what he wanted. It was enough for now to revel in this second chance. A second chance to be himself with Theo. That is what he told himself.

As before, the thirty minutes went by too quickly. The Impersonator produced an enigmatic smile and said, "You'll have to go now, Bob."

Wrong again. Robert stood up, picked up his jacket, his tie. Suddenly he felt unwelcome, foolish. The figure in the chair was looking at his watch, tapping his foot, staring absently out the window. Robert's face began to flame. He left money on the bureau by the front door and walked down the four flights to the street.

He was astonished by the ordinary colors of the afternoon. The grimy stoops, the snarls of traffic, the children playing. The world had been going on all the while. He thought of where he had just been. One swore off in shame, one ran back in sweet surrender. The litany of addiction.

A silent ambulance traveled slowly by. When they didn't use the siren he always wondered if it was because the person inside had died. He looked at his watch. A tutorial with that rather bright young woman from Bombay. Then a drinks meeting with his editor. He crossed the street at a sprint, his long, athletic legs quickly covering the distance to the corner, where a cruising taxi had paused for a red light.

The instant Robert had quit the apartment, the Impersonator carefully removed his false fingernails and took off his silk blouse and linen trousers. He put everything he had been wearing—including the wig—into a large plastic garment bag and wedged it into the crowded closet that held all of Marly's and his things. He took out a makeup box and carried it to the bathroom. He pulled off his false eyelashes, creamed and wiped off the foundation and the blusher, and held a hot washcloth to his face for a long time.

He began to cry a little, angry tears that made his eyes red, so he took a bottle of drops from the cabinet and, tilting his head back, let the cool liquid flood into the corners of his eyes. Then he left the bathroom with the makeup box, slipped in the money that Robert had given him, put the box away at the bottom of the closet, and turned on the television set. John Wayne again. Four inches of him, riding, fighting, loving. He got into bed and pulled the fur rug over him.

When Marly came in he was asleep. She stared at his milky eyelids and wanted to scream. She had never known anyone who slept so much. On purpose she made a lot of noise unpacking the grocery bag she had carried in with her.

His eyes opened and he looked at her with an air of sleepy bewilderment. A bit of the fur blanket had slipped so that one bare, sculpted shoulder was exposed.

She said with an edge to her voice, "If I'd known you were going to be around, you could have got the groceries. I have to work the early dinner shift tonight."

No reaction. Instead, a redolent silence that promised she would soon find herself in the wrong.

"I don't feel well," he said, and shivered. "Will you feel my forehead?"

She replied in a fury—suddenly she didn't give a fuck, she really didn't—"I guess that means you didn't go look for a job like you promised. And you know what? I've had it. I told you two weeks ago I was sick of living like this, but every day you've come up with an excuse." She paused uncertainly, remembering that two of those days he had devoted himself to a thorough cleaning of the apartment, waxing the floors, washing the walls, polishing the furniture. He had also filled the place with flowers; it had been like coming home to a bower—and he had made wonderful spaghetti and then massaged her feet and read to her from Byron. But that was exactly the problem. He would do anything to postpone the future.

"I want to make something of myself," she continued, on firm ground again. "I'm almost thirty years old and nothing has happened. You promise to change but you never do. I want to break up." She took a wavery breath. "I want you to go. I mean it."

He closed his eyes and lay still as death. The last time she'd said that, he'd had to go stumbling around their revolting neighborhood making up stories about looking for work and he'd met a girl who had a brother-in-law in the Village who was just getting a club started and would probably take on cheap nonunion entertainment. He'd really had no choice but to do the only thing at hand, put on the red wig and go on as Theo, sick unto his bowels with fear.

Marly resumed unpacking the groceries. She put the nectarines and the grapes and the plums into a bowl. Where would he go? What would he do? Was it fair to turn him out without any money? She put the rest of the things into the little refrigerator and began to fold up the bag, which they would use later for the garbage. Her hands were shaking. She wanted a life. Was it selfish, unreasonable, to want a life?

Behind her, she heard him get out of bed. Then the light tread of his bare feet on the wooden floor. He was holding the fur rug around him like a cape. It trailed behind him and he looked very wan and tall. In a moment, she thought, the lighting technicians would begin the storm. Incredible how he could create a stage for himself anywhere. He knelt at her feet, bowed his head.

She felt his tears falling on her bare toes, which were sticking out of scuffed sandals. "Do I at least," he asked huskily, "have the right to say I love you?" He took one of her hands, kissed the palm, then folded her fingers tightly around the place he had kissed.

They had been together for longer than any other couple they knew, never separated except that summer he'd had to help out his uncle with his logging business in northern California. Yes, she wanted to imagine a life without him, but for today, for today her resolve had already begun to dissipate and she felt only the sadness of him, of them. Sighing, she ruffled his hair.

An hour later he was playing racquetball at his friend Keith's gym, a square of sky-blue cloth tied as a headband around his patrician forehead, his thick hair wet and curling over it. He played with savage grace. Keith glanced at him enviously. How could that delicate-looking frame contain so much strength?

"You want to get a beer?" Keith asked when they finished their game and headed for the showers.

"Sure," the Impersonator replied, eyeing a couple of Lovelies who were coming toward them. He looked each girl over with the same dedicated concentration with which he had just been slamming balls and with which afterward he regarded his own reflection in the locker room mirror. Later, when he picked up his beer to drink it, his friend Keith took note of the particular movement. Really, there was nothing to picking up a bottle of beer, except as performed by the Impersonator it became a perfect act.

"Been to any auditions?" Keith asked, sticking as usual to the Subject. They had not seen each other in a while.

"I go with Marly to hers." He gave Keith a look. "You know I'm her coach."

Keith sipped his beer and pondered this puzzling remark. In principle, his unfathomable friend didn't have the experience to justify being anyone's coach. But again he envied him, this time for his silvery way with words. He could dress the most mundane, even the most mendacious information by shifting the content ever so slightly, as if he were moving a mirror in order to catch the best possible light.

"Marly's having a crisis of confidence." There was a concerned frown. "I do what I can to help."

Keith, who had heard from his own girlfriend, Sandy, that Marly had had it with having to support an able-bodied man and was thinking about living life on her own, was not sure how to reply. So he inquired, "Sandy said you had some kind of gig at a place downtown?"

"I decided to drop it." There was a pause, then he continued smoothly. "Working a club is like doing floors and windows."

Another mystery. What amateur in his right mind would pass up the chance for that kind of exposure? Keith sipped his beer. "So how come you're not going to auditions?"

"I draw the line at begging. At kissing ass."

"What other choice do we have? Besides," Keith added generously, "you're probably going to make it."

The Impersonator's expression was hooded. "I only decided to get into acting because that's what Marly was studying when I met her. It was a way to be together."

Keith stared. "You're kidding me."

"I don't burn with a bright flame. I never have. I need inspiration or I sink." What did it matter if he gave Keith a few tidbits of the truth? Keith couldn't hurt him.

He scowled, thinking of recent events. The latest barrage had begun in earnest two weeks before. Marly, who did not know about Robert's visits, nevertheless sensed in that deeply unsettling way women had that something was being concealed from her. Frustrated and made to feel guilty by his clear-eyed and reproachful responses to her as yet vague suspicions, she had exploded in another, even more dangerous direction. What was he going to do about his life?

"You think because you're handsome and charming I'll spend the rest of my days working in a fucking restaurant so you can lie around all day watching TV and waiting for your career to be handed to you on a platter? You think standing around naked at that art school showing off your cock for practically no money and loving every minute of it is a contribution to this household? You think I believe that you walked out on the nightclub job?"

At least for today he had managed—again—to hold on to her.

He now said to Keith, "You want to take a day off next week? Get out of the city and go fishing?" Blessed trees and silence. This grotesque city would crush him. He hadn't wanted to come, he had been frightened, he would have preferred to continue putting on Thornton Wilder and Tennessee Williams at the little community theater where they had met, where they had spent their first years together in a gentle, pastoral New England landscape, but Marly had wanted to come to New York and be a star.

"Fishing? God, I'd really like to," Keith said, "but I'm working two jobs at the moment. Sandy and I are in deep shit with our Visa and MasterCards." He looked at his watch. "Fact is I got to be at the answering service in forty minutes."

The Impersonator took the subway home. There were plenty of seats at this hour, but he stood in order to get a better view of who among the passengers he might develop a temporary fantasy relationship with for the duration of the journey.

At the first stop a woman got on, holding the hand of a little girl of about four who had soft black eyes and fat little Shirley Temple ringlets. He began to stare at the little girl with fierce concentration. His intention was to inhabit her, to actually become her.

The staleness of the subway car now dissolved into the cleaner air of the past. Gingerbread cookies, ironing starch, morning dew. Green fields with grass waving under a perfect summer sky. Safe. Safe in the tall grass with the warm breeze blowing and every fantastic wish about to come true.

A kind Stranger with sad eyes now approaches through the grass. The Stranger kneels, reaches under that tiny skirt, gently pulls down those tiny panties—

Thus did the Impersonator, encased in the body of the little girl with the ringlets, have loving oral sex with himself in the softest of remembered green meadows as the filthy train car carried him through the underbelly of Park Avenue. Also thus was he mercifully prevented from engaging in another of his subway fantasies— peering through the window into the blackness, looking in dread and cynical resignation for the alligators he had been told inhabited the foul bottom of the city.

Robert sat in a taxi next to his editor, Phil Simonetta, a graying, athletic-looking man with ulcers and a fondness for Robert that had recently begun to give way to impatience.

Phil looked down at the manila envelope in his lap that contained Robert's manuscript. "It's not only late, old pal, but it looks thin."

Robert was staring out the window. "It's not all there. Sorry. Two more chapters to go."

"I don't understand," Phil proposed agreeably, "why it has taken you so long to collect a series of lectures you've already given—and now you tell me the manuscript isn't complete?"

A few days later Amos Miller was less indulgent.

"I should think," Amos dryly remarked, having just been brought up-to-date on Robert's week, "that the

least productive place for you to work out your unresolved ambivalences about Theo—assuming that's the
problem—is in the apartment of this transvestite."

"You keep harping on that aspect of it. I'm surprised
you haven't asked me if I've ever had a homosexual
experience. If I'm actually having one now."

"Most men have." Amos gave Robert a mild look.
"Or at least in the sense they've wanted it at one time or
another."

"I fooled around in prep school. It wasn't really my
taste—then or now."

"So what's the attraction? What keeps you going
back to him?"

"I told you I haven't touched him. And he hasn't
touched me." Robert added, "I suppose I go to see him
because it's like being with Theo. I get to have her
back." He had now told three half lies. No, he hadn't
touched the Impersonator except in torrential waking
dreams of sacramental passage. No, the Impersonator
had not touched him, not touched him sexually except
through sly suggestion. As for Theo . . .

But Amos was posing another question. "You mean
you get to have Theo back in a more manageable, more
attractive way than before?"

"What do you mean?"

"You get to have her back as a man. As a man would
want to conceive her. As you might even have preferred
her. It's possible you may have stumbled upon the actu-
alization of what might be the ultimate male fantasy—
one we don't even want to know we have—that is the
wish to create our women as we would secretly like
them to be. Feminine. But not female."

Robert gave Amos a prissy, scholar's look. "That's
pretty cynical, isn't it? Even distasteful?"

"Why distasteful?"

"You're saying we don't really want women, don't really like them?"

Amos's glance was humorous. "It's entirely possible they don't really like us either," he said, and then wished he hadn't. He promised himself he would never again take on a friend for clinical consultation. One was more relaxed and thus more easily provoked into meandering into untried speculations. Unhelpful. Risky. The fact that Robert gave lectures in philosophy was no guarantee that he was emotionally ready to apply the notion of abstract hatred between the genders to his own messy dilemma.

Amos took a sip of his diet drink. Had there been, all this time, throughout all these centuries, only the one remedy for the male fear of powerlessness? Either to destroy women or to create them—and was it the same?

He glanced across at Robert, set down his drink. Were women so terrifying that it had always been ultimately less threatening to will a goddess to spring from one's head than to risk the untidy mortality of a maiden?

He resumed his professional air. "As I remember it, Robert, at the end you and Theo were living mostly apart. She was at the Russian River. You were here on the East Coast. You told me at the time you weren't getting along at all."

Robert stared at his shoes with a puzzled air, as if trying to remember the facts.

Briskly Amos continued. "Could we sum up where we seem to be so far? You come in here—what is it, six weeks ago—with this . . . situation. You're not prepared to give it up. But you want to talk about it. You want, in effect, an accomplice. Just in case."

Robert's look was bland but slightly uneasy.

"As your friend," Amos went on, "my first thought is to protect you from possible consequences by inviting you to realize what they could be. You're playing a dangerous game with a stranger. Someone you've never even seen as his real self. You don't know where he comes from, who he lives with, what he does when he's not taking your money. Whatever personal information you give him, even the fact that you visit him at all, he could use in ways that might damage you publicly, hurt Jane, and make an unholy mess of your lives."

The outer door opened and closed. Amos glanced at his little clock. "Notwithstanding the fact that the police closed the case on Theo, it remains an unwitnessed death. This guy goes to the press, they'll have a field day. Grieving Widower Employs Transvestite Séance Medium to Discover Truth about Star's Mystery Death. You want to put Jane through that?" He looked at his appointment book. "Sorry, I have to throw you out now. You want to drop by at the end of the week?"

"We're going down to that thing at the White House." Robert stood up. "Listen, Amos, I appreciate your caution. I'd want to do the same for you." He paused. "I just hope I'd have been a little more sensitive."

Pleasantly, Amos looked up. "No shit."

"I wasn't born yesterday," Robert said quietly. "If I want to trust him, that's my privilege. I can help him. I can open doors. He's never had a proper chance. I could make the difference in his life."

Love, Amos thought, after he had shown Robert out. Love.

Some three hours north, the Impersonator, with a beer tucked between his knees, had been doing eighty miles an hour on the expressway. He now turned off, drove down a steep ramp, went a scant one hundred and fifty feet mostly in a circle, and arrived almost immediately at an entrance through a scrubby hedge to a three-story Victorian-style house, its fanciful period trim polluted by age and fumes from the highways that encircled it on all sides. The property itself, once a hundred acres of rolling countryside, had been reduced to one, barely enough to contain the house, a few dilapidated out-buildings, and the traffic-whipped garden.

He parked by the front steps and reached into the backseat for his jacket. A young man in stiff dungarees and a neat Brooks Brothers shirt came out the front door.

The Impersonator smiled up at his younger brother. "Hey there, Ethan."

"Hello, Bro."

Ethan had been calling him Bro ever since the younger boy had been sent to prep school, courtesy of their Great-aunt Charity, who had also paid for the Impersonator's two years at drama school after he'd met Marly.

It was during the prep-school period that Ethan had started ordering Brooks shirts and wearing his hair the way he did now—short and squared off—and acting real serious and quiet for his years and kind of old-maidish too, the Impersonator had thought but did not comment. He preferred to accommodate his brother's individuality, and anyway hardly anyone ever saw Ethan except the inmates of the house and the delivery people and the plumber and the state inspector. Ethan ran Brawley Manor like a tight ship and rarely left the grounds except to get a haircut in the shopping mall.

Two years earlier Ethan had traveled to a friend's wedding in another state and had been away for three days. When he got back he said he wished he hadn't gone, and when the Impersonator had asked why, he had replied, "I like it here," and turned on the televi-sion, picked up a *National Geographic* magazine, and settled down on his bed, which was covered with an ivory satin comforter he had ordered by catalogue.

"You ever see any girls?" the Impersonator had once asked Ethan.

"Nope," Ethan had replied, and added with one of his droll looks, "boys neither."

They walked through the house, went into the fusty Victorian parlor that was never used except at Christmas, funerals, or to receive visiting relatives, of which there were few remaining. The boys had another great-aunt, who lived in Nebraska and whom they'd never seen. Then there was Dear Old Dad, as they called him with much hilarity when they spoke of him at all. He'd recently married again and neither brother had seen him for years.

They entered another, smaller parlor where a tiny, sweet-faced, very old lady sat staring at a television set.

The Impersonator leaned down, kissed her on her forehead. "How you doin', Aunt Charity."

"Well, I'm just doing fine." Charity gave him a pleased look. "It's been a coon's age since I saw you. Guess you're doing all that fancy acting in New York. How come we never see you on the TV?"

He smoothed her hair, straightened the plaid lap rug over her knees. "I'm in the theater, Aunt Charity."

"I guess I forgot. I forget things now. Ask Ethan."

Ethan guffawed. "You remember everything you really want to, Aunt Charity, and that's a fact."

Charity's eyes went back to the television set. "Look at that. Everything's so ugly. Charles and Diana getting married, now, that was grand. You think they'll repeat that?"

"That was millions of years ago. They got a baby now." Ethan chucked her under the chin. "You want a cookie or something? More coffee?"

The Impersonator had walked into a small room just

off the parlor. A middle-aged hunchback sat at a little school desk, staring down at his hands.

"Hiya, Tommy," the Impersonator said cheerfully. Tommy did not turn, did not look at the Impersonator.

Ethan appeared in the doorway. "He's been depressed all week. Couldn't get him to help me with the chores, and he'd been doing great lately, did I tell you?"

The Impersonator lit a cigarette, blew smoke out of his beautiful nostrils. "We'd be depressed too if we'd been retarded since we were born and lived most of our lives in this room." He looked down. "When are you going to fix this linoleum? He could trip and fucking kill himself."

"Could you identify the problem?" Ethan asked with a deadpan look as they left the room and started down a small hallway. "You speak as if his death would be some kind of universal loss."

The Impersonator burst out laughing. Ethan had already started to giggle. They began to choke with merriment. Gasping, they climbed the stairs to Ethan's room. Ethan turned on the television set, threw himself onto his ivory satin quilt. His brother sat down in a rocking chair nearby, crossed his legs, fleetingly admired his own ankles.

"How come you're not wearing socks?" Ethan inquired in some dismay.

"Loafers with no socks are in."

"Looks fruity."

"Fuck you."

"How come you're here, anyway?"

"Hadn't seen you in a while. I'll stay till after breakfast."

"How's Marly?"

"Okay."

An hour went by. They did not speak to each other except to comment on the action. During the commercials Ethan worked his remote to monitor what was playing on other channels. When the program was over he got up. "It's Rhoda's turn for a bath tonight. You want to help? It'll go quicker. Then we can put Charity down and come back here for the late movie."

His brother rose, took off his shirt, removed his watch. "How're the girls doing, anyway?"

"Patsy and Hester had this fight over one of the dolls. In the end I had to throw the damned doll away, it was the only way to make peace. Come to think of it, it was the doll you gave Patsy two Christmases ago."

"Marly picked it out." She had also paid for it with her Visa card.

They got Rhoda into the large white institutional-looking bathroom, took her clothes off, helped her into the tub. Ethan made sure the water was just right as it began to run in, testing it with the inside of his wrist. The Impersonator repinned Rhoda's hair so it wouldn't get wet when they washed her neck.

They set themselves to giving Rhoda a good scrub. She weighed one hundred and sixty-five pounds, had big brown eyes and a remarkably unlined face for a woman over sixty.

When the Impersonator said, "Reach for the sky, Rhoda," she smiled flirtatiously, lifted up both her arms. He sponged soap into her armpits. "Good girl, Rhoda."

Ethan was rinsing her back. "Have we done her ears?" he asked his brother. "I have a routine, but when you're here I get mixed up."

The Impersonator began to wash Rhoda's ears. She didn't like this. He chucked her gently under the chin, winked at her to distract her attention. His glance dropped to her desiccated breasts. Dispassionately, he examined them. He wondered if her family ever thought of her. They were Cabots or Vanderbilts, something like that, from long ago. Brawley Manor, in fact, owed its inception to those great American families who since the turn of the century had been now and then obliged to hide away an unfortunate daughter or son and had come upon Aunt Charity's parents, who had promised a noninstitutional institution that guaranteed that the poor things would be treated with kindness and individual attention, be given good food and medical attention of the highest order. This guarantee had been scrupulously, if sometimes informally, observed.

"You haven't been here for months." Ethan pulled the plug and they helped Rhoda to her feet.

Ethan wanted to say, "You only come here when you want something or when you're in trouble," but he couldn't. His brother was the only person who had ever bothered to try to understand him, and failing that, to accept him. His brother was the only person in the world he could call on the telephone when he was feeling depressed. During these conversations they never talked about what the problem really was, but that was okay. They talked about what Ethan had ordered from a catalogue that day, what he was planting in the garden, and Ethan would recount the latest dramas and incidents concerning the residents of Brawley Manor. The Impersonator would allow Ethan to chat on about inconsequential matters—television programs he had seen, how he felt about certain world events, and so on. Ethan would feel better by the minute.

They dried Rhoda, put a fresh nightgown on her, and led her back to her room, which she shared with two other aging child-women, who were already in bed. They tucked Rhoda in. They both kissed her on the cheek, patted her on the head. The Impersonator turned out the light. "Should we look in on Frank?"

"No need." Ethan's eyes twinkled. "Let's go back to my room and I'll show you."

He had ordered an intercom system. He switched it on and the Impersonator heard snores. "It's hooked up to the girls' room too," Ethan added. "I don't have to make rounds at night anymore. I don't know why I didn't think of it before." He looked at his watch. "We still have Charity."

They went downstairs. Aunt Charity had washed her face and brushed her teeth. She was arranging some pillows on the sofa. "You're such good boys. I don't need a thing." Fully dressed, she lay down on the sofa. Ethan put a pillow behind her head, covered her with a blanket. The Impersonator took both her hands, rubbed them in his.

"Nighty night, hon."

"You know I haven't slept for twenty years?"

"I know, Aunt Charity."

They left one light burning and went into the huge kitchen to get milk and cookies. There were ten bedrooms in the house, but Aunt Charity had been sleeping on the sofa ever since they could remember. She had started doing this after her husband had died because she was now alone with "the children" and wanted to be in a central place—and ready—should anything be required of her. Some thirty years later, when Ethan decided to postpone college and to go up to western Massachusetts and help out at Brawley Manor, Aunt Charity could have resumed sleeping in her bedroom, but the habit was ingrained. She lay on the sofa, gazing through the window, looking for stars most of the night, fantasizing about a lover who would come and make her life, finally, something to be remembered.

The brothers, who did not know of Aunt Charity's desperate loneliness, fierce romantic and sexual desire, and unswerving hope (and why should they?), went upstairs. In Ethan's room they closed the door and settled down to watch more television.

The Impersonator felt himself relaxing. Funny, this was the one place in the world where he felt really okay. Fucking riot, really. A loony bin. Sitting here with his brother, eating cookies out of a box from the grocery store, warm and comfy inside this creaky old place that had been in his family since the turn of the century. Around its perimeters snaked the highways, the off ramps, the vertiginous flashing lights, but inside the house was safe, trusty as a fortress.

Sometimes he envied Ethan's life. Ethan didn't have to live up to anything or anybody. All he had to do was take care of the Children. There were only five of them now, and they were all on tranquilizers, so they weren't too much trouble. Even when occasionally one of them fell down the stairs, the medication required by the state—even for private institutions—kept them so physically relaxed they rarely suffered anything more than a few bruises.

Ethan didn't approve, philosophically, of the tranquilizers. He felt that with less blurring of the senses the Children might enjoy better, more rewarding lives, and had lately been sending away for information, hoping to educate himself on the subject.

The Impersonator preferred not to dwell on the fact that it was a bizarre way for a twenty-five-year-old to spend the first decade of his adulthood. When people asked about his brother with raised eyebrows or just plain curiosity, he merely smiled and replied, "It's a family business. Ethan's helping out Aunt Charity." When queried further as to whether Ethan had had any prior training in institutional work or planned to make a career out of working with the mentally retarded, he would smile again and say, "Ask Ethan, why don't you." He declined to participate in any speculations that proposed that Ethan at a tender age had been so horrified by life in general that he had escaped into the safest haven available.

The phone beside Ethan's bed rang. He reached for it. "Hello? Hi, Marly."

The Impersonator scowled. Whenever he did this, Ethan noticed, something ugly happened to his mouth, which was on the verge of being a bad mouth to begin with, but this was hardly ever remarked upon because of the classically fine nose and cheekbones, the smoky eyes, the darkly handsome eyebrows, the perfect skin.

"How's everything, Marly?" Ethan continued. He listened briefly and handed the receiver to his brother. "She wants you."

The Impersonator took the phone. "Hello," he said in a beautifully modulated, cool tone. So different, Ethan marveled, from the down-home way he talked when he was at Brawley Manor.

Marly's breathless rush of words poured into the Impersonator's left ear. He felt his brain heating up. With his will he tried to shut her out. Finally he said reassuringly, "Listen. I'll be home tomorrow." He waited briefly for it to sink in. "Gotta go, babe." And he hung up.

Ethan pressed the volume button on the remote box and the sound amplified again. He held out the bag of cookies to the Impersonator, who took three and began to munch. Some minutes later a commercial came on. With understanding and tenderness, a husband and wife discussed the husband's diarrhea.

"Marly says she thinks she's got a lump in one of her breasts," the Impersonator said. "I guess you could say she's hysterical."

Ethan looked back at the commercial with frantic attention. What would he be asked for now? He didn't want anything to do with Marly's lump. He liked

Marly, she was always nice to him, she was always fun, they talked often on the telephone and the check she got from her parents every month had for years relieved him of being asked too often for money by his brother. She carried Bro's car insurance and took care of his tax returns (what a laugh those were!). But he really resented this latest piece of information. He didn't want to think about Marly's breasts. He had never seen them, never wished to, they had nothing to do with him. Now, on top of everything, one of them had become diseased and would probably have to be lopped off. As his mother's had been. Both of them sliced from her body. And more stuff from under the arms. A year later she had died. What was the point of breasts anyway? They disgusted him. Clearly they never disgusted Bro, who had been quiveringly offered every pair he had ever wanted to lay his hands on since the age of seven or eight.

In anguish, Ethan reached for another cookie. No use thinking about the early days, Bro always being the favorite and all wherever they went, Bro being cruel to him, frightening him when he was little. Things had changed. He, Ethan, had become a responsible adult, far more responsible than Bro. He just hoped Bro wasn't going to talk anymore about Marly's lump or Marly's breasts. One of the good things about Brawley Manor was that one didn't have to concern oneself with breasts.

In the morning Aunt Charity sat as usual at the head of the long mahogany dining table by a bay window hung with machine-made lace café curtains she and Ethan had ordered from a catalogue. She poured out cooked percolator coffee into three thin porcelain cups. The brothers took their places at the table, one on each side of her. A comfortable silence settled over them as they drank the coffee and ate white toast spread with margarine.

"I'll mow the lawn after breakfast, Aunt Charity." The Impersonator helped himself to more toast. "Might do a little pruning on the forsythia too."

With bony fingers Aunt Charity was tapping her worn bird book lying next to her plate. "That red cardinal that was here yesterday, remember, Ethan? Think he'll come back today?"

Ethan was thumbing through a catalogue of silver plate. "That was last year, Aunt Charity."

With an encouraging look the Impersonator patted Aunt Charity's hand. "Let's sit real still-like and watch for him." He lit a cigarette. If time would only stop, he could be at this table forever, with the morning sunlight showering the grain of the mahogany, lighting up the sweetness of his brother's serious young face and all around them the peace of this warm haven. It was what all his life he'd felt around Aunt Charity.

"Used to be more birds when I was younger." Aunt Charity fingered the smart black binoculars that were next to the bird book. "Ethan and me ordered these from—what's the name of that place called, Ethan?"

"The Museum of Modern Art, Aunt Charity."

"That's the place. It's in New York City." She looked at the Impersonator. "Where you live. Want to look through them? They're much lighter than that old pair I had. Better for my arthritis."

The Impersonator picked them up. "Pretty swell, hon."

"Snappy design, hey?" Ethan asked with a possessor's pride. "Aunt Charity, what do you think of this serving tray?" He passed the catalogue to her and pointed at a picture.

"Well, we got a lot of silver trays, Ethan. We only use them Christmas. How many trays we got?"

"Twenty, maybe."

She considered. "Well, you're right. This one's mighty pretty."

The Impersonator was looking through the binoculars at the bereft garden. He wondered if Ethan had ever explained to Charity that the reason there were no longer birds to be watched at breakfast time was that the house was now completely encircled by expressways. Maybe he had and she just forgot over and over. It broke his heart, her sitting here pretty as a picture, her silver hair tied jauntily with a polka-dot bow, with her bird book and her binoculars, waiting for the cardinals, the thrushes, the robins, the hummingbirds that had been part of every morning of her life.

Behind them there came a snuffling noise. Tommy stood staring at them from a few feet away.

"Damn," Ethan said quietly. He started to push back his chair.

"Why, Tommy," Aunt Charity said brightly. "You know you're supposed to be in your room. You've already had your breakfast with the other Children."

The Impersonator got up. He said to Tommy, "Ethan's been telling me that you're turning into his right-hand man. Helping out with the wood and in the kitchen and all. Told me you made the sandwiches last week. Gosh, we're proud of you. Come on, let's take a mosey over to your room. I want to see your car collection."

Tommy allowed him to take his arm. As they walked away together, Aunt Charity said to Ethan, "Your brother's always been so good with the Children. He has a gift. And he's so handsome too, isn't he? Like a movie star."

In the little room where Tommy had spent all of his days since he was eleven he now sat at his little school desk, his head bent slightly forward. Behind him the

Impersonator stood, gently massaging the base of the little man's skull. Tears came to Tommy's eyes. He remembered those strong, gentle hands from before, many times before. Tommy liked Ethan, Ethan took care of him good, but Ethan never touched him like this fellow did, never made him feel like this.

The Impersonator, a natural at giving massages, worked at the muscles at the base of Tommy's head and stared over the hunchback out the window at a dying white beech, and beyond that the expressway. Another hour or so and he would have to become part of that traffic, headed back to the city, the brilliant scorpion of his nightmares, evil and suffocating. Dirt and fear. Winter. Robert de Peña. Marly.

He mowed the lawn, pruned the forsythia, made a big batch of fudge for the Children, played a few games of gin with Aunt Charity, and kissed her good-bye. Ethan followed him out to the car. The brothers never kissed, never embraced. They hadn't touched each other for years. Their partings were therefore always slightly awkward, hands in pockets, lots of standing on one foot, then the other.

"She mentioned the will again," Ethan said. "Everything as before."

The Impersonator ground a pebble into the dirt with the tip of his shoe. "But you haven't seen it."

Ethan also kicked at the ground. "It's still locked up at the bank. I told you. If I could get my hands on it, I would."

The Impersonator looked at the garden. "I remember when she used to cut the grass herself. Sitting on that tractor in her jeans, her face glowing like a girl's. She was up at five every morning baking pies, putting up fruit, and at midnight she'd still be ironing tablecloths just as bright as anything. The house was always full of that brightness. Remember how grateful we always were whenever the folks came up here and dropped us off to stay with her?" His eyes went to the bare flagpole over the porch. "The old flag used to be flying up there, and there weren't any of these highways, just green everywhere you looked."

It embarrassed Ethan to see his brother's eyes had filled with tears. Bro had always been known as the emotional one. Everyone always said he was so sensitive, so poetic. Ethan himself was very sensitive, probably a darn sight more than Bro, only no one had ever noticed. He knew most people just called him "sweet" and sometimes "strange." Ethan kept his own counsel. He had begun that practice at the age of four. Now he didn't really know any other way to live.

"How come you don't fly the Stars and Stripes anymore?" his brother was saying, still emotional, still staring up at the house. "Remember the Fourth of July party she used to have for the Children? I mean, damn. I guess after Vietnam everyone's ashamed."

"She's getting deaf," Ethan said, sticking to the point. "Did you notice?"

"I noticed you shouting at her. But she understood me when I talked normal to her."

"How do you know? She smiles back at anything anyone says to her."

The Impersonator looked taken aback at this quick retort. Then he chuckled. Ethan also chuckled. They gave each other conspiratorial looks and continued to laugh. For a frightening moment each wondered whether their hilarity was going to get out of control. They stood there guffawing, toeing the ground, joined in chaos and suffering, trying to check it, trying to wind it down. Finally there was only silence.

The Impersonator's city voice sliced through the pale gray air. "Ethan old chap, I must be off." He slapped an imaginary pair of gloves against an imaginary pair of riding britches and Ethan marveled at the way his brother could change voices.

The Impersonator got into his car. "Later," he said with a grin. Over the noise of the motor he added, "You call if you need me, hear?"

"Like for what?" Ethan realized this had not hit exactly the right note. He sucked in his breath and produced an awkward laugh.

The rich, smoky eyes looked him over.

"If Aunt Charity gets worse, I meant."

Ethan gave him a finicky look. "She's not sick, she's just old."

"I meant her heart or something."

"Doctor says she could last for years."

"You going to try and find a way to look at that will?"

"I told you. I'm not worried."

After a pause the Impersonator said, "A half a million dollars plus this property and the business and you're not worried?"

"Who else besides us does she have to leave it to? She wouldn't will it to Dad. She can't stand him."

"Who can?"

There was a droll pause. They began to guffaw again. They couldn't stop. The Impersonator began to choke. Tears streamed down his face. With a final wave he drove away.

Ethan remained waving until the car disappeared. He tried to imagine his brother's life in New York City but he couldn't. He had never been able to imagine his brother's life anywhere. Trying to conjure up a memory of him was like trying to conjure up air.

He went up the porch steps, relieved to enter his own life again. His brother's visits provided glamour but there was plenty to do here that was interesting, and plenty to think about. His life was full.

Aunt Charity was in her chair, watching a soap opera on the television. Ethan patted her on the head and
shouted, "Can I get you some more coffee?" She nodded and smiled. Ethan went into the kitchen, whistling,
busy, important.

The Impersonator drove toward Manhattan. But reaching its sullied periphery, he abruptly took a turn that
freed him. He headed down a route that would take
him farther south. Of course he wouldn't go all the
way, he was only flirting with the idea, he'd have to
turn around in a minute.

But he didn't. It was a stunning day. The light was
perfect. He caught his breath with sadness and fear.
What would become of him?

Soon there were a good hundred miles between him
and the apartment where Marly was waiting for him. In
her kimono. Munching on something. That beautiful
face. Waiting to blame him. He jammed his foot down
on the accelerator. She had naturally cystic breasts. It
would be nothing. They had been through this before.

Toward late afternoon familiar soft green pillows of
landscape encircled him. He rolled down the window
so he could smell the sweet grasses of home. Well, one
of his homes. He looked at his watch and calculated
what each of his old acquaintances might be doing at
this moment. Mary Louise, for instance. She'd be lying
in a hammock reading a cheap book. Or rolling out a
pie. Or grooming her horse or teeing off on the second
nine or having her hair done downtown. He should
have married Mary Louise. At the end he'd tried. Asked
her to be engaged to him. She'd looked very surprised
and said that she guessed she sort of loved him but that
she couldn't possibly marry him. The following week
she'd gone with her parents to Sardinia for the summer.

He was passing Billy's horse farm. Two hundred acres and Billy was practically a moron. Christ, it could make you sick the way some people inherited the earth. Billy's sister Susie wasn't overly burdened with intellect either, but she'd had those pointy tits. He laughed out loud, remembering the day she first let him play inside her blouse, and then her little panties. She had become an obsession. He would follow her home from school, wait until she went out to the barn for chores (even rich kids had chores then), and then cajole her sweetly into lying down with him so he could excite her and in the process die a little himself. They'd never gone all the way because she wouldn't let him and anyway she was a lot older, thirteen, while he was only eight. But she loved him. That he knew. Later they'd sent her to a prep school (how they got her in, nobody knew) in Connecticut and she'd committed suicide.

And then Lily had come home. Lily, who taught him everything.

Lily. Forget it. Forget it.

He slowed down the car, pulled over to the side of the country road, lit a cigarette, and began to watch some horses grazing in the distance. The Hanleys had been buying again. Arabians, no less. He squinted, trying to see them more clearly. The money in this town. The low-key recognizance of rank. Worn boots, old jackets, plain cussing, meanwhile coins jingling in Swiss banks. Women who went to the collections in Paris every year did their own mucking out, changed their own tires, oiled their own guns, and planted petunias outside their back doors.

His father had never really got the hang of any of it, not that either of his parents ever got the hang of much anyway. They'd always been outside, looking in. From town to town his father had dragged the family, announcing each time it was a fresh start, but it was always the same. Outside, looking in.

On family drives, whenever they passed a particularly attractive house with curtains at the windows and smoke coming out of the chimney, his father would say peevishly, "Doesn't it look cozy in there?" Then there would be an accusatory look at his wife, at the two boys. "Bet those folks have a real nice life."

He and Ethan would remain silent, not really understanding why what their father said was pathetic, why it stamped him as a failure, but they knew profound shame for him. Shame for the family sickness. Outside, looking in.

Lily had understood that. She had understood everything. The sweep of her eyes, like God's eyes, missed nothing, even if she was only laughing or eating a candy bar or kicking off her boots, or sitting in church in one of her slinky silk dresses. Lily, who had practically invented him, created his manhood, given birth to his soul.

He turned on the motor again, gunned the accelerator. Dust flew, birds scattered, and in the distance one of the horses lifted its head at the sudden noise. *Vroom vroom vroom.* He would ask Julie and Tad to put him up. Or the Bartons over at Highacres. It was Saturday. There would have been a hunt. There'd be a party somewhere tonight, for sure.

That evening in the Middlebrooks' chestnut-paneled living room with its ancestral portraits and silver bowls filled with black peonies, a visitor from New York, a tall, large-boned woman of more than forty with a long dark braid wound at the nape of her neck—unfashionably yet not unattractively—was examining the well-modeled face and smoky eyes of a stranger across the guest-filled room. She had been in the Middlebrooks' handsome Federalist mansion for two days, studying, taking notes on, and photographing—for a regional New England museum—the interior architectural and design details of an upstairs room in which, in the process of redecoration, four walls of rare and original stenciling of a kind unusual for the area had been discovered. The woman, Sara Alessio, gazing across the room, said to her host, "Who is that young man talking to your daughter?"

"Has he been giving you the eye, Sara?" Middlebrook glanced unenthusiastically at the Impersonator.

The black-haired woman sipped at her mineral water. "I take it he's the local Casanova."

"No longer local. He moved away. Look at the cigarette holder and those fairy Italian shoes. He says he's an actor now. Told my wife this afternoon he's about to sign a contract to be in *Chorus Line.*"

"It's a fascinating face." And indeed Sara was still warmed by the Impersonator's brief but complimentary appraisal of her a few minutes before.

"He shows up every now and then. Gives the girls a thrill."

"His family's still here?"

"Moved away." There was the briefest of pauses. "We were never on a social basis with them."

"Yet you were with their son?"

"He went to school with our kids. He's still very popular. As you can see."

Across the room two young women and a young man were enthusiastically greeting the Impersonator.

Sara saw her host was monitoring this with a pejorative look. Amused, she asked, "Have you got anything good to say about him?"

"Always wanted long eyelashes myself." He took her

drink. "Let me freshen this for you. In my absence I'll
bet you a million bucks he moseys on over to talk to
you."

"Why would he want to do that?" Sara stroked her
still-beautiful neck and counted her years.

She remained standing where she was, annoyed at
being left, annoyed at her host's assumption that she
was interested in a nameless young man at least a decade her junior with no credentials except his face. He
was thin, too thin, and there was a hot glitter in his
eyes, a cheap glitter. His coat sleeves were too short.
She didn't like his mouth. She turned her back on the
room and looked out the window at the rolling land
with its trees of money, its yapping dogs bred for the
kill, and the curved picture-book horizon turning a perfect pink at the end of the day. Dixie. They could have
it. She had plain hated Detroit because it was too many
shades of gray and her parents had been poor—too
poor to send her to art school, too poor to understand
why she had to go—but the South left her mildly irritated, mildly intrigued. She waited for him to come to
her.

A few moments went by, but he did not appear behind her as she had expected. Nor had her host returned. She turned around to face the room again. Her
glance went straight to where the young man was
standing, but he wasn't there. Her eyes quickly swept
the room. Then she felt a hot flush begin to rise from
her neck into her face. He was now sitting on the arm
of a sofa. And he had caught her looking for him. He
acknowledged this with the barest flutter of his eyelids.
An ascetic young cardinal denying the randy nun. He
now turned his head to talk to a young woman sitting
next to him, giving Sara the opportunity to examine his
profile.

She realized he was posing. Someone had told him

she had arrived with photographic equipment. He had taken her for a journalist. Transparent as an amateur, he had been working hard to provoke her interest.

Bunnie Middlebrook appeared, handed Sara her refilled glass. "Henry sent me with this and his apologies. He's been waylaid by late arrivals."

Sara looked about the room, feeling her separateness. "These women all look so—for want of a better word—frilly. Hard to imagine them having spent all day engaging in a blood sport."

Her hostess fingered the enormous cabochon emerald at her throat. "The South has always struck folks from other places as different." There was a fully rounded pause. "I reckon we're glad to be."

"What would you say sets you apart more than any other thing?"

"I suppose it's pride. Would you like a canape?"

It was like they had the Holy Grail. Sara preferred them bewigged and in taffeta, in portraits and in miniseries. Covertly she glanced at her watch. Maybe another hour before dinner. God, how these people drank. She excused herself and went upstairs to what everyone referred to as the powder room.

Afterward, on her way down the exquisitely proportioned staircase, she saw Casanova on his way up. She paused, let him come abreast of her. He also paused. She watched him look her up and down as if he were the romantic lead in an old black-and-white movie, like Cary Grant or Jimmy Stewart.

Unprepared, as yet, for life. Brought up in front of a television set. Potential misfit. Inviting but dangerous. Pity. He was, in his way, so beautiful.

The Impersonator, since childhood a master in reading the reactions of others, gave her a curt nod and moved up the stairs. He was stung, furious. Bitch. She'd eyed him down there in the living room, strung him along, but just now there had been that curve of the lip and he had watched her tearing his brief history into little pieces, throwing them to the wind.

He reached the landing, went down the hallway. Sara continued down the stairs.

Very early the next morning she was up with one of her headaches. They came less and less now that her life had become more orderly, now that she had made the choice to pursue her course independently, leaving behind her a life littered with men she had left, thrown out, asked to go. Once the initial me-Jane-you-Tarzan phase saw itself out, she always became bored. She had had three husbands, and since then several longish affairs. She'd been—she thought—in love with all of them. The last one had been a married man.

"But why?" he had asked in dismay when she told him she was finished with him. "I could see you more. We'll take trips together. I know my being married is hard for you—"

But the only hard part had been displaying a semblance of passion once she no longer felt it.

"Maybe you've never loved anyone," her first husband—still a friend—had commented when she told him of her decision to live as a single, even chaste, woman of dignity and serenity.

"Maybe I never have." She had given him a droll look. "But how would I know?"

He had looked at her for a moment. "Maybe you only know how to love yourself." He had grinned and added, "Listen, maybe you should bottle that."

Now she got out of bed and pulled aside the heavy flowered curtains to see if it had gone light yet. She looked out at the misty, rolling green acres. Casanova was in the paddock. Cowboy boots. Red polo shirt. Sunglasses. Wet hair curling wildly. Bathed but unshaven, like a Sicilian in mourning. She had never seen a man break a horse, but she understood that that was what he was doing. A wizened groom stood by, watching.

Her new resolution was six months old. She dressed and went outside, across the sopping wet grass to the fence, leaned against it. The groom nodded at her. The sun began to inch its way up.

"Always had the touch, that boy." The groom offered her a stick of gum. "Always."

She didn't know how long she had been watching.

When Casanova was done, he handed the long reins to the groom. He came though the gate like a matador walking out of the ring so that the picadors could go in to do the dirty work.

He acknowledged her with the briefest of nods.

Sara introduced herself, said in her straightforward way, "What did you do to that horse? I must know."

She watched him draw a long breath, compose himself. Was he so thrown by her?

He asked her if she wanted to go to the local roadside dive for breakfast, and he decided not to take her in Marly's car, cheap and dirty; but in young Wade Middlebrook's white Eldorado. He knew the keys would be under the seat.

"You've got to be kidding," Sara commented as he helped her in. He did not disabuse her of her assumption that the long, flashy car was his. For a few minutes they drove in silence along the country road. She glanced at his muddy boots, at his profile, far more interesting in the daylight than seen through candlelight and peonies. Or her own bad temper.

"You're staying with the Middlebrooks?" she asked.

"Staying with the Bartons. Bunnie, Mrs. Middlebrook, that is, asked me to give them a hand with that uppity little horse you saw me working with. In theory she's been broken, except somebody rushed it.

In theory the same person should stay with her all the way, but I told them I'd stick around a few days and work her up to a saddle maybe and then give her back to the trainer."

"The trainer was the man watching?"

"That was one of the grooms. The trainer is over at the next farm drinking bloody Marys."

"Bloody Marys? It's only eight o'clock in the morning."

"So." He raised his eyebrows. Then gave her his slow, cowboy smile.

He was real, real tired. After the guests had gone home he'd spent part of the night making love to Bunnie Middlebrook. They'd started doing it fifteen years ago when he was part of her daughter's crowd. Every time he came back they greeted each other with grave politeness and somehow found a way to find each other later, even if it had to be—as it sometimes was—a quick stand-up fuck in the john. Bunnie was sixty now and still one of the better addictions of his life. Sexually she was completely selfish, as opposed to her daughter, who, trained by magazine articles and self-help books, took her carnal responsibilities to her partner so seriously as to be really boring.

At the diner, steamy with bacon and overcooked eggs frying on the grill, Sara noted that as he entered the place he seemed to have grown leaner, taller, and even princely; at least everyone looked up and watched him walk in. Or at least that is the way she remembered it. But when they sat down she thought he looked sad and hollow-eyed and she asked him what it was.

"The woman I've been living with for nine years wants to split up. She says she still loves me but she wants things I can't give her. She's very structured and materialistic."

Interesting. The same woman for nine years? Sara

couldn't for the moment make it go with everything else. What would the woman friend be like? Someone confident enough, evidently, to cast aside a commodity that was at a premium in New York. A presentable heterosexual with all his faculties intact.

Did she herself want him? Definitely not. Even if she hadn't made her resolution to live life on her own, she wouldn't have dallied with him anyway. Something about him bothered her. She scanned the menu. She would have eggs, sausage, potatoes, toast, jelly, oatmeal with cream. Waffles too. With syrup.

Normally her breakfast consisted of a grapefruit and black coffee. She took a cigarette from him, smoked it, drawing deeply, deeply. She ordered a glass of milk. She couldn't seem to get enough of anything. But she would deny him. She was friendly, extremely friendly. She gave him advice about women. Dispassionate advice. Maternal advice. Humorous advice. To herself she said, *Who needs this cowboy?*

When they were done, the waitress brought the bill. He let a charming beat go by. Another. Sara insisted on paying it. To herself she said, *Why am I doing this? He invited me.* She put down the money. She added an ostentatious tip.

On the way back he asked her questions about her life as if she were from another, brilliant planet visiting this lesser, meeker one.

"How do I get to be like you?" he asked with a slight smile.

They had reached a crossroads. He slowed the car. The sun beat down and they were surrounded by blazing yellow fields. She indulged herself. Glanced at him. He sensed it and gracefully turned toward her. With one finger he nudged the bridge of his dark green sunglasses so that they descended an inch lower on his nose. Over the rims he surveyed her, let her survey him.

When she saw him looking at her Like That, she affected to misinterpret, to not understand. She kept to her pleasant, maternally interested, strictly wholesome manner.

He was not intrigued by her scrupulous rejection of his suit. He was rarely drawn to women who didn't want him. By sundown he would have forgotten her. Still, there *was* something about her. She kept her own counsel, a rare thing in anyone he had ever known. She seemed to keep it not in the manner he had always kept it himself—as secretiveness—but as strength.

He glanced at her. He fantasized that she would start unbuttoning her blouse, that she would say quietly, "Find a place where we can pull over." She would say it like that.

"I'll give you my card." She gave him a nice smile. "We could have a drink sometime in the city." Then she was very quiet, as if she regretted having offered him even that.

6

Robert and Jane had also gone south. There was to be an evening for artists and literati at the White House, to which Robert had been invited. He and Jane had come down from New York that morning, both in temporary good spirits, Robert because he was flattered (though he denied this) at being included in the President's list, and Jane because one of her brothers, an adviser to the President, would be present at the party. But what continued to flare unsaid between Jane and Robert had begun to make the most ordinary conversation dangerous.

"Are we to think it odd," Robert remarked as they were in their room at the Madison getting ready, "that until now I haven't met any of your family?"

Jane stared into the mirror, fluffed out the sides of her hair. "One floating Jesuit and one on-the-go politician hardly constitute any kind of a blazing hearth to have taken you to." She gave him a wifely smile. "Time to go."

Acting, always acting, dragging the subtext to their marriage as a ball and chain. Could he not see how unhappy she was? Did he think the way they had lived since the night at The Touch Me Club constituted closeness? What possible kind of relationship could he and Theo have had that might have led him to think this was the way anybody would ever want to live?

Robert straightened his tie, checked his cuffs. "If you were close to them, you'd have wanted me to meet them right away. Like we did my parents."

Indeed. They had gone down to Coral Gables to visit the older De Peñas a few weeks after their arrival from France. Robert's parents were tall, handsome, with flashing eyes, wildly pleasant, wildly social. There had been a lot of card playing, champagne, bands, swimming, and siestas. It had been like staying at a beautiful, impeccably run club.

"My brothers and I *are* close." Jane was becoming heated. "We're close in ways that—" She paused, thought better of continuing. "Robert, we're going to be late."

"Finish the thought." He smiled back at her pleasantly but there was an edge to his voice.

Briefly she played with the gold bangle on her left wrist. She had bought it in a little shop behind the Piazza San Marco and then returned to read a book and have coffee in the square, in a life before this. She remembered that for a moment, just a moment, the sun had turned everything persimmon and silver.

"Hal and Jerry and I don't really agree on much that you could print in the newspapers. There's deeper stuff we share that's important. Stuff we believe in."

"Stuff like what?"

"Commitment. Seeing things through. Loyalty—"

"You *admire* Hal's loyalty to that asshole in the White House?"

She picked up a small beaded purse and walked toward the door. "I don't understand what Hal does or why he does it. I don't want to. If I did, maybe I couldn't talk to him anymore. What he and I have together came to pass a long time ago." She took a breath. "Our parents' blood and a billion grains of sand and this steel bar we have to chin ourselves on when the earth falls away." It was out of her mouth before she could stop herself. "Maybe you could take a tip from us."

"Meaning?" His tone was sharp. Her look had verged on contempt.

She caught her breath. "We're late." She went out of the room.

He followed her down the hall to the elevator, having a fantasy in which he shoved her against a wall and slapped the life out of her. The elevator came at once, and there were several other people in it, all wearing evening clothes.

In the car Robert said in a low voice so the driver wouldn't hear, "I'd like you to clarify that last thing you said, in the room."

She turned and looked him full in the face. "Maybe it's you who needs to do some clarifying."

Levelly, Robert stared back at her. The street lights, glistening in the rain, intermittently lit up his stolid gaze.

She concentrated on breathing evenly, hoping to stop the pounding of her heart. *So now he knows I know. Only I don't know what I know, only that there are lies.*

And indeed it had not occurred to him until then that she might have noticed anything. His hours, days, weeks, had been full, entirely contained by his beguilement with the Other. Had she been counting his absences? He now said with a quizzical look, "So that's it.

Can't I keep *anything* secret? Women are amazing. It's pathetic how we try to get around you. We miss a breath and you notice."

She remained regarding him.

A moment went by and he continued. "I felt I needed to tie up some loose ends I never got around to in my therapy. Nothing to do with you and me, darling, more of a tuneup, really. Amos has been fitting me in once a week. You know I've been having trouble with the book. Trouble sleeping. It's all intertwined, I suppose. I didn't want to worry you because there's nothing to worry about. I realize now"—he smiled apologetically —"I should have told you."

The car had come to a stop at some gates. The driver showed a slip of paper to a guard. Robert took Jane's hand, put it to his lips. "I loathe your brother already. He's made us have a fight over nothing."

I am a suspicious shrew, Jane said to herself as she walked into the first house in the land.

"It's less ta-ta-ra-ta-ta-ta than I imagined," she was saying to her brother a few minutes later. "I expected there to be trumpets to announce us." She looked around at the relentlessly sprayed heads and the dozens of pink and red taffeta dresses.

Her brother, older by ten years, eyed her with impeccably concealed interest. "Only one couple here gets the trumpets."

Robert, examining his brother-in-law, had the impression of complicated inner wiring. Hal's smile was quick, generous, and his manner was warm and—perhaps studiedly—informal, but the inky pupils of his dark brown eyes were extraordinarily opaque. Little blackout discs. Not a pinpoint of information behind them. Hal saw but rarely told.

"Still subscribing to radical causes?" Hal gave Jane an indulgent look.

Jane looked up at him. "You're so dreary and old-fashioned I can't believe it." To Robert she said, "By 'radical' he means I mix furniture from different periods in the same room, and send checks to Amnesty International."

"Don't start, okay?" Hal's handsome wife, Carole, said pleasantly enough, shifting a loyal inch or two closer to her husband. She had not joined in the conversation since the introductions but had stood gracefully by, a bourbon in her hand, the topaz necklace on her well-sculpted collarbone glittering in the light from the chandeliers.

Hal still had Jane fixed in his gaze. "Basically, it's amateur bleeding hearts like you who'll bring us down."

"We had this discussion in 1968, wearing our school ties, as it were, and we're all still around, though it's not specifically thanks to you and yours."

Unruffled, Hal turned to Robert. "I suppose she's told you about our brother Jerry." He jiggled the ice in his drink. "I'll be damned if I understand the Catholic Church anymore. Priests should wear black skirts, take confession, say Mass, and occasionally play football with the guys." He paused to smile and wink at a passing couple. "Our brother is a Jesuit who spends half his time in Paris painting nudes and riding around on his Honda. The other half of his time he spends drinking martinis and writing political pamphlets advocating the impeachment of our President." He looked at Jane. "That little shit. I held his hand. I wiped his nose. I taught him how to shoot craps to win. I didn't let the big guys gang up on him. Now he's trying to bring down my government."

"Someone has to do it," Jane said.

"You want to be President?" Hal shot back. "I'd like

to see you last one fucking day. How about one fucking hour? What about a fucking minute?"

"Really," Hal's wife said.

"They say he dyes his hair." Jane stared across the room at the President. "Including the hair under his arms."

"They're always like this," Hal's wife said to Robert. "Then they stay up all night playing the piano and singing and getting tears in their eyes about how brilliant and special they are."

When the dancing began, Hal whirled his wife around the floor a few times. Next he danced with Jane.

"Your husband seems like a nice fellow," he said. "Does the press still bother him about, uh, his former wife?"

"Occasionally."

"Is there anything to the rumors that the cause of death was definitely not what came out in the newspapers?"

"We've never discussed it. Why don't you ask him, if you're so interested?"

"It just came to mind."

"Nothing ever just comes to mind with you."

With a slight pressure of his hand against her back, he guided her into a half turn, then led her in a snappy traveling step she hadn't done since she'd been a teenager. Hal danced well, just as he skied, sailed, rode, and played golf and tennis well. They had been expected to excel at all those things—and many others—as children. Unaccountably, her eyes misted over and she was overwhelmed by nostalgia. "Oh, Hal, what's to become of us all?"

But he was nodding cordially at someone over her shoulder. "What?" he asked.

"I said I have a bomb in my purse."

"That's not funny, Jane. Anyone from Security heard

you, they'd have you stripped right down to your panties in two seconds flat."

"It's not in my panties. I told you. It's in my purse."

He stared at her for a moment, then allowed her a slight smile. He led her through a complicated series of steps.

"When's your book coming out? I'm looking forward to reading it." He gave her a genial look.

"You mean Carole will read it and tell you what to say."

"Carole's one girl in a million."

"I think there's going to be a television version."

He looked interested. "How much do they pay you for that?"

"Not much. It's public television. But I'm really excited. Seven parts, one hour each."

He was frowning, already thinking of something else. "There's a question I've been wanting to ask you."

"Shoot."

"You think Jerry's a homosexual?"

"He's a priest, Hal."

"Do you or don't you?"

"He's over twenty-one. He can do what he likes."

"No he can't, goddammit, he took vows." He took a breath. "I have to go through another security clearance."

"New job?"

"They might be around asking you some questions too."

She glanced at him with irritation. "Why should they care what Jerry does with his life, or me with mine? I thought that kind of witch hunting was all over."

He gave her a patient look. "They need to know anything Jerry or you could be blackmailed for, or I could be blackmailed for on his or your behalf. Anything that might come out and be embarrassing for our government should one of you be taken hostage. Should I be taken hostage."

The music had come to an end. Jane looked up at her brother and said with passion, "Jerry regards himself as a patriot. And you know it."

Hal's opaque discs took her in. "The CIA hates fairies."

"How do they feel about tragic incompetence, megalomania, and lies?"

Hal took her arm and they left the dance floor. He steered her across the room, smiling at this person, that person. "Truth and beauty are not the responsibility of a government." He chucked her under the chin. "It's never been any different."

In New York a few weeks later while riding in a taxi, Jane saw Robert walking across East 71st Street.

"You can let me off here," Jane said to the taxi driver. "Thanks." She flung too much money at him and jumped out. Robert had said he would be at Columbia University all day. Over forty blocks away.

She followed him. She realized she was staying too close—if he turned around he would see her—but she couldn't stop her drunklike momentum. Her legs had a will of their own. If he saw her, what would she say? She was conscious of her left hand gripping her purse, but why did her right hand feel empty? What should she have in her right hand? She flexed the fingers of that hand.

Through the thick membrane that now separated her from her life before this, she perceived that she had left her briefcase in the taxi. Research notes. Reading glasses. Appointment book. Gold bracelet with broken clasp to be repaired. Correspondence.

Her legs moved forward some twenty feet behind her

husband, who was now opening the front door of a neat brownstone.

Walking toward her from the other direction was a youngish man in a threadbare coat, three-day-old beard. He was going to ask her for money. She opened her purse, fumbled frantically for some change. He was coming abreast. He was walking as unsteadily as she. His bleary eyes looked her over. "Piss on you," he said quietly, and kept going. Tears began to spill down her cheeks.

Another few steps and she was at the door of the brownstone. She opened the door to the entry. There were four brass nameplates. The Sinai Travel Agency. Harold Ralston. Bernard A. Miller. A. Ross. A. Ross could be a woman. She pressed the buzzer. Her heart pounded. A woman's soft, educated voice suddenly came over the intercom.

"Yes?"

Don't let me faint, prayed Jane. She opened her mouth, formed the words. "Robert de Peña."

There was a pause. "Who?"

"De Peña." Jane leaned her forehead against the cool brass of the nameplates. Her eyes were level with the neat white card that announced: Bernard A. Miller.

"You've got the wrong apartment." The woman's voice crackled and then there was silence.

Jane was still staring at the card. Bernard A. Miller. It was Amos. Robert's shrink. It was not another woman, it was Amos!

Not Another Woman lasted until that evening, when she asked Robert if he'd had lunch and if so where, and he replied he had been at Columbia all day. He was sprawled in a comfortable chair, making notes from a book. He looked up at her and his smile was as slick as glass.

Later she found an excuse for asking him what day

he usually saw Amos. There was the briefest of pauses, then "Didn't I tell you? I haven't been going. I've graduated."

And Jane understood that nothing would ever be the same as before.

7

As a child the Impersonator had been nicknamed "Beau" by his mother, Eva, a wispy girl from Nebraska whose romantic fantasies had come to ruin by the time Beau was born. Eva's good-looking husband, Richard, of the flashing eyes and officerlike mustache, had made her a string of golden promises and had kept none of them. So the empty pear-shaped place behind her left breastbone that Eva identified as her heart had to be filled with the lives of fictional characters. Thus, as Melanie Wilkes had called her son Beau, so did Eva. The name stuck, and it would be many years before he re-adopted his real name.

By the time Beau was five it was evident that he was gifted. In just what way was more difficult to describe.

"He glows," Eva said to herself, watching him through the frosted-over window. Out in a vast field of snow, Beau was making angels. First he lay on his back, his arms tightly at his sides, to form the main impression of the angel's body. Next he moved his arms outward to make the wings. Then his feet, which were close together, would be moved in a fanlike motion to form the skirt. He would get up very carefully so as not to mess up the snow picture. On one foot he would hop about five paces, and then lie down on his back again and begin another angel.

Eva turned back to her ironing. There were now over a dozen life-size angels out there in the snow. She understood, in her way, from the set of his little chin, from the stern, finicky manner in which Beau was going about things, that he wasn't just passing the time until supper. He was on a holy mission. He was reinventing the universe.

Eva turned the plaid shirt on the board so she could do the sleeves. She pressed the hot iron to the fabric and the smell of steam rose from it. Mixed with the residual odor of detergent and now the vapor, there came from the shirt a smell that was familiar, determinedly male. She continued to iron it, resenting its presence in her life. She had ironed it the day before yesterday and would iron it again two days hence. And again.

Fish sticks for dinner with mashed potatoes from a box. You mixed all these little flakes with boiling water. Time went by and you never even thought of real mashed potatoes, the kind her mother had bought, peeled, boiled, and mashed. Eva had never been to a fish store in her life or bought meat directly from a butcher. Her mother had done all this, but times were better now. You went to a supermarket and picked out what you wanted and could afford. Almost everything the family ate came in boxes and cans. It wasn't a question of economy as much as disinterest. Eva was not a good cook, and by the time dinner came, Richard had had too much to drink to care one way or the other what he ate.

Thus were they silent partners in a growing collec-

tion of transgressions they were unwittingly to perpe-
trate against their two sons. These transgressions, particularly including Richard's whoring, set the stage for
a series of not unrelated consequences that would ultimately find the Impersonator wearing a wig, makeup,
and women's clothes, playing a game of necro-prostitu-
tion, and which would also find Ethan, at twenty-five,
the sole and untrained custodian of a state-approved
houseful of mentally retarded old people.

Eva folded the plaid shirt and began on the oxford
striped one her husband liked to wear for occasions on
which she was usually not invited to accompany him.
She looked out the window again.

Beau had now completed almost twenty angels. He
was lying in the snow, moving his arms in a wide arc to
make yet another one. She was wondering whether he
had been out there too long in his thin jeans and the
cotton socks that would be sodden by now. The boy
never seemed to get cold. Except, when she came to
think of it, at the oddest times. Suddenly his teeth
would begin to rattle and he would shiver—inexplica-
bly—even on a hot summer day. At these times he
would appear even thinner, so thin and wavery that
there was a spectral transparency to him that caused in
her the (surely) irrational fear that he would disappear
altogether.

These fits never led to illnesses of any kind, not even
a scratchy throat or runny nose; they just came on of
their own and disappeared on their own. When they
occurred she wrapped him up in what was really, she
supposed, the most splendid thing she and Richard
owned, a big fur traveling blanket that had belonged to
her grandmother and was still wonderfully thick and
comforting because of its black and silver pelts, which
felt thick and luxurious to the touch. Once wrapped in
its rich warmth, little Beau's expression would become

less congealed and the odd redness that rimmed his eyes would disappear. He would stop shivering and become dreamy. Eva would open a package of cookies for him and let him watch television.

Television was such a wonderful invention, it made Eva's heart glad just thinking of it. Television was the steady beating heart of the house, it was the ardent wallpaper of their existence. She could not imagine life as a wife or a mother without that small magic glass in its beige plastic casing.

Her peppy, once very interesting girlhood lay behind her, on the far side of memory. Summer nights. The smell of jasmine, the creak of the porch swing, the crackle of a radio dance band—these images were no longer as reliable as the reality of the trustworthy television in the front room of their small creaky-floored house, the overseer's quarters on an estate in New Hampshire.

Eva was twenty-six, not a heroine, not even much of a survivor. What imagination, what fight she had, what time she had left, she would use—when she could—on behalf of her sons, though on that wintry day she knew only that there would be fish sticks for dinner and television afterward and that she had just discovered a come stain on the front—way down at the bottom—of Richard's shirt.

She pressed the hot iron down on it. Richard made love to her only when they were in bed, never when he was wearing his best shirt.

Out in the radiant snow, Beau was on his twenty-fifth angel. His blood sang with the perfection of his work. The crystal air was soft with chill, his world chaste and silent. He would make a hundred angels, a thousand. They would cover the earth.

Eva looked through the window again. She put down the iron and pressed her face to the glass. She had heard the muted sound of a motor coming through the snow. Now she saw a moving blur zigzagging across the white field. Richard had bought a pickup truck on shaky credit and was showing off what it could do. Instead of approaching via the driveway, he was cutting through the field. Eva saw Beau frantically waving his arms to warn his father off. He desperately pointed to the snow angels. He held up his hands in unmistakable warning and supplication. The pickup truck kept coming. Coming.

Eva quickly turned from the window, resumed her ironing, tried to frame her thoughts so that they might be bearable. *Richard has put us further into debt by buying this new truck. This stain on his shirt happened with someone else, not me. He's been drinking again or he wouldn't be driving so crazy across that field. He has run over and ruined Beau's angels. We will not talk about any of this. He'll talk about the truck and I'll put the dinner in the oven and maybe I'll have a drink too because I feel so bad about Beau's angels. Maybe I'll let him watch TV later than usual.*

Out in the snow, Beau, his little face set, was trudging away from his home toward the horizon, toward the end of the world. When it got dark and he still hadn't come in, Richard went looking for him, and when he finally found him, gave him a terrible licking.

There were other places after that, other houses to be secured, disappointed in, and then abandoned for what was always promised by Richard to be greener pastures.

The family of four—by now Ethan had been born—moved steadily south. They traveled always at night like fugitives. One of Beau's earliest memories was waking in the night, being taken from his bed, wrapped up tightly in a blanket, placed for a few moments on the top of a trunk or a table in an emptied-out hallway where the front door was already open to the dark future.

On the long drives through the night to the new state, the new town, the new house, Beau always wanted to watch the stars. He would crawl to the space behind the backseat and arrange himself on top of the luggage and household goods with his face pressed to the cold black glass and look up at the vast, still universe and pretend he was flying through space in a cloak of silver.

Maryland was sunny and golden yellow, warm with fresh smells of cut grass and soft rain and spiky magnolias and pungent stables and—Richard knew—money. It was April when they arrived. Beau was eight. Six weeks later they moved to Virginia. Then it was Kentucky. There were three more moves after that, all on the same circuit. No explanations were made to the children.

Three days after his thirteenth birthday Beau met Lily. He had been worshipping her from afar for some time. Around those parts everyone worshipped her, including her aging guardians, who spent most of their time sitting on the porch playing dominoes and wishing she would come home and throw white light on them. Lily was simply beautiful. When she appeared in church, or the filling station or the drugstore, people fell excitedly silent, even people who had known her since she had been a little girl. She was twenty-three now, with a great mass of russet-colored hair, a mouth shaped like an open piece of fruit, and further, Beau thought when he saw her fishing by the river, naked to the waist (shocking!), the torso of a goddess.

She had spent much time away. Lily did what she liked. The money was hers, the guardians merely administered it and were in bed by nine. She had spent a year at some drama school in London. There had been a pilgrimage to India. She had lived briefly in New York. Everyone wondered what she would do next. She was seen riding, she was seen fishing and dreaming. On rainy days people saw her going into the little public library downtown. She turned up at a few of the parties but she appeared not to be dating anyone, and this was no surprise, for who was good enough for her?

The hundreds of acres that made up her property bordered at one point on the one and a half Richard had bought (heavily mortgaged) to make yet another one of his fresh new starts. There had been the natural back and forth exchange between the neighbors and Beau was given a part-time job working in the stables on Lily's property.

After a few months Lily's guardians proposed that Beau, who seemed to have a special knack with horses, be "loaned" a filly named Daisy that he would be permitted to keep in the small barn on his father's land and to care for as his own. Lily had been away so long it seemed a shame to her guardians that she insisted on keeping three horses waiting around for her to ride. And it would mean one less horse a day for the staff to visit, exercise, and generally tend. The little boy next door was wispy and sad and appeared quite lonely. It would be nice for him to have Daisy. They were sure Lily would not object.

The guardians had no idea that the wispy, sad little boy had already had various forms of exciting sex with one of their exercise girls, with their housekeeper's visiting sister, and with the local vet's wife, who had had too much to drink and had been stumbling around her flower garden and had come across Beau, who had just climbed down some wisteria from the bedroom of her own daughter.

To be fair, he had not actually initiated any of these adventures; that is to say, his opening contribution had been limited to his mere presence, and a certain expression in his beautiful gray eyes that managed to combine soulfulness with dirty promises. His adolescence gave him heat, his grateful partners, license. He began to experience himself sexually as a unique gift and was becoming, quite unconsciously, an accomplished tease —a quality generally associated with females, but this only seemed to add to his already odd attractiveness. The fact was that in the heat of matters no one could be more masculine than Beau.

Lily had been away for a year. Nobody yet knew she was back except her guardians. On the second day she noticed the absence of Daisy and was told that the horse was boarding with the neighbors' son. She said she would walk over there soon and say hello and then for a few days she forgot about it.

Very late Sunday night there was a loud knocking at the front door of the big house. The guardians had gone to bed and the servants had also retired for the night. Lily went down the stairs, crossed the large reception hall, and opened the door.

Richard stood on the threshold. In the first moment Lily had no idea who the very good-looking man smelling of whiskey was, and she was about to close the door.

"Sorry it's so late," he said, "but I need your permission. My boy's horse—I mean your Daisy—took sick all of a sudden—that was yesterday—and now the vet says she should be put down."

"Wait," she said finally, and went upstairs to dress. She hadn't asked any questions because she now realized who he was and that he would know about animals. She herself had known the local vet since her childhood, and the fact was, Daisy had been plagued with infections all her life.

In his father's barn, by the pale grubby gleam of a

lantern, Beau sat with Daisy, his arms trying to reach around her neck. The air in the barn was close, but both the boy and the horse were shivering.

Lily walked in, followed by Richard. Behind them, through the open door, a bolt of lightning came and went in the jet-black sky.

"Hello," Lily said to Beau. "I'm Lily." He did not, could not, reply. Lily got down on her knees next to him and examined Daisy. Then she looked up at Richard and nodded.

"Beau," Richard began firmly. "I know this is hard for you, but this little lady here agrees it's got to be done, and after all, it's really her horse. It's not your fault, I told her that, and she's not blaming you. Now, you just get up like a little man so we can get on with things."

There was a brief, violent shudder from Beau. He pressed his face against the horse's neck.

Behind Richard, Eva had entered with Ethan. He was in his pyjamas and she was carrying him. Silently she took in the scene.

"Beau," Richard went on, "here's your mother. Show her what a little man you are."

Eva tried to give Ethan to Richard so she could go to Beau.

"No, mother," Richard said. "He's not a baby. He's going to get up out of his own free will, aren't you, Beau?"

Eva and Lily—who had never met—exchanged a glance. Ethan was making baby noises. The first raindrops fell on the roof.

Eva stared at her husband. "Richard," she began quietly.

He crossed to her, and whispered in an angry mutter, "Don't you look at me like that. Is it my fault this happened?"

His voice carried. Lily reached for one of Beau's hands. Her fingers felt for his. He would not return the gesture, but he allowed her hand to close over his.

Richard crossed again to Beau with a no-nonsense look. He shook the boy's arm. "Come on, boy."

He was answered by Lily. "Why don't you folks go on back to the house? Beau and I want to be with Daisy for a while."

Richard measured her cool, authoritative look. "Come on, Eva." He took her arm and they walked out of the barn, Eva carrying Ethan against her hip. Years later Ethan described the scene to Aunt Charity, who was amazed that a five-year-old could have remembered so vividly.

Eva and Richard went the hundred feet to the house and entered by way of the kitchen. Richard went immediately to the refrigerator. He took out an ice tray.

"You'd better not have any more to drink," Eva said with a sharp look. She was weary, she didn't feel well, she wanted only to sleep. "You still have to finish the horse."

Richard was pouring bourbon into his glass. "The girl will do it. She's got a gun with her."

In the barn, Lily and Beau sat side by side in the straw with Daisy.

"I hear tell you and Daisy were real pals. That you trained her good." When in the South, Lily said "good" instead of "well." "People over at my place, they said they used to hear you hollering and whooping. Having fun. What were you doing?"

His look was bleary. "Making up things."

"Like what?"

"I was a knight. Go ahead and laugh."

"In armor?"

"Well, I made a spear. A lance. I'd rescue ladies from the burning stake."

"Princesses?" Lily looked gravely interested. "Tell me."

"I'd make a bonfire. I'd ride away, then I'd gallop in on Daisy. Gallop around and fight every last man and then I'd kill them. I'd swoop up the lady in my arms and carry her to my tower."

"Where's the tower?"

"My room."

"What else?"

"In summer I'd be an Indian. I took off my shirt and rode bareback. When I had to baby-sit Ethan I'd tie him to a post and gallop around him with my bow and arrow. I'd shoot arrows all around him while the flames licked at his feet."

"Wasn't he afraid?"

Beau looked puzzled. "I guess. Mom got sort of mad."

"Did you go places on Daisy?"

"We'd run away."

"You mean really?"

After a struggle Beau came clean and said, "We always came home for supper." He rested his head against the horse, squeezed his eyes shut. "She can't die." Hot tears coursed down his cheeks.

"Listen." Lily stared into space, thinking. "We'll plant a tree for her. Down by the creek."

His words came in a blubber. "If she dies, I don't want to live."

"Tomorrow we'll get the tree. A willow. A weeping willow. It'll get real tall and have soft, droopy branches and we'll sit under it and tell stories about Daisy's life for as long as we live."

He had opened his eyes. A puny little flame, but a flame nevertheless, began to lick at his heart.

The new architect of his soul continued. "It'll be sacred ground." Lily was frowning in concentration.

"We'll be able to make wishes there always and forever because Daisy's spirit will be there blessing the earth, the air, the sky. Your love for her and my love for her will bless it too." She paused and looked at him. "Beau, she hurts too much to live."

She had brought him to the fold.

"Oh, Daisy," he whispered. "I'll miss you so bad. So bad."

She took a gun out of her jacket pocket and placed it on the straw between them.

"Do you know how to use one of these?"

In a very small voice he said, "My dad says I'm not old enough."

She gave him a casual glance. "Your hand over mine." She picked up the gun. "So you can always say, When my horse needed me I was there." She took one of his hands and placed it over hers. "Just rest it lightly on mine."

"Let me say good-bye!" he cried. "Daisy, I'll never love anyone like you, never, never—"

"Now," Lily said quietly. "Now."

In the kitchen, drinking their bourbon, Richard and Eva heard the shot. They braced themselves for a second one. None came. "Snooty as all get-out," Richard commented, "but she shoots straight."

Lily took Beau in her red convertible to the all-night drive-in. For Daisy's wake, she said. They had fries and hamburgers and onion rings and root beer floats. Then they drove around the dark rolling landscape listening to the radio until the sky was a pale purple and Lily saw Beau's eyelids were drooping and she drove him home.

That summer Beau became Lily's creature. She taught him to shoot and to drive a car, and she got him some riding togs and taught him how to ride correctly. Jumping was next. She showed him how to sit motionless in the grass or high in a tree in order to see—really see—nature. She took him fishing and they would sit where they had planted the willow for Daisy. On rainy days she played the piano and taught him songs and told him stories. Sometimes Beau's eyes would want to fill up with tears, he was so happy.

And proud. His relationship with Lily took place in a framework of mutual respect. He knew Lily admired his steely precision in learning any task, his penchant for performing reckless feats of derring-do, his astonishing strength (where did it come from?), and his natural physical grace. He had learned none of the above from his father. He had learned it all from Errol Flynn movies on television.

What he had learned from his father he was as yet unconscious of. At thirteen, Beau was already a chipped glass. Like Richard. But inside the chipped glass was a magic trick. Beau would always know how to make it ring like crystal.

During that first summer as Lily's acolyte he never consciously picked up the scent of his father's interest in the relationship.

Richard's pleasure in the alliance was great. The rich older girl had taken a maternal interest in his son, and this could almost certainly be parlayed into various agreeable directions for the whole family. There would be educational and economic advantages for Beau by way of his being exposed at the right level to the ritzy horse world and the right people. Lily might even provide a scholarship of some kind. Richard, who had always optimistically felt that the world owed him a living, was not—now that there was a money tree there to shake—above expecting the same for his son. The pleasant adjunct to Beau's good fortune was that he, Richard, would clearly benefit socially. Richard looked forward to being included by divine right in weekend gatherings at the big houses.

He said as much once or twice in Beau's presence, and was either shushed by Eva or suffered by Eva. Beau had appeared not to understand his father's gist and Eva was relieved, but the record would later show that the cupidity of his father's fantasies had infiltrated the boy's consciousness and remained.

There was another bequest from his father, though he was unconscious of this one as well, and the root of it was simply this: Rooms required a woman. Because women were interchangeable, without histories, without futures, the only crucial thing was always to have one for the bed, for the kitchen, and—in one's absence —for the window, so there would always be someone to come home to. Richard's hysterical, unremitting requirement of Eva as companion, whipping boy, nurse, field hand, and daily repository for his domestically emitted semen left only contempt for Eva's soul, and the boys understood early that she was Richard's before she would ever be theirs.

Silently Beau and Ethan would eat their cornflakes or their fish sticks and then escape to their rooms, or outside, or to school, leaving their clown of a father and his ragged, victim accomplice—their smoke-stained mother—to play out beyond their earshot yet another infernal marital scene.

Beyond earshot, but noted. Beau would have liked to love his father. Instead, he was secretly ashamed of him. His feelings for his mother were more complicated. She was more consistent than Richard, that is to say, she never sprang those horrible surprises on him, and she often took Beau's part—to a point—and he suspected she cared about what was fair. But as he entered his teens he began to notice that her primary role was as his father's passive collaborator in failure. And this made

Beau almost as resentful of his mother as he was of his father.

Lily, on the other hand, was beautiful and accomplished and successful at everything. Beau abandoned his sexual forays and turned chaste. He thought only of Lily. He resolved they would marry. He kept that vow to himself and waited. He never asked himself why a twenty-three-year-old girl would choose to spend so much time with a boy who was barely in his teens, let alone someday marry him. He accepted it as divine right. He saw himself and Lily as Lancelot and Guinevere. Love that was true.

It was in the stars.

So he was embarrassed, very embarrassed, when she made him pass himself off as a girl. They'd driven down to a horse show over the state line and there'd been a scarcity of rooms at the motel Lily wanted to stay in. She'd given Beau a silk Hermès scarf to tie around his head, lipsticked his mouth with Revlon's Really Pink, and tied a sweater around his shoulders, knotting it in front to hide his chest. She held up a mirror to him and the simple transformation was so incredible, they dissolved with laughter and he got over being mad and paid attention to the way she walked so he could mimic it.

They took turns in the bathroom, like being together was the most natural thing in the world, then got into bed, each scrupulously leaving a wide white channel down the middle, and watched television for a while before turning out the light. She fell asleep instantly. Beau was sure he'd be awake for hours, but the next thing he knew it was morning, and he could hear her splashing in the bathroom.

They repeated the charade a few weeks later when they drove up to D.C. because Lily wanted to walk in a civil rights march, and this time Beau fell into the spirit of his temporary role right away. He was dedicated, jokey, outrageous, and brought on peals of laughter from her. He would do anything to please Lily, even if it meant dressing up like a girl and marching for Negroes.

In the fall she went away again. He resumed all his old habits and waited for spring.

She returned and it was as if she had never been gone, except he was taller. And bigger. Encouraged and funded by Lily, he acquired a new obsession, polo. Like everything else that required sensitivity to animals, physical grace and flair, and exceptional riding skills, he took to it naturally, even though he was still very young and it was difficult finding opportunities for him to play at it; but because Lily was who she was, the occasional door opened, and his prowess took care of the rest.

Over their iced lemonade on the porch one late afternoon, Lily's guardians brought up the subject of Beau. "What do you plan to do with this boy?"

"Do with him?" Lily leaned against the open woodwork of the railing and sipped her drink. The sinking sun backlighted her russet hair. She looked earthy, fine, made of ginger and gold, and her guardians sighed, as they always did, at her beauty. "I told you. People around here my age, they're boring. All they want to do is get married, shop for tablecloths, and stay drunk. That little Beau, now, he's a treat."

"He's a fair horseman." There was a grudging pause. "So are a lot of folks."

"He's more than that. He's got lots of other qualities."

"Just what we're asking, honey."

Lily lifted herself onto the railing and began to swing her legs. "He understands things most other people around here don't."

"What things? He's only thirteen."

"Fourteen." Lily turned her clear, frank gaze on them. "I think he's special."

There was clearing of throats. "It's dangerous to give someone like that hopes. His parents, for instance, they'll start assuming things, like maybe you're going to do something about his education too. Fact is, his father doesn't have the best reputation hereabouts."

Lily replied with patient good humor. "Beau didn't choose his father. And if someone doesn't help a kid like that, he ends up selling used cars, or working the track. Fact is, Beau could make it to the American team."

There was a silence, then, "You think he's got the character?"

Lily gave her guardians a sharp look. "What do you mean?"

The guardians exchanged a glance. "In order to be a sportsman, a man must be a gentleman."

Lily laughed. "Give him time, will you?"

"The boy already has quite a reputation."

"For what? What are you talking about?"

"Like father, like son."

She stared at them. "Beau doesn't drink."

"It's not liquor we mean."

"Then what?"

"He's quite the little Lothario."

In that moment Lily—she was still looking at her guardians—might have actually been seeing the sweet depression where Beau's collarbones met, and the sun-burned angle of his jaw. And the gold flecks in his young eyes. And the long, skinny legs he was so ashamed of.

The next morning dawned hot, abuzz with flies. Lily and Beau went fishing.

"You got a girlfriend?" Lily asked him.

Something happened to Beau's eyes. Suddenly they

were like translucent marbles swiveling beneath delicately bluish, half-lowered lids.

"Who. Me?"

"Yes, you."

After a moment he replied, "I'm always with you." And they fished in silence for a while. He felt her eyeing him.

"What you want to know for?" he asked. His body felt becalmed. He was conscious of the weight of his arm holding the fishing pole. Was he in the lap of the gods? His eyes flickered over her. For a voluptuous, prayerful moment his lids closed. Then he opened them. She was still looking at him.

Sharply she said, "You do that just like a girl."

"Do what?"

"Bat your eyelashes like that."

He smiled at her sweetly, sadly, and looked away. He was not only offended but confused. What did she want? Her voice had had an angry edge. He weighed this against the instinct that had been telling him the moment had come.

Once they got started he was sure it would be all right, but how to begin? He looked at her out of the corner of his eye. She was sitting quietly, staring into the water.

Wretchedly he considered the situation. Up until now he had steadfastly tried to avoid all thoughts of sex with Lily. Up until now it had been a dream that belonged to the future. If it happened today, here by the river, he sensed he would have only one chance. If he failed in some way, the first time, he would lose her. What should he do? She had put the thought into his head. He was pretty sure the thought was in her head too. He was also pretty sure she wasn't going to be anything like the others. They'd been easy. He hadn't had to talk them into it or get them ready, though he'd wanted to. He'd dreamed about it, he'd always thought he would like that part, but he still hadn't experienced it.

He began thinking about how it would be to do it for Lily. The getting-her-ready part. He began to understand he couldn't wait.

"What are you doing?" Lily stared at him.

He was unbuttoning his shirt. Then he kicked off his sneakers, unbuckled his belt, tore off his shirt, and was out of his jeans in a moment and standing before her, fanatical, completely naked, ready for inspection or execution, hard as a man and wearing the expression of a hero ready to do or die.

He fell to his knees in front of her, buried his face in her lap, murmuring, "Let me, please let me."

He heard no reply, only her breathing.

He pushed her roughly on her back, lifted her T-shirt, and began to suck her nipples. He was weeping with fright and lust, and Lily, who had felt the wetness between her legs the instant he had stood before her naked, let him do what he wanted. Moments later, with a skinned young knee planted on either side of her, he eased off her shorts and underpants with trembling hands, covered her belly with hot tears, and entered her. He rocked back and forth on her like an orphan, and she began to rock with him.

That day, in his own eyes, Beau became a young god.

8

The Impersonator, dressed and made up as Theo, sat framed by the high dusty green velvet curtains that hung in their usual heavy sprawl in front of the rain-splattered window.

Robert had just given him a large, expensive book. "One of those coffee table books," Robert said. "Mostly pictures. There are some great ones of Theo. It's coming out next month. Someone sent me a copy and I thought you might like it."

The Impersonator handed the book back to Robert.

"No, thank you," Theo's voice said. "It may not have occurred to you that I didn't want to die, that in fact I passed away under violent, heartrending protest. I certainly didn't want to end up in a coffee table book with lots of grungy lies in it about famous people, including grungy lies about how they died."

His heart began to pound. Why had he departed from his routine? Why? He was losing it. He was fucking losing it. Was there no safety anywhere? Not even inside these clothes, this makeup? Was there no place he could belong, ever?

Marly had left in a bad mood for her job at the restaurant, and he knew when she came home she would begin berating him for whatever she was angry about today. He envied her the way she had structured her life. She had walls around her, whereas he had only netting, flypaper, air. She had her auditions, her diets, her network of female friends, her singing lessons, her self-help books, and her dreams. And of course there was her job.

But most of all he envied Marly because she was female. The advantage was to *them*, always had been. They only had to use their tits, tell their little stories, and walk a certain way, and they got what they wanted. They didn't have to *do* anything, whereas a man was castigated and considered a failure if he didn't want to *do* something. Unless, that is, the man had money to begin with. But he had never had money, at least, never money of his own.

When he was sixteen his parents had given him a gas credit card. He had been prouder of this than anything he had ever possessed. But then his father had gone into one of his slump periods, and Beau was asked to return the card.

Even now the Impersonator felt sweat in his armpits. He had gone berserk. He had screamed, "It's mine, you gave it to me!" And when his mother tonelessly remarked, "Things are hard right now, we have to pull together," he heard the words but not the meaning; he was incapable of connection to his parents' troubles. He had wanted to kill his father.

There had been other times when he'd have happily seen Richard dead. When his father—in a drunken rage —had pushed his mother down a flight of stairs, the Impersonator had actually tried with his bare hands to snuff all the breath out of his father. Ethan had tried to pull them apart, while their mother—in a heap at the bottom of the stairs—struggled to her hands and knees and crawled over to help Ethan save her husband's life. By then she was in the middle stages of the cancer that was ultimately to kill her. Her hair had fallen out and she normally went around with her head tied in a scarf, but during the fall down the stairs it had come off.

Now he suddenly realized that several minutes had gone by and that Robert was staring at him. Maybe he should flirt with him a little. He languidly recrossed his legs, slung an arm across the back of the chair, meanwhile producing the radiant, famous Theo smile. He asked, "Would you like a song?"

"I'd like to know why you looked so sad just now."

Airily the Impersonator replied, "I miss earthly things. Pastrami sandwiches. The January sales."

"I meant you. Not Theo."

The Impersonator gave Robert a Theo look, a brittle laugh. "The young man you're speaking to does not exist. He's a figment of his own imagination."

Robert raised his eyebrows. "He's sitting here in front of me, Theo, dressed up as you, so he must exist."

"Wrong again. I'm pretending to be him, dressed up as me." Inside he was on his own hellish roller coaster. Why didn't he stick to the script? Where was this taking him? He smiled provocatively across at Robert. What did this overprivileged jerkoff want for his money? Absolution? He resolved never to let Robert have it. He should have stopped these meetings long ago, before the man had become addicted, before he himself—he realized with dark satisfaction—had also become addicted.

A dead woman, radiant still, her heart beating steadily in a corner of everybody's mind. But what to call this corruption, this creature he had become for money, for thrills? Hiding in a woman's clothing, inhabiting a swollen, water-logged ghost, enjoying every wanton step of the way the temptation to drive Robert to the edge of the ambivalence he suspected every man—including himself—harbored.

Had his own unconscious objective from the beginning been to appropriate female power in a way that would entice and inflame Robert into desiring him more than the man might have ever wanted Theo herself? The sheer piquance of the notion thrilled him. And really, none of it was his fault. He hadn't singled out Robert. Robert had come looking for him. Once in hand, the situation had shown itself to be too profitable, too alluring to resist.

Call it sport. He shuddered. What would Theo have thought? Intellectually she might have been fascinated. What had made her so famous was her consistent, intuitive take on the odd, hidden byways of human nature. She had somehow known every terrible thing there was to be known. Yet until the very end, even with the flowering of her own inevitable narcissism, she had been straight as a fine Indian arrow, true blue as the high summer sky. Flooded with the remembrance of her bright spirit, he felt a sickness in his gut. Did everything always end in betrayal?

He suddenly saw her clear, even gaze. From somewhere in time Theo was looking him in the eye. Theo, who had been born Lily Theodora Buckley.

9

All Jane had to do now was to wring proof from the universe that she was not falsely accusing Robert. On a particular Tuesday morning she went to the drawer where she had put the envelope containing the telephone bill, including an itemization of local calls she had requested. She took out the telephone bill, sat down at a desk, and began to go through the list of local calls. Those she recognized she drew a line through. Those she did not, she commenced to dial. After an hour had passed her face was flushed. She had dialed Bergdorf Goodman, 47th Street Photo, her dentist, three movie theaters, four takeout places, the Department of Motor Vehicles, Lincoln Center, the library, TWA, Eastern Airlines, a flower store, an optician, a pharmacy, Robert's publisher, half a dozen restaurants, and Phil Simonetta's office. She was almost through the list. She dialed a fresh number.

A youngish sounding, actressy female answered hopefully, "Hello?"

"Good morning," Jane said immediately. It was without a doubt the same voice who had answered when she had called the number inscribed on the matchbook from The Touch Me Club. "I'm afraid I have the wrong number."

Jane checked the bill. The number had been called three times. She checked her appointment book. The first call had been made the day after they returned from Washington. The second the week afterward. Same day, Thursday. She checked Robert's appointment book. It indicated nothing on either date, nor for last Thursday. Nor today.

Robert was with the Impersonator. He had just arrived. He sat in his usual place and looked across at the immaculate reproduction of his dead wife. "Not Theo today, please. You. I want you." He said it in his elegant way, with a slight smile. He felt it important to go about this lightly in case he was rejected. He was very frightened.

The Impersonator gave him an appraising look. He remained silent. Finally he said, "Methinks you'd better go," but there was an odd glitter in his eye and he was watching Robert carefully from underneath his long, thick eyelashes.

He's intrigued by the sexual gamble, Robert guessed, and his blood rose.

"You've been leading me on from the beginning," he said next. He was no longer sure this was true, but he was past caring.

The answer came on the end of a breath. "I've never loved with a man."

"Neither have I. What difference does it make?" Robert's voice was raw, reflecting his desire, which was now uncheckable. He stood up, stood over the Impersonator, looked down at him.

The Impersonator looked up at Robert. Then slowly, very slowly, not taking his eyes from Robert, he removed his wig, let it fall to his lap, then to the floor. Casually he ruffled his hands through his own beautiful, silky thick brown hair.

This man was a prostitute. Of this Robert was now certain. *I can change him,* Robert said in his heart. *Make him as beautiful as he really is. He will be mine. I will be his.*

Robert placed his hands on the Impersonator's shoulders. The Impersonator, still looking up at Robert, made to remove his false eyelashes.

"No," Robert said quietly. "No." He took the Impersonator's face between his hands and bent to kiss him, to taste at last his mouth.

A man like me. The enchantments that followed were not strange, not strange at all. *For the first time, someone of my own. A man like me.*

Late that afternoon Jane heard the front door open and close. The cross breeze fluttered the long filmy white curtains in the living room, where she sat cross-legged and barefoot with a large map of the Mississippi River spread out before her on the thick Oriental rug.

The angle of a handsome old mirror on the west wall allowed it to reflect in part another antique mirror in the foyer, both of them De Peña heirlooms, so that hearing Robert had come in, Jane got up from the rug, saw him in the mirror, and instead of proceeding farther, paused and stood very still. *Here it is,* her heart told her. *You had to have proof? You had to know?*

Robert had not advanced into the foyer. He had closed the front door and was leaning with his back against it. His eyes were closed and he was taking deep breaths. He thought he was alone.

After a moment he opened his eyes. With the languor of the satiated, his left hand dropped his keys onto the little table to the left of him, but he remained leaning against the door in an exhausted, relaxed manner, his head lolling back luxuriously.

From the living room Jane, the stone statue, watched him in the beautiful old mirrors Robert's ancestors had brought to the New World from Castile.

Robert uttered now a little moan of pleasure. He clenched his eyes shut again as if in some exquisite memory. There was a deep exhale. He smiled. He opened his eyes.

And saw Jane. She had walked into the foyer and was quietly looking at him. She was very still and he knew she had seen it all.

A very long time passed in silence. A space of time with no choices, really, except the one that had been marked out for them by the radiant smile of the dead Theo.

Wordlessly Jane left the foyer. She didn't want to know his infernal tale. She went to her study and closed the door. It took some time to unearth the phone number she was looking for—she had written it down in Brazil but hadn't put it in her book. It would be on a loose piece of paper somewhere in one of the folders. She opened a drawer and went through them. Some minutes later she was dialing a number in Switzerland.

When Hanna Spengler came on the line, Jane said, "It's Jane Donovan de Peña. I wonder if I could ask you something. I know it's terribly late there, and I'm sorry."

There was a brief silence. "What has happened?"

"Do you think men are, first of all, capable of being faithful?"

"The historical indications have been scant, possibly even apocryphal." There was a dry pause. "Testosterones, I suspect, are destiny." Another pause. "It's such a big conversation. Is there someone—I mean right now—who can stay with you?"

"You think I'm hysterical. Is that the way I sound?"

"I know something has happened that you don't choose to share with friends or family, or you wouldn't be calling someone you had a drink with in Brazil. Do you want to come here? You would be very welcome. You could fly to Geneva and I could drive down to pick you up."

"I don't know."

"Does your present distress have to do with your husband's late wife?

"How do you know?"

"One senses, I suppose, an unquiet grave."

"Robert's been having an affair. It had started when I met you. I don't know whether it's with a woman or a man."

"Does the gender make a difference to you?"

Jane looked out at the Hudson. "To betray me with another woman, he betrays our love. To betray me with a man, he rejects my race."

Hanna was silent a moment. "What's your next river? Perhaps you need, more than anything right now, to work. Not in the sense of burying yourself in it to forget or to postpone, quite the contrary—it's just that doing our work and doing it well can create a happiness that's authentic on its own and that we can never get from anyone but ourselves." There was another pause. "Do you know that horrible German proverb about life? 'Work, build house, die.' Can you imagine the dreary asshole who composed that?" There was an irrepressible chuckle. "Doesn't it make you grateful for

your own glorious imagination? My dear, truly you
have everything you need to get through."

Hanna Spengler kept Jane on the phone for an hour.
The next day Jane moved out of Robert's apartment.
The following week she began her journey on the Mississippi River.

10

Robert did not tell the Impersonator that Jane had left him. He didn't mention her at all. He never had. Her departure from his life had left him shaken and angry in a muddled sort of way that he planned to think about later. His feeling for it didn't come in the same vivid colors as his obsession for the exquisitely buttocked Theo/boy whom he had taken in transports of terror and joy last week, and whom he had looked forward most of his waking hours since to taking again.

The following week Marly caught them. Putting her key in the lock, turning it, she was expecting Twinkies and a back rub maybe.

The room was dark. The dusty green velvet curtains had been closed against what light was left of the day. The air was very still, very thick. She heard him crying out in a way that was strange to her. She understood she was being betrayed in her own bed, but in the first moment her imagination stopped short of perceiving her replacement as having a male body. Then there came another voice, low and handsome. She scarcely saw him but what she saw was enough. She turned and ran out, leaving the door wide open, the keys dangling in the lock.

The men were not quite finished. Close to victory, they called out their terrible words of love and Marly heard them as she fled down the stairs.

Robert was the first to notice the shaft of artificial light coming through the open door from the hallway. After that there was only the blur of haste and hurt. Walking home, Robert folded and refolded that part of it, reassuring himself that the next time they saw each other there would be a clearer perspective, there would be the shared experience behind them instead of how it was now, Robert walking across the city alone.

He had been ordered by the Impersonator to get out. Marly could come back any second, he had said through his teeth. Robert had quickly dressed. There had not been what one might call a good-bye, only Robert asking, "You'll call me?"

The Impersonator had not replied but only turned his back. He had covered himself in the fur rug with the black and silver pelts. He was waiting for Robert to go.

Robert walked to the door—since closed—and opened it.

"Don't forget to leave the money," he heard his lover in the black and silver pelts say.

Crossing the avenues, he wore his anguish on the outside of his skin and shrank from inadvertent contact with passing humanity. Walking the sidewalks, past the ledges of the drunken, the hopeless, the dead, he felt he paraded his own shame.

He let himself into the foyer with the mirror that had come from Castile. He walked into his large handsome living room with the long filmy white curtains blowing, the thousands of books, and across the way, the fiery blast of New Jersey. What, who, would fill the empty afternoon? There were hours yet before dark. And then? What, who, would get him through? Robert's recourse was limited. No one in the world to tell. The heterosexual brotherhood's standards were high, and besides, in extremis, one had always wept on the shoulder of a woman.

In the apartment with the green velvet curtains, the Impersonator, now dressed in a clean shirt, jeans, and cowboy boots, looked down out of the window at the sidewalk. Forty black plastic garbage bags, a plaid sofa with its springs exposed, and a toothless woman in a rakish Easter bonnet and rags on her feet. No Marly.

His sexual interest in Robert had been contextual, exploratory. His personal interest in the man had been scant. There had been in addition the danger that Robert would find out the earlier connection with Theo. Now that Marly had gone running out to the street knowing God knows what, his choices were further narrowed. He leaned his forehead against the glass, and suddenly saw her crossing the street. Coming home.

That same evening down in TriBeCa, Sara Alessio was enlarging some photos in her darkroom when the front buzzer sounded. She crossed the theatrically bare space of her minimalist loft, opened a window, looked down into the street. Three floors below she made out the features and graceful stance of the young man she had met down south.

"I was passing by," he called up with a beguiling smile.

When she opened the door she saw he was holding a deep blue iris. "I thought you might be more of an iris person than a rose person or a daisy person or a lily person."

She took the iris and crossed to the open hundred-thousand-dollar kitchen to find just the right vase for it. "What do you do in life, anyway? Did we ever get around to that? I think you said you were an actor?"

They had got around to it. She remembered everything he'd said, everything she'd said.

"Yes, but I've always been more interested in period architecture and interior design and photography."

She laughed. "Get out of here."

What he liked about her already was her good humor, her generous spirit, unlike Marly, who was mean and small.

"Cross my heart," he went on with a sincere look. "I didn't tell you the first time we met because I was too shy." Really, he had had no choice. A nest had to be found and it had to be found tonight. He hadn't dared to try to bunk in with any of his and Marly's friends, or even ask them if he could. He hadn't known what Marly in her hysterical state might say to them.

He glanced around the huge loft. So this is what they looked like. He'd seen layouts of them in magazines. He supposed all this iconographic restraint indicated social confidence. Still, why anyone with lots of money would want to live on a revolting street with warehouses and grungy sidewalks instead of near a park or a river or in the country, he could not imagine. He wondered where the bedroom was and if there were two bathrooms or one. He had never had his own bathroom.

He returned his gaze to her. "If I had the nerve I'd ask you if you could use an assistant or apprentice. I'd do anything."

Sara felt a twinge of pricked vanity. He hadn't come looking for her, he'd come in search of a job. "Would you like a drink?" she asked pleasantly, waving to a tray set with bottles and glasses. "Maybe you'll make me a scotch and water—no ice." She continued

agreeably—*give him a drink and get him out of here*—
"I'm afraid I can't afford an assistant."

She watched his hands, pouring the liquor into the
glass, recapping the bottle, lifting a pitcher of water,
pouring, setting down the pitcher. She remembered him
training the horse.

He handed her the glass. "Could I talk to you,
please?" He sat down beside her. "I've broken up with
my girlfriend," he said with a twisted smile.

She eyed him. What would he ask for next? First it
had been a job, and now sympathy. She said, again
nicely, "You told me that it was imminent. Remember?
She's moved out?"

Lightly he cleared his throat. His heart was beating
so fast he thought Sara would surely hear it. He stared
into his glass, languorously stroked the rim of it with
one finger, hoping she would think he was imagining it
as the curve of her body.

Sara decided—on the basis of his youth and inexperi-
ence—to forgive him this antediluvian courting ploy.

He was now looking at her, his expression suffused
with misery. "She can't afford her own apartment right
now, you know, paying to move her stuff, and the security deposit you always have to pay. I felt so sorry for
her. It was simpler, really, for me to let her have it till
she gets on her feet."

"How chivalrous."

He added with a sigh, "Marly'd have been better off
with a lawyer or a corporation type so she could have
wall-to-wall carpeting. Matching silver. A furniture set
from Bloomingdale's." He glanced around the room.
"I've always wanted something like this. I was never
really comfortable trying to strive for the world she
wanted. Marly's sweet but there's a lot she just doesn't
get."

He was feeling slightly sick at this betrayal of Marly,

but he continued to tramp through the squalid mud of revisionism. The ire with which Marly had thrown him out indicated he would never be allowed back again, therefore there was no benefit in his being loyal or telling the truth.

He must press on, he must shut out the vile things she had shouted at him when she'd come in, gasping with rage, with tears. "Get out and get out now and don't try to talk me out of it this time because you can't. Everything I've done for you, all your promises and new leafs, none of it ever meant anything to you."

He had stayed cool, very cool. It had been the only way to protect himself. "Maybe you have standards not everyone can live up to. Some of us don't have your strength. Or your toughness. When my horse died, I—"

He thought she would go berserk. "I don't ever want to hear about that horse again! Or any of your other pathetic stories! You think you're the only person to ever have anything bad happen to them when they're a kid?"

"If you'd just calm down," he said through his teeth. "I was desperate. This person was in a position to help me get a job—" But he couldn't go on. Even he recognized the thinness, the cheapness of his excuse.

"Job?" she shouted. "You wouldn't know a job if you fell over one. Working in a restaurant is a job. Working at the answering service or in a department store is a job. Being President of the United States is a job. Playing fuckface with some guy in my bed isn't a job, it's playing fuckface with some guy in my bed because you're lazy and conceited and you think the world owes you a living!"

She would never understand, he reflected, that exploring sensuality was a country of its own, something he had never thought he should deny himself. She insisted on seeing what had happened as a personal be-

trayal of herself, whereas it had been merely the hard-
ness of himself in a completely new fashion. De Peña
had instructed him to receive, to give as a woman
might, and so the Impersonator had come to understand many things.

He now looked covertly at Sara's legs. Not perfect,
but a damn sight better than Marly's.

Over their drinks he told Sara the standardized version of his life. She cooked a simple dinner for them.
Cooked! He couldn't get over it. Pots and pans. A salad
spinner. A special brush to wash mushrooms. A real
dining table with lighted candles.

She was intrigued when he asked if he could sleep the
night on her sofa—and then did just that. She had been
cynically prepared for the usual gambits: "It's cold, I'm
too long for it, couldn't I just lie beside you like a
brother, I promise I won't touch you." She had been
greatly relieved to have been spared rejecting him. She
had also been much impressed. Not Like Other Men. In
the morning she made coffee for them and left the
house for a long day of appointments, giving him permission to stay and use the telephone to make his arrangements for a place to live. When she returned late
in the afternoon he was very busy in the kitchen, trying
to cook dinner. He was shirtless, and dancing to rock
music on her stereo as he stirred. He looked up as she
came in, turned the heat down under a pot, and announced with a grin, "I washed my shirt and it's in the
dryer. I'm happy. Do you know how long it's been
since I've been happy?"

He put down the wooden spoon he was holding and
began to swivel and thrust his hips to the music.

She laughed out loud. He was refreshing. It was a
nice change to see pure naturalness, boyish energy in a
man these days. The ones she knew were all so tired, so
uptight, so wrung out with the getting of power.

Exuberantly the Impersonator had begun to juggle four grapefruit. He was skillful. Encouraged by her rapt attention, he followed this by standing on his head, lifting himself up on his hands, and walking around the kitchen upside down, reciting Kipling with a German accent.

She had better be careful. The situation was harmless enough, and he was quite entertaining; still, there was that indefinable filmy translucence to his personality. Try to put her hand through him, it might come out the other side.

A half-hour later she again revised her opinion. Why had her earlier one been so negative? He was merely starved for good company, that was all. He was the brightest of spirits, who had been forced to wander in the wilderness for too long and had temporarily lost his way. Having him at the other end of her table felt right. Afterward they sat down to read, she in one pool of lamplight, he in another. It was uncanny the way he fit into the room, into the evening. She had said, "If you'd rather watch television?" He had shaken his head. "I rarely watch the tube." He had scanned the bookshelves. He chose a volume of Auden's poems and a big book with pictures of frescoes by Fra Angelico and settled himself to read.

He slept on the sofa again. Sara was sure he would show up in her room at some point. He didn't. She had difficulty getting to sleep, but finally drifted off. In the morning, when she went into the living room, he was already sitting up on the sofa. He had remained fully dressed but was wrapped from head to toe in a blanket. His hair was tousled and curly.

"I should get out of your way," he said, then added apologetically, "The trouble is, I'm getting addicted to you."

"It's been fun," she said sincerely. "What are you going to do?"

He looked puzzled.

"About your life," she prompted, and wondered if he'd been thinking about his life at all, if possibly he had been staying here in order to avoid it. On the whole, it might be a good thing he was leaving.

"I wrote a poem last night. After you went to bed." He picked up a slip of paper he had taken from the telephone pad and handed it to her. The handwriting was childish, unformed, and it was not a good poem, it was scarcely a poem at all. It was couched in limp imagery and was entitled "Self-Loathing." She read it with dismay.

Her first thought was to heed the warning bell that was ringing in her head. She was not the Salvation Army, he was not her responsibility, and the words he had written smacked of a dark, rudderless meandering she didn't like at all. Her second thought was to argue the case. Had she herself not gone through periods of muddle and despair at his age? She thought of all the people who had helped her through it. Did he have no one?

"I guess," he was saying, "I'll bunk in with one of my married friends. I'll get odd jobs, stuff like that." He began to put on his shoes.

"Why not a real job?" she asked impatiently. "And this poem. It's not clear. It's not clear and it's drenched with resignation."

"I was down. I was scared. It was four o'clock in the morning. I don't live anywhere." He stared out the window, his back to her. "Could I come back sometime?"

Let him go, Sara intoned from a deep place in her gut. His neediness would engulf her. He was trouble. In a few weeks she would be bored and then what? She examined the wistful way he was looking at her. *Un-*

dressing me in the nicest, most respectful of ways. Now he's looking away, embarrassed.

"Good-bye," she said nicely. "Let me know how you make out."

He looked at her briefly, sadly. "Anon," he said, and left.

He descended the three flights of stairs to the street. He had his hands in his pockets and he was whistling. He would drive up to see Aunt Charity and his brother for a few days.

"You stupid prick! You little child!" Marly was screaming at him a half-hour later. "You destroy me, you destroy what we had together, and now you're having a tantrum because you can't use my car and my gas credit card to spend another day jerking off and telling lies?"

His chest was tight. His brain was heating up. He hadn't thought for years about its being not his car but hers. She was truly gross when she got like this, even the veins in her fat neck stood out. He felt a wave of pity for her, that she would never be as classy as, say, someone like Sara. Sara, he had noted, used cloth napkins even for breakfast, and knew how to pronounce foreign expressions without stumbling or sounding pretentious.

Marly, staring at his cold, handsome mask, burst into tears. She sank on the bed, a crumpled mess of kimono. "I loved you." She sobbed and beat her fists on the bed.

His voice was cold. "You told me to get out. I did."

"Do you have any idea how much you hurt me?"

He was silent. Fury continued to boil up inside him. He wanted the fucking car.

Marly dragged herself off the bed, hurled herself against him. "I loved you."

He felt her arms around his neck and the wetness of

her tears on his chest. Poor Marly, poor sweet Marly. The nine years of their life together ran backward like an empty hallway compared to the richness of the enticing hours just passed with Sara, during which he had outgrown Marly and everything she represented.

Marly waited for him to say something. A wave of fresh anger washed over her. She pushed him away. "Where have you been?"

"Sleeping on friends' couches," he snapped.

"What friends? No one's seen you."

She wasn't going to let him have the car, he wouldn't be able to go up to see Ethan and Aunt Charity, and he couldn't go back to Sara yet. He lit a cigarette, sat down on the edge of the bed, and turned on the television.

Marly stared at him. "What do you think you're doing?"

"I'm resting. It's tiring not having a home."

She sat down next to him. After a trembly moment she asked, "Do you love me?"

He looked at her with a pleasant expression. "You threw me out and now you won't even let me have the car so I can go up to my brother's and have a few days of peace and get my head together."

"What about what you did to me?"

He continued to stare at the four square inches of television. Cary Grant and Katharine Hepburn. Sara looked a bit like Hepburn. Except for the legs. He couldn't call her back or go to see her for at least three days. He had to give her time to chew on her ambivalence. He had to give her time to begin to miss him. Two nights in her apartment and she hadn't made a move toward him, not a single one. He had waited for hours on that sofa.

Beside him Marly continued to snivel. He turned off

the television. He took both her hands and looked into her eyes for a long moment. She began to quiet down.

"Marly," he said quietly, "let me have the car for a few days so I can cool out at Ethan's and you can cool out here. Right now all we'll do is hurt each other."

Her expression was a mix of suspicion and hope. "How many days is a few days?"

"I'll be back on Thursday." He kissed the top of her head. "Scout's honor." He was still holding her hands.

"And then what?"

"The future is still the future." He kissed her hands. Both of them.

Turning teary again, she asked, "Had you ever done it with a guy before?"

"No."

"Did he ask you or did you ask him?"

"He asked me."

"Did you like it?"

"Some."

"Better than . . . with a woman?"

"No."

"Will you see him again?"

"No, honey."

So there was no reason at all, Marly decided, to tell him about the phone calls that had been coming in daily, always at the end of the day when it was getting dark, from this guy who said his name was Bob. He didn't sound fruity but he sounded old like her father and the whole thing was disgusting. If he called again she would say that the person he wanted had moved away, leaving no forwarding address.

At Brawley Manor the Impersonator helped his brother with the chores and they watched a lot of television. On the second night, during a commercial, he announced, "Marly and I broke up."

Ethan looked horrified and embarrassed. After another few commercials went by he said, hesitating, "Was it about her breast?"

The Impersonator looked confused for a moment, then, "Oh, that. It was just a lot of those cysts that she gets. Nothing. Like last time."

"Is it all right for me to still talk to her? I mean, I've always liked Marly. Anyway, she's the only girl I know." He stared at his brother. "What happened?"

"We don't want the same things anymore. I met this real interesting woman. Guess I'll be moving in with her."

"Won't it be weird? Having to start all over with someone you don't, like, know?"

The program came on again, and the Impersonator did not reply. The brothers resumed staring at the screen. Two days later the Impersonator telephoned Sara. He heard her quick intake of breath and then a pleasant "Hello."

"Could I come over for a drink tomorrow night?"

There was a slight hesitation. Then, "That would be nice." He loved the way she talked. It was always considered and gracious. It was not put on, it was natural. He decided to practice talking like that.

The next afternoon he was lucky to find a parking place only two blocks from Marly's apartment. He scribbled a note: "Car is in front of laundry," wrapped the keys up in the note, and put them in her mailbox. Then he sprinted down the street toward a subway. In the moment Sara opened the door to him he saw his future and it was golden.

He would go carefully about the evening. It was all in the pacing. There were two buttons, one marked on, the other marked off. You pushed one, then the other, and you kept it up, mixing the sequence after a while.

His assumption all along had been that all he had to overcome in her was what he guessed was a lack of sexual confidence. What he didn't dream of was how much the best part of her didn't want him. What she didn't dream of was how very, very simply he would get her.

When morning came, he opened his eyes and thanked his God. He reached for Sara's sleeping body.

She opened her eyes and smiled. "Hi."

"Hi," he said. This would from now on be his bed, his duvet, his apartment, his cosmology. He was fully erect.

She inspected him with interest and then glanced at the clock. "I wish I didn't have to go."

"We'll be together tonight." He gave her a reassuring look and slid her body under his for a quick one. "Again. And again."

"I'm leaving for Mexico today."

Temporarily his breath left him. A few seconds went by and he was able to collect himself. It wasn't all bad news. He could stay in the apartment while she was gone. Yippee!

But this was not to be. Her sister and brother, she explained, were having their apartment painted and had ordered the work to coincide with Sara's trip so they would have someplace to stay. Sara would be away for three weeks. She asked him to give her a phone number. He told her he would bunk in with this friend, that friend, so it would be difficult for her to call him. They arranged that at the end of the first week he would call her in Mexico City. She wrote down the number for him. He stared at all the digits. He had never before made an international call. They said a tender and romantic good-bye.

He took the subway up to 29th Street. His handsome mouth was turned down at the corners. Would he never have a home he could call his own?

A sullen Marly greeted him. "You got a nerve. I let you have the car and you disappeared."

He put his arms around her. "Hush." He continued to hold her, nuzzling his cheek against hers, looking around the room. It was familiar and sweet. Marly's head rested against his shoulder. She would be afraid to risk losing him again. He probably had all the time he needed.

As the first week went by the image of Sara receded. The world again became his fur rug, television, an occasional racquetball game, and Marly, who was bursting with plans as to how they could improve their lives. She was going to go on a diet. She was going to ask her parents to increase her monthly stipend. She was going to make a list of job ideas for the Impersonator.

His lethargy was greater than before. He sank so deeply into himself he forgot to call Sara on the appointed day. By the time he remembered, he was unable to reach her. She had checked out, left for the next city. He lay under his rug, watching television and carefully considering his situation. Sara had been for those few days his only ticket to a safe new life, but now that Marly had taken him back, he had a choice. Did he have the energy to be the personality he would have to maintain for Sara? He put a grape in his mouth and considered the pros and cons.

A few days later he called Sara at the second number she had given him. Her confident voice came over the wire. "Where are you? I'll call you back in two hours— give me the number."

Marly wouldn't be back until nine. He was safe. He gave Sara the number. Possibly it was the hesitation in his voice that caused her to ask, "Where's that?"

Although he was good at inventing elaborate lies on the spot, he drew a blank and realized he must get over letting her intimidate him. "My old apartment," he had to say, furious at himself because nothing else would come to him.

"Oh?" Sara's tone was cool.

"Marly had to go to the hospital. Nothing serious. A D and C. I'm just here taking care of the dog." There was no dog. "If I send you a kiss over the wire, will you fold it up in your fingers and save it for when you really need it?"

Slightly briskly, she came back with "I've really got to go. Talk to you in two hours."

An hour later Marly came in. She examined his look of surprise. "I only work till seven on Wednesdays." She was taking off her clothes. "Can I get in with you and snuggle for a while?"

"Sure." But his face had turned sulky. She dealt with his disinterest by beginning with a profoundly reverential blow job. He began to stir. They made love for a time. When they were done she got up to go into the bathroom and he instantly pulled the telephone plug out of the socket and scattered some magazines on it so she wouldn't notice. She came back and he pulled her to him. She didn't have his new girlfriend's grace, she didn't have his new girlfriend's elegant bawdiness, but she was sweet, tireless, and he loved her, he'd loved her for nine years and she knew him better than anyone. He tried not to think of Sara calling, calling, getting no answer. What could he do?

The next day he went out and called her from a public phone.

She was really cool this time. "As you no doubt know, there was no answer at your apartment."

He explained that Marly's sister had dropped in to pick up some things for Marly at the hospital and had stayed to chat and he had unplugged the phone. It would have been impossible to talk openly to her, Sara, with the other woman listening.

Having had some success with this scenario, he began, over the next few days, to invent one for Marly. His version was this: By a lucky fluke he had been introduced to a successful photographer who had broken her leg while on a job in Mexico and needed someone to assist her physically as well as administratively, at her loft, in her darkroom, and to drive her and accompany her to places she needed to go. The job would probably last a month, it unfortunately would be a twenty-four-hour-a-day thing because of having to play nurse, and it would definitely benefit both himself and Marly.

"How?" Marly asked.

"She knows everyone we only read about in magazines. She'll open doors. It's our chance to get somewhere. Let's go over your pictures, I want to have them with me so I can show them to her."

By the time Sara returned to New York, Marly had accepted the coming absence of the Impersonator for the period of a month while he did his stint with the woman called Sara, whom he described as middle-aged, hardboiled, and really a riot.

While Sara had been away she had suffered profound misgivings about her new boyfriend. It was the lightweight aspect of him that troubled her the most. But after ten minutes with him she wondered how she could have forgotten the sweet impact of his attentions, his sensitivity, the utter freshness with which he looked at everything—the starry night, the shape of a teacup, a bird on the sill, and herself. He was a wonder. And she would have him.

He brought some clothes, his sterling razor, and a crystal decanter in which he said he liked to keep Chivas Regal.

Two weeks went by and he had received no phone calls, nor had he made any as far as she knew. He seemed to have no past life and very little baggage. Where, for instance, were his books, personal papers, mementos, *stuff?* Didn't he have winter clothing? A raincoat? A suitcase? He'd brought his things in a lot of plastic bags. But when love is new it is its own belief system. Sara readily accepted his explanation that most of the things in the old apartment had been his and that rather than strip the place he'd wanted to give Marly time to start putting together stuff of her own.

Sara admired him for his generosity. That he seemed not to have a life of his own—he had instead thrown himself enthusiastically into living hers—she ascribed to the fact that his love for her was absorbing him so much that for this initial period he only had time for that.

Meanwhile, Marly waited each day for his phone call. It usually came between nine and nine-thirty, which was the time Sara usually took her bath, but Marly didn't know this and could not have suspected it because frequently he would say, "Hang on a minute, honey," and then she would hear him call, "I'll be with you in a second, Sara. I'm talking to Marly."

This always warmed Marly. She liked the idea of her new connection—even if second-hand—to someone so successful as Sara. Marly continued her life, working at the restaurant, going to general auditions, and waiting for him to move back home when the job was over. She suggested a few times that they should have lunch or a drink, but he explained—and she understood—that Sara expected him to be on call every second of the day.

The initial, loving agreement made between the Impersonator and Sara was that since he was temporarily insolvent (he explained that he had felt compelled to settle his last few thousand dollars on Marly to get her started), she would tide him over until he found work that would suit his talents. She set up several introductions for him. Apparently none of these went well. The Impersonator supplied her with explanations, once accompanied by angry tears. This one had been bitchy, that one had kept him waiting and then not given him more than a few minutes. Another one had been inattentive, and the final one was a fag who had tried to hit on him.

Without telling him, Sara telephoned the first person he had seen.

"Darling, he's an amateur" came the explanation, and then there was a short laugh. Not a nice laugh.

"Come on," Sara said. "He was probably nervous."

"His experience is zilch. And sorry, Sara, but I don't have time for actors who come in and put more energy into playing up to me than they do to reading their lines."

Sara hung up. Nasty, frustrated old bitch.

The Impersonator took over the cooking of the meals and the housework. "Let me at least run the house for you until I get myself organized," he said, giving her a long kiss.

At last, a male without an image problem. Like most women her age, she had had to spend a good deal of her life finding it prudent to playact, and it was such a relief now to have a completely natural, loving, equal partner.

They preferred to eat at home because it saved them the awkwardness of having a meal in a restaurant for which Sara would invariably pay. Once or twice he had reluctantly produced a Visa card. She assumed he was having difficulty paying the balance on it and was afraid of being refused. She grew more and more protective of him in every way. Their life settled into a pattern. They were very happy.

He less than she. There was still the break with Marly to administer. He had thought it prudent to postpone this while he waited to be sure of Sara's commitment to him. There was now little doubt of this—unless he did something really stupid—and anyway he knew that he would have to tell Marly soon because once he had stopped calling her, she had begun calling him. Happily, so far Sara was unaware of these calls, but the conversations themselves were getting more and more difficult.

"When am I going to meet Sara?" Marly would ask, or "Did you show her my pictures?" When she asked whether Sara's leg was healing and when the cast would come off, he did not for a moment know what she was talking about. He began to be ashamed of Marly for being so stupid, so gullible.

One evening as darkness fell, he was in the kitchen preparing a tray of hors d'oeuvres and Sara was in the bedroom, dressing. In half an hour the party Sara was giving to introduce her friends to him would begin. The phone rang. Before he could get to the kitchen extension he realized Sara had picked up the call.

He knew, somehow, it would be Marly. He continued to place slippery little slices of smoked salmon on buttered brown bread, but his hands were shaking.

Sara came into the room, zipping herself up, carrying her earrings. "It's your ex-girlfriend. She seems to know an awful lot about me. She's also under the impression that you're my employee. She's worried that I won't let you off next week. She's expecting you to drive up to Vermont with her for her parents' anniversary party." Her delivery had been icy. She looked him in the eye.

"Tell her I'm not here," he muttered. But he couldn't

bear the way she was looking at him. He turned and rammed his fist into the wall.

"I think on the whole," Sara said, "this is a call you should take." She picked up the extension on the counter and handed it to him.

They exchanged a long look, his expression hot with misery, hers still steady and pleasant. Guts, he thought. Style. Not blubbering all the time like Marly. He had to get rid of Marly. He put the receiver to his ear. "What is it, Marly?" he asked curtly.

Marly's voice was a little breathless. "Well, she certainly sounds nice, like you said. But I'm glad to be talking to you."

"What's the problem, Marly?"

There was a shocked pause. "Listen, the first problem is why are you acting so weird?"

He glanced at Sara and took a deep breath. "It's really inappropriate for you to be calling here."

"What?"

"When something's over, Marly, it's over."

"What's over? What the fuck do you mean 'over'?"

"Sara and I would prefer if you didn't call again." He hung up the phone. He smiled at Sara. "Sorry about that." He sighed. "When Marly can't take care of herself, she really can't take care of herself. Can I make you a drink?"

Sara began to screw in her earrings. "What gave her the idea that you're working for me?"

He was ready for that one. "I wanted to let her down easy."

"But you told me that she was the one who wanted the separation in the first place."

"Yes, but she changed her mind."

"When?"

"Honey, I don't remember. By then I'd met you. I just tried not to think about it."

"What's this trip to Vermont?"

"It's something we did every year. I guess she just can't get it through her head that things are different between us."

"Have you called her since you moved in here?"

He shook his head, poured himself another drink. What would he do when the phone bill came in?

The phone rang. Sara walked over to the answering machine and switched it on. The phone continued to ring. After six or seven rings the machine clicked on. When the beep sounded, Marly's voice came over the wire. "I know you're both there. I have a right to talk to my boyfriend."

Sara and the Impersonator stared at each other. He crossed to her, put his arm around her. She smiled at him nicely and removed it. Marly's voice took over the room. "Answer! Pick up the phone, you coward!" All three of them waited in silence. A few more seconds and the beep cut her off.

Sara said quietly, "This is appalling."

He would have to throw Marly to the fire. "Poor Marly," he began with a sad smile. "It's probably impossible for you to understand someone like her. You're so totally different. She doesn't have your strength, your wit, your style—"

He was preparing to go on when the sharp ring of the telephone silenced him. They stood like two condemned people as the outgoing message played and the beep sounded. Marly's voice filled the room again.

"I'm in my bathroom. There's a silver shaving mug and a shaving brush and a silk dressing gown hanging on a hook and a box of lotions and creams. None of these articles belong to me." There was barely a pause, then, "Now I'm in the living room, which is also the bedroom—kind of crowded but try as I might I just can't afford a swell loft in TriBeCa like some people

because I work six nights a week at a restaurant so I can
support my boyfriend. I see a fur bedcover and a cam-
paign chest containing rifles, pistols, riding trophies,
yearbooks, and also there's a closet half full of men's
clothes. They belong to my boyfriend, who told me he
was going to work for a rich middle-aged woman
who'd be able to open some doors for us so we could
get acting jobs. The morning he left he made wonderful
love to me."

The doorbell sounded. The first guests had arrived.

Marly's litany continued. "I want my Visa card back.
The bill I got this month showed a couple of swell dinners at restaurants I've never been to. I want the five
thousand dollars you borrowed from me. I want you to
come and get your stuff or I'll have the Goodwill pick it
up. I want you to know I don't understand how anyone
could hurt someone the way you've hurt me." There
was a final pause, and then the sound of her hanging up
the phone.

Sara went to the door to press the button that un-
locked the street door. Over her shoulder she eyed him
with contempt as she said, "Turn off the volume, pull it
out of the wall, I don't care."

Trapped like a rat. He felt skinless, hideous, un-
manned. He looked at his wrists, his hands, expecting
them to be the milky blood color of a skinned rabbit.
Think. Think. Marly would, he knew, take him back.
And maybe that's where he belonged. It had been exhil-
arating with Sara, but it was also exhausting having to
stay ahead of her. Maybe it was just too hard. Maybe it
was impossible.

He said, his eyes on the floor, "I'll go pack my stuff."

There was a knock on the door and cheerful voices
outside.

Sara gave him another look of contempt. "These
people are expecting to meet you. You will stay for the

party. You will be gracious and charming. When it's over, you can go back to your girlfriend. I'll tell my friends you died. I never want to see you again."

She opened the door. "Welcome," she said with a warm smile.

Within twenty minutes the living area of the loft was filled. Sara felt as if her eyes were covered with flies. Someone lightly touched her elbow. She turned. It was him—stoic, beautiful, his gray eyes veiled. He was holding a glass of wine he had poured for her. "Would you like this?" He spoke her name gently. "Sara?"

She took the glass, wondering how his simple pronunciation of her name could affect her so. She raised her eyes briefly to his. He was regarding her with grave concern.

"Thank you," she said crisply. "Have you met the Malloys?" She indicated the couple she had been talking to.

She excused herself and went to attend to other guests. She felt his sweet, grave gaze on her as she went. It was as if by sheer will he was trying to reverse their roles, as if she were in greater need than he, as if he, the foul betrayer, had become her protector, her only protector in the room, her only protector in the galaxy.

She had cleared out such a bright space in her heart for him. True love at last, she had lately dared to think. That space was now empty, cumbersome with loss. She heaved it around the room with her. She wanted to be alone so she could weep. Instead, she laughed, conversed, and saw that her guests had everything they wanted to eat and to drink.

Those who had cynically examined the Impersonator's handsomeness, his youth, assuming he would be vain or dull, had been surprised. He said very little, but instead listened, asking only now and then a quiet, very interested question. He paid close attention to the men, what they said, how they spoke, where they had been, what they professed, what they wore. If he hadn't been feeling so bloodied, he would have been thrilled to be in the company of such people, who inhabited a layer of the city he and Marly had never had access to.

It was as if a new emerging self had taken over, born of Sara, nurtured by Sara. He wished desperately to remain in this company. He realized Marly and their friends had kept him back. This is what he must have. This woman, this chance.

So that when a second later he met Sara's eyes across the room the residual blaze of his intensity and desire still marked his expression. Sara understood this signal of what was clearly passion and quickly looked away, unable to bear her own.

As the evening went on, there seemed to be a physical force drawing them closer and closer to each other as they circled the room in their deliberately separate orbits. When once they passed within inches of each other, he touched her lightly at the waist. This almost brought her to tears of confusion and desire.

But when the door closed on the last guest, she was still resolute. She saw he was picking up glasses. "No need. Mimi will be here in the morning to take care of all that." She paused. "Thank you for being so gracious to my guests. And now you may go."

He did not reply but only looked at her, desperate for inspiration. How to get past her dark, female logic? How to win her back?

She said as if divining this, "I didn't tell the lies, I didn't make the phone calls, and I didn't trick my way into this relationship. I just had the party. And it's over."

He closed his eyes. A low moan came from his throat. "Please. Give me another chance. Please."

He opened his eyes and saw her looking at him with

displeasure and he understood he would never get her back by groveling. He took a quick breath. "Whatever I did was because I'm so crazy in love with you."

" 'Whatever'? Is that how you describe lying to me, lying to her? At what point were you going to tell her you were living here as my lover? When you'd got everything out of me that you wanted—whatever that may be?"

"Stop." His teeth were rattling and his face was ashen.

She wanted to control herself but she couldn't. "What makes you think that I, who've been working since I was thirteen, who've earned every last cent I have myself, that I, who treasure my independence above all else, am interested in buying love? In supporting a cheap trick?"

He fell on his knees before her. "Help me."

She turned and walked away. "I want you out of here." She remained standing with her back to him, her chest heaving. She desperately wanted him to go. He was weak. He would drag her down.

Lightly, he cleared his throat. "I know you despise me." His voice was low, husky. "And in many ways I deserve to be despised, but not when it comes to how I feel about you. When I came here that first night, everything changed for me. Forever. I began to feel confidence in my talent again. I began to feel pride. I began to feel like a man. I knew I was falling deeply in love with you and I wanted more, more, all I could get of you. Not your friends, not your life, not this place, but you. I lied to Marly because I thought it would be the kindest thing to let her down slowly. I'm going to ask you to understand that I couldn't cut her off at the knees just like that. Maybe I loved you more specially than I ever loved her, but that's not her fault." He smiled painfully. "I didn't have the courage to tell you that underneath all my happiness with you I was often heartsick and worried about her. I was afraid you'd get jealous or angry and want to send me away. And that's exactly what has happened. You're breaking off our relationship because of the loyalty I still feel to someone I was with for nine years and feel a certain moral responsibility to. I plead guilty."

He concluded his speech. "It's true I want things from you, Sara. I desperately want you to want me. I desperately want to make you proud of me." There was a pause. "I desperately want us to be together always."

She turned away again, not wanting to look at him while she considered.

He is a flawed spirit and unbelievably clever. There are holes in his story I don't even want to think about now, but we've been happy, and we've been good for each other, surely that counts? Can I believe he loves me? I think it's the only thing I do believe. But it's something to build on. I could make the difference in his life. I could help him be everything he wants to be. The only thing he's done wrong, really, is to handle his breakup with that girl very badly, but really, she sounds so neurotic and childish. Clearly much of the blame is hers.

And so Sara and the Impersonator tasted of peace and union and joy.

Two and a half years later, standing aimlessly in her kitchen, Sara picked up a nectarine and a small sharp knife to peel it with, paused a moment, closed her eyes against her anguish, and rammed the knife into her chest.

She had only meant, really, to cut him out of her heart.

PART

2

11

Theo Buckley's eerie radiance was everywhere. It had started with a reverential BBC documentary that spawned a less fastidious, not very good play in the West End called *And Never, Never Think of Me,* which crossed the ocean to off-Broadway just as no less than three books about her were being readied for spring publication. Two of them were large with sumptuous collections of photographs and minimal text. The third was an unauthorized, flagrantly skimpy biography.

This flurry of interest in Theo generated its own momentum. There had remained a whiff of mystery and a collective public longing to be informed and satisfied as to what might have really happened in the moment of her death. For a gifted, beautiful, famous, and still quite young woman to have died so oddly, with no witnesses and no absolute certainty on the part of anyone that the coroner's reports or the speculations of those closest to her constituted the last word on the matter, had been

fodder for a shocked (and thrilled) world, a public not
only saddened and titillated but unsatisfied.

The current revival of attention was provocative in
the sense that questions were again being asked—first
by the documentary, then by the play and its audiences
and its reviewers on both sides of the ocean.

When the play came to New York, a ticket was held
at the box office during preview week in the name of
Mr. C. Jacklin, who picked it up ten minutes before the
curtain, took his aisle seat in the third row, and read his
program with attention. As the curtain went up, he
took out a pencil from his breast pocket, evidently to
make notes. Despite his hastily knotted, off-center tie
and longish hair, he wore that indefinable stamp of
coming from a life that mattered. Those seated around
him (particularly the women, for he was far from unat-
tractive) might have imagined him to be not an ordinary theatergoer like themselves but a young impresario
of some kind.

At intermission he did not leave his seat but remained musing. He thought about how young people,
much more at the call of isolated, exterior events than
more mature personalities tend to be, often allow a single circumstantial whim to redirect the entire course of
their lives. In her mid-twenties Theo had taken the train
to Chicago to spend three days as part of a wedding
party on the North Shore. In her apple-green taffeta
dress with dyed-to-match apple-green taffeta pumps,
she had been eyed by the gifted, chronically suicidal
leader of the seven-piece combo—moonlighting students from Northwestern University—hired to play for
the wedding reception. She had eyed him back and after
that, in a sense, disappeared. At least that was how
everyone back home had seen it. She disappeared into a
world of gigs, clubs, cross-country bus trips. No one
who had known her before witnessed her struggle, went

on that journey with her. No one knew whom she had used, who had used her; at least no one ever came forward to tell tales of any kind—even after she was famous. When three years later the bandleader who had spirited her away into his world died by his own hand in a borrowed bathtub late one pale afternoon at the Beverly Hills Hotel, Theo handled things with the police, the hotel, made the funeral arrangements, washed her hair, drove to a little club on Sunset Boulevard near the corner of Laurel Canyon Boulevard, and walked in on time to do the ten o'clock show. There hadn't been time to tell the musicians that the act was now a solo. For the rest of her life she walked into the spotlight alone.

Not a bit of this was in the play. Jacklin had himself pieced it together.

Jacklin was not connected to the production or to the theater world at all. He was a detective. Reserved, unimpeachable, used to traveling in high circles, he had recently been asked to embark upon what he knew was going to be a long, twisted, possibly even hopeless journey.

Amos Miller also went to one of the first previews. He went alone, sat in the second row, wholly absorbed, then returned to his apartment, where he poured a drink, cooked a simple meal for himself, and made an entry in one of the notebooks he kept:

Theo once told me her main problem was that there were so many versions of herself, all of them true and most of them in conflict. "If I die young," she said, "it will be because I garroted myself with one of those versions without benefit of having been saved by the others." I asked her to give me an example and she said she couldn't and anyway she'd just been making a joke. "I wouldn't garrote myself, I'd probably do whiskey and water like my parents. But I'd have to have someone to do it with. I mean I couldn't do it alone."

I'd heard the story. It was like a movie with Scott Fitzgerald characters directed by Buñuel. Theo's racy, loving, beautiful mother and dashing, hero father had drowned (what else could you call it?) off Key West. They had taken a boat out after a party given to welcome him home on leave from his aircraft carrier in the Pacific. Their bodies had been found together, tied at the wrists with a silk cord. Theo's mother had been shot through the heart.

"I mean, what was the dialogue?" Theo continued. "And what were they wearing? I was so young, by the time I grew up and asked, nobody remembered. When I see it in my mind's eye, she's wearing satin. Had to be satin. And he'd have had on his dress uniform. Epaulettes and gold braid but with the tie loosened and the collar slightly open at the throat. Sailing through the night to the bottom of the sea with their trusty silver cocktail shaker. And his .45. Saying witty things. Wonderful and terrible witty things."

I thought she had dodged my question altogether, but she was coming back to it. I could see her trying to start at the point where her answer would be the most clear. It was always as if she felt a social responsibility not to bore me. *"Say I talk to you and give you my version of a single feeling or single event. After we say good-bye I think wait a minute, there could be different interpretations of that, and I feel remiss for not having mentioned them. I start to argue with myself as to whether the version I gave you has any legitimacy without being taken into consideration with the others. I become convinced I've bent memory, twisted it. I mean if you turn the glass half a millimeter, everything looks different. Of course you know that, Amos, because of your work."*

I miss Theo even though I didn't know her all that well or all that long. I miss her complications, messy tempers, and *fundamental honesty. I miss her carefulness. I miss her mind.*

Amos got up to put his few dishes in the dishwasher. He thought of the slick play he had just seen. Theo painted on glass, her spirit barely discernible behind the ritually catalogued events of her life—the affair with the aging, married theater director, the dual flop they had made, her loyalty to him during his long illness, her political activities, her automobile accident and rebuilt face, her obsessive concentration on her career, the possibly imprudent coda of her marriage to Robert, and, as climax, an untimely, mysterious death.

The play's construction had relied on fixed externals. The framework had been obituary, tying the public persona of Theo around the known facts in a series of neat little knots. Not one warm Theo breath had been expelled. Yet the piece would very likely succeed because of the sly question it raised. Taking advantage of dramatic license, the playwright had chosen as his theme the troubling suggestion that Theo's death had been neither accident nor suicide but foul play.

At the time, Amos himself had speculated on the same, as he supposed had others who were close to Theo. At a somber lunch he had had with Robert the day after the New York memorial service, he had waited for Robert to bring up the matter, but he had not. Robert had apparently chosen to believe that it had been a tragic accident, that Theo, exhausted from overwork and keyed up, had had a few too many vodkas, gone into the water, and . . . Horrible.

What had always nagged Amos was that it was not a death that in any way became her. It was not so much tragic as offensive. That she could have been so careless, that she could have gotten so muddled. That she had traded depression and a few drinks for the several decades of life she still had coming to her.

Unless. At the time he had gone over all the unlesses. Then he had put it all out of his mind until a little over two years ago, when Robert had come to him with his story of that impersonator fellow. Within the context of Robert's obsession for the young man who could get himself up as a dead ringer for Theo, Amos had found himself speculating again on the circumstances of Theo's death. Had Robert known something all that time? Was the impersonator somehow connected to that? Had Robert been lying?

But after a few sessions Amos had been satisfied that this was not the case, that the source of Robert's bizarre attachment to the young man had to do partly with the unresolved nature of his marriage to Theo and partly with plain novelty lust. What man of appetite could have resisted the lure of that particular trick of gender played upon him by the beautiful and obviously wily impersonator? Any suspicions Amos had had on the other questions were laid to rest. There had been no blackmail, no aggression. Insofar as he knew.

Amos took a book and went to bed.

Since Robert and Jane's divorce, Amos had seen Robert only once and Jane not at all. Robert had chosen to avoid him, Amos knew, and this pained him on the professional level. Regularly he made lunch dates that Robert—always politely—canceled twenty-four hours before the appointed time. Amos finally sent him a card on which he wrote, "Come on, already."

They had met on a dark, raw day at the Madison Pub. Robert, Amos observed, was behaving over-brightly, very much like a man given to speaking rapidly and smiling rapidly in order to hide some terrible thing he was being forced to hold in his mouth. In this case, Amos suspected with compassion, it was his life.

"I'm sorry we haven't seen much of each other," Amos began. "You know I'm always available if you want to talk things out."

"I see all of the past as a closed chapter," Robert said. He studied the menu.

"And Jane?"

"She cut her hair and went to China, I heard. I don't see anyone we used to see together. I'm in a new pack."

"What sort of pack?"

"I escort substantial and worthy women to the opera, to the ballet, to benefits, and on country weekends. Sometimes I fuck them, sometimes not. Most of them don't seem to care one way or the other. It's just something they've always done at the end of the day."

Amos had winced. "That's ridiculous. You've lived in this city for twenty years. You've always had lots of friends, lots to do."

Robert was looking pleasantly at him. "I'm fine, Amos. I'm with people who know the score."

"Hey. What fucking score?"

"That life doesn't have to be unbearable. That it can merely be glossed over."

"Let's talk about what we're really talking about, okay?"

Robert stared into his drink.

"What happened? At the end?"

"When Jane moved out I hardly noticed. I sat waiting by the phone for his call. It was like that, Amos. Like that. Okay? I never heard from him. I don't even know what he looks like when he's not in drag. I know the feel of him, I remember that. We were naked together a few times. But there were heavy curtains. It was quite dark." For a moment Robert closed his eyes.

"What do you suppose he really wanted from you?" Amos asked.

"If you don't mind, I'd like to preserve the notion,

pathetic though it may be, that what he really wanted was me." Robert gave a short, bitter laugh. "Shall we order? Could we talk about the America's Cup? The elections? You?" Gracefully he held up one finger to summon the waiter.

Amos had given up. When they left the restaurant they had walked a block or two together, then paused at a corner to say good-bye. They had shaken hands and Robert had said with an ironic look, "I'm not the same. Well, you can see it. I don't suppose it matters all that much." There was the short laugh again. "Before that I'd had a good run."

"You're still in your forties, for Christ's sake." Amos paused in some frustration, oppressed by the obsessive wedge of the city up against him, people stampeding past to step off the curb, the surge of elbows and shopping bags freshly arrived from across the street.

"Did you know," Robert had said with that bright, pained look he'd had before, "that when a shark bites he leaves his teeth imbedded in the thing that he bites?" He gave Amos a ghastly smile.

Either that, Amos had thought, watching Robert walk away, or Theo had had a very long arm. Either that, or between them Robert and the impersonator had gone God one better, creating the perfect companion for man.

Afterward he'd looked up the thing about sharks. They later grew new teeth with which they could bite new prey.

That had been over a year ago. Amos closed his book, turned out the light. He had a very early appointment in the morning, an emergency. After that, two patients who were in severe depressions. Then a bright spot. It was his afternoon off. He would take his usual stroll through Sotheby's and then have a good lunch.

He was examining an eccentric little rococo mirror when he saw behind his own reflection a woman who looked like Jane. He turned and saw her standing with two men, one youngish, the other slightly older, with prematurely gray hair. He recognized this as one of her brothers. Not the politician. The priest. Amos had met Jerry Donovan only once, at a group show downtown that had featured some of his paintings. He was impossible to forget—piercing, smoldering eyes, Rasputin eyebrows, a tall, strapping, athletic body.

Amos walked over to them.

"Hi," Jane said, and hugged him a little shyly. "You know my brother?" she asked. "Jerry, you remember Amos Miller."

"Happy to see you again," Jerry said. Amos felt himself being quickly examined. "And this is Barrett Rossignol." Jerry indicated the younger man, who gave Amos a cordial nod and a firm handshake.

"Can I take you people to lunch?" Amos asked impulsively. "If you've no plans." His glance politely included Barrett. He was not sure whether the young man was with them or a functionary of Sotheby's.

"What fun," Jane said, accepting. They walked to the restaurant, a few blocks away, Amos and Jerry together just behind Jane and Barrett, who were holding hands.

"That's Jane's new fella," Jerry said quietly, anticipating Amos's curiosity. "He's transformed her. And apparently she he. He was also in a bad relationship. It's a new start for both of them."

"How did they meet?"

"Improbably." Jerry grinned. "On the Yangtze. The People's Republic invited three groups of American artists, writers, film people, and so on to come over and see the new democratization. They ran them all over China. Jane and Barrett started out in different groups, but on the last week there was a trip down the Yangtze on a romantic little riverboat left over from the twenties and all the groups got together for that. Jane and Barrett took one look at each other across the deck of that boat and lightning struck. I believe in that kind of baloney. I suppose you don't."

"It's almost the only thing I do believe in."

"I thought psychiatrists had demythologized love."

"That theory comes in handy after the divorce. Helps patients make the emotional separation. But enough of that. On Saturdays I hate all emotions and all patients." As they turned the corner he asked, "What are you doing with yourself these days?"

"Teaching. And running a kind of street group-therapy thing for bad boys."

"No time for painting?"

"I do it on the fly." Jerry ran a hand through his thick hair and smiled ruefully. "Maybe our charmed lives are over. Dappled sunlight on the Arno. Pitchers of golden wine. The seventies seem like a century ago. The eighties seem to have taken a wrong turn. I don't know how we get back, and if so to what, so I guess we have to plunge ahead. And love each other."

At lunch Amos examined Barrett, found himself approving of the younger man's well-pitched, educated voice, his open expression, his modestly engaging manner, and was happy for Jane.

He temporarily lost track of the conversation and came in on Jerry saying to Barrett, "Would you say your own values have altered in the same period?"

"Now that I have Jane in my life, I can't remember what I was like before." Barrett looked across at her and they exchanged a lovers' look.

Jane, teasing, asked, "What if I left you, what would you do?"

"Put my head through a plate glass window." Gravely, he took a strand of her hair, yanked it.

Passion. Newness. Amos felt a pang of envy. Jane and Barrett were joined to each other's nerve endings. A cabal of two. He thought of Plato's theory that two divided selves became one, and he realized that after a week of angry, depressed patients he wanted very much to believe that Jane and Barrett's love would last forever. He suddenly wished he could revise the facts of his own careful history. He wished there had been more sun, more castles. He remembered that really, all things are possible.

Such was the bright power of Barrett and Jane.

Jerry was also looking at them. "You two are so mushy. You'd make most people sick." He cuffed Barrett gently on the chin.

Basking in their warmth, Amos felt privileged, joyous, inspired. Accustomed to providing daily hope to his patients, he felt happy to be on the receiving end. Glancing at brother and sister, he thought what a particularly attractive family the Donovans were. He inquired about the other brother.

"Oh, him." Jerry smiled. "We're so much more fun, don't you think?"

"Will he be running for that Senate seat?" Amos wanted to know.

"I doubt it," Jerry said. He dropped a small bread roll down the inside back of Jane's blouse.

With some difficulty she fished it out. "In any case, he'll never get *me* on a platform with him, smiling and waving, wearing a Bill Blass suit and a gallon of hair spray."

"That's one thing I don't have to worry about."

Jerry ate the olive from his martini. "He'd never ask *moi*."

Barrett looked at Amos. "They'd both walk on their knees across the Appalachians if he needed them."

Amos asked Jerry, "Why don't you think he'll run? Isn't it perfect timing? An opportunity to represent his state, now that the seat is empty and he's made such a good name for himself backstage, as it were?"

"I suspect," Barrett said, with a deferential look at Jane and Jerry, "that Hal wants to get where he's going in a different way. He doesn't want to spend the time and the energy it takes to get elected. He's been very lucky so far with appointed positions." Barrett paused. "I'd say he's been brilliant the way he's parlayed all that. His gift is not with the grass roots as much as with the guys who really matter. He knows how to work that. I can't see him shaking hands with miners, wearing funny hats, and eating tacos and blintzes." He paused. "Unless it were for the top job."

"My clever boyfriend," Jane said. "First he figured me out, now he's figuring out the family."

Jerry was looking curiously at Barrett. "You could have a point. Thought you met him only once."

Jane smiled across at Amos. "When Hal met Barrett, he assumed, because Barrett doesn't talk like a cowboy and know a lot of dirty jokes and has the face of a poet—"

"Do I?" Barrett smiled at her. He took her hand, kissed it very slowly.

She also smiled, let him prolong it, then continued. "He assumed that Barrett was a sissy. Was *he* surprised when Barrett practically outpokered him, outfished him, and outshot him."

"Hal's surprisingly traditional," Barrett said with a quizzical look, "considering the rest of the family. But he's a great sport and a great gentleman. Funny as all hell when you weren't around, Jane."

Noting how generously Barrett had chosen to deflect any further talk of his sporting victories over the older Donovan brother, Amos felt himself drawn all the more to him. Barrett had a courtliness that was not in the least prissy, in fact very much the opposite. Favored and lovingly nurtured as a child, Amos guessed. He glanced across at Jane. She was staring raptly at Barrett, who had taken a spoon, placed the bowl of it on his nose, and now rested his hands on the table. The spoon hung upside down from his nose. He regarded the other three with modest triumph.

"You've stuck it on with something," Jane accused him.

"I did not." Barrett moved his lips carefully so as not to disturb the spoon. "Bet you can't do it."

Jane, riveted, nudged her brother. "You try it."

Jerry regarded Barrett and the spoon hanging from his nose. "I am a man of the cloth. The fact that I'm wearing a T-shirt that says HOOT and am on my second martini could be taking things far enough. Don't ask me to hang a spoon off my nose in public as well."

"It must depend on some kind of suction," Amos said. He picked up his spoon, tried to hang it on his nose. He took his hands away. The spoon clattered to the table. "What's the trick?" he demanded of Barrett with a laugh.

"Warm it up first. Rub it hard. Get up some friction."

Amos rubbed the spoon, then quickly placed it on his nose. It stayed put. He was immensely pleased.

"I can't stand it," Jerry said. He looked at Jane. "I'll race you." He picked up his spoon. Jane grabbed hers and they began rubbing furiously. A moment later all four were solemnly staring at one another, spoons hanging from all of their noses.

A woman at the next table said to her companion in a low voice, "How rare it is these days to see people having simple fun."

Amos hadn't had such a good time in ages.

The season turned. There were several crisp mornings in a row.

"We hardly had a summer," Jane said. "I'm not ready for fall."

Barrett looked at her in amazement. "Splashes of yellow. And blazing reds. Cider. Bonfires. Chipmunks." He blew out his cheeks into two perfectly round, puffy balls. "Little mouths stuffed with winter provisions, streaking around to hide them. When I was little I used to worry myself sick that they would forget where they hid all their stuff." He drew her into his arms, kissed the top of her head. "Horses wearing their winter coats. Pumpkins. Bringing in the wood. Tulip bulbs. Blankets. Starry nights. Winter coming. Scary, scary and beautiful."

"Like us?" Tears welled up in her eyes. He made her so happy.

He took her wrist, looked at her watch. "I said we'd be there by twelve."

An hour or so later on the parkway, Jane looked at Barrett's profile. "What are you thinking about? You haven't said a word for ages."

"I'm pretending I'm an Italian race car driver."

"How so?" she asked, amused.

"I'm wearing my leather jacket. And the shoes I got in Rome. I feel sleek and dangerous and sexy." He turned to her, waggled his tongue obscenely.

She put her hands over her eyes. "Revolting."

"My virgin queen." He patted her hand.

"If I'm the virgin queen, what do we call you?"

"Lancelot. Did you know that according to Malory, Lancelot was very ugly? Do you think that's more romantic or less romantic than if he'd been handsome?"

"If I give the answer you want, will I get a prize?" She smiled and reflected that on the whole it was more fun getting to know someone like this. From the beginning Barrett had shied away not only from his own past but from asking her about her own. Their relationship had a clean, crisp language to it, based as it was on their own brief history as a couple, rather like two six-year-olds having just met, rowing across a beautiful make-believe lake together. What she didn't understand about him she was willing, even excited to wait for.

"Look at that sycamore." He was glancing out the window. "Look at that beech, those willows." There was a brief pause and then, "Christ, it's good to be out of that filthy, fucking city."

She was taken aback at the bitterness of his tone. "I thought you liked it. You always say you like it."

"Sometimes I lie so you'll keep on loving me." He squinted through the windshield. "Want some coffee? I feel like a hit."

They turned off the parkway and drove down into a small hamlet. He parked the car in front of a small drugstore. Jane didn't want coffee but she went inside with him. The place smelled of damp and of old. She wandered through an aisle of shampoos, antacids, toothpaste, plant fertilizer, dog collars, trusses. She picked up a package of Q-Tips and went to join Barrett at the counter, where he was waiting for a young woman wearing overalls and dangling brass earrings to fill a Styrofoam cup with coffee.

Barrett had been staring at a little girl who was on the verge of crying because the bearded young man with her—obviously her father—had just said, "I'm telling you for the last time" that she couldn't have the small orange plastic pumpkin she had been lovingly fingering.

Big tears began to roll down the little girl's face. Her lower lip trembled violently. Underneath her tiny pink T-shirt her chest heaved.

"Quit that, okay? Just quit it." Her father turned and began to examine a display of disposable razors.

Jane glanced at Barrett. He was standing very still, watching the little girl. A few seconds ticked by. Jane asked herself, *Why do I desperately want Barrett to stop looking at that little girl?*

The young woman behind the counter held out the Styrofoam cup to Barrett. "Sir?"

A few seconds ticked by. Then Barrett turned to the counterwoman, took the coffee, reached into his pocket for some money to pay her. Jane put down the Q-Tips and walked out of the store. She waited outside in the colorless light. *It's ugly here,* she thought, looking at the skimpy trees, the dead gray sky, the oily gas station, a couple of nasty-looking shingled houses up the street with their paint peeling and their roofs in disrepair. She looked down at herself. *This skirt makes me look fat. Why did I wear these stupid shoes? I look definitely off today, just when I wanted to look especially nice.*

Barrett came out of the drugstore. They got into the car and headed for the parkway again. The air was deathly still.

A few drops splattered the windshield. A moment later a theatrical rumble came from on high. For a time nothing else happened. They continued to drive north into the stillness, tall trees flaring into nothingness on either side of them. Quietly, the deluge began. Jane stared out the window at the prim shape of New England wet and black. Churchmen, spinsters, hat makers. A race of clock winders, witch burners.

She was experiencing a ludicrous difficulty. Whereas before all had been one—herself, Barrett, the car, the landscape—now everything had separated and she was alone and unprotected. In front of them and behind them the watery stream of the decade's boxy, gracelessly conceived vehicles carrying thousands of strangers denied all possibility of deliverance, of escape.

The rain was falling in sheets. With one hand she touched the top of her head, feeling for the large taffeta bow that had once been there. She had been small, compact, with sturdy legs and a stout heart. She had been absolutely positive that everyone in the world understood that the most important thing was to always try to be as good as possible. The erosion of that jejune philosophy had been taking place all these years. Why should she so sharply feel the utter, anguishing loss of it just now?

She realized Barrett had said something. What? What did she really know about him? Six months ago they had been strangers.

He touched her hand. As slowly as if she were obliged to resist the weight of tons of water, she turned her heavy, heavy head to regard him. He had picked up danger signals. He had sensed her removal. How did she know this? Had it happened before? She couldn't remember.

Barrett pressed the defogger switch. He was frowning slightly, squinting through the windshield. She stared at his profile, the fine crinkles around his eyes, the deep indentations beneath his cheekbones, and the mouth that somehow didn't go with the rest of his face.

He turned to her and said quietly, "The rain is blessing us." He held her glance for a moment as a sorcerer might. She felt restored to sanity. She moved closer to

him, put her head against his shoulder, felt the magic
come flooding back.

His right arm encircled her. "You scare the hell out
of me when you do that."

"How?"

"You go away from me in your mind. You build a
case. I become a victim of your past." He added with a
dry smile, "Your fierce, unforgiving past."

She was struck, as always, by the unerring beam of
his inner eye. She felt the guilty weight and corruption
of her own dark imaginings. *Truly I am neurotic. I've
been distrusting Barrett's purity because somewhere
along the way I lost so much of my own. That little girl
he was looking at in the drugstore, the rain, my own
insecurity—it was a combination of that, nothing to do
with Barrett at all, only to do with me.*

"I love you," she said, and touched her finger to his
lips.

They continued, now in a more westerly direction.
An hour later they turned off an expressway and
headed down a ramp, then Barrett made a sharp turn
into not a road but a brambled driveway, black and
thin with elderly shrubs and awash in mud. Thick
sheets of rain obscured Jane's view of the house.

From the front door a figure emerged and stood
waiting.

Barrett turned off the motor and remarked with an
affectionate expression, "He's been at the window,
looking for us. His hair is all slicked down. I'll bet you
that's a new shirt." He turned to Jane with a gentle
smile. "Well, you're about to meet my family."

Ethan, wearing the saddle shoes he had ordered from
L. L. Bean and holding a snappy English umbrella that
had been mailed out to him by Abercrombie and Fitch,
was coming down the steps to greet them.

12

Sara's tutelage had been thorough. Loving, impatient, sarcastic, generous, and determined, she had, over the nineteen months she and Barrett spent together, filled him with her energy, her taste, her information, her support. Always a gifted learner, he had absorbed though his pores and often with his heart the riches she scattered his way and had become—even he himself believed it—the well-informed, well-traveled, confident Barrett whom Jane was to meet on the top deck of a riverboat that had just left Chonquing harbor for a week's journey on the Yangtze down to Wuhan.

An hour or two before this encounter Sara, on her second whiskey, had been raging in their cabin. What was she going to do with Barrett? About Barrett?

Get rid of him. Get rid of him or perish. But did she have the strength to cut the sinewy, passionate bond between them?

She sat in a rattan armchair by the large square window. The tassels on an orange silk lampshade swayed with the almost imperceptible rise and fall of the boat. The ceiling had been fancifully decorated with flying, painted white birds against a pale blue background. She stared through a fine rain at the picture-book river traffic, at the steep tiers of the wet, gray-washed city, at the ridge of the black hills above with their trees finely brushed against the blank sky and finally, as a fanciful puff of mist moved, a tiny inky pagoda. Chinese paintings didn't lie.

Did Barrett have enough skills to survive? Could he make something of himself on his own? She saw him always in her mind's eye as a boy beguiling a horse, handing her an iris, preparing her for love, so it was a shock when the cabin door suddenly opened and he stepped inside. Before her stood a man who wore his air of understated elegance with naturalness and grace. She took it all in. Shirt, Paris. Jacket, Milan. Handmade shoes, Rome. Billion-dollar watch. The Leica. The copy of *The Dream of the Red Chamber* tucked under his arm. Her Barrett. She took another swig of whiskey. She had never in her life wanted to drink in the morning.

"Honey?" he said. "We're about to pull out. It's thrilling. Shall we go up to that little deck on top and see everything?"

"I'll experience it from down here, thank you." Damn, she had slurred her words. Not that he would ever express criticism. That he secretly judged her and told only the avenging angels, she was certain. But he would not voice it. His existence, she had been finally forced to acknowledge to herself, was still dogged by survival, obsessed with acceptance.

She was left to be critical of herself.

He crossed to her, bent down on one knee, took her hand, looked at her with concern. "Are we all right?"

Wordlessly she gazed at him. The Sweet Prince and

the Drunken Ogre. The ship's bell rang. For a moment Barrett rested his forehead on her knee. "You know I love you."

She announced without much grace, "I want to be alone."

He got up and walked—beautifully, she noted—to the door.

"I'll come back and get you just before we start moving."

He reached for the door handle. She saw him take a quick, preparatory actor's breath. "Your imagination conjures up far worse things than are ever really true." He gave her a sweet sad look and went out.

Zing. Ball to her. Smooth. Not dumb. He had never been dumb, merely neglected. His mind, she had found, was capable of trying on anything, but she had come to doubt that he was long on original thinking. His gift— and it was impressive—was to appropriate. His borrowings were rarely prompted by intellectual curiosity but rather in animal preservation of his territory. He smelled out other people's brains and hearts very much as if he were a biological throwback desperately on the track of surviving the coming centuries.

His life with her had afforded him the luxuries of being comfortably supported, entertained, accepted by a substantial number of people, and profoundly loved by her. But she was beginning to understand that he had not even after all this time really let down his guard. His rabid desire to please one and all, she feared, was pathological. Either that or she had taken into her life a prostitute.

She got up again, refilled her glass.

She sat down and put her head in her hands. Or was she, as he had provocatively suggested just now, overreacting to everything?

How to wind back again the empty spool?

They had been traveling all month. China was vast, stubborn, horrific, breathtaking. It shimmered like green satin and ran with blood. It had always run with blood, it was incomprehensible, it was fiercely exacting, it was wide and clean as fields the color of golden straw, fragile as a teacup, garish as a painted opera, rank as a one-thousand-year-old egg. The rules and restrictions were maddening, the officials inscrutable, the restaurants often dirty, and toilets unspeakable. More irritating to Sara than anything was having to travel in a group.

"Like being in goddamn kindergarten," she muttered to Barrett after the first day. "I didn't realize we wouldn't get to go where we liked and for as long as we like. And why should I have to have breakfast, lunch, and dinner with these same people every day?"

Perplexed, he had regarded her. "They're interesting. They're successful. Some of them are famous." Gingerly. "That's why you were invited."

She decided not to grumble anymore in order not to spoil his fun. She had seen that he liked being part of the group. He had set out to charm them, one by one. She had followed his progress, marveling as always at the deadly skill with which he fine-tuned himself.

But her patience had snapped at the end of a day in Xian, provoked by the grotesque heat, the dirty hotel room, and her own emotional state after that shattering first sight earlier on of the ghostly army of dust-blinded terra-cotta soldiers at the excavation.

She had found herself shouting at him. He had forgotten to load her second camera and thereby prevented her from getting the pictures she wanted. "The soldiers are the most beautiful thing of my life. Of my *life,* it was my only shot at them, maybe ever, to see them just that way." Did he understand her anguish?

His reply had been delivered with injured dignity.

"They told us photography wasn't allowed. You had me scared to death while you were shooting that first roll."

"So did anybody see me?" She had wanted to put her hands around his throat. "Since when did you get so goody-goody about rules and regulations? I asked you to load both those cameras before we went in. I asked you and you said you would."

He had stared at her. "I'm sorry, but have you any idea how you confuse me? For the past two years you've lectured me on responsibility, and then you go and take pictures in a place that the Chinese government expressly asked us not to."

Had this happened in their first months together, she might have thought it naïveté on his part. An overly literal mind. But it was not that, it was anything but. It was one of his seemingly artless excuses, which he had calculated with the speed of light would best diffuse the issue of his having neglected to load the camera. The scenario she knew would follow was that she would very soon come to feel in the wrong for shouting at him and upsetting him. Barrett the innocent. Barrett the loved one, whose only desire was to live in the service of her endless happiness.

Speechlessly she had stared at him.

What she was equally as angry about she hadn't so far had the courage to accuse him of, because as with most of his transgressions, he flat out denied his culpability. She couldn't ever prove it, she would rage, he would withdraw in heroic, injured silence and then go about passive and wan—sometimes for days—until she ended up by apologizing for her anger because it was the only way to get him back from death. No one issue was ever resolved.

There was a gay film producer in the group who had clearly developed a crush on Barrett. This in itself was nothing new; people everywhere developed crushes on Barrett. What had begun to nag at Sara was that Barrett had not only done nothing to discourage the man's attentions, but was allowing the situation to flourish, and even, Sara had noted, provoking it.

Barrett's louche behavior was a betrayal of her, a public embarrassment to them as a couple, and an act of gratuitous contempt toward the unfortunate man—whose name was Lesley—and his unrequited passion. She liked Lesley. He was intelligent and amusing and his yen for Barrett would never, she was sure, have openly flowered had there not been tantalizingly mixed signals back from Barrett.

A little later on the same evening Lesley had knocked on their door to return the binoculars he had borrowed from Barrett earlier in the day. Barrett opened the door and Sara observed with heartsick dismay the superbly grave and finely honed flirtatiousness with which he greeted and spoke to the man.

The instant the door had closed she had gone off into another rage about the unloaded camera, this time flinging at him the rest of the story. "When I realized you hadn't loaded the Minolta I looked around frantically—there were only a couple of more minutes—and you were nowhere. Nowhere with all my film in your pockets. Nowhere with Lesley. When I finally saw you on the other side of the excavation tripping along with your boyfriend, Christ, I couldn't call out to you, not in there, not over those heartbreaking faces, not over the heads of that army. Those soldiers had been dead there in the dust for a thousand years."

She had paused as if for breath. Barrett had whispered with a frantic expression, "The walls are like paper. Everyone will hear you, honey."

Maddened by his refusal to engage the issue, she had yelled to the heavens, "I don't give a fuck."

He had fled to the tiny bathroom. She had followed him, yanked at the door he was about to close. It had fallen off its hinges and clattered to the floor between them.

Barrett's face had turned white. He had stared down at the door as if looking deep into his own grave. But Sara, ever susceptible to the absurd—in this case the comedic interruption of the cheap jerry-built door in the jerry-built hotel in the heart of ancient Cathay on a night like this about fairies and cameras while a thousand dead soldiers slept down the road—had burst, incorrigibly, into laughter.

This might have turned the moment, might have headed them off from disaster, but Barrett, pale, his gray eyes frosted with ice, had said, "I know that when I met you, my manners weren't all that wonderful. You've taught me which fork to use and how to tip a headwaiter and how to write a thank-you note and when to take flowers myself as opposed to when to send them, but now you're embarrassing us in a way I never have and never could. Everyone on this floor heard everything you shouted at me." His pallor was ghastly. "And now we've broken a hotel door."

Then she was off, stung, furious. "You're worried about a door? Why don't you worry about your immortal soul? About us? About poor Lesley? About your cheap behavior? Batting your eyelashes at him like a girl, brushing against him by pretend mistake—you think I don't see? In addition to supporting you right down to your shoeshines, must I also pay for this relationship in pain and humiliation and betrayal?"

He had turned from her and thrown up into the toilet.

She had gone and sat on the bed. He had turned her into a virago.

Was she really as intolerant, overdemanding, impossible to live with as his wounded silences often implied? Yes, but what about him? What about his passivity, his promises, his litany of excuses—his fear of failure, his alcoholic father, his horse that died? What about it indeed. The fact was, Barrett had managed quite well so far, without ever having stood on his own two feet. Everyone had always taken care of Barrett.

She heard the shower being turned on. She looked at the sterling traveling clock she had bought for him. They had an early start in the morning. She picked up the door, which was still on the floor, propped it against the flimsy-looking wall of the room. She undressed, got into the hard, narrow bed, turned on her side. She stared out the curtainless window at the stars.

All her life she had dreamed of coming to China. Marco Polo. Silk and rubies. Kubla Khan. Barrett's enthusiasm for the preparations had matched hers; in fact, at one juncture she had decided she really couldn't take the time off and was going to cancel their trip but he had begged her to reconsider. So they had bought language tapes, history books, gone to seminars. They had been as excited as children.

If only he could be as enthusiastic in a direction that might generate a practical future for himself. She employed him as an assistant only because it helped them save face for each other. Regularly she urged him to want to generate a life of his own. He would enthusiastically agree. And do nothing. She remained mystified by a personality who seemed so easily to have relinquished the course of his own life.

She heard the shower being turned off. She closed her eyes. A few moments had gone by. She heard him coming across the thinly carpeted floor, checking to see if the alarm was set, then the sound of him getting into the twin bed pushed up against hers. She heard a comb going quickly through thick, wet hair. Then the one lamp in the room was turned off.

Darkness and silence. She had tried to breathe evenly. After a moment she had heard him lightly clear his throat. This meant a brief announcement was about to follow.

"Sara."

She knew he had been rehearsing it in the shower. Not for Barrett the spontaneous approach, the impulsive outburst or confession. He led his real life in secret. She had understood this early, had been fascinated by the overwhelming ambiguities of his personality, and had remained stuck fast in the conflicting machinery of her own feelings for him. Had she not known him so well, she might not have forgiven him, something that already she knew she was going to do. Whatever he planned to say—about Lesley, the cameras, the door— was irrelevant. She would forgive him because she believed in her love. What had pulled her in and still held her. The promise. The man-boy. The angel.

She would forgive him and they would go on. He would leave his bed, slide into hers, and they would both cry with relief at being reunited. They would speak their love. That, they had.

Now, two weeks later, the riverboat bobbed on the muddy yellow water of Chongquing harbor and Sara, sitting by the picture window, tried to reach a decision.

That time I was away and he pulled his bad knee out of joint, getting out of a taxi, he said, and I didn't twig until I saw my American Express bill and there were hundreds of dollars of charges at two dance spots that night. When I blew up he said he'd been lonely without me, and the dancing hadn't been his idea at all, those two stewardesses on the second floor had talked him into it and frankly he couldn't remember if the knee happened on the dance floor, it may have started there

*and even if it had he didn't understand why I was so
mad—wasn't he allowed to have fun without me?—and
anyway he'd pay me back. And I said, "With what?"
And so on. It's always my fault. There I was shrieking
at him and he's lying there in horrible pain from his
knee and then there was the operation that I had to pay
for because his brother had stopped carrying his medical insurance, being under the misapprehension that I
was now carrying it. For five weeks Barrett lay on the
sofa watching television. I bought him those earphones
so I wouldn't have to listen.*

She got up, poured another few inches of whiskey.

During that period the guy at the Times *came to do
that interview on me and I asked Barrett if he'd let me
have the living room. After fifteen minutes Barrett hob-
bled in wearing his silk dressing gown open to his navel
and he lounged on the sofa opposite us like Marlene
Dietrich, complete with cigarette holder and sexy languor. What could I accuse him of? He didn't do anything, expose himself or make coarse remarks. He just
lolled there, pretending to read, saying it was too hot in
the bedroom. Even the way he turned a page became
more interesting to the* Times *guy than me.*

What had happened yesterday she had thought—at
first—would change things. A telegram from Barrett's
brother had been waiting for them in Chongquing.
"Great-aunt Sue in Nebraska (remember Mom saying
we still had folks out there?) left 35 thou to you, 35
thou to me, let's not tell Dear Old Dad."

"Why not?" she had asked him with a puzzled look,
ready to ask a lot more than that.

"Do you mind if I answer that at another time?" had
been his only reply, and she thought she shouldn't pursue it then. She smiled encouragingly. "So you're sort of
loaded now. Congratulations."

But he was not happy. He had been eyeing her oddly. "I guess this is your chance to get rid of me."

"What?"

"You can tell me to go without feeling guilty about how I'll survive."

Anguished by his ongoing insecurity, she had not been able to speak to it, not then. Instead, she had said frankly enough, "I was thinking along other lines. That a big wad of cash like this just now maybe isn't the best thing. An inheritance isn't exactly an incentive. It's another gift."

He had assumed a dignified expression and had not replied. After a morning touring the city the group stopped at a store for shopping. Barrett had tried on a good-looking leather jacket.

"Why don't you get it?" She had asked, suddenly heady with relief that he was now going to be able to buy things for himself.

He was revolving slowly in front of a mirror. He had put up the collar and his hands in his pockets, fashion-model style. He had revolved some more.

"It's a hundred dollars," he had said, looking at her anxiously.

"It would be zillions of times that at home; of course you have to get it, don't be silly."

He had taken a breath. "You're right." He had shrugged out of the jacket, indicated to the young saleswoman that he would take it. They had gone to the cashier. Barrett had put the jacket down on the counter, reached for his wallet. He had handed one of Sara's credit cards to the cashier, turned back to Sara with his handsome smile. "Thanks, honey, for getting it for me. I'm crazy about it."

He had caught her look. One second, two, three had gone by. He had turned crimson. She had remained very still, gravely regarding him. He had looked away.

The cashier had taken the jacket to the wrapping desk. After a moment Barrett had very carefully looked back at Sara. His expression was suffused with suffering, martyrdom, silent accusation. Apparently she had ruined things again. She was a bull in the china shop of their relationship.

"Lest you forget in times to come," she had said evenly, "this moment was not about money."

He had signed the credit card slip, taken the wrapped jacket from the young woman, and turned on his heel. She had followed him out of the store. They had walked back to their hotel in silence. Once they reached their room, he had gone into the bathroom and shut the door. For some fifteen minutes there had been only deep silence. He had come out, picked up his guidebook, and sat down with it, crossed his legs, turned pages.

She had thought she had never been so defeated. "If I'd been the recipient of the kind of generosity I've shown to you," she heard herself begin, her voice dry and weary, "and I'd just inherited some money, I would have run out to the street, crawled on my hands and knees over broken glass to get you a rose, a ring, a pledge, something in representation of what I might now, at last, be able to do for you."

He had looked up, stared at her from behind his sad mask, then looked down at his book again.

There had been a knock on the door. The group director's voice had come through. "The bus that's taking us to the boat is here."

Barrett's voice, beautifully modulated, had rung out. "Thanks, Lina," he had called, smiling brightly at the closed door, then even more cheerfully, "We'll be down in a sec."

To Sara he had spoken anxiously. "You haven't finished your packing. We don't want to be late." He had got up, looked around the room, checking to see if he'd left anything. The paper bundle containing the leather jacket was on the bed. He had put it into his open, packed suitcase and slammed the lid, begun strapping it up.

From sadness to anger, that was the way he always brought her. She licked her wounds alone, every one.

"I have long been aware," she had said, going down the danger chute again because it was the only opening available, "that the male gender lacks the gene required for the mouth to open and the tongue and larynx to work in combination so that the words 'I'm sorry' can come out, but I had hoped, even expected, that you would have found it possible during the last half-hour to acknowledge the issue between us."

He was giving her a frantic look. "You heard what Lina said. We'll be late. Why do you always do this?"

A moment had gone by. "I will go downstairs," she had announced coldly, "when I fucking please." She had sat down on her bed and stared at the wall. She would keep to herself the certainty that he had driven her mad.

Barrett had waited, pacing, giving her smoldering looks, uttering inarticulate sounds. She had ignored him. With the air of a suffering martyr he had picked up his suitcase and left the room.

Some twenty minutes later Sara had stepped onto the bus. There had been several delegations sent to fetch her. She had answered their entreaties politely, always saying she would be along in a while. She had remained sitting staring at the wall, asking herself what she was going to do about Barrett. She had decided at last she would make up her mind when they got on the boat.

The faces in the bus were mildly curious as she entered and made her way down the aisle toward the empty seat next to Barrett. As she sat down she had seen Lesley—sitting directly across—exchange a covert look with Barrett. The man's eyebrows were raised slightly and his glance was sympathetic, conspiratorial. Barrett's answering look, also covert, had been one of grateful acknowledgment and heroic suffering.

As the bus pulled away, Sara had wondered if there was anything in her purse that might serve as a weapon, but there was nothing sharp enough. With her fingernails she had dug discreetly into Barrett's arm, starting at the wrist, slowly leaving a trail of broken skin all the way to the crook. Barrett had not flinched. He had merely shifted a little, crossed his legs, looked out the window at the sights.

Tears had rolled down Sara's face. She had put on her sunglasses.

This had happened some three hours earlier. Barrett had still not referred to it.

She rose abruptly, went to the small sea chest of drawers at the foot of his bed. With a humorous glance she looked up at the ceiling.

God, please, this is an exception. I've never looked at anyone's private papers before, I know it's wrong, but there's a lot at stake. Am I living with a monster or am I the monster? I've changed my life for him, I've shucked off old friends who don't like him, I've humiliated myself in front of others, begging them to give him a job, and I've poured most of my energies into rehabilitating him. Without realizing what I was doing I've allowed my career to slide and meanwhile I've spent so much money supporting the two of us, I could be in trouble very soon. Don't I have the right to know?

She took his diary back to the armchair by the picture window and sat down. The notebook was handmade, beautifully bound, the paper was hand-tipped. She had bought two of them in Florence, a red one for him, a blue for her. On the eve of their trip to China they had resolved to take the notebooks with them as journals of their trip and on their first evening had further resolved to read their entries to each other at the end of each day. This had been fun. Despite the fact that they had been together every minute, the individual choices they made as to what to record and how were always different. She loved his painstaking recital of tiny detail. He loved her broad, bold brushstrokes of flamboyant description.

At the end of each entry she had made a habit of recording private thoughts which she did not read aloud, and she presumed he had done the same. Maybe she would find some key to the puzzle of him if she read those now.

She opened the book. The front page said *Barrett Rossignol. China 1985.* She turned to the second page. It was blank. Quickly she turned the page again. Blank. She riffled through some more pages. Nothing. She turned the book over and started from the other end. Blank.

He had made up his entries and "read" them to her as if they had been on the page.

She closed the book and returned it to the sea chest. She felt a vibration under her feet. The engines had started. She glanced out the window at the churning brown waters, the darting sampans, the grubby dock, the stony layers of Chongquing. They had been told that on the way out they would see the old airstrip used by the Flying Tigers in World War II. Barrett had been thrilled. He had a surprisingly thorough knowledge of that time and that war. He had acquired all of it, she knew, from having watched the old black-and-white movies on television. Heroism and romance were Barrett's favorite subjects.

His knowledge of general history was ragged, impressionistic, and stopped dead at the year he had been born. It was as if once he had appeared on earth, there had no longer been any need for outside events to be recalled.

She had asked him about Vietnam.

"Never drew the unlucky number. Anyway, my mother would have paid for me to go to Canada."

"When did she die?"

"I guess I was nineteen."

"Were you with her?"

"Not really."

"What does that mean?"

"What I couldn't get into my nose or my arm in those days, I swallowed."

She had waited for him to go on but he did not. He had begun to make love to her. "Love me," he whispered, "love me."

She thought about the blank pages of the diary. He had "read" at least a dozen entries to her so far. She recalled in particular a lyrical description of the waves of lavender they had seen at the Great Wall. And another one—the apricot-cheeked peasant woman riding a bicycle along a dusty pink road between emerald-green fields holding a large black umbrella. His entries had touched her, made her smile. She had been impressed with his clear, uncorrupted powers of observation.

A cold fear gripped her. All the times she had forgiven him for his lies and betrayals, had he forgiven her for catching him in them? Had he been silently adding up the accounts? He never said—as she had pointed out that morning—"I'm sorry." Instead, he would say, "I'm sorry that you think that of me." Or "I'm sorry, but when you upset me I get so paralyzed I can't think." Or "I'm sorry, but maybe I just don't have it in me to be what you want."

The door opened. Barrett had returned. The

scratches on his arm were terrible. She looked at them. He saw her looking at them.

He took a glass, poured some whiskey for himself, gave her a wistful look. "I know you can't help yourself, Sara."

"Sit down." If she was ever going to do it, she knew it had to be then. Let the moment go, and they would destroy each other.

He sat down, crossed his elegant legs. His actor's eyes watched her coolly enough, but his hands trembled. He knew. He always knew.

Woe is us.

"You know that I love you," she began.

His chest appeared to cave in.

He stared at the floor. "You want us to break up because of the leather jacket. I just didn't think, that's all."

"Knock-knock," she said. "Is anyone at home, Barrett?"

He remained silent.

She was in charge of everything, even this. "You've done nothing to take advantage of the opportunities you've been given. Instead, you get all your oxygen from my bloodstream."

He shifted restlessly. "I wanted to be with you all the time. I admit that's a weakness. I love you."

She wondered if sawing off her legs would bring as much anguish. "It's over. I'm sorry."

Sullenly he raised his eyes to her. "You're very demanding, you know. It takes a lot of energy out of me just keeping things peaceful. You're a difficult person to live with. A lot of the time it's a full-time job. It hasn't given me time for anything else."

"I decline to take the blame for your inertia."

"Not everyone's as lucky as you. Maybe I just don't have what it takes to be anything more than I am." He got up, began to pace in the tiny space between the sea beds.

Having heard all this before, she said nothing.

Next he burst out, "What will I do?"

"You've got thirty-five thousand dollars. I started my life with ten."

He was staring at her, bewildered. "Use my money to live on? I wanted to husband that money, I want to invest it wisely, make it grow."

"While continuing to live off me? I don't believe this conversation!"

He continued to stare at her as though he didn't understand.

"Tell you what." She paused. "Get a job."

"You hate me, don't you?" he asked bitterly.

"Sometimes. Just like you hate me sometimes."

He gave her an uncertain look and she went on. "The difference is, I say it in words but you collude behind my back with secretaries, waiters, dogs, children—"

He interrupted through clenched teeth. "I've watched you torture yourself with your insane jealousy. I've lived with your pathological possessiveness, your hysterical suspicions, and been appalled, not knowing what I could do to help you."

"I've never been a jealous person in my life! Ask my parents, ask my boyfriends, ask my ex-husbands. Ask God. How dare you!" This time she thought she *would* go mad.

He fell to his knees. "I'll make you proud of me," he said in a low voice. "I'll earn your love, because it's the only thing in the world I want."

Old promises they had already bloodied themselves on. But she could feel herself stirring. She could sense a stirring in him. Over the loudspeaker came an announcement. "We are leaving Chongqing. We are leaving Chongqing. There will be an orientation meeting in the saloon in fifteen minutes."

Saved. Sara turned away. "I want to change. I'll see you there."

"Honey?" He paused at the door, and she saw for the first time the tears in his eyes. "You can throw me out, but nothing can ever kill our love." And he went out.

Barrett stepped into the corridor and closed the door behind him. She, with her boldness, her righteousness, her successful career, her swell friends, her comfortable, easy, interesting life, was planning to hurtle him into the fucking darkness.

He went up the little companionway into the odd yellow light that reflected through a brown mist, the sinking sun on the river. They were well on their way. The banks on either side were rich, pungently green, the Yangtze itself very swift. And low at this time of year. Their passage, he noted, was dotted with rocks and reefs.

He climbed to the top deck, just a small space with some sailors' clothes drying. It was deserted except for a woman about his age standing at the rail, holding a notebook against it, looking up at a farm terraced in a dozen shades of green all the way from the bank to the hilltop, then writing something in the notebook with a silver pen. He knew she was from one of the other invited groups that had joined them for the trip down the river.

He also knew who she was. He accepted this, with his chronic passiveness, as his extravagant fate, a dictate—or perhaps a sly joke—from his demons. He had seen her name all those months ago on the VIP list sent to Sara along with the initial invitation.

What was he going to do without Sara? What would become of him? He strolled toward the woman at the rail. Without Sara he would become air. He would be transparent. He would cease to exist.

He slid his panic behind a hastily assembled, handsome mask, but interesting traces of strain and sadness still etched his features and Jane saw these when she turned. And was intrigued.

"Hello," she said with her lovely smile. Some part of her acknowledged an arcane remembrance which later, when she fell in love with him, she would put down to their having known each other in a previous life.

Ethan shook hands with Jane. He liked the way she looked, and hoped she would be friendly and not too put off by Aunt Charity, who was skin and bones now, half blind, and who never spoke. Her heart, of course, was ticking away just fine. The doctor came by every week and complimented Ethan on the way he was taking care of her. Ethan asked the doctor if she'd lost her wits and the doctor said she had. So Ethan kept her clean, well fed, and comfortable. It was a lot of work, but he had no other choice, and besides she was going to leave him all that money and some to Bro too. And anyway, he guessed he loved her.

He decided his brother looked older, more good-looking, kind of scary. He wasn't Bro anymore, he was like the hero in some old movie. The collar of his raincoat was turned up just so, and he was making a big deal out of tapping his cigarette on a silver (it looked real) case, then lighting it with a heavy gold lighter.

Ethan led them inside. He had made sure the Children were all in their rooms. He wasn't sure how Jane would take to them. Bro, when he'd called, hadn't told him a thing about her. But he was proud of the way the house looked. He'd been vacuuming and polishing silver since early morning. He'd carried Aunt Charity upstairs to one of the rooms that had a double bed and made her pretty with a pink duvet and a spray of grasses in a vase on the nightstand.

"Have some coffee?" he asked Bro and Jane. The question, of course, was rhetorical.

"Tea, I think." Barrett glanced at Jane.

"That would be lovely," she said.

"I don't have any tea." Ethan felt his brother's eyes surveying him. He felt as if he had failed some sort of test. He offered in some misery, "I've got chocolate cake."

Jane gave Ethan a warm look. "Coffee will be fine. And cake too. Perfect. Thank you."

They sat down at the long table that Ethan had already set with plates, cups, saucers, and silver-plated cake forks. There was a snuffling and snorting behind them.

"What's that?" Jane turned in alarm.

Ethan got up. "Tommy, I told you to stay in your room." The wizened, hunchbacked man was approaching the table, making unintelligible sounds.

"Hi, Tommy," Barrett said, and sliced off a piece of cake. "Now, you take this back to your room and I'll see you later."

Tommy shuffled off with his piece of cake. Barrett smiled at Jane. "You okay?"

She smiled back. "Sure." She turned to Ethan. "I told Barrett on the way up here that I was a bit nervous about meeting the . . . Children."

Ethan wondered what Barrett and Jane's life was like. What they talked about. He hoped he'd get a chance to be with Barrett for a while before they left, even if he was acting like a spoiled sissy.

A moment later there was a sudden and then prolonged bumping noise. Then there was a sickening thud, and silence. Barrett and Ethan exchanged a glance of pure hilarity.

"Hester's fallen down the stairs again," Barrett explained to Jane.

Ethan put his napkin down, picked up his slice of cake, took a large bite, put it down, and left the room.

Barrett chuckled. "She does it every month before the full moon. Like clockwork. Worst she's ever done is knock a tooth out."

Over the next hour Jane made a heroic attempt to be at ease. She felt smothered, locked in time. Barrett had prepared her. He had told her about Aunt Charity, Ethan, the Children, the history of how it had all come to be, but she now realized that he had lined his tale in colors of his own. He had made Brawley Manor sound so extraordinarily warm, so special, as if it were America's last authentic slice of blueberry pie. The humor with which he had described it had not hinted at its desolation but made it sound instead delightfully eccentric and wonderfully cozy.

But it wasn't. It was bloodless, a waxy still life, coolish to the touch, Jane thought, like the dark green linoleum and the giant black glass screen of the television that had been crammed between a carved Victorian sofa and a whatnot table laden with awkwardly painted jugs and souvenirs from Atlantic City. There was no hope here at all.

Barrett had described the few remaining residents and Jane remembered that the woman called Hester was in her late fifties and had been placed in Brawley Manor at the age of seven. Neither Barrett nor Ethan knew why, and Aunt Charity had forgotten over the years, but a substantial check from the family still came in regularly. When Jane pressed him for details, Barrett mentioned that Hester frequently mentioned an "Uncle John."

"Gibberish mostly," Barrett had said. And Jane had felt a chill. Centuries of avuncular fumbling and no one except a mad seven-year-old to pass on the tale.

"What do you think?" Barrett was now asking her with a humorous look. Meanwhile in the hallway there were grunts and the patient voice of Ethan. "Now, Hester, we'll just get you up to your room real fast because you don't want to miss cookie time."

"Fascinating," Jane managed in reply.

"Aunt Charity used to have Fourth of July parties. We drove up for one once when I was real little. It was always outside, with hot dogs and lemonade and potato races and stuff. The local school band was there and they played 'America the Beautiful' and 'The Battle Hymn of the Republic.' And I cried." He gave her a slightly abashed look.

She took his hand. "Ethan is lovely."

And he was. Shy but warm, with a quiet manner and an odd charm completely different from the sleeker one possessed by his brother. But Ethan's only discernible role was to fit noiselessly into the still life. Isolated, and encircled on all sides by the dirty, whizzing, noisy swirls of traffic, Ethan reigned with total absorption over his domain. Kitchen cupboards stocked with Jell-O, canned goods, cereal, and graham crackers. Cartons of tranquilizers. On the bookshelves three sets of Encyclopaedia Britannica going back decades, in his bedroom the *National Geographic* magazines for the last thirty years, and in the hall three- and four-foot-high stacks of mail-order catalogues.

"Does he really never go out?" Jane asked.

Barrett looked defensive. "Once in a while."

"He's still in his twenties," she said, "and he spends his whole life here, like this?"

"Maybe he wants to." Barrett picked up the binoculars, looked through the windows for birds.

"But you couldn't live like this, could you?" she pursued.

He looked around slowly, his gaze caressing for a moment a beam of sunlight on the linoleum. "Some of my best days have been here."

Ethan came back holding a book. "Did you happen to read this? It's great. I've read half of it already. A woman in Africa who is studying gorillas."

"Ethan's a great conservationist," Barrett said.

"I believe she died." Jane looked at the photo of the author on the back cover of the book. "She was murdered."

"Not by the gorillas?" Ethan looked shocked.

"Apparently some tribesmen."

"Oh, by people." Ethan looked greatly relieved. He handed the book to his brother. "Take a look. Maybe I'll lend it to you." He paused. "Maybe I won't. You'd probably never give it back."

Barrett, already absorbed in the book, did not reply. Jane did not understand why but she felt pierced to the heart by Ethan's last remark. She glanced at him and found him looking at her. In the moment something as inarticulate as it was profound was exchanged between them. An acknowledgment of an acknowledgment. It happened in a flash and then it was gone.

When they left, Jane had mixed feelings. Longing to escape the dead air of this lifeless house on its poor bit of discarded land, she was at the same time reluctant to part from Ethan, to see him walk up the steps, close the door, and resume his life in the sanctuary he had chosen for himself.

Barrett was pleased with the day. Driving back to the city, he said, "Ethan really liked you."

Jane surprised herself by responding with heat.

"Ethan needs a girl. A job. A shrink. He needs to get out of there."

"Ethan is Ethan," Barrett said indulgently, and turned on the radio. He sang along with Edith Piaf. He was terrific.

Jane stared out the window, thinking of the long table by the window, the birds that no longer came to be fed, the shuffling sound of the inmates, and the ghostly, miniature old woman with the sweet face lying under the comforter. Barrett had kissed Aunt Charity's hands as gallantly, as languorously as a lover.

At Brawley Manor Ethan hauled in the American flag (he'd ordered it specially and Bro hadn't even noticed), went inside to put the coffee cups and saucers, the cake plates, and Barrett's brimming ashtray on one of the beautiful silver plate trays. He carried it all—including the flag—into the vast, silent white kitchen, which smelled of insecticide and antiseptic. With a group of inmates like this, who hadn't been out for forty, some of them fifty years, it was crucial to keep the house as germ-free as possible. Ethan began to wash the crockery in the large double stainless-steel sink. He looked at his watch. Another hour before the Children's dinner. Cereal, cookies, and tranquilizers.

Barrett was so like Dear Old Dad. He wondered why he had never noticed it before. Barrett had added refinements to the basic personality—the artiness and that way he had with people, and also he was much better informed—but the bottom line was that neither Barrett nor their father was a responsible person when it came to relationships. He, Ethan, had never had a relationship, it was true, but should he ever, he knew he would be nicer than his father, nicer than Barrett.

He finished the washing up. He went into the living

room intending to turn on the television, but instead, driven by his thoughts, he continued through the room into the entry and climbed the stairs to his bedroom.

During Barrett and Jane's visit he had taken his brother aside while Jane was in the bathroom.

"I'd better give you those letters from Sara," Ethan said.

"I don't want them," Barrett said through his teeth. So Bro hadn't changed, hadn't changed at all.

Ethan said, "I'm sorry I never got to meet her. Two years and I didn't see you at all. I only got to talk to her on the phone once, about your car insurance. And I guess your tax returns. Anyway, these came in care of me; well, I told you that. I guess it's been months. Remember? I said I'd forward them and you said wait till you came up."

"Throw them away," Barrett said.

Ethan stared at his brother. It was incredible how ugly Barrett's face could become in certain moments. It could stop your heart. "There could be something important in them."

"Get rid of them." Barrett turned away. Jane could be heard coming back. And that had been the end of it.

Ethan now opened a drawer, took out a manila envelope neatly labeled by him CORRESPONDENCE TO BE GIVEN TO BARRETT. He looked at his own neat lettering with pleasure. At the bottom of the envelope he had listed the dates of arrival of each letter, all within a few weeks of one another.

He opened the envelope, took out the letters. Fine fine stationery. A bold and scrawling hand. He went through them, selected the first in the sequence, and opened it. It would be interesting to see what women wrote to men and anyway, fuck Barrett. He arranged himself comfortably on his satin comforter and began to read.

Dear Barrett,

You will recall your hysteria when I asked you to move out, how you begged me not to take down any of the photographs of you. I remember your words, "Don't make me invisible. I'm coming back as soon as I've made myself independent and worthy of you." In the period that followed I enjoyed the occasional times we met for a drink —at your instigation—because you glowed with your progress, your new job, your sessions with a therapist. I was looking forward to seeing your new apartment as soon as it was fixed up. You told me you wanted to surprise me, remember?

Ethan reached for the bag of cookies and read on.

Yesterday, as you also know, I found out that you don't have a job, you don't have a shrink, and you don't have an apartment, and that you have been having an affair with Jane Donovan which you began in China and that you told her I had got you in my power and used emotional blackmail to keep you and that you only stayed with me because you felt so sorry for me. I was told all this by a friend to whom Jane had said (not knowing the connection), "Poor Barrett, he has nightmares about that wretched woman he used to be with. She's unbalanced and a drunk and still mad for him and won't leave him alone. I've told him to simply cut her off, but he's so sweet and gentle he wouldn't hurt a fly."

When I called you last night literally on my knees with horror, you told me please not to bother you and Jane anymore.

Anymore?

Barrett CAN YOU HEAR ME?

Ethan's heart was pounding. He looked at the last two lines.

I don't believe you said those things, I can't. Please call or write.

Ethan threw the letter on the floor. He reached for another cookie and thoughtfully munched it.

Crueler even than the break with Marly. Higher stakes? Deeper guilt? He knew why she had addressed it here in care of him. She knew she wouldn't be able to get directly to Barrett, any more than Marly had. Ethan remembered asking Barrett once what Sara was like. "She's one glorious tough broad" had come the ready reply.

Not that tough.

He wondered what Sara had written after receiving no reply.

Dear Barrett,
I can't imagine what Jane offered you that could have been so valuable that you would trade it so quickly, so silently, so viciously, for a case of amnesia about me.
Still, I hope you can put your attention to the following. When I gave you my grandfather's walking stick—the one with the silver knob that conceals the little flick knife —it was in the spirit of what I believed was the continuity of our life together. You had proposed marriage, and while I felt that was a premature notion (I need not explain), the joint assumption was that we had a future together. It just isn't appropriate now for you to keep this family piece of mine. I loved my grandfather and I would like to pass this memento of him on when I die, so that it can be kept in the family. Could you please let me know—just leave a message on my machine—when it would be convenient and I'll send a messenger to pick it up.

Ethan folded the letter and put it back in the envelope. A walking stick with a silver knob and a hidden knife. Just the thing for Barrett the Dandy. He definitely did not want to look at the third letter. His brother made such messes. Ethan looked at his watch. Time for the news. He turned on the television.

But in the morning he was unable to shake off his troubled connection to the woman stranger. He took a fresh manila envelope and put the letters inside with a note: "As Ma used to say, God might strike you dead." He gave the envelope to the mailman for special delivery to his brother, and hoped Barrett wouldn't be too furious. Barrett's way of punishing was so secret, you didn't know until a long time after.

When Sara's suicide occurred later that autumn, an obituary appeared in the *Times,* but Ethan never read the *Times*. He didn't read newspapers at all, there was plenty of news on TV.

13

The detective, Jacklin, had come to see Robert. His manner on the telephone the day before had been low-key; he had introduced himself with impeccable politeness and he had offered his credentials. He was calling, he said, because "I thought you might be able to identify someone for me."

Jacklin took off a battered raincoat and dropped it on a chair but kept the professorial green canvas book-bag he'd had slung over one shoulder.

Robert glanced at the face. Cool, very cool. I Am the Captain of My Soul. Not a pill-popping shit from Chilean aristocracy like himself. Inwardly he grimaced. Well, he'd been having a bad day.

He noticed a slight limp as Jacklin followed him into the living room and wondered whether it was a recent injury or whether the man had always had it.

Jacklin produced a black-and-white photograph, the subject of which had evidently been enlarged. A bearded young man in jeans. A little out of focus.

"You know this man?" Jacklin asked.

Robert reached for his reading glasses. "I don't think so. He looks familiar, but he's a type, wouldn't you say? The kind of guy one sees in advertising shots, hiding an erection in his Calvin Klein underwear."

"Take your time." Jacklin reached in the green canvas bookbag and produced a magnifying glass. "Try it with this."

Jacklin's system was not ever to follow a system. Handsomely paid by clients who rarely asked procedural questions, he began, once he had thoroughly informed himself of the basic spread of a case, with the more provocative aspects of solving each new puzzle, flirting with guesses and allowing instinct to come into play ahead of settling down to the more boring and detailed work of investigating by rote. A big guess often saved him a lot of time. When the big guess didn't work, he had, of course, to resort to going back to square one and doing it the accepted way. But his track record was good. And life was so very, very short.

Robert held the magnifying glass over the man's grainy face, which was turned away slightly. He felt a stirring of unease. He thought of the darkish room with the green velvet curtains and of shame and rejection. "I'm sorry. Am I supposed to know him?"

Jacklin took the photo from Robert, slid it into a folder, and put the folder into his bookbag. "His name is Barrett Rossignol."

Robert took off his reading glasses, stared uncertainly at Jacklin. "I believe that's the name of the man my ex-wife is living with."

"You've never met Rossignol?"

"I haven't seen Jane since we separated. Look, if this involves her, you'd better tell me what it's about." He could not shake the feeling of uneasiness.

"It doesn't involve her at the moment, and may

never. I'm in the preliminary stages of a larger investigation." He stood up, picked up his canvas bag. "I may be in touch again."

"With me? What for?"

"I always say that. Even when I promise myself ahead of time I won't." With a slight smile he held out his hand. "There's a theory that Americans don't know how to just say good-bye."

"Is there?" Robert asked, shaking hands. "That is, of course I know that—most Americans don't know how to say a simple hello either—but I didn't know it had been elevated to a theory."

"I read it in a book. Thanks for seeing me," Jacklin said.

Robert let him out and then went to the telephone. He dialed Amos's number. The answering service picked up. He left his name. He went into his study, sat down at his desk, and pretended to work. He did this every afternoon. In the mornings he took two Valium, and if it was Monday or Wednesday gave a lecture and then took a two- to three-hour boozy lunch where nobody knew him, at an uptown saloon with tile floors, real waiters, and natural light that came through high, old-fashioned windows. Sometimes he read the newspaper, sometimes he talked to people or bought them drinks. Then he would take the long walk home, enjoying it—because it, too, made time pass—until the final unspeakable stretch, the hellish rot of the last two blocks he had to cross to get to the river, to his good-looking, comfortable perch above it.

Weekends he spent guesting, sunning, cooking, and drinking in the Hamptons or in the country. He hadn't published a book since his divorce from Jane. He couldn't decide on a theme. Everything was pointless. Meanwhile he was admired, sought after, envied, and thought to be happy.

An hour later Amos returned his call.

"Do you ever see Jane?" Robert asked at once.

"Not since last summer."

"A detective was here asking questions about her boyfriend."

"Barrett?"

"You know him?"

"I've met him, yes."

"He showed me a picture. I guess it was him. He wanted me to identify him. Why?"

"Could it have to do with Theo, do you suppose?"

Robert's heart stopped. "Why would you think that?" But he had thought it too. With all of Jacklin's casualness, he, Robert, had been carefully examined.

"Detectives are like shrinks. They encircle areas of information on false pretenses. And there's been a revival of interest in the last year in the alleged mysterious surroundings of Theo's death. You can't have failed to notice."

"I noticed. Why can't people leave it alone? There was no mystery except how she could have been so stupid. What do you think of him?"

"You mean Barrett? I ran into them and we had lunch one day."

"Well? I hear he's young and beautiful."

"I liked him."

"You didn't feel anything was wrong? Something shady?"

"On the contrary."

"Well, I'm glad Jane is happy," Robert said, because he felt he should.

But for the first time in their relationship, Jane and Barrett were not particularly happy.

Some months before, they had made an impulsive

decision to move from New York to a house in the country and had described the decision to each other as destiny. They had spent a weekend with friends of Jane's in a pretty rural area upstate, several hours from the city, and on the Sunday the friends had mentioned that there was an charmingly sited little house nearby on a large piece of land which was about to go on the market. Did Jane and Barrett want to see it?

"Let's," Barrett had said at once. "I love to look at houses."

The place was indeed intriguing. Hidden, thickly wooded, sweetly simple, and only a few grassy green feet from a wide, silvery brook that rushed here, meandered there, through the property.

"Magic." Barrett had looked at the encircling woods. "It's us, honey."

She had replied with a laugh, "Don't tempt me."

On the way back to the city they had talked about the week to come, the dinner party they wished they could get out of, their plans for getting a carpenter to build more closet space in their apartment. Jane mentioned a movie she wanted to see. Then there was a silence.

"It needs a lot of work," Jane had said.

He had taken one of her hands, squeezed it. "I can't get it out of my mind either."

"I really don't have to be in New York more than once a week. It would be perfect for me, but not you. You have to be around. You have to be available."

Jane, as Sara had, cooperated in the fiction of Barrett's acting career because she was in love with him and willing to believe in anything that would not rock the boat of that love.

"There's an even bigger obstacle," he had said. "You know I can't afford to put anything into buying a house. It would be all yours. I'd be a guest, like I am at the apartment." She had watched his jaw tighten.

They hardly ever spoke of this because of course the imbalance in the relationship was only temporary until he was able to get his life together.

"Let's not worry about that side of things. You know I have faith in you." She had rested her hand on the back of his neck. "That ship of yours is bound to come in. But maybe the house is a crazy idea on its own. We saw it only this morning. Suddenly we're talking about changing our lives."

"I think it called us." Barrett had worn a sad smile. "I know it did."

"Yes, but there's a pair of shoes on Madison for five hundred dollars that have been calling me since I saw them on Tuesday, but I'm not going to buy them either."

He had not replied and she had gone on. "I've never owned a house. I've never even thought of living in the country. I'm a city girl."

But I'm a country boy. It had not been said, but it had lain, wispy and redolent, between them for the rest of the drive.

On Monday morning at breakfast Barrett had stirred his coffee with one of Jane's handsome little Georgian spoons and looked at her. "I'm pretty good with my hands. That could be my way of contributing. Rather than hire a contractor, let me be the contractor. I've done carpentry, I can paint, wire, I know something about plumbing, and I probably know everything there is to know about building fences, fixing barns, clearing land, dredging ponds—what I can't do we'll hire people for, but it would save a lot of money and I'd feel like an equal partner."

As if anticipating her next question, he'd said, "I've been wanting to tell you this for some time, but I didn't want you to think I'm a quitter. I just don't want to be an actor anymore. Yes, I'm good at it, but it offends me to have to beg for work—it always has. And"—he took a breath—"there's that play I've been wanting to write. I could do that in the country."

She had never heard of this play, but she had welcomed the idea of it as she would have welcomed anything that provided Barrett with a focus other than their relationship, and that made the idea of the house possible.

Meanwhile he hadn't finished outlining his idea. "I figure you could get everything done at the property for much less than if you had to hire a contractor. I mean I'll just charge you for my hours at a modest rate"—he had smiled—"just so I'm not working for nothing."

They moved into the house.

And their life was perfect. They tramped through the snowy woods, built roaring fires, and planned their enchanted garden. Spring came and they began skinny-dipping in the icy brook. Then the telephone call from Jane's older brother, Hal, came.

They had been out by the lilacs. Barrett had said they should be pruned, and showed her how he would do it. When they came in there was a message on the answering machine. "Jane," Hal's brusque, authoritative voice announced. "Why don't you give me a call."

Barrett thumbed through a gardening catalogue while Jane dialed Hal's number in Washington. "Power to the people," she said when he came on. "How are you?"

"Question. Did your boyfriend have some kind of relationship with Theo Buckley?"

Jane stared through the chestnut mullions of the window at the bright silver slashes the wind was making on the surface of the brook. She felt quite unwell. "You must be mistaken."

"Ask him."

"Not here," she lied, and didn't know why. She avoided looking at Barrett directly but was conscious all the same of the sudden change of atmosphere in the room. Out of the corner of her eye—she was sure she was not imagining it—his figure had gone rigid.

"What's this all about, anyway?" she asked.

"You know how the press loves to mix sex with politics. One of my colleagues, Horace White, had a few dates with Miss Buckley just before she died."

"Everyone knows he took her out, it was in the papers at the time, and anyway, what does that have to do with—"

"What it means," Hal interrupted crisply, "is that there's going to be question-and-answer time. White is up for reelection to the Senate in the fall, and problems like this he doesn't need. There's been a rumor going around that there may be a reopening of the investigation into her death. He put a private detective on it the minute he heard."

Jane, who had been standing up, sat down now, and with her left hand began to pluck at some furry, browning leaves on an African violet that was obviously getting too much sun and would have to be moved. She poked her finger in the dirt around it to check the dampness.

Barrett kissed her on the top of the head and went out. She waited a few seconds. "If your pal White has nothing to hide, why does he need a detective and what does this have to do with you? Let alone me? Where did this information come from? And wouldn't it be more to the point to talk to people like Robert, for instance? Barrett would have told me if he'd ever known Theo Buckley."

Her brother's tone was impatient. "Why don't you be a good girl and just ask him the question, okay?"

"Why don't you piss off?"

"Why do you always get so emotional? I'm just trying to save time. If it's not your Barrett Rossignol whom the detective's interested in, we'll be home free."

"We're home free anyway. And I still don't know how you got into this."

"I'm on White's team, as it were. He's shown me the information the detective has checked in with so far, which is basically just a list of people who might have been at the Russian River around the time she died." He paused. "Haven't you seen anything about the possible reinvestigation on TV lately?"

"We don't have a TV."

"Jesus, you're a snob."

"We don't have TV because there's no reception here."

"That's ridiculous." In the way that one can read silences coming over the telephone wire, she felt the sudden quickening of his interest. "I didn't think there was a place left in America where there was no reception."

"We read books. We're fine."

"When will Barrett be home?"

"Soon," she replied coolly. "Believe me, the whole suggestion is bizarre."

"Call me back."

Jane put down the phone. She could hear the ticking of the kitchen clock. She could hear her own breathing. Not a whisper of traffic, they were miles from that. Out where the brook was, there was a sudden sharp splash and then silence. A kingfisher savaging the water for food had swooped down and gone. She put her head in her hands. Now what? Would Theo's eyes never close?

Jane got up and brought some water to the African violet. She patted the earth around it. Naturally she had wondered about Theo's death at the time. Everyone had. After her meeting in Abu Simbel with Robert she hadn't given it much thought; Theo, yes, but not the manner of death. After she realized he had become obsessed in some dark way with that impersonator, she had never wanted to think of Theo Buckley again. But suddenly a new, very cold idea had been introduced.

Did Hal's call about Barrett reflect some oblique tangent on the part of this detective by which he was trying to get to her in order to get to Robert, who would, after all, she supposed, be a suspect—if there were to be suspects? She patted the earth some more. Robert a murderer?

Jane went into the garden, looking for Barrett. She heard a *thwack thwack*. He was practicing with his bow and arrow. She crossed over a little wooden bridge Barrett had painted Chinese red, and made her way through a massed clump of oversized azalea shrubs with creamy apricot-colored blossoms (they had looked in the books and couldn't identify the species), then around some silver beeches and stepped into a mossy clearing. He hadn't worked on his "play" in a week.

Thwack thwack. The circular canvas target was set up several hundred feet away. He was hitting the bull's-eye every time, his face grave with concentration. He was playing Robin Hood. He really was. It was one of the things she had fallen in love with.

He paused to set another arrow in the bow. She walked toward him. Arriving, she leaned against him for reassurance. "Hi."

"Hello, sweet." Then he sighted, despite the fact she was still leaning against him. *Thwack*. Bull's-eye. "What did brother Hal want?"

She sighed. "Have you ever been to the Russian River?"

He fitted another arrow to the bow. "That's the one in California?"

"Hal had this bizarre idea that you might have known Theo Buckley."

"Theo Buckley?" Barrett was smiling at her. Heroic shafts of silver sunlight poured through oak trees and American beeches. There was something funny about his eyes. "I met her. What's the big deal?"

Jane understood—in the way that we always do—that a hitherto concealed crack had been introduced, and leaking through was the tiniest bit of unwanted light. There had been an omission, yes, but an omission that clearly had nothing to do with her because if Barrett had actually *known* Theo Buckley, well, for instance, he would of course have told her long ago. It would have been the only honorable thing to do.

Met her how? She wouldn't ask because he would tell her. No use jumping all over him, he would tell her in a moment, tell her it was nothing and make it all go away.

Thwack thwack. Bull's-eye. *Met her how.* Jane, waiting, soon began to feel relieved. *Met her* and it was nothing, obviously. There in the clearing with the wavy ferns, the birdsong, the lichen on the ancient stones, Hal's roughshod invasion of their privacy was offensive, his very questions surreal.

Jane took a breath. "Well. I *told* him he was barking up the wrong tree."

Barrett slung an arm around her. "Let's go in. I'll pick up my arrows later." He kissed her and she forgot her complicity.

They walked back toward the house. Barrett squinted at the roof. "I can't believe I didn't notice that corner before. Some of those shingles are rotten. When we go into the village later I want to stop at the hardware store."

While he was taking a shower, she phoned her brother. "He met her once, so blow it out your hat," she said crisply, and hung up. Immediately she dialed him back. "I'm sorry. Really."

"You know what you are? Butt boring." He hung up. Jane giggled.

At the hardware store, a tall, spare man with a weathered face listed the purchases to be charged to Jane's account. Jane and Barrett stood by, holding hands without really being conscious they were doing it.

"One carton of shingles. Flashing. Spatula. Three clematis. One bag of bone meal. Six batteries. Two extension cords. Twelve closet cedar bags. Sprinkler attachment for hose. Outdoor thermometer. Two floodlights. One bag of charcoal. Six citronella candles. One bag birdseed. One shovel. Three tarps."

Jane, mentally running through her grocery list— they were going to the market next—noticed on the periphery of her vision the back of a young woman with dark hair who was wearing a shiny red rain slicker. Jane continued with her list. Tomatoes. *Next year I'll grow my own.* Zucchini. Lettuce. Grapefruit. *Mustn't forget trash bags.*

Barrett, still holding her hand, moved his middle finger against the inside of it in that way that when everyone had been teenagers they thought was dirty.

The man with the weathered face was still listing. One hardwood chopping block. Three humidifier rods, two dozen pink light bulbs.

The girl in the red slicker had turned. Her face was round, pretty. She was exchanging what looked like a covert glance with someone. Her expression was bold, conspiratorial. Jane realized it was Barrett the girl was looking at, and turned to catch the tail end of his reaction—a seemingly provocative glance—before he shifted his gaze away.

Barrett squeezed Jane's hand again, and did the dirty

thing with his finger again. The hardware store man added up the total. "Two hundred dollars and ninety-five cents," he announced, and held out the charge slip and pen for Barrett to sign.

Jane stood there in a muddle, thinking, *I must have imagined they were looking at each other.* There followed a moment when she, Barrett, and the man with the weathered face seemed to be locked in a freeze frame. Nobody moved, nobody breathed. Jane came to, saw the man was waiting and Barrett was flushing.

"Actually," Jane reminded the man with a quick warm smile, "we have this account in my name."

She took the charge slip and the pen, signed her name. Barrett stood still as a statue, smiling handsomely at the top shelf behind the counter, which held a row of shiny galvanized watering cans. The girl in the red slicker passed close to them. Jane looked up and saw that under the girl's heavily made-up eyelashes a curious, knowing look was being directed at herself.

When they were outside, loading their purchases into the back of the station wagon, Jane asked, "Who was that?"

"Who was what?"

"The girl in the red slicker."

Barrett put the last things in, slammed the back lid. "One of the town tarts, I suppose." His mouth wore that sullen expression she had noticed once or twice before and didn't like.

Jane got into the car. "I didn't think this town had tarts. It doesn't have stoplights or sidewalks or a bar."

Barrett also got in, behind the wheel. It was her car but he always drove. "Every town has tarts." He turned on the ignition. He looked up at the sky. "It's going to rain."

She waited for him to close his door. An unlit cigarette clenched in his teeth, he slammed the car into reverse and, holding the door open with one hand, leaned his head out and backed the car at high speed for some thirty feet before he braked. Like a valet parking attendant giving himself a thrill in someone else's expensive car. Jane asked abruptly, "Do you know her?"

Barrett turned to her with a patient smile. "No, honey."

The rain began to come down in sheets. After they left the market, Barrett headed the car for home. "Dry cleaners," Jane said.

"Do you want to skip it? It'll take half an hour there, half an hour back." There was no dry-cleaning establishment in their own little village, and they had heard of one in Rigby Creek, a neighboring hamlet. Before leaving for the hardware store they had piled in clothes and a rug that needed cleaning.

"Let's get it over with," Jane said, and then added irritably, "God, stuff like this takes up so much time." In a moment she was complaining again. "We left the hammocks out and didn't close the windows upstairs."

Barrett took her hand, lifted it to his lips. "Cranky," he said. His fingers were cold as ice.

Their first impression of Rigby Creek was a leafy, shaded main street lined with Yankee-simple, gracefully proportioned eighteenth- and nineteenth-century houses, some of them with their original fencing, and a grand few with hundreds of velvety rolling acres of farmland behind them.

Barrett whistled in admiration. "Glory, glory." But a moment later they exchanged a quick glance of dismay.

To be sure, lovely old houses continued to line the street, but now, sandwiched between them, appeared first a flat-roofed modern bank, then a cheaply built brick structure with a lighted sign, DISCOUNT LIQUORS, and a little way farther, between two particularly pretty houses with wide verandas, there was a convenience store advertising a paper towel sale in its windows. There was also a video rental store in the downstairs of a house with a gambrel roof, and several lots that had been cleared and sported signs announcing the construction of a shopping mall.

Barrett was taking it to heart. "A town that lets this happen to their ancestors, Jesus." He banged his fist against the wheel.

The dry cleaners was on the ground floor of a somewhat ramshackle pewter-colored Victorian-style house with white trim. It was right on the street, but there was a narrow driveway to the left of it, shared with a two-pump gas station. When they entered, carrying their load of things, they found themselves in a small room with a freestanding electric heater and a small vinyl-topped counter with a cash register, a jar of safety pins, a pot of dusty artificial flowers, and a call bell. They could hear a television blaring from behind a cloth curtain. No one was at the counter.

Barrett banged his hand down on the call bell and said to Jane, "I desperately want to go home."

A young woman, not at all in the local country mode but evidently devoted to following the latest fashion magazine fads for hair, makeup, and wardrobe—and had it all wrong, Jane mused with sympathy—came from behind a curtain. While Barrett handled the transaction, Jane, out of boredom, continued her examination of the woman. Overmoussed hair, iridescent makeup, plastic earrings. Synthetic blouse with too many brass buttons.

Jane glanced at her watch. Home by four. Leave the hardware stuff in the garage if it was still raining. Unpack groceries. By five she could do something worthwhile. Like work or read.

"Your name?" the young woman asked Barrett in a flat country whine.

Barrett cleared his throat. Jane paid for everything, so everything was in her name, but the girl was waiting and Jane seemed not to have heard. "Rossignol," he said.

"How do you spell that?" She giggled nervously, meanwhile not missing out on his good looks.

Impatiently, Jane stared out the window.

In his beautiful, slightly husky tones, Barrett spelled his name slowly and distinctly for the woman, who now looked boldly at him. "Are you an actor?"

"No, my dear," Barrett boomed in his stage voice. "I am a dangerous pervert."

Jane sucked in her breath. "Oh, Barrett," she said, then saw that the young woman was not in the least offended. Rather, she was looking at Barrett as if she couldn't believe her luck. She made a slow, flirtatious business of handing him the receipt slip.

"Good-bye," Jane now said crisply, taking Barrett's arm, and they left.

They ran to the car in the pelting rain and got in. Barrett started the motor. "I suppose you're going to ask me if I know her too."

Jane was getting out of her wet coat. "Did you see the goopy white shoes? Minnie Mouse forced by white slavers into a bordello. But really, what possessed you?"

"I have a coarse streak I try to hide from Guinevere. When I see a cheap girl like that, I want to rut until I die. Fuck her against a wall. Behind a gas station. Make her ask for unspeakable things. Command her to remain partially dressed so I can keep my eyes on the Minnie Mouse shoes."

Off guard, she caught her breath. "Oh, Barrett."

He was laughing. "I love it when your eyes get all round and you catch your breath and you say, 'Oh, Barrett.' I love it when you say it like that." He encircled her tightly with his right arm and drove the rest of the way home with one hand.

Jerry came up from the city for the weekend carrying a bulging pillowcase. "Is that all you brought?" Jane asked when they met him at the bus stop some thirty miles from where the house was. There was no train to where they lived either.

"Shirt, underwear, painting materials, a Sacher torte from that place on Seventy-second for you, and for you, Barrett, since you now live in the woods by a body of water, a copy of Thoreau. The pillowcase is because I lent my last suitcase to one of my students."

When they got to the property he looked quickly around, breathed in the country air. "Paradise."

They showed him the grounds first, the willows, the brook, the dogwoods and the golden chain trees, the star magnolia, the water iris, a pair of visiting ducks, a hollowed-out place in some tall grasses where a mysterious creature they had never seen slept at night. They stood very still to hear the frogs, the phoebes, the crows, the swooping sound of a kingfisher.

"We have a prehistoric giant turtle," Barrett said. "We pray he'll come out of the water while you're here. We'll show you the place where we found the loon. We'll pray for the blue heron to show up. He's bigger than Jane."

"We have trillions of apple trees too." Jane pointed up a gentle slope to a pretty, meandering orchard. Above the orchard was a thick, military line of trees that completely hid any sight of the property from the road. Jerry looked at his sister and Barrett in the sunlight filtering through the tall hickories, the beeches, the oaks, with the sounds of summer all around.

"I'd like to paint you while I'm here," he said. "Up there in that tall silver grass under the apple trees."

"I'll wear white." Jane was pleased. "Droopy linens and a floppy wide-brimmed hat with trailing ribbons."

"I want one too," Barrett said. "What the hell."

Jane had not planned to tell Jerry about the call from their brother. She hadn't wanted to think about it all, but the fact was it teased her at every turn.

Jerry and Barrett went for a walk on their own. She decided to talk to Jerry when they got back. When they came in, Barrett went off to take a shower and Jerry came into the kitchen where she was washing salad greens and sat, draping his long legs over the arm of a pretty Shaker chair, and said, "We had a great walk. Great."

"You were gone for ages."

"I guess it's the first time we've ever spent more than a few minutes alone. I like him more than ever. There's a grace. A spirituality."

She reached for some tarragon she had picked earlier and began snipping.

"He told me a little about his past. Interesting mix, that personality. All that fragility. All that toughness."

Alert with curiosity, Jane wondered how to lead Jerry into telling her more. "About his childhood?"

"Bits of everything." Jerry glanced at her. "He loves you a lot."

The phone rang. A neighbor. Then Barrett wandered in, in a big white towel wrapped around his hips and trailing behind him like a train. He had come for a piece of fruit. He picked up a peach, ate it in sacramental fashion. There was no opportunity to talk to Jerry after that. The three spent the rest of the evening together.

In the morning Jerry said he wanted to start painting. Jane wore floppy white trousers, a thin white silk shirt, a long white linen coat, and a droopy straw hat.

She and Jerry started for the orchard together. Barrett, who was still dressing, appeared in a few minutes in a white linen suit and a smocked white linen shirt (all made for him in Hong Kong, courtesy of Sara) and one of Jane's straw hats. "I wanted to be very Proustian," he explained. Jane applauded.

Jerry looked him over. "Perfect. Stand over there." He pointed. "Under the low branches. Jane, stand facing Barrett but look off a bit. Let your coat flap open. Barrett—" He had started to give instructions but saw he needn't. Barrett had assumed a naturally graceful pose in the exact spatial relationship to Jane that Jerry had had in mind. Perfect. Spooky.

With a reedy bit of charcoal Jerry began a preliminary sketch. The day was warm. There was the rhythmic chorus of wood sounds. High overhead a hawk circled. Barrett and Jane remained as still as pictures.

Jerry grinned. "I'm hot today. I'm getting the shape of it on the first try. I want it to be fantastically romantic. I want it to be out of time." He became absorbed in his work.

The branches were heavy, warm and sweet with fruit. Barrett's breath had become slightly uneven. His eyes, on Jane, seemed to want to enfold her into the moment. She tilted her head slightly, examining him with curiosity, wondering.

"Will there ever be," he asked her very quietly, "ever again, this summer, this place, this us?"

Why was he facing her in that way, looking as if he were waiting for some invisible guillotine to fall? Why was her heart pounding? Did this ground they were standing on, this land, her land, enclose them, shelter them from doom? Was she so incredibly fanciful, so given to aggrandizement even, to wonder if their story was larger than what time they had been given?

Sitting several yards lower down on the grassy slope,

Jerry caught the moment between them—fierce, mysterious—without ever hearing the words. He tried to control his excitement. Much earlier than he had planned, he reached for his paint box and began to wash the page with color.

August had turned. Chipmunks were busy. In the late afternoons a little wind would appear and put frills on the surface of the brook. Jerry's watercolor, simply framed, stood on a pretty old easel to the right of the fireplace.

And Hal had just called again. There had been no levity this time between brother and sister. "According to our detective," Hal began bluntly, "your boyfriend lived next door to Theo Buckley when he was a teenager. She took him under her wing and they were inseparable. What I'd like to know is, why has he been lying to you?"

Jane, suddenly in charge of this inexplicable state of affairs, said a dazed good-bye to Hal and then without preamble spoke across the room to Barrett. "You looked me in the face and told me you'd met her. Just met her."

Barrett was leaning, as if for support, against an open doorway. His face was ashen. He made no reply.

"You lied to me, you made me lie to my brother, you made a fool out of me, out of him—" She stopped, not knowing where she was going.

Barrett sounded as if in another few seconds he would strangle. "I wanted to forget my past. I didn't know why he was asking. I didn't want to hurt you."

"What do you think you're doing now?"

His only answer this time was a sullen expression. Jane's heart died a little. Beautiful Barrett. Not brave, not true. She was afraid she would cry as she had done as a child when betrayed by the angels. That primitive, unbounded state of nonbeing. Nothing to go on. Nothing. Unbearable. Unbearable.

He looked young and thin, dangling there in the doorway, knowing that before him was the potential miracle of her forgiveness. *How well he understands me,* Jane thought. *He knows I'm pitifully ready to twist my intelligence into any contortion necessary for believing that he never meant to deceive me.*

He said with a desperate look, "Let's not let this bring us down."

She tried for coolness, looked away. "I think it already has." But what she wanted now more than anything else, more, even, than the tidy explanations she so desperately hoped he would produce, was declaration. Love me and I will be healed. Bring back the crystal ball, the sounds of summer. The silvery grass. The white linens.

She waited in the silence, still looking away from him. The quietness began to grow a sound of its own. She turned. He had disappeared. Crept away on Indian feet. She went to the window, raised it, stood looking out. She did not see that the brook ran with platinum or that the feathery cimicifugas were waving their white five-foot plumes or that up the hill a deer had paused daintily to listen.

Thwack thwack.

He had gone out to play. Faint-hearted Robin Hood. Would he not even fight to win her? She looked at her watch. She went to the telephone, dialed the number of the school in New York where Jerry taught, and left a message. Twenty minutes later, without saying goodbye, she drove the car down the driveway, paused at the road to wait for some stray cows from next door to pass, and then, carefully maneuvering around them, she headed for the city.

She left her car in a parking lot on East 82nd Street, where there had been a killing the day before, they told her, and walked the few blocks up to the city-blackened school building that adjoined the church. She heard the bell ring just as she came around the corner. Hordes of uniformed boys poured out onto the sidewalk. She leaned against a wall, waiting for Jerry.

She did not recognize him at first. He was wearing his priest's clothes. He seemed much taller, and not as friendly.

"Where do you want to go?" he asked, coming up to her, swinging his battered briefcase. Two of the boys walked by him, boldly smoking. Deftly, he had a hand around each of their necks and was not too gently knocking their heads together before they realized what was happening. They choked and spluttered. He held out one hand, palm open, while he continued his conversation with Jane.

"Think of a place. Obviously we can't go to a bar with me all rigged up like this."

The taller boy put a crumpled pack of cigarettes in Jerry's hand and he and his friend ran off.

Jane looked bleakly at her austere brother, wondering why she had made the impulsive journey, wondering if he would help her, wondering if anyone could help her. "There's that horrible coffee shop on Madison."

"The one with the guy who never writes the order down and then brings you a fried egg with bacon and a glass of buttermilk when you've actually asked for a tuna salad and an iced tea?"

"The very one." Her eyes brimmed with tears.

Jerry looked down at her. "Come," he said gently. They walked the three blocks to the place, passing the handsome limestone mansion where they had grown up. It was now a consulate. Neither of them commented.

The coffee shop wasn't busy at that hour. Three booths were occupied, all, Jane noticed, by elderly women alone, well enough dressed but with mangy hair and musty purses and cloudy eyes, and lives that were over. One of them was elegantly shrugging and mumbling to herself. *That's me, that's what I'll be,* Jane knew.

She and Jerry sat down and ordered tea.

Jerry regarded her. "It's the coincidence that's thrown you. When you get used to that, you'll see your feelings more clearly."

"I may never get used to it. Tell me how many women have had their marriage wrecked by a dead ex-wife, only to fall in love with a man who was also involved with her."

"Hold it." Jerry touched her hand. "Theo didn't wreck your marriage. Robert did. All that's happened now is that you've found out Barrett also knew her."

"And lied about it."

"Have you never told a lie, Jane?"

"Not like this one." She played with her spoon, grasping it with her fingers, trying to bend it. "He wouldn't even, wouldn't even—" She was about to cry.

"Is that what's hurting you the most?"

"I didn't finish my sentence."

"I'll do it for you. He didn't even apologize. He didn't give you an explanation that might satisfy a grown-up woman. He didn't take any stand at all. He crumbled and fled."

Anger got in the way of breath. "He called you."

"He was pretty upset."

"He had no words for me, but he managed to slouch over to a phone to talk to you."

"He figured you'd come here. He wanted to know if you were planning to go back tonight. Or ever."

"It would be wildly mysterious of me not to return, don't you think? It's my house."

Jerry regarded her silently.

"It was shoddy of him to call you," she added bitterly.

"Why? You jumped in a car and drove over two hours to discuss the same problem."

"You're my brother, not his. He's using you. Dammit, Jerry, can't you see that?"

"I know you're very angry, but aren't you distorting things? He called because he loves you and he's very upset."

"What did he say?"

"That you'd found out he'd known Theo Buckley. That he hadn't ever told you about it because he'd been afraid of exactly what is happening right now."

"First he cons you into feeling sorry for him, then he presents a version carefully tailored so that not only will you continue to admire his character but you'll do his work for him. Thus he avoids any further confrontation with me, thus he avoids having to answer any unpleasant questions. Thus he counts on you, a man, a priest, to send me home contrite and guilty for having caused him so much pain. It has cost him nothing. Not even the phone call. I pay for that."

Slowly Jerry stirred his tea. "And this man, this deceiver, this parasite, this coward, this manipulator and liar, is the man you love?"

Jane rested her elbows on the table, put her head in her hands. "Could we do without the Jesuitical flash?"

"Peace," Jerry said. He took out the crumpled pack he had confiscated and lit a cigarette.

"I thought you gave that up."

"I did, but I didn't mean it." He inhaled deeply.

"Why don't you go home and love Barrett? Let him love you? He lied because he was scared."

"Do you think he knew who I was from the beginning? Do you think he singled me out because of my connection to Robert and therefore Theo?"

"He told me when he walked across that deck in China you introduced yourself as Donovan and he made no connection at all."

"Do you believe him?"

Jerry ignored this. "When he realized shortly afterward who you were, of course he was hesitant to tell you of his own link to Theo."

"Yes? Why?"

"Come on. Insecurity. He obviously comes from a very damaged childhood. He bears all the marks."

"What about us?" she threw back. "By what stretch of the imagination would you describe our upbringing as normal? And do we run around telling lies and behaving in a shitty way and blaming it on our damaged childhood?"

Jerry smiled. "You know what Barrett said to me that weekend I was up at your place? 'Jane's brilliant but she's got a lot to learn.' I asked him what he meant. He said, 'She thinks everyone can be as strong as she is, and if they're not there's something criminally wrong with their character.' "

Jane looked stonily at Jerry. "So there's no problem under the sun except me. My fault? My blindness? My lack of generosity?"

"Shut up, okay? Some people are able to take the dysfunctional and run with it. Beat it, remold it into an asset. You, me, Hal, I guess we could be examples of that. Others—Barrett, and from what he told me, his brother as well—can't seem to manage it like that. They drag it around with them for a long time."

"He told you about his brother?"

"Yes. And there's something else to take into account if we're making comparisons here, and that's privilege. We grew up with silver spoons et cetera. A rotten father who is also a wealthy rotten father is in the position to offer his children counterbalances to his abuse. We grew up with access. The best kind of education, travel, culture, and the company of people with spirit and experience who have all of the above. *Options* is the key word. A rotten father whose failures, poverty, and anger are basically all he has to offer can strangle the growing child and spawn an adult wrapped in a blanket of shame and fear."

"But what about character?"

"Yes, I was waiting for the moral-fiber speech."

"Fuck you."

"Let me finish. Barrett's only attractive role models were flickering shadows. Errol Flynn. Montgomery Clift. Double image, double bind. What I wonder is, did he aspire to be the actor or the part? Did he possibly not even discern the difference? A childhood produced by Hollywood, presented on a series of television sets in a series of houses in a series of towns, parented by a drunken, promiscuous, debt-ridden father, a crushed mother, and a great-aunt who ran a loony bin? I think on the whole he turned out remarkably." Jerry took Jane's hand. "And you know what, baby? I believe he's capable of being more loving than either of us."

Uneasily, Jane looked inside herself to find Barrett's face staring out at her.

"We don't do loving so well, you and I," Jerry was saying quietly. "We add up to two divorces and an alleged life of celibacy. Do you suppose the problem is that we want 'perfect'?"

"Do you think Hal wants perfect?"

"Hal's life is as indecipherable to me as a bucket of

nails. As mine is to him. But he's smarter than you and me. He knows better than to expect perfect."

"How am I going to explain to him why Barrett lied to me?"

"Why should you explain anything? Hal's not the police. So Barrett knew her. So what? He didn't murder her. That we both know. You want more tea? You want a muffin?"

As Jane drove north she kept an eye on the speedometer, didn't waste a moment. She wanted to get home. Jerry was sure that Barrett loved her.

PART

3

14

Jacklin had never even seen a photograph of the Russian River. It wasn't one of those spots that got featured a lot in the Sunday supplements or in the travel press, as did other vacation places in the area around San Francisco, such as Big Sur and Mendocino, but the Russian River had once had its lush day as a lazy, off-the-beaten-track weekend retreat for San Franciscans who could afford a second home. Jacklin knew that much and that in the seventies it had attracted hippies and other free spirits, who were eventually joined by entrepreneurs with dreams of development. But Jacklin's image of the area remained stubbornly untouched by this last piece of information; in his mind he saw mansions, he saw rich kids in swimsuits having a whale of a time swinging from tree ropes while their rich parents drank gin fizzes and talked about Franklin D. Roosevelt. Simple, healthy summers in the lap of nature. Such as he had never had.

So he was pleased as he drove his rented car through

the peeling, forest-green gates of what had once been
Theo Buckley's hideaway house, to find that everything
conformed with his illusions. He was out of time. He
had never thought of Theo as someone who would
want to be out of time, but here was the proof. The
driveway was unpaved, long and winding, down down
down through dark, rotting overgrowth. Dangling
branches of old trees, vines, and untidy shrubs spilled
from an unseen sky.

Nice.

He couldn't see the water from the grassy little level
area where he parked his car because of the junglelike
growth, but he could hear it below, loud and swollen
with the rains of last night. He took a few steps and
found himself looking up at the house, white with the
angles and trim of Monterey Victorian. Perched right
over the water.

A graceful old wooden deck—teak, not that redwood crap they used now—encircled the house on three
sides. He hoisted himself up, walked a few feet, turned
the corner of the deck, and came to what he realized
was the real front of the house, facing the river. He
leaned against the railing and looked down a steep in-
cline of some dozen feet leading to the water. The house
was situated quite prettily in the crook of a gentle bend.

The late afternoon sky was colorless, the river a
pearly gray. Not very wide here. A good swimmer
could get across in a dozen pairs of strokes. He wondered how deep. He would determine that before he
left. Was there a boat? Oars?

There was a smallish white wooden structure in con-
siderable disrepair where the driveway had ended. He
went in. Damp and dark. A wooden boat, dark green.
One oar. He looked for the other one, couldn't find it.
He had to keep reminding himself to stop looking for a
murder weapon. There hadn't been a single mark on

her. In a corner there were what looked like several sets of outdoor furniture. A pile of green-and-white striped cushions, mildewed. A lantern, a hose, a barbecue, several inner tubes.

He left the garage, went back to the house, let himself in with the keys the caretaker, who lived down the road, had given him. Apparently Robert had all the money in the world, keeping the house on all these years, never coming here himself.

The enormous cantilevered living room was all white, including the grand piano. There were handsome slipcovered sofas and chairs, books and magazines piled on low tables, wood stacked by an enormous fireplace. He picked up one of the magazines. Seven years old.

He walked across the long space of the room into a white hallway and through double doors into a kitchen. Cooking pots, plates, glasses. He opened some drawers. Stainless steel cutlery. He opened the refrigerator. Canned and bottled drinks. He took out a beer.

There were four bedrooms and three bathrooms. The beds had coverlets but no bedding and there were no linens in the closets. What had obviously been Theo's bedroom was connected to the deck on the river side. The bed was king-size and over it there was a canopy, its filmy white curtains open. Jacklin found the pull, pulled, and the curtains silently slid along a track until they completely enclosed the bed.

He looked in the closet. Two long, sparkly dresses hung side by side and on the floor was a shoe rack with several pairs of very high-heeled shoes in various shades of red and pink. He examined the rest of the closet quickly, found a few odd bits of things, then slammed the door shut, giving the rest of the room a quick once-over and quitting it in some relief. He didn't like looking in dead women's closets.

He walked back to the living room, sat down at the

edge of a plump white sofa, and took a swig of beer. It tasted fine. He could hear the sound of the river from here, even with the doors and windows closed. He took another swig of beer and began to think about his current obsession. Barrett Rossignol.

He knew that Senator White would be best satisfied if it turned out that no one had killed Theo, that it had been what it seemed at the time, an accident. But he, Jacklin, had sensed muddle and violence from the beginning.

Theo had drowned in the Russian River between 10:00 P.M. and 2:00 A.M. on September 3, 1979. She had not been found for two days. There had been disagreement down at the coroner's office as to the actual time, one opinion being that death had taken place earlier. She had been wearing a halter top, shorts, and a little necklace of pearls she had worn every day for most of her life. There was no evidence of a struggle.

Theo had never known how to swim. Jacklin was not sure who, besides himself and the person who had told him—and the possible murderer—was aware of this fact. Athletic in all other ways, an excellent horsewoman, shot, tennis player, and gymnast, she had successfully covered up her fear of water throughout her life. There were photographs of her frolicking in the Aegean, playing in the surf at Malibu, and so on, but in every case she had either been in water only deep enough for wading or someone had been with her.

"If there was someone with her, she was always all right, but she couldn't be in deep water alone."

This crucial bit of information Jacklin had obtained early on from Theo's theatrical agent, Barnaby Gibbons, a graying, dignified, and cultured man who had looked after Theo during her entire career. Gibbons added, "I wondered whether I should mention it to the police. Not that I thought there had been foul play—

who would have wanted to kill Theo?—but I wondered if I should make it clear to them that there was this factor. I went back and forth with myself about it. Ultimately I was afraid that it would only add a further exploitative element. The press would run with it and the thing was, nothing could bring her back."

"Do you know who else knew?"

"I assumed those who were close to her must have known."

Jacklin was not a man to be seduced by the obvious, or he might have spent a great deal more time investigating the widower, Robert, who would surely head the top of any suspect list compiled by officialdom, if it was indeed determined that there had been foul play. De Peña inherited the money. He and Theo had been unofficially separated at the time of her death. Et cetera. But whatever else Robert might be guilty of, Jacklin was convinced it wasn't murder.

Through the high, slanting windows he saw the day was brightening. He got up and went to the window. The river had turned a jewel green. He glanced at the sky, wondering if there would be a rainbow. He waited there at the window. Rainbows were not a dime a dozen.

This Marly person whom he had questioned in New York. Breathless, actressy, she had flirted with him a little. He wasn't flattered. She was lonely. Poor kid. What happened to girls like that when they got too old to pretend they were still what they had wanted so desperately to be? Marly was over thirty for sure, yet when she crossed a room she didn't walk like a woman, she kind of ran with teeny, fluttery little steps like she was on a stage. But he had seen the despair behind the transparency of her bright chatter. He had seen it before. *I must be as darling as I can and maybe this man will want me.*

He had told her he was trying to track down a
woman by the name of Ann Sykes, who had inherited
some money but could not be found.

Marly had smiled like a six-year-old Mata Hari and
had almost pirouetted. "How exciting. But why come
to me?"

Ann Sykes was a complete fiction, just to get him
through Marly's front door. "One of Ann Sykes's childhood friends was"—he pretended to consult his little
notebook—"Barrett Rossignol. Who I believe you
know."

"Knew," she corrected him. Her face had clouded
over.

"This is the last address I have for him. That is, if
he's the same Rossignol. You wouldn't happen to have
a picture of him?"

Her eyes strayed to a photograph stuck in the mirror
over an old dresser littered with cosmetics, a clump of
loose change, a half-eaten candy bar, several pencils.

She colored slightly. "I really forgot I still had that."
Her shrug was worldly. "You get used to things, you
don't notice them anymore."

"May I?" he asked politely. Years had gone by, and
she still had a picture of him.

She got the photo and gave it to him. One edge was
curled, and here and there were faint discolorings. A
young man on a horse, the scene swathed in morning
mist. Jacklin stared under the racing helmet into the
eyes of Rossignol.

"Maybe it's not the same man." Jacklin frowned. He
dug into his green canvas bookbag and pulled out an
envelope containing a snapshot. "This is what I'm going on."

Marly looked at the snapshot. Beard, long hair,
ponytail, lumber jacket, hands in pockets, slightly out
of focus. "That's him."

"You think so?" Jacklin's expression remained doubtful.

"It was before he had his nose fixed and his jaw restructured. And caps on his teeth."

"When did he do that?"

She paused and thought. "Right after we met." She added defensively, "He was real good-looking to begin with. This just made it perfect. He'd broken his nose several times riding. With actors it's not vanity, it's just good business."

"Of course." He put the snapshot back in his briefcase. "It must have been expensive. How did he pay for it?"

She thought again. "He had this aunt . . . Listen, where did you get that?"

"It was on file."

"On file?" She looked troubled. "Like where?"

"When a case isn't exactly closed, they keep copies of everything."

"Who does? What case?"

"I'm not involved in it. I'm just looking for Miss Sykes."

She was waiting for her answer. He pretended to be puzzled. "Oh. The case. Well, it has to do with Theo Buckley."

She gave him a prissy look. "She's dead."

"Those folks down at the police, I guess they were never satisfied that her death was an accident." He smiled but got no reaction. "Now. Did you ever hear Mr. Rossignol mention Ann Sykes?"

The rainbow had not materialized. He turned away from the window, from the river, and surveyed Theo's living room again. He would finish here, have a good dinner in the city, go to a movie, and in the morning he would go to Los Angeles.

He went into the kitchen and began methodically to go through every drawer, every cabinet. People always left things in the kitchen. There was always a drawer filled with miscellaneous things that had not been pilfered by relatives and servants or had not found their way into packing boxes. He picked his way through extension cords, screw lids, tacks and nails, loose paper, receipts, phone numbers, appliance instructions, all kept for good reasons and in the aftermath of the house's life abandoned or forgotten. He found nothing of interest.

After he finished in the kitchen he took on the nasty job of the afternoon—sloshing around in the damp undergrowth and mud down by the riverbank. There were two pilings where the boat had once been tied up. He noticed marks on a massive branch that jutted out from a great tree over the river. At one time there had been a tree rope. In his mind he saw again the laughing summery people swinging out on the rope over the river, with all the world before them and all the time, then dropping into the deliciously cool water. The smell of suntan oil, steaks on the grill, a striped umbrella on the deck, jokes, plans, a future.

He looked up at the house with its girdle of deck over the water. It looked wise, the house. *Now you've lost it, Jacklin. A wise house?* But really it was an enchanted place, and he thought he understood why she had chosen this cozy, child's river. That she had died in this place had not been her fault, had not, perhaps, even been in the cards. If that was the answer, then what would be the question?

———•———

The next morning a plane took him on a choppy ride over the scrubby, foamy coast, then down through pink layers of sky garbage into Los Angeles. At noon he stood on a hot West Hollywood street outside a bland pair of iron gates and pressed a buzzer marked 2-C. It was almost a hundred degrees. The air you could gag on.

He announced himself. The gate buzzer sounded. He went through and entered a bunker-shaped courtyard constructed in colorless slabs and stucco. With difficulty he found the elevator, which he had taken at first glance for some kind of gazebo. The glass cubicle carried him up silently, the glass door opened silently, and he stepped out into a duplicate of the courtyard below. Gray slab, oatmeal-colored stucco, a few dry, dusty ficus trees in redwood tubs.

The silence, so different from the lush quiet of the house at the Russian River, got to him. It was sterile, faceless, devoid of the slightest clues.

A pair of massively deceptive, cheaply made double doors. Walnut veneer with reproduction brass hardware. He pressed the bell. One of the doors was immediately opened by Una, Theo Buckley's former secretary.

"I was her P.A.," Una corrected him. "Personal assistant. I did everything. I ran her life."

"I hope she left you something in appreciation when she died," he said agreeably, looking her over. He would do his hardboiled detective act with her. Otherwise it would take too much time, getting around her to the information he wanted. The cream-colored shirt opened to the third button, the long, shapely, bare brown feet with impeccably manicured toenails in a light shade of beige, the freshly washed long brown hair, were the silkiest of camouflages and didn't fool him for a moment. Hard as fucking nails, she was.

Bemused by his instant distaste for her, he looked around. Chunky wooden shutters ran the length of the room. The louvers were tilted to allow only a minimal filtering of harsh sunlight. Thick, bland, expensive carpeting in pale beige, lots of Lucite: vases, figurines, boxes, bookshelves. Lucite on the bar counter. Dozens of Lucite-framed photographs of herself with famous people propped up on little tables. One truly terrible, very large iron sculpture.

He eyed it all with dull attention. He had been to Los Angeles before.

Una was answering his question. "Theo wasn't all that generous a person, but her husband was. He let me sort of pick some things out." She led him into a pink and beige kitchen. "Would you like something cold to drink?" She opened the gigantic refrigerator. Jacklin looked inside. It was a toss-up between flavored Perrier, which he hated, soy milk, tropical fruit cocktail, and Piper-Heidsieck.

"Some of the Perrier," he said. "What sort of things did you pick?"

She opened the bottle for him and poured the drink into a thick crystal glass that had cost a hundred bucks minimum. "That can't be why you're here—to ask me what I have that used to belong to Theo."

"I was just interested. Nobody ever left me anything."

She handed him the glass.

He wandered back into the living room. Fake fireplace filled with spiky succulents. No books. The television would be in that low cabinet. "How do you mean she wasn't generous?"

"What I said was, not *all that* generous." She had followed him in. "I didn't mean to imply she was stingy, you couldn't say that. A lot of the time she just didn't think. She'd always had everything she wanted."

He asked casually, "Do you think someone killed her?"

"Maybe you should show me your identification," she snapped.

He gave her a friendly look. "Gladly, gladly." He produced his private investigator's license, his driver's license, flipped out some credit cards. "How'd you ever get to be so suspicious?"

"It's an interesting story how I got to be so suspicious." She sat on the edge of a sofa. "But it's not for sale."

"Could I look around?"

She said pleasantly, "Get a warrant."

"I love asking you questions," he said. "I could get addicted to it." He walked around, looking at the photos. "You ever do any writing for Theo?"

"She had a writer. And of course she did a lot of it herself."

"The writer's name was Emma Grace? I'm hoping to see her while I'm in L.A."

"She's in Morocco."

"You two still keep up with each other?"

"I saw it in the trades."

"What are you doing now?"

"I freelance. A European star comes over to make a movie, for instance, I take care of them while they're here." She paused. "Why don't you get down to asking me what you really came for? It can't be any of this. You said it was for Senator White."

"If you were to make up a list of suspects who might have killed Miss Buckley, would you put Barrett Rossignol's name on it?"

She reached into a glass bowl and grabbed a handful of peanuts, then smiled politely. "Excuse me. Would you like some?"

"No thanks."

"If you came to ask me about Barrett, I can't help you. I haven't seen him for years."

"Were Barrett and Theo lovers?"

"A long time before," she said abruptly.

"Before what?" he asked. First time he'd seen her rattled.

"Before she became famous."

"How would you describe him as a personality?"

"Wimpy." She reached for another handful of peanuts.

"You're suggesting he's too chicken to have committed murder?"

She recrossed her legs. "It was just the first thing that came out of my mouth. You know, you say Pinocchio and I say nose. You say—"

"Marly Durban."

"Who?"

"Damn. We were going good." He gave her a friendly smile. "I thought you'd known her. In what way is he a wimp? What made you think of Pinocchio?"

"How should I know?"

"So are you going to recant and say that Barrett really does have the guts to have committed murder?"

She gave him an even look and then laughed. "You're dangerous."

"Did you and he have an intimate relationship?"

"Are you kidding?"

He looked across at her. He had only once before run across a woman who was so poised under questioning. "Could I take you to dinner tonight?"

"Sorry," she said. "I'm busy."

He stood up. "Then we may not see each other again. Frankly, I enjoyed talking to you."

She did not comment. He followed her to the door, admiring the backs of her knees and the well-shaped ass. Her good-bye was diffident. She looked him in the eye for a moment. He felt her dismissing him.

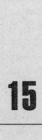

15

An anonymous letter had arrived for Barrett. Plain paper, block capitals. YOU SHOULD HAVE KNOWN THAT SOMEDAY SOMEBODY WOULD CATCH UP WITH YOU.

Standing in the little country post office, he had opened the plain square envelope with some curiosity. He so rarely received mail; it was always for Jane. Jane, looking through her letters, glanced up and saw his expression. "What is it?"

His smile was forgiving. "A shoe sale. They rig these things to look like it's personal mail." He ripped up the letter and the envelope and threw them in a trash bin. They walked out of the post office. The air smelled of fresh-cut grass and maple syrup.

"Shoe sale where?" Jane asked as they got into the car.

"That place on Madison. Near the Westbury."

"Where we got your boots. When is the sale?"

"I don't remember." He started the motor, put the

gear into reverse, backed out of the parking space. His glance swept her briefly as he put the car into first gear and took off. He said, not looking at her, "Your suspicions demean both of us."

Stung and embarrassed, she said, "I was only asking." She fell silent, stared straight ahead. Had she imagined seeing him glancing in dismay at the letter and flushing? It was the second such scene they had had in the past week. First there had been the matter of the two hundred mystery miles on the odometer of her car on a day she had hitched a ride from a neighbor into the city and Barrett had remained at home to "work on his play." He had had a ready answer for the two hundred miles as well. She was mistaken, he had insisted. He had gone into the village to get a newspaper, that was all. He didn't realize she checked the odometer on the car every time she left him alone.

"I don't! I just happened to notice. The car was in the service station the day before yesterday, don't you remember? And I stood there with the guy and we looked at the mileage and someone commented it had come up four zeros all at once."

He said, looking at her evenly, "I have no explanation for that. I only know that I didn't put those miles on the car and that your jealousy is bringing us down."

She talked no more to Jerry. How to describe quicksand? It was inconceivable that there was another woman, other women, and so what was her suspicion? She couldn't give a name to it. It was Barrett's darkness, where he kept the secrets.

She would catch him watching her sadly, wistfully. Once or twice he collected fat bundles of peonies and yarrow and laid them silently in her lap. He was more tentative in his affections, more needy. Sometimes during the day he would pull her toward him and just hold her.

Meanwhile she had her own secret. She no longer liked him to touch her.

One evening she looked across the dining table at him, watched him through the tall candles. He was cutting gracefully into a lamb chop. Dreaming of something. He had spent most of the day in his alcove pretending to work on his play. She knew he had long abandoned it. It could have been, could have become, something of his very own. He had so little.

He saw her looking at him and she knew that he knew the tenor of her thoughts. He knew her, just as she knew him. Once they had exulted in this magic. Now he returned her look almost politely, in wordless acknowledgment of their new shared plight.

The next day she was walking on the other side of the brook and saw him shooting with his bow and arrows. Fiercely he would empty his quiver of arrows into the target, walk the hundred feet, yank out the arrows, replace them in the quiver, go back to his position, and begin again. In the midst of chaos, a simple occupation. She experienced a wave of tenderness and longing mixed with familiar despair.

He's taking a passive role. He's not fighting, he's accepting everything as if he were some kind of martyr saint. And I, the Inquisition. Am I the corrupt one? With my moral straitjackets, my fire and brimstone? Was it not that odd purity in him that first touched me?

At last, she had said to herself when she met him, a man who is every inch a man in the most glorious sense. Spiritually unfatigued, unmarked by traditional taint. In that sense Robert had been finished by the time she met him. He had long before accepted the mantle, the rights and penalties of his malehood. Barrett, on the other hand, fiercely declined to give to gender what was not admissible to his soul.

She stood there in the sunshine. Their sunshine. How

could her heart have been wrong? Hadn't she always trusted in it? She walked over to him. She didn't have to say a word. He looked at her for a moment, put down his arrow, his bow, put his arms around her. Tears spilled down his cheeks.

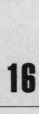

16

The shuttle to New York was delayed. Hal Donovan stood at the boarding gate. Irritably he looked around. He had already inquired what the problem was and had been met with smiles and "Just a few more minutes, sir."

It had already been twenty. Now there was a wave of commotion. Some two dozen people, herded into a group, were being led by a smiling man in a jogging suit through the boarding gate. Everyone else was held back. Hal scanned the faces of the boarding group. They didn't look like tourists. Or an orchestra. And they weren't prisoners.

A few minutes later the regular passengers were allowed to board, and the pilot, speaking over the intercom, solved the mystery. "Ladies and gentlemen, we have aboard with us today the graduating class of the Fear of Flying School. They are taking their first flight ever and we'd like to welcome them."

Hal opened his briefcase. Just what he needed today.

The Peepee in Your Pants flight. He took out a copy of Ciaran Jacklin's report. Ciaran. Was that Celtic? How would you pronounce it?

"And there's more good news," the man in the seat next to him was saying dryly. "The captain gave up smoking this morning. They say he's a basket case."

The plane rolled down the runway, picked up speed. Across the aisle a woman whimpered. She unbuckled her seat belt, tried to get up. She was thrown back into it again. The plane was hurtling toward liftoff point. Hal reached out his left arm, and with one hand tried to get the woman's belt buckled and couldn't. Next he contorted his body, got two hands across, and quickly fastened her belt just as the plane, shuddering and whining, left the earth. The woman began to sob.

"Don't be a baby," he said crossly, and shook his finger at her.

He resumed looking at his copy of the detective's report. He read through it with his customary impatience and was pleased to find it lucid and concise. The man had come highly recommended to Senator White as clever, discreet, and possessing a "complete operational portfolio." Hal wondered for a moment if that last bit meant he could bug, commandeer aircraft, shoot to kill, and all that kind of crap. He turned a page. He had never thought about it in particular, but an investigation of one single event, i.e., Theo Buckley's death, was a fairly exhaustive project and could fill volumes. It was obviously a long way to the jackpot, if there was a jackpot at all.

Hal liked to solve problems, he didn't like to chase after answers to questions that would never be answered. It was a waste of time to ponder those large, powdery issues that Jane and Jerry, for instance, did *ad nauseam*. He himself knew better. He had his work, Carole, the kids, his buddies, his tennis, his shooting, his acres. And of course his devotion to his party and to the administration. He guessed that Jane and Jerry thought they were anointed children of the gods while he, Hal, was merely a crass politician. Still, the fact was, whenever they were all together it was rare and great. And one had to admit Jane was good company, but with this Rossignol business she was looking more and more like a loser. Like Jerry. How could they live such untidy lives?

The plane took a sudden dip. There were screams from most of the graduation class, but not, he was pleased to notice, from his acolyte across the aisle. He glanced at her. Proudly, desperately, she gave him a brave look. She was his.

Jane couldn't pick men, she simply couldn't. She was probably supporting Rossignol. And she had gone through half of her money. It was so foolish. She was still in her thirties. What would she do in her old age? This house in the country had better be the little jewel of an investment that she had described when she razzle-dazzled the trustees into allowing her the money to buy it. Oh, he was sure it would be as artistic as all hell. He, Hal, would start by looking at the basement. You could always tell by the basement.

The plane began to rock. Everything rattled. The Fear of Flying School had everything they had always feared to contend with and were doing, for the most part, poorly. Hal checked on his new friend. She had been waiting for him. Her face was dead white but she produced a plucky smile. He held up one thumb and smiled back. He thought he could love her. In the end, bravery was all.

They continued to be violently buffeted about. His seat companion, a House member from Florida Hal had recognized from the outset but hadn't acknowl-

edged—he never struck up conversations in airplanes—
said, "They may never want to fly again."

The congressman had recognized him. Fine and
dandy, but the man had better understand he wasn't
going to get into any goddamn conversation about the
price of grapefruit, the Cubans, dope, or whatever else
they were forever frantic about down there. He often
wished planes had private compartments; the fact was,
one was a sitting duck when traveling.

"How do you feel about flying?" the representative
asked conversationally. "Ever scared?"

"Never think about it," Hal said, and opened up the
Washington Post wide. He disappeared behind it. Hal,
who had been a jet pilot and had survived two air
crashes, saw no point in sharing this information with
his seatmate, nor the fact that his parents had been
killed in a private plane that had exploded over the
Sinai Desert—because the goddamn pilot had forgotten
to check some simple little thing—when he had been
twenty-six, Jerry twenty, and Jane sixteen.

When later that day he arrived at Jane's house, having
prepared himself on the drive up from New York (how
could she live in a place there wasn't a plane to or even
a train to?), he found only Jane at home.

"Barrett should be back any minute," Jane said. "Let
me have your coat. I'll show you around. Or maybe
you'd like something to drink, or eat," she added politely, realizing that his large, demanding presence in the
delicate space she defined as home was putting her off
kilter, reducing her to good manners. "Too bad Carole
couldn't come," she added.

"It's not exactly a social visit." He looked around,
already appraising.

Surprisingly, he warmed up to the house, even approved. She was able to tell by his expression, though he said little, his eye methodically examining the rooms, detail by detail. She took him outside and they walked over the property. On the way back to the house he said, "Nice piece of land, kid. You did well."

In the kitchen she made tea. "I can't imagine what's keeping Barrett," she said.

"Just as well. You and I have to talk." He took the cup and saucer she handed him. "I never did get the drift of what Barrett does."

"What do you mean?" She turned away, rearranged some pretty canisters on the kitchen counter.

"His income. Where does he get his money?"

"He's in a slack period. I'm helping out."

"Does he contribute anything at all? Has he ever?"

"I'm not sure I want to be interrogated like this, Hal."

"I know you don't. But maybe you'd rather that I ask the questions you don't want to answer instead of this detective we hired. He sent in a report last week. There's quite a bit of information in it about Barrett. He was going to come up here to ask Barrett some questions. I asked him to hold off until I talked to Barrett myself. Our detective is the rah-rah type. He takes this case to heart."

"What case? Do the police know that innocent citizens—Barrett, myself, and God knows who else—are being harassed over a closed matter that hasn't been officially reopened? Do I give a damn about Horace White's extramarital relations with Theo Buckley, which he's now trying to whitewash?"

"Not whitewash," Hal responded without rancor. "It's part of the record and he'll have to live with it. What he doesn't have to live with is even the tiniest suspicion on the part of anyone that he had anything to do with Theo's death. In assuring that, he may have to point the finger at someone who did."

"*If* anybody did."

"Six years from now, White's going to run for president. This coming election is crucial to him." He paused, seemed to consider. "Maybe to me too. There's been talk about getting me ready to run on the ticket with him."

Jane knew he hadn't wanted to disclose this, not to her, not to anyone. And yet in the context of the seldom-called-on but inviolate trust between them he had chosen to do so.

"What we don't want," Hal continued, "is to have this Theo specter raised between now and November with us unprepared. Don't think that the opposition isn't waiting to use it just at the right moment. They spring it on us, we want to be able to say, "Here's the proof, here's what really happened, so fuck off." He stared at her levelly. "My friend White was seen with Theo the day before she died. He's one hundred percent clean, but we have to prove that. If Barrett was involved in any way, I have to know that now."

"Of course he wasn't. They were childhood friends, that's all."

"He hasn't told you they were lovers?"

Jane thought she might faint. She replied coolly, "I didn't ask."

"Did you know that he has a tidy little sum of money salted away in a money market?"

"I don't believe you."

"It's not a fortune; still, it doesn't seem gentlemanly to me that a fellow who's living off my sister, a fellow who pretends he doesn't have a dime, is collecting interest on this thirty-five thousand dollars and putting it right back into the account without ever taking her to dinner or buying her a posy."

Barrett had been sick with anger all day, ever since Jane's brother had called (at 7:00 A.M.) from Washington to say he was coming to spend the night, ever since Jane, flustered at this impromptu visit from a loving foe, had sent him scurrying into the garden to tidy things up while she went to the market, and then dispatched him upon her return to pick up a cake, to get the wine she had forgotten to buy, and to drive all the way to Rigby Creek to get her best tablecloth, which was at the dry cleaners.

It was as if the king were arriving. Barrett, who depended upon his role as lord of the manor, felt displaced, violated, and afraid.

His last stop was the dry cleaners. He had driven there in a murderous rage, a beer can between his knees, his foot pressing the accelerator to the floor. He hurtled along the winding country roads not caring if he hit somebody or somebody hit him. He had kicked open the door of the cleaners sullenly and childishly.

Now, some twenty minutes later, he was still there. It was soft and steamy inside the little room, and the poor stupid broad who ran it—he had by now been told her name, which was Dora—was a perfect foil for his black mood. He even, momentarily, wished himself attracted to her, but the featureless contours of her face under its coat of makeup, her flat monotone, and her coy aggressiveness made that an impossibility. He eyed her huge tits with faint distaste. He liked Jane's breasts.

Misinterpreting his languid examination of her mammaries, Dora gazed back in hot pleasure. With shrewd artlessness she inquired, "That woman you came in with. Are you married?"

"I shall never marry." He studied the effect on Dora. It was cheap fun, titillating this dull tart, wasting his soul on her literalness, but it would pass the time, put more space between this moment and the inevitable return home, where he would be asked to kneel at the feet of King Hal.

He continued to loll against the counter, watching the effect he was having on the breathless, avid Dora. It was child's play. Ater Sara, after Jane, this was ridiculous. Dora was as gullible as Marly had been at the start. On the other hand, Marly had often been refreshing and even surprising, and Dora would never be that. What Dora would be forever was already written.

"Well, I'm divorced," Dora announced provocatively, as if she were sharing the news that she owned a ten-room apartment facing onto the Place des Vosges. She giggled and sighed with the same breath. She gazed at him soulfully. He gazed back sternly. He was driving her wild, he knew.

And his pain was great.

On the drive home he indulged himself in the fantasy that upon his arrival Jane would greet him with the news that Hal had had a heart attack on the plane and was now dead. He and Jane would go to Washington to the funeral and he would wear his new navy blue suit. There would be photographers, and the next day Sydney Pollack and Francis Ford Coppola out in L.A. would see the pictures and want him for a starring role in the respective movies they were casting at the moment.

Instead, he and Hal exchanged a studiedly cordial greeting and then, in the silence that followed, Barrett and Jane made forced domestic conversation. He could tell by her manner that Hal had already been up to no good. Bile rose in him.

"You got the wine?" Jane asked brightly.

Barrett examined her with concealed resentment. "And the cake and the tablecloth."

"Good." She racked her brain for something else they could talk about.

"Ran into some bad news," Barrett offered. "Got to chatting with our little friend at the dry cleaners and she told me the place is closing down next week."

"Life in the country." She smiled at Hal. "You worry about the balance of payments. We worry about where we can get our clothes cleaned or something photocopied."

"Nice place Jane's got herself here," Hal said to Barrett.

Barrett's color rose. "Will you excuse me?" he said. "I have some things to see to before it gets dark." He turned and left the room.

Jane eyed Hal. "There'll be none of that. If you want to talk to Barrett about the Theo thing, talk to him and be done with it. But not one more nasty innuendo. What I do with my life is my business. I remind you that Barrett is your host."

Hal studied her. "Fair enough."

She continued pointedly, "Jerry adores Barrett."

"He would."

The phone rang. She went into the hallway to answer.

"Hello?" Someone asked for Hal.

"For you." She held out the instrument to her brother.

"Yep?" There followed a longish silence while he listened with increasing irritability.

Jane went to the other part of the house looking for Barrett. His bathroom door was closed and she could hear the sound of the shower. She knocked. And waited, but there was no answer.

She returned to the living room. Hal could be heard laying down the law. "There's no way that bastard's going to be allowed into the country. You call Rafe over at State and tell him I said so. I don't give a fuck what the *Washington Post* thinks or the Intellectuals for Freedom think or what your grandmother thinks. Hear me?" He hung up.

God help us all, Jane said dully to herself, and went to set the table. She took no pleasure in it. From the long oak server she got the soup spoons, the butter knives, the lobster picks.

The dinner show. I am tired, very tired of it all. My brother, my lover. Yet really, I am alone. Hal has just denied a visa to a popular hero, Barrett is masturbating in the shower, and I am only here to serve.

In the bathroom Barrett wiped the condensation off the mirror. The steam, soft and drifting, enveloped him. Tenderly he stroked his powerful arms, one by one. His eyes were filling with tears. Wrong, always wrong.

Hal was in the living room, examining the watercolor Jerry had done in the orchard. He wished he were home with Carole, home where he belonged, not in this unfathomable nest his sister had made with yet another man who was going to cause her grief.

She came back in with a drink for him and one for herself. A few minutes later Barrett appeared. Jane thought he seemed to have recovered himself. He appeared relaxed, confident, and very much the agreeable host. Jane felt a surge of pride.

Barrett showed Hal a few pieces they had bought at a local antique show. He pointed out the fine details, dated them, speculated on where they might have come from, and Jane smiled to herself, seeing that Hal was bored and frustrated but also making a herculean effort to appear riveted with interest.

"Oh, and there's another gem I should show you," Barrett said. He went into the hallway and returned with a handsome old walking stick topped with a silver knob. "This was my grandfather's," he said, pausing in the center of the room. Hal was sitting on a sofa a few feet away.

Barrett said to Hal, "Bet you've never seen one like this."

"Very nice," said Hal.

Barrett was holding the stick in his right hand. He raised his arm until the stick was vertical, pointed at the ceiling. Then, still holding it at arm's length all the way, he brought it down, slicing through the air as a duelist might a sword—very quickly, with a snapping motion —to point it at Hal.

Inches from Hal's jugular there was now the sharp point of a tiny, nasty-looking blade about three inches long, which had been concealed in a spring underneath the silver knob.

The hostility of this act, and the foolish risk Barrett had taken, had stolen Jane's breath, and she felt she might become ill. Had Barrett miscalculated by more than an inch, Hal might be dead.

Barrett stood still, as gracefully as a practiced duelist, skillfully maintaining the distance between the point of the blade and Hal's throat. His eyes glittered and were joyous.

Hal looked back at Barrett, who perhaps did not understand that he would never forget this. Hal's mouth smiled. "Fuck you," he said.

Barrett still didn't move but laughed in triumph.

Jane said in a cold voice, "Put that down. This is unconscionable."

Barrett withdrew the walking stick, flipped the blade back into the little hiding place inside the silver knob. Hal, who had been captured by the Vietcong after his first plane crash, tortured, and had his back crushed before managing (by garroting two guards) to escape, felt his joints bothering him and made himself more comfortable. He put a pillow behind his back, crossed his legs, and picked up his drink.

"How could you be so childish?" Jane now shouted at Barrett.

His stance was cocky. "I calculated the distance, hon. I'm an experienced swordsman."

Where? When? Jane stared at him. She saw that under her castigation he was turning sullen and beginning to flush. She knew he was furious at her. Furious at her for not applauding his having put her brother, the enemy, in mortal danger. And so she learned, as she did every day, a little more about Barrett.

"Barrett, ol' boy," Hal said pleasantly. "Reason I came up here was to go over some business with you. Why don't we do that now while Jane rattles things around in the kitchen getting dinner ready."

"Usually I rattle things around with her," Barrett somewhat piously replied. "I don't believe women should be stuck with all the housework."

Apparently Hal decided this did not require an answer. A moment of silence ticked by. Jane said, "There's really not much to do." Her brief, noncommittal glance included both of them.

"I gather Jane has told you the general subject." Hal looked at Barrett. "About the detective. And such."

Barrett leaned casually against the fireplace. Jane could tell by the way he was breathing, trying to control his inhalations, that he was very nervous. He looked across at her and remarked with sarcasm, "Your brother wants you to leave us. This is going to be man talk."

Was he pleading with her to stay? Then let him say so. She waited. But he only stayed posing handsomely there by the fire. She left the room. From the kitchen she heard the muted murmurs of their voices, so low she could barely distinguish Barrett's from Hal's.

She did nothing about dinner. She went into the garden. The moon was almost full. She walked along the little stone path that encircled the house. She paused by the large bow window and from the blackness looked into the living room. Barrett was still at the mantelpiece. She could see only a bit of Hal's face, partly obscured by a lamp. She walked on.

Turning the corner of the house, she saw a gleam of metal some ten yards away. She went closer. Barrett's bicycle. He had forgotten to put it away. He usually kept it in the garage. She went toward it, wondering when he had had time to ride it today, and thinking she had better get it under cover. The radio had predicted rain.

The bicycle was behind some shrubbery. She had only spied it because of the moon glinting on a handlebar. Reaching it, she stopped. It was loaded, packed, ready to go. A duffel bag, obviously stuffed with clothing, was strapped to the back, and tied to that were his bow and arrows loosely wrapped in newspaper and bound with a string. His leather jacket hung over the handlebars. She picked it up and looked in the pockets. Wallet, sunglasses, sterling traveling clock, penknife.

She replaced the jacket on the handlebars. With an orphan's mentality he had prepared himself for banishment, for losing the home that wasn't really his, for losing her. He had been prepared to flee, a bad boy on a bike striking out through the night into nowhere. Turning his back on what was ultimately not worth fighting for?

Maybe he had never loved her.

She sat down in the grass, looked at the moon, and listened to the woodsy chorus of nightsounds. Of course he loved her. She hated that destructive part of her that rose up and doubted him. Whatever had turned up in the detective's report, whatever he may have done and been in his past, it might not be pretty, but it wouldn't be murder. She realized that his strange and hostile behavior to her of late—and the packed bike as well—reflected fears of rejection that had come about as a direct result of Hal's vile agenda—which had poisoned and unbalanced her own role in the relationship as well.

A screen door slammed. Her name was called. Barrett, his voice edgy. "Jane?" She could hear him coming around the side of the house.

"Honey?" She saw his figure moving toward her. He dropped on his knees beside her. "What's the matter? Did you hurt yourself?"

She looked at him for a moment, then pointed to the bike. He glanced at it, then back at her. He said with a painful smile, "I'm always too ready to accept rejection."

"Why?" she asked with sudden impatience, and realized she wanted no more of shifting mirrors.

"Maybe I can never be what you want." He turned from her and stared at the moon.

"I only want you to love me and be loved by me and make a life together."

He got up, put his hands in his pockets, kicked at the grass. "You say that, but you don't act it and you don't like me to touch you anymore."

"I think I've been afraid to trust you."

He gave her a bitter look. "I've satisfied your brother. But I can't satisfy you. I'll never satisfy you."

Over to her.

"It's been a horrible day." She stood up. "Let's put the bike back in the garage. It's going to rain."

Together they walked toward the garage, Barrett wheeling the bike.

"You want to give me a brief version of the inquisition?" she asked.

"Hal doesn't think I'm good enough for you. That's what it's really all about. He asked a lot of insulting questions. For the sake of peace and brotherly love I answered them. It was very unpleasant. I haven't lived the life of a saint. I guess you figured that out a long time ago." He kicked his foot at the ground. "By his standards I suppose I haven't much to show for my thirty-five years on earth. He reminds me of my father. Dad was a failure and Hal's a success, but they're the same man. They traffic in rituals I find barbaric. They never heard a bird sing. They never had a fantasy that wasn't about sex. Put them in a room by themselves with nothing to do and they'd go crazy with fear and despair."

They had reached the garage. Barrett pulled at a cord that switched on the fluorescent lights. He propped up the bike on its stand.

Jane stared at the paint cans, the gardening shovels, the badminton set. She turned and looked out at the night. The boy who had been prepared to flee on the bike and the man who had just spoken had different voices. And there were other voices, she knew. Ultimately, were there so many floating bits of roles that the sum of them was too poor and fragmented a thing ever to constitute someone who could with sureness and trust be called Barrett?

She turned around and faced him. "I want to know about Theo."

He was surprised, discomfited. They stood there in the glaring fluorescent light, surrounded by cold cement walls. She heard herself saying on behalf of the sturdy six-year-old she had once been, "If you lie to me this time, I'll kill you."

His laugh was uneasy, his look perversely intrigued. "You? Kill me?"

She said nothing, merely gazed steadily at him.

A few moments ticked by. Down by the brook the nightly chorale of frogs had begun, loud and comical, playing mating and power games.

"Theo was my first love." He lit a cigarette, closed his eyes for a moment. "She was years older than me, but she let me have her." He opened his eyes, looked at Jane. "At fourteen I was a man with her." He took a drag on the cigarette. "She was everything."

Under the unmerciful lights Jane reviewed her own inadequacies and character flaws and waited for him to go on.

"When I was seventeen I got her pregnant." He paused, absently stroked his waist with two hands. "My baby in her belly." He looked at Jane. "I wanted to quit school and for us to get married. I didn't think about practical things like our ages, I just loved her so much." His eyes were wet and he paused again to blink at the tears. "She went away and got an abortion. I was too young to take it, to understand that her ambition, her career, were the things that drove her, all that ever drove her." Again he looked at Jane. "That little person growing in her womb was mine. It wasn't right."

He fell silent.

Jane walked out of the garage, stared up at the navy blue field of stars.

From inside he spoke to her. "We didn't see each other again until years and years later—that summer at the Russian River. She was famous, she'd had those two long affairs and who knows what else, plus a marriage. A lot had happened. She'd found out where I was, asked me to come. I didn't want to, but for old times' sake I had to. I had to lie to my girlfriend about why I was going out there." He took a breath. "You girls get so mad at us when we lie, but you'll ask us for anything —*anything*, like it was your right—and not give a damn what we have to do to someone else in order to live up to that."

He turned out the light in the garage. "Anyway, I went. She cried a lot. She apologized over and over about the baby and how she'd hurt me when I was so young and all."

"Why didn't you tell me this?"

"I've never told anyone." Behind her he had stepped out of the garage. "She'd hurt me more than she could ever know. Women do a lot of hurting, they do it all the time. Maybe they don't mean it, but damn, they'll say anything. Maybe there's a myth among all of you that we can take it. Maybe that's why you always get so shocked and surprised as all hell and don't understand why there comes a point where we usually have to start loving someone else.

"Men aren't as uncomplicated as women think," he went on quietly. "They're not as stupid, either. I'm not saying that in a hostile way, honey, it's just real relevant. I know that our egos seem like a giant jokes to you. When you're not laughing at us for them and making cracks among yourselves, you're despising us for what we have to do to preserve them. But you have to be careful"—she heard him pause and take a breath—"because it's like if we were to laugh at your breasts. Or if we were to despise them." There was a longer pause. "Or to imagine we could live without them."

He had come up behind her. He began to kiss her neck. His hands went around the front of her, touching her nipples. "These are as holy, as vulnerable, as absurd, as my ego. They can't be reasoned with. They can't be dismissed." He turned her around to face him. "Don't you understand? I'm in as much danger from you as you are from me."

They returned to the house, made very civil and agreeable conversation with Hal over dinner, and were profoundly relieved when, after coffee, he said he had some reading to do and disappeared into his room. Jane and Barrett could not wait, could not wait, to get to theirs.

In the morning Hal left for Washington. As they were saying good-bye, the telephone rang and Barrett went to answer it. Jane took the opportunity to say to Hal with a triumphant look she couldn't disguise, "I hear you're satisfied."

Hal looked at his watch. "Gotta go." Stiffly he kissed her and walked to his rented car.

Uneasily, Jane followed. "You are, aren't you? Satisfied?"

Hal got into the car, fiddled with the key in the ignition. He was staring through the windshield. "Sorry," he said at last. "I think he's trash."

Jane went white. "Get out of here." She turned and walked back to the house.

On the way to LaGuardia, Hal stopped and telephoned Jacklin, asking him to meet him there. He wanted to get a look at the fellow. He was being paid exorbitant fees, Hal told himself, let him get his ass out there.

There was a traffic snarl-up on the expressway, and Hal was delayed almost a half-hour. When he got there, Jacklin, who was sitting on a bench reading a book, looked up and recognized him. Hal glanced at the title. *The Hotel New Hampshire.*

He shook hands with Jacklin. Except for reading novels in the middle of the goddamn morning, he looked and talked okay.

"We've got ten minutes," Hal announced. "I didn't want to do this on the phone." He didn't explain.

Jacklin, who had moments before been posed for a

long time over a particular line that the author had
written about sorrow, knew he had been summoned to
be examined, did not resent it in the least, and clicked
into the situation.

"What did you get out of him?" he asked Hal.

Hal looked around restlessly, checked his watch.
"He told me about his unhappy life, his terrible father,
how insecure he had been, how he's never been able to
get himself together, and now he has real hopes because
he says his relationship with Jane has changed him."

"What about the thirty-five thousand?"

"He says that's put aside for his brother, who's
younger and even less confident than he is, and might
need it down the line."

"What a sweetheart."

"He was real shocked I knew about the money."

"What about Sara Alessio's suicide?"

"He said she was an alcoholic, a manic depressive,
and threatened his life, and that's why he broke off the
relationship." Hal paused. "Did you find out whether
she left him anything?"

"Thirty pieces of silver."

Hal peered at Jacklin. "You mean silver bars?"

"Coins. She wasn't so alcoholic and manic depressive she didn't know how to make her point."

Hal continued to stare at Jacklin. "You don't think
he killed Alessio."

"He didn't have to."

"Well, what about my sister? Look, Jacklin, you
came highly recommended, with kudos from kings and
all that, but this is my flesh and blood and I don't fucking need guesswork."

Jacklin's expression was professional, uninsulted. He
was looking thoughtful. "With all his flash, maybe he's
not as bright as everyone has assumed. Or he lives in

more terror, maybe more complication, than I've conceived of. Sorry, I was just thinking aloud."

"Just don't put stuff like that into the report. I mean, who has time?" Hal looked at his watch. "He's real convincing. I began to think you had us barking up the wrong tree and I was making an ass of myself. I began thinking maybe I should apologize. The red flag didn't go up until I was almost through."

"Tell me."

"He implied that Robert de Peña could be our man. He saw this caught my attention and began to embroider on it. I led him on a bit and he fell right in. A six-year-old could have seen through it. Fucking amateur." Hal got up. "Walk me to the gate, will you? My gut tells me he's incapable of murder. I ask myself why. I have no answer."

"You spoke of a red flag."

Hal hesitated. "A personality thing." He hesitated again. "He's not living with your sister."

Jacklin waited.

"I don't trust him," Hal said finally. "I'll never trust him. Not as long as I live."

He shook hands and said good-bye. "Let's get this wrapped up as soon as possible." He nodded and walked through the gate.

Like a head of state. Power was palpable. Jacklin watched him exchange pleasantries with the young woman who was checking tickets in the doorway, and then disappear into the boarding tunnel. He did not begrudge Hal his manner or whatever fiefdoms he might control. The man was rough, demanding, irritating, and when it came to things that counted, solid as a rock.

On the plane Hal buckled his seat belt, nodded at an acquaintance across the way, opened his newspaper. Jacklin wasted no time, and his information-gathering was discreet and impressive. He looked you in the eye, and at the same time Hal detected a deep vein of maverick. He hoped it didn't run to prima donna. People like that could and did make costly mistakes because they talked only to themselves.

But on the whole he was satisfied with the man. He was also satisfied with his decision not to tell the detective what the red flag had been. At the time, with Barrett draped elegantly against the mantelpiece, his well-sculpted arms flung out, resting on the polished wood, Hal had experienced a crawling sensation and the knowledge that his own face was flushing as he wretchedly wondered whether the younger man was actually trying to flirt with him.

The plane started down the runway. Hal folded his arms across his chest and stared into the seatback in front of him, monitoring, without being aware of it, the pilot's performance, the possible age of the aircraft, the direction of the winds.

Barrett hadn't actually *flirted* with him, that was too strong a word. But there had been a corruption. The languid, posed way he had stood there, the long, meaningful looks out of knowing, ironic eyes, the hushed pauses in which he presented his dreamy profile before answering Hal's questions. *Look at me. Want me.*

Jesus. The plane took to the air. Hal glanced out the window, willing himself to be in Washington. The real world. There was something disturbingly gossamer about Jane's house, Jane's life. He began to think with relief about his own.

In the 29th Street apartment Marly was pacing, eyeing the phone. Should she or shouldn't she? What would he sound like after all these years?

She went to the phone and dialed the number. Barrett answered and she found herself gasping, "Hello? Barrett?"

"Yes?" Very cool. But he knew who it was and she knew she had caught him horribly off guard. She looked around the room and thought of them together in that bed.

"I'm sorry to bother you." Why had she said that? Nothing but empty air on the line between them now. She took another breath.

"Barrett, there's something weird going on. I don't really get it, but I thought I should give you a call."

"Yes?"

Over the years in her loneliness she had recreated him, gradually filtering out all the things she did not want to remember, so it was a shock to understand he was the same. She could plainly see the sullen expression on his face and feel his resentment toward her, a long-since-exiled outsider.

She realized that this phone call had been a mistake in judgment, but now she would have to go through with it. "There was a detective here asking questions. He said it was about someone called Ann Sykes. Do you know someone called Ann Sykes?"

"I'd rather you not ring me if you have nothing to say."

La de da de da. Even his inflection had gone up the ladder of success. She imagined him in a cashmere cardigan, holding a leather-bound book, drinking a sherry. *And me still a waitress. And still caring enough to make this call.*

She struggled on. "Then he called again yesterday. He asked me to dinner, so we went out. He acted like it was completely social. And so we played Getting to Know You, naturally." She laughed nervously. "He already knew who you were, because of this Ann Sykes."

The silence on the other end of the phone had been

intensifying into a terrifying void. "He asked about, well, all our years together. I can't remember how it came up, but I told him about your act. You know, when you got to impersonate Theo Buckley at The Touch Me Club."

She heard a sharp intake of breath. She rushed on. "He said he'd always been a big fan of hers and did I have any pictures of you made up as her?"

Barrett had answered the telephone in the kitchen. Jane had just stepped into a shower to wash her hair, but after a moment of standing in tepid water that refused to get hot she realized there was something wrong with the hot water heater again. It had happened the day before. Irritated, she turned off the water, stepped out, put a towel around her, and went looking for Barrett to ask him to go to the basement and flip the switch or whatever had to be done. She heard his voice coming from the kitchen. As she made her way there, she heard a snarl. That couldn't be Barrett.

It couldn't be.

It was. "All those years with you, you kept me back," he was saying into the phone. "I only wanted to escape. Now I've got a life, and you want to destroy it."

Jane entered the kitchen. Barrett was sitting in the Shaker chair. He had his back to her. He was momentarily silent—evidently the person on the other end of the line was saying something. Now he burst out again. "I'm trapped like a rat. It's her brother who hired the detective. And you, for the price of a meal, spilled your guts. Cunt."

Then it was as if he knew, as if he sensed her there, and he whirled. And understood she had heard.

He jumped up from the chair, knocking it over. His eyes were rolling, and he seemed to have lost control of his limbs. He crashed into the kitchen table, fell across it, and screamed—whether into the now dangling phone receiver or to Jane it was impossible to tell. "See the man with a thousand faces!" he shouted. "See him, touch him!"

Pulling himself upright, he yanked the phone out of its jack and threw it against the far wall. Uttering agonized, shattering howls, he began to tear off his clothes while he circled the kitchen, kicking at the stove, the refrigerator, the cupboard. He tore off his trousers, his shoes, his socks, everything, until he was naked, then he unstrapped his watch and hurled it against the wall. He turned to face her. She could feel his breath on her, and smell perspiration. His chest was heaving, she saw all his ribs—he suddenly seemed so thin—and there were dry sobs coming out of his throat.

"I'm filth," he howled at her. He flung his arms out to the sides. "I'm slime. You'll never know what it is to be me."

She tried to fathom what had brought it on, who had called, what had brutalized him into this vicious, naked boy who stood in her kitchen in a pose that could have had him hanging from a gibbet, howling out his self-loathing. It occurred to her that he wasn't even seeing her, that she could be anyone, that she could be everyone, that in his extremity there was no one in the world except himself. Perhaps there never had been.

He began to quiet. He grew, it appeared, quite cold. He began to shiver. He quickly collected his things and left the kitchen.

Jane sat down in the Shaker chair. She rewrapped her towel more tightly around her. She heard him in the hallway making a brief telephone call. She could not hear the words. After a while she went to find him. He was packing. He was still naked.

She said, "I already know about your different faces. When you love someone you pay attention."

He fitted the walking stick in, closed the lid of his

suitcase, snapped the locks. "If you know what I am, why can't you leave it alone?" A second ticked by, and he screamed at her, "Why can't I have peace?"

How did one converse with a murderer? She gave it up and left the room. He did not say good-bye. She heard the front door open and a few seconds later close quietly. The local taxi was parked in front of the house. The driver loaded the suitcase and the duffel bag into the back. Barrett, wearing his white linen suit and his cowboy boots, got into the taxi without a backward glance. The taxi went up the driveway, disappeared.

Jane rested her forehead against a cool windowpane. When later in the day she went to the garage to get the car out, she saw he had left his bow and arrows, and his bike. Apparently wherever he was going he wouldn't want them. Already they belonged to his past.

She talked to no one that day. Or the next.

Jacklin showed up on the third day. He was surprised to find Barrett gone, discomfited by his own mistiming, and somewhat intimidated by Jane's polite, unshakable demeanor. She would not allow him past her front door.

"As a courtesy to my brother and to the hapless Senator White, I'll stand here with you for a few minutes. That is all." She smiled and looked him in the eye.

Impressed by her straightforwardness, taken by the look of her face, and studiously avoiding looking at her sensational legs—she was wearing shorts—he inquired, "Is Mr. Rossignol staying in the area, or has he gone back to New York?"

"I have no idea."

"You've broken off the relationship?"

"By mutual agreement."

He found he didn't like having to ask her any of this. "Did the break have to do with aspects of this investigation?"

"I wouldn't call it an investigation. I'd call it a man on my doorstep. I'd call it politics. I'd call it being on the short end of other people's former fun and games." Again she looked him in the eye.

The Donovan family was beginning to interest him. Would the priest also be fearless?

"Did Mr. Rossignol ever say or do anything that might make you suspicious about his past?"

"I am always suspicious of men's pasts." She paused. "They get around so much."

"I meant specifically, Miss Donovan."

"No."

"Do you find it odd that the last two men you've been involved with both had relationships with Theo Buckley?"

"Perhaps she got around quite a bit herself."

"What do you think of the extraordinary coincidence?"

"I think it's an extraordinary coincidence."

"Thank you for your time." He hadn't needed her anyway, and he was convinced she didn't know where Barrett was. Yet part of him didn't want to go, didn't want to leave her there in the woods, in the middle of fucking nowhere. It wasn't danger he thought she was in, or he would have put on a man to watch the house. It was something else.

Before he got on the expressway he called a stringer he had over the state line and asked him to come up to the area that afternoon and do some nosing around. He then drove back to the city, feeling depressed and irritated.

Jacklin had begun to doubt himself. Why? Five minutes on Jane Donovan's doorstep? Had his instinct been wrong about Barrett? Looking at Jane, it had been hard to imagine her with the Barrett that Marly had described. Or that Una had dismissed.

Or that he had pieced together for himself. The picture he carried in his head of Barrett—and he was experienced enough to know that its dark, exaggerated irrationality would not necessarily preclude it from emerging eventually as the guess closest to the plain truth—was that of a seedy young circus performer, wiry, pale, with glittering eyes, naked to the waist, wearing cheap trousers, holding a long whip, standing in the mud and muck of the circus grounds between performances.

But now he could not connect that image to Jane. Jane was class. Sara, according to all accounts, had been too. But betrayed, she had been unable to hold. He suspected that Jane betrayed would hold. She would crack most horribly, but she would see herself through.

In the city he garaged his car, stopped at the Chinese place around the corner from his apartment to order takeout, and leaned against a wall, reading the evening paper while he waited, listening to the chatter around him from the garrulous, friendly countermen. It had been so quiet in the country. Standing on Jane's doorstep, he had been struck by the soft stillness with which nature amplified its own sounds. The wistful plaint of the phoebe. The swish of an unseen brook. There would be tall trees on either side of it and in winter it would freeze over. You could probably skate on it.

He turned a page. Senator White's sincere face stared out at him from a photograph. He had made a routine speech the day before, yet it got coverage. Jacklin wondered whether Theo had been the only woman for whom he had temporarily deserted his bright, attractive wife.

Jacklin himself had once had a bright, attractive wife, with long, silky brown hair that used to swing whenever she moved, and Jacklin had loved to watch it. Walking across a sunny street at the age of twenty-six in a peach-colored sweater and a white skirt, she had been hit by a car driven by an insurance salesman who had had too much to drink at lunch.

Jacklin's wife had taken an hour to die. She had died without him. Their car had been in the shop, which is why she had been walking across that sunny street. Jacklin, unable to find a taxi when they called him—the President had been in town and everything was tied up —had run the twenty blocks to the hospital. He had flung himself across Kathleen's warm, dead body. They had not been able, for a long time, to pry him away.

Jacklin had immersed himself in his work. The lives of his clients, suspects, witnesses, became a useful over-all replacement for his own, which in his heart he no longer had. He decided to fill up the rest of his spare time by further educating himself. Anyone talking to him might have reasonably assumed he was a college graduate, but in fact his formal education had stopped at the eleventh grade. He now began taking night and weekend university classes, choosing his subjects on the basis of what, from case to case, there was to know that he didn't know. Outside his business and his school he saw no one. He grappled with his grief and slept alone.

The following year an ex-associate of his father's recommended him for a cushy, "kind of screwy but sensitive" job, the older man said, which would take him far and wide, and none too soon. "You need to lighten up," he told Jacklin. Intrigued by the opportunity—and the pay—Jacklin took on a longish stint as a special officer and exalted personal bodyguard to the wife of a certain head of state, and so on planes, yachts, in luxurious desert tents, palaces, royal suites, private train cars, and country houses he came to know some very interesting people, picked up a great deal of interesting and entertaining information, and had the time as well to read novels, biographies, and books on cave paintings, religion, fox hunting, estate gardening, czarist Russia, mountain climbing, cosmetic surgery, military history, psychiatry, structuralism, and theater.

After a year he had returned to America, and been hired to conduct a long, discreet investigation concerning certain wrongdoings by one of California's great families. His work on this was impeccable and well rewarded by the beginnings of a reputation as well as by the generous fee paid him. He began to take on only those cases that intrigued him, that promised fresh news, and he continued to take courses at night and on weekends. His small apartment on East 52nd Street was crammed with books and papers.

He came in now, carrying his bag of mushu pork, butterfly shrimp, and egg rolls. The first thing he did was to feed his fish. His aquarium was a thing of beauty, sleek and spare. No plastic palm trees or coral, just the brilliantly hued, plump, bearded, fantailed, spotted, speckled, and striped fish moving in stately, fixed trajectories. Iskan, the flamboyant woman he had guarded, had liked to skin-dive and snorkel, and Jacklin, who until then had never really thought about fish one way or the other, had met, head-on, deep in the heavy, hushed water of the sparkling Red Sea, a school of fantastic polka dots, flashing silver and black, coming toward him in exquisite formation. He counted it still as the first moment in which he understood that the universe held wonders that might inform personal loss.

He changed into neatly pressed shorts and an old shirt and sat down with his Chinese boxes. He lost himself in the fish. Watching them, he was once again reminded of how closely basic human behavior aped that of the fish in the tank. How none of us have all that many directions in which to go.

"Was she depressed over her career?" Jacklin had

asked both the agent, Gibbons, and then Robert, whom he had gone to see for a second time.

"She had been melancholy for some time," Gibbons supplied. "Theo wanted to be more. Having reached one rung, she always scrambled for the next. She wasn't satisfied being an international cabaret star, recording star, plus frequent appearances on film and TV. She wanted to write and direct a movie, star in it, and produce it. She couldn't get the backing. She was very bitter over the continued rejection. She said over and over again that women were still being denied what was given naturally to men. She cited Woody Allen, who was allowed to do what he wanted. She said she was every bit as funny and talented as he was, and she had a point. Theo's stage character, Fanny Lou, was in many ways the female counterpart to his own film persona—quirky, modern, fresh, but an old soul. She wanted to make a movie in which that character loved, sinned, failed, and triumphed."

"Instead," Robert had further filled Jacklin in, "the movie executives patted her on the head, told her how great her act was, and offered her cameo parts for astronomical sums in comedies and film musicals. She wrote a script, as I recall."

"Does the script still exist?"

Robert looked blank. "I don't remember." Then he added, "You can't imagine the piles, rooms full of paper that were left. Remember, this was before computers were in general use. I gave all the papers to Una to sort out. They're in storage, I guess." He looked at Jacklin. "When someone dies there's always a lot of stuff left that you don't know what to do with. Some of the things you don't want to look at at all. Too awful, too sad. In the case of someone like Theo, who belonged, as it were, to the public, it's even more complicated. I was overwhelmed. I decided to let Una—who was fantastically efficient and loyal—do the major sorting out. At least catalogue the stuff and then store it and I would deal with it later. I never have. It's the same with the houses. I sold the one in France last year, finally. But I can't get myself to do anything about the river place."

"Do you think she was capable of committing suicide? Or of getting so drunk she couldn't swim or handle herself in the water?"

"I've thought about it a million times. No one around her had any reason to want to kill her. It certainly wasn't a stranger, or there would have been signs of a struggle. In the end one has to accept that she did have too much to drink and decided to go in the water." He looked at Jacklin bleakly. "And as you say, was too far gone to swim."

So Robert hadn't known—or was concealing the fact he knew—about her fear of water.

Theo would not have gone into the water *unless someone was with her*. Yet according to everyone who had been questioned, all of those who admitted to having been at the Russian River that day, at some time or other, no one had been at the house except Theo after eight in the evening. And not a single one of them had an unimpeachable alibi. They had alibis that had been accepted by a police department that had not been investigating the death as a homicide. In a crunch, Jacklin knew, none of them would hold up.

Including Senator White's. On the matter of his infidelities he had been matter-of-fact. "I'm not saying I haven't had a girl here and there in my twenty years as a husband, but it's always been discreetly handled. My attraction to Theo was different from anything that had come before. I was fascinated by her. If she hadn't died, maybe I'd have made an ass of myself, I don't know. The facts are, as you know, I was with her the day before she died. I was speaking in San Francisco and I drove up to the house at the Russian River in the afternoon. I noticed nothing unusual in her demeanor, though in hindsight she may have been a bit quiet. There were several people at the house—two of them I'd met before. Her secretary and her writer. I briefly saw a young man who could be the same one as in the photo you showed me—I'm not sure, and I'll never swear to it because I can't. He was outside pruning shrubs, that kind of thing, and I assumed he was the gardener. When I arrived, there was also someone else, an early computer whiz who had come to deliver an electronic typewriter that Theo had ordered and was very excited about. After he left, Theo and I played with the machine a little. Those things were still a novelty then. After getting back to San Francisco I remained in the city until the next day and flew back to Washington later that night. What else do you want to know?"

"Did you sense any tension in the household while you were there? Pick up an undercurrent of any kind?"

"Frankly, I don't remember."

"Did you have a meal while you were there?"

"Theo and I had some lunch on the deck. The secretary laid everything out and then disappeared."

"Wasn't there a housekeeper?"

"Yes, I forgot. I mean, she'd been there on previous occasions, but apparently it was her day off."

The housekeeper had died three years after Theo, of cancer. The computer whiz, now living in San Diego, recalled his visit to the house that day in some detail, which added nothing new to the picture Jacklin already had.

Jacklin opened the white boxes, fetched a plate, a fork, and a napkin. The next two people he would talk to were Theo's writer, Emma Grace, and Father Jerry Donovan. Theoretically he should have interviewed them both before setting out to see Barrett, but Emma was not due back from Morocco until the following day. Father Donovan he could have seen at any point, but he had put it off several times. Donovan was not really relevant, he had never known Theo; however, he had known Barrett of late. It seemed to Jacklin it was worth half an hour.

The phone rang. It was the man he'd sent to the country. "I checked the bus station when I got here. The bus station, get this, is in a trailer, talk about boondocks. Nobody remembered anyone who looks like Rossignol buying a ticket."

"Maybe he rented a car."

"There's only one place he could have done it, and I came up with zero there too. Lucky for us there's only one taxicab for the whole area. He picked up Rossignol at the house and dropped him off at a gas station. I guess he called somebody and that somebody picked him up."

"Okay. Take the evening off and—"

"And do what? There isn't even a coffee shop."

"There's an inn over by the lake. Ask. Tomorrow morning I want you to go to a place in Massachusetts called Brawley Manor." He flipped open his notebook. He gave the man the address. "Rossignol could be there."

But he wasn't.

After the man had come looking for Barrett, Ethan went up to the attic and gazed at a locked blanket chest. Bro had brought it up ages ago and dumped it, maybe about the time he'd gone to live with Sara. Ethan guessed Bro had had it when he was with Marly and didn't need it anymore.

But Ethan was sick of guessing about Bro and never being told anything and just being used. He hadn't seen

Bro since Aunt Charity had taken so bad and he'd
called Bro and Bro had said he'd come when he could,
not that day, he was having problems with Jane, maybe
in a few days. When he did come, Aunt Charity had
taken a turn for the better. Bro said he had to get back
home that same day but that he'd come for the funeral.

He didn't. The funeral had been yesterday and Jane
didn't know where Barrett was, said he'd gone. Ethan
walked behind the coffin alone. He was an impressive
young figure—the answer to a maiden's prayer, he had
announced somewhat drolly to his mirror while getting
ready—in his three-piece navy blue suit, white shirt, rep
tie, and spit-and-polish dress shoes. His hair had been
neatly brushed, he held his five feet eleven erect, and he
carried in his hand the binoculars Aunt Charity had
used to look for birds every morning at breakfast. He
was going to put them in the grave with her. He had
chosen the music, the service, the coffin, the flowers,
and he had asked them to place the coffin in the ground
so she'd have her back to the expressway.

Ethan couldn't help thinking that it was as if Barrett
had *known* the hysterically funny part of the whole
thing. Aunt Charity hadn't left a dime to either of them.
You could split your gut. There was just some old will
she'd made thirty years ago leaving everything to the
Catholic Church. Ten years of his young life taking care
of her and the Children, and she hadn't even left him a
toaster. He didn't like the idea of all those silver trays
and everything going to the Catholic Church—all those
things they'd ordered together. He hoped he was going
to be allowed to keep his duvet, but he'd been too embarrassed to ask. The lawyer and the parish priest and
even the people from the state were already acting as if
he didn't exist.

Ethan understood that Aunt Charity had just plain
forgotten about the will, and he supposed he should

forgive her. Still, the state was probably going to take over Brawley Manor if the Catholic Church didn't, and he would have no place to live. Not to have Bro around to talk to about it was the worst part. If he'd left Jane, that meant he'd made a mess again and gone on to a new woman.

Ethan went downstairs and got a few tools, climbed back up to the attic, and started working on getting the chest open, all the time wondering where Bro had gone and why this guy who said he was with a security company had come looking for him. Seemed like a lot of people were looking for Bro and wanting his phone number, Marly for one, and after that an agent with a job offer for an off-Broadway part.

He got the chest open. There was that beautiful old fur rug with the black and silver pelts that the folks had given to Bro instead of to him. Trophies, yearbooks, a polo helmet, two rifles, a pistol, a hunting knife, long underwear. Nothing of interest, really, except a makeup box which he opened and was momentarily taken by. Actor's stuff. Powder, lipstick, eye shadow, a little tube of gold sparkles. He pawed through the colored confections in awe. There were also some women's clothes wrapped in a garment bag that felt heavy. He investigated. A pair of women's shoes. And a red wig.

For fun, he put on the red wig and got up to look at himself in the hazy mirror of an old dresser against the attic wall. Jesus, it made him look just like Lily.

He stood there a long time in front of the dulled-over mirror, looking at himself with the red wig on his head, thinking about Aunt Charity's sweet dead face and him having no money and no place to go, and Bro, who'd had Lily, who'd had everything, who'd always had everything—

And he began to cry.

17

Jane had been in the city for two days. She came back in the late afternoon, and when she let herself in she was sure that someone had been in the house during her absence. It didn't feel as if anyone might still be there; the silence was definitely that of someone come, someone gone.

A silk scarf she had left over a chair in the dining room had slipped to the floor. The glass door to the pantry was closed. She was sure she had left it open.

She opened the doors to the garden, looked across the brook, up the slope. Her land lay quiet, undisturbed. She came inside again, walked through the rooms one by one, her glance sweeping them. All was sweet and familiar. Nothing she could prove, yet her sense of his presence lingered.

"Barrett?" she said aloud. She knew he wasn't there. She only wanted an answer to the mystery. Who was he? Had he really loved her?

She took a walk in the garden, sat on a stone bench

to watch the sun sink, willing herself not to think about Barrett but about her life, her work, her future. She went into her study to work.

At ten o'clock she took a book with her into the bedroom and began to undress. The hours of concentration had resulted in a slightly more balanced outlook. Since Barrett's departure her imagination inflamed easily. It was highly possible that she had exaggerated the wispy bits of evidence into too ready an assumption that he had been in the house. In her heart she wasn't done with him, therefore she saw him in every corner.

She dropped a nightdress over her head. *I thought I knew him but I didn't. I must get through this somehow.* She took off her watch and laid it on the bedside table. And saw that a single China-blue iris had been placed in the slim silver bud vase which was always stored—when not in use—on a high shelf in the pantry.

She told no one.

In New York, Jacklin was in a rising elevator at the Mayfair Regent hotel. A pink-cheeked, white-haired woman in a gray uniform and white gloves opened the door and he stepped out on the seventh floor. He walked down the discreetly elegant hallway, paused before a door, and buzzed.

Emma Grace opened the door. Plain face, nice face. A big white T-shirt that said FIJI in fuchsia sequins. Shorts and running shoes. Punkish haircut, drop earrings, no nail polish, no makeup.

She led him into the living room of the suite. There were several flower arrangements in baskets, a bowl of fruit, two buckets of champagne, each on a separate tray with two glasses. The television was on. There were piles of newspapers, magazines, books, and thick manila envelopes.

In a row under the windows were over a dozen filled shopping bags, including an enormous one holding, obviously, a new suitcase.

Jacklin looked around. "I thought you just got here last night."

"I did. Sit down. I've got orange juice, diet Coke, and beer in the fridge. I can order you anything from downstairs. Would you like something?"

"No thanks. Tell me, how did you accumulate all this stuff in less than twenty-four hours?"

"There's more stashed in the bedroom." She grinned. There was a slight gap between her front teeth. "A friend of mine once said that every one of her needs could be translated into merchandise. It's a goal I'm trying to attain."

The phone rang. She went to another extension, dialed one digit. "Operator? Can you pick up for me on my other line? And hold any other calls for the next half-hour? Thanks a bunch."

"Half an hour is all I get?" Jacklin asked, thinking that she was quick and nervously alive and he was glad at last to be able to talk to her.

"I have a dinner at half past ten." She sat down and gave him her attention.

"You know what this is about?" he began.

"The gift from God."

"The what?"

"That's what Theodora means in Latin, or maybe in Greek. We used to call her that—some of us—behind her back, naturally. The Gift."

"You didn't like her?"

Emma stared into space for a moment. "The longer she's been dead, the more I've come to chastise myself for not having just enjoyed her more. But for about five years I had to be with her almost every minute, and that put quite a strain on any propensity I might have had toward adoration, let alone perspective."

"You were around her more of the time than, say, Una?"

"Una? Do I have to talk about Una? That *will* be depressing." She grinned, offered him a chocolate from a little round box tied with a gold cord. He smiled, shook his head. She eyed the box for a moment, then put it down. "Una spent more actual time with Theo because she had to do everything for her. Letters, phone calls, appointments, chauffeuring, making drinks, and all that—and what a devious little creep she was. My work for Theo was on a different level. I had to crawl around the inside of her mind." She paused. "Writing for her was the hardest work I've ever done. I'll never again work in that kind of situation, writing for only one character—two, actually, Theo and her alter ego, Fanny Lou."

"You did most of it?"

"Theo and I did it together. We were a real sloppy act, but that's the way she operated. She'd wake up in the middle of the night and make little notes. Or she'd have a few too many drinks and make little notes. Or she'd be making love to some guy and make little notes in her head. Which she would later dictate to Una. Then she'd bring me all the little notes. She'd have forgotten the exact point of them. 'It was in my unconscious,' she'd say. 'We've got to find out what I meant.' When we finally did, it was usually something usable, sometimes eminently usable, occasionally staggering." She stared off into space again. "She was very talented. I've never believed she committed suicide. She may have thought about it. God knows, we've all thought about it. But in Theo's case, only the knowledge that she had a fatal illness would have led her down to that river that night."

"Do you think someone knocked her off?"

She shrugged. "I mean, but who?"

"Was she a good swimmer?"

Emma seemed to hesitate. "I guess so." She frowned. "I really don't remember."

"And in your case? When you thought about it?"

"Swimming?"

"Suicide. You said we all have."

"Hey." She finally took a chocolate. "Is that relevant?"

"Try me."

"My heart was broken."

"Sorry." His glance of sympathy was sincere. "Did you get over him?"

"Her." She smiled. "I've been gay since I was three. Theo was never quite comfortable with that aspect of me. Sometimes she'd look at something I'd written and say, "I don't understand how you can write for me so well when the published fact is you hate men."

"Do you?"

"It's more complicated than that. Or maybe less complicated. Aren't we getting off the track?"

He opened his little notebook. "The script she wrote. The film she wanted to make. You have anything to do with that?"

"Who told you about it?"

"Her widower."

"Darling Robert."

"You didn't like him either."

She picked up a pencil, fiddled with it. "I don't know."

"You'd be hell on a witness stand, Miss Grace. The words *yes* and *no* don't seem to be in your vocabulary."

"I suppose Robert also told you that the script vanished?"

"Did it?"

"Some of my best stuff ever was in that script. We wrote it all at the Russian River, that last summer. It was still in progress when she died. I asked Robert for it. I said I wanted my material back, it was only fair. He told me to ask Una, that he'd put her in charge of all Theo's papers that had to do with her work."

"And?"

"Una claimed she didn't have it, that it wasn't in the boxes that were in storage. She was lying, of course. I spoke to Robert about it again. He wasn't very helpful. He asked me what was he supposed to do, confront Una and accuse her of lying? It wasn't real important to Robert. He couldn't connect with the fact that a lot of my life's blood was in that script. I had my agent call. Then he called Gibbons, her agent. Nothing worked."

"How do you know Una was lying?"

"She was a crack secretary and never lost a piece of paper in her life. In fact, I saw her personally typing the script on Theo's new typewriter before I left to go down to L.A. She had the only existing copy."

"What is your allegation?"

"She wanted the material for herself."

"Why?"

"Because she's like a dog with a bone about every goddamn little thing. Maybe she had fantasies. Maybe she planned to eventually pass some of the material off as her own." Emma put her head in her hands. "I can't tell you how it frosts me. The particular way we wrote that, I mean we wrote it out loud, so to speak, Theo and I, day after day, talking it out, acting it out, and we'd call Una in to take it down. I had a couple of monologues in there I'd give anything to have back— the thing is, in writing comedy, in writing anything, that first burst of inspiration, it's incredible how it can elude you later if you try to recreate it. For example, one of the longer bits was based on the idea that the two most famous characters in literature created by women are Frankenstein's monster and Peter Rabbit. I took that idea and I ran with it and the way I sequenced it was what held it together and you know what? I've tried a dozen times to recover that inner sequencing and it's gone." She looked at him. "Sorry. I know that's boring."

"Let's have a chocolate."

She smiled and handed him the box.

"When's the last time you saw Una?" he continued.

"At the Russian River. Theo's second to last day. Senator White gave me a ride into the city and then I went straight to the airport to go to L.A., which is basically where I live. My later conversations with Una—about the script—took place on the telephone."

"What do you remember about your last day at the river?"

Emma sighed. "As you said, I'd make a terrible witness. I remember things only impressionistically."

"Who was there?"

"Theo. Me. Una. The housekeeper was off for a few days, so we just had someone who came in for a few hours in the morning. The senator. And a guy called Barrett Rossignol."

"What can you tell me about White's relationship with Theo?"

"It couldn't have been more banal. He was drawn to show biz. She was drawn to power."

"Now, this Rossignol. What was he doing there?"

"Fucking Una, mostly."

Jacklin tried to hide his surprise. So he'd been on the wrong track. But this new one might lead him home just as neatly.

"How long had he been there?"

"About a month. Theo flew him in from the East Coast. They'd grown up together, had a special relationship, she said. I never saw anything too special about it, let alone healthy, but I didn't mention that to Theo. Live and let live."

"What do you mean?"

"Theo had a lot of fantasies she simply wouldn't let go of. This happens more to famous people than most because without being conscious of it, they pay people to assist in perpetrating those fantasies. She was pushing forty, she'd ended yet another relationship with a man, she had a wildly successful career which she was frustrated over, she couldn't find anyone she wanted to be in love with, and she'd decided Rossignol was probably her best friend in the world. And it's true that anything that Theo wanted, Barrett did. Barrett was a study in responsible adoration. Meanwhile, he and Una were having it off. Upstairs, downstairs, in the garage, back of the house, underwater, in the backseat of the car, you name it."

"Tell me more about Barrett."

"You want Peter Pan or Dorian Gray?"

"Are there others?"

"Billy Budd. Elvis. Heathcliff."

"A multiple personality?"

"That's what he's not." She looked at her watch. "I forgot I had to change. I could dress in there." She indicated the bedroom. "And we could yell back and forth to each other." She was already taking off her shoes.

He smiled. "Hit it, kid."

She walked to the bedroom and disappeared. "A multiple personality is involuntary. Barrett isn't a host to a lot of different people with different voices. Barrett is nothing. I studied him. I was fascinated. Can you hear me?"

"You're doing great."

"He's great company. The best. He's whatever you want him to be. It's like being with yourself under the most ravishing of circumstances. Or with the person you always wanted to meet but who didn't yet exist. Barrett would be that for you. He's so brilliant at it, you just don't bloody know what's going on."

"How did *you* know?" Jacklin got up, picked up a straight chair, moved closer to the bedroom door, sat down.

"I guess partly because there wasn't the sex thing between us and partly because being a writer, I pay attention. Being with him was like looking in the most flattering of mirrors. Not that he didn't bring fresh gifts of his own. He was damned intelligent and could be very funny."

She now appeared wearing a different T-shirt, gold sandals, and a big glitzy flower in her hair. "I don't say this lightly." She paused. "I believe Barrett is the most tragic character I've ever known."

"Why?"

"I told you. There is no Barrett. I don't think even Barrett thinks there's a Barrett."

"It seems to me," Jacklin replied, "he's made some very shrewd choices."

"Not choices. He's never made a clear choice in his life. What he does is commit last-ditch, desperate acts."

"What do you think makes him tick?"

"Fear."

"Of what?"

"Fear there is no Barrett."

She went to one of the shopping bags, rummaged in it, took out a little box, opened it, removed a pair of earrings from tissue paper.

"You think he might have killed Theo?" Jacklin asked. "Not premeditated, but, let's say, in passion?"

Emma laughed. "Passion requires commitment. Obsession. Love and hatred in a combination that's so overpowering that an extreme act is the only choice. Excuse me for lecturing you; of course you know stuff like that."

"But I don't know Barrett."

"Passion simply isn't in Barrett's portfolio. If he's on your suspect list, you might as well wipe him off." She began to screw on her new earrings. "Why should Barrett kill Theo when ultimately it didn't matter to him whether she lived or died? The only person Barrett ever worried about dying was himself."

"What were he and Theo like together?"

"They had their own little universe. They pretended the world hadn't turned out the way it had. They were children together. In fact—"

"This may be a naïve question, I just don't know where the hell I am. Did they sleep together?"

"He spent time in her room. The assumption was, yes, they did."

"How did Una feel about this?"

"As the summer went by, he spent much more time in her room." She looked at him and smiled. "You're going to ask me what Theo thought about that. She didn't know."

"How is it possible she didn't know?"

"You don't know Barrett." She looked at her watch. "And now I have to go." She held out her hand. "Call me whenever. The L.A. number will always reach me eventually."

As they shook hands he saw her examining him curiously. Caught, she grinned. "I've never met a private eye. You're really cool, you know?"

"It's been a pleasure," he said gallantly. And meant it.

Going down in the elevator, Jacklin was already beginning to figure out how much his theories had been shaken by Emma's theory. Emma had nothing to gain either way, by protecting Barrett or damaging him. As a lesbian, she would have had no designs on him. What she had produced for him just now was character analysis, not proof of any kind, but it was looking as if this time his own instinct had failed him. Compared to Emma's, his analysis might have been hasty, possibly overly subjective.

He walked through the small lobby. A heroic-sized arrangement of fresh flowers. The bejeweled, expensively scented sound of Italian, French, and Los Angeles. At least two security men discreetly placed, in really terrible herringbone suits. He went through the revolving doors and nodded at the immaculately fitted out doorman.

He decided to walk home. On the way he would think about the missing script. It was only a detail, but it would occupy his time while at another level he pulled himself together. Once he got home, instead of discounting Emma's opinions and searching for ways to refute them in order to preserve the legitimacy of his own hunch, he would see if he could incorporate them into the overall picture. Mix them around. Maybe something would jump out at him.

At the hotel Emma was herself now descending in the elevator. It stopped at the fourth floor. A theatrical-looking woman, immensely tall, with a fur draped over one bony, powdered shoulder, stepped in. Emma eyed her. There was something that didn't quite parse. Emma looked harder. Was she possibly a transsexual? The elevator reached the lobby. Emma, watching the woman slink across it, remembered something she had been about to tell the detective before she had been distracted by something else. It wasn't important, it was just that in detective work, as she knew, a single detail could work as a bridge between one seemingly isolated element and another.

If Jacklin called her in L.A.—or maybe she should try to remember to call him—she would tell him how Theo and Barrett had, in fun, one rainy weekend, cooked up an impersonation of Theo by Barrett. Barrett had been fantastic. Theo, delighted at having spawned this living duplicate of herself, would call on it sometimes in the evenings to entertain herself. She would command a performance. In preparation she and Barrett spent hours at a time picking clothes, wigs, songs. She made him listen to her records. She coached him, insisting on perfection.

What Barrett thought about all this was anybody's guess. Did he like putting on shows for one, at the most two or three, at the Russian River? Dressing up like a woman? It seemed so bizarre now. In the context of those days it hadn't at all. The Russian River was like location, it had its own exclusive cosmology. And who ever knew what Barrett thought anyway?

One night she had heard Barrett on the telephone talking to someone who apparently, she realized as she shamelessly listened, was his girlfriend in New York. Even forgetting about Una, what kind of girlfriend would let a guy spend a month with Theo Buckley? Emma decided to tell Barrett she had heard the conversation. He then told her he'd told the girlfriend that he was spending the month helping an uncle in the logging business, and that he was up at a camp with no telephone and he could only call her once a week when he went into town.

He explained to Emma that he'd created this masquerade because he'd hoped that what Theo had had in mind in bringing him out west was to arrange acting parts for him in the movies. He'd arrived to find it wasn't that at all, she only wanted a courtier. He told Emma that his girlfriend in New York was getting suspicious and was demanding that he come back, and meanwhile Una was getting so possessive, he was afraid she was going to make trouble.

Poor bastard. Emma went through the revolving doors. The Russian River seemed so long ago. Talking about it just now had brought back the whisper of the trees, the sound of the rain. She'd loved Theo, wildly, desperately. Theo had known, she had been generous, she had been immaculate. And one day Emma had got over it. Ah, well.

She nodded at the doorman, stepped into the back of the waiting car.

The following day Jacklin had an appointment with Father Jerry Donovan. They were to meet in Central Park. "If you don't mind," Jerry had said on the telephone. "I'm supervising a softball game at four. If we meet at three-thirty?" There was a slight pause. "I doubt I have any information you don't already know."

Jacklin watched the tall, craggy man in the jeans and a purple T-shirt walk toward him. He knew instantly it was Donovan. Not so much a physical resemblance to Hal and Jane, but there was a family air, a family walk, what the hell was it?

"Now I've met you all." Cordially Jacklin shook hands with Jerry. He saw Jerry was giving him the once-over. Priests and doctors. First thing they always did was check out your eyes. "Shall we walk?"

They fell into step. "Your brother, Hal, told me you'd got quite close to Barrett Rossignol."

"Doing what I do, I get close to a lot of people. As I imagine you do."

"I get near, Father, but rarely close." Why had he said that? Jerry gave him a quiet, searching look.

Jacklin continued. "I guess you know he's disappeared. Has he contacted you?"

"No."

"Would you let me know if he does?"

"Probably not. Your objective, I gather, is to clear Senator White of any involvement in Theo Buckley's death. Do you have any proof that anyone *was* involved?"

"With respect, Father Donovan, our time is so short, do you mind if I ask the questions?"

"It seems to me that Barrett has been gratuitously persecuted."

"Why did he run, then?"

"Could we say he may have needed some peace from you people?"

Holy shit. Maybe the priest was hiding Barrett. Throughout history Jesuits had done as they damned pleased.

"Could we say," Jerry continued, "he has every right to disappear if he so chooses? There are no charges against him."

Irritably Jacklin came back with "His whole life is a pack of lies."

"Is it?" Again Jerry gave Jacklin the once-over.

They were passing a bench. Jacklin sat down on it, stretched his legs, examined his shoes. Jerry looked down at him silently.

Finally looking up, Jacklin said, "Could we start over? First, I didn't create this investigation, I agreed to conduct it. Second, it's my responsibility to talk to everyone who is connected to it. Third, I went to Catholic school. The nuns beat me with sticks, forced me to write with my right hand when I am actually left-handed, and every week the priest at confession asked me if I had been masturbating. I have a horror of the church, the saints, the incense. As it happens, this is the first time I've had to question someone of the cloth, and apparently I'm so freaked I'm not handling it well."

Jerry sat down beside Jacklin, crossed his legs. "Okay. Let's start over."

But it didn't work. Jacklin (who had been reared without benefit of any formal religion and who had never talked to a nun or a priest except occasionally on an airplane) realized after a few minutes that nothing was going to work with Jerry, not confession, not charm, not man-to-man stuff. Jerry was clearly offended by the investigation. He would be polite, he would be adroit, and if he was hiding Barrett, there was no way on earth Jacklin was going to be able to catch him out.

18

Barrett stared into the darkness. That bitch, Una. How many times had he dreamed of burying her? He wanted to beat his fists on the pillow, kick his legs, howl. But he lay still, so as not to disturb the sleeping figure beside him. He had bothered that body enough, taken enough liberties for one night. Now he had been lying awake for hours. Trapped in his boiling mind.

Thinking about the past always provoked the very feelings he could least tolerate. His separateness, his terrible sadness. He had kept so many secrets, told so many lies, there had never been anyone with whom he could share the tatters of what had gone before.

Some people were lucky. The Donovans, for instance. Look at them. Jane, Hal, Jerry. They had everything. They strolled through life, choosing what was theirs. The Donovans would always take the winning cup.

Actually, that wasn't entirely fair to Jane.

But he didn't want to think about Jane! He made a

picture in his head. He squirted Jane's face with black ink until she was obliterated. And now he wanted desperately to stroke, just for a minute, the flesh of the body beside him, if only to feel the warmth. His fingers were so cold. His mother had had the same thing. Cold extremities. He would die young, he knew it, he had always known it. Death. His mother, bony, bald, weeping. Theo, half buried in the rich silt of the Russian River.

Would he die in this bed? On cheap, no-iron sheets? In the darkness there was no one to see his self-mocking smile. His women had educated him in little luxuries. Theo had loved satin. Sara had used only cotton. Jane had antique linens. She had down pillows, and everything done in hand-worked lace.

He touched the cheap, papery synthetic blanket, drew it closer around his shoulders, turned on his side. The moon, plump and cold, had appeared from behind the clouds and flooded the room with imperious light. Barrett eyed the impassive globe through the thin curtains. Like a woman, the moon gazed back at him. He closed his eyes.

Una. The fucking irony of it. She was going to destroy him. She had promised she would. Then the years had gone by and he had slowly allowed himself to be lulled into a sense of security, until she had turned up in New York at The Touch Me Club that night. And he was sure she'd been the one who had sent the anonymous letter.

The fucking irony. She had been an aside. A light lunch on the road. He was now smeared with it—and her. He had made the biggest mistake of his life, thinking so little of her, this crass young mariner, this shadow of Theo, this basically unimportant, sick person. The horror was that he had shown more of himself to her than he ever had to anyone. He had not moni-

tored his performance. She hadn't been worth the effort, she didn't count. She was Theo's secretary. A ser-
vant. Like himself.

He groaned aloud. The body next to him stirred, was
still again. Okay, Theo hadn't treated him like a ser-
vant, but he'd felt like one. He never told her that he
had gone out there expecting that she would introduce
him to an agent and launch him on his career. How
could he have been so naïve? Instead, at her court he
had been half man, half retriever. A beloved jester—in
high heels and pearls. And in off moments, in order to
assuage his pride, he had trashed Theo to Una, had
begun making love to Una, to prove to Una—who
didn't matter except as release and receptacle—that he
had a magic cock, a magic spirit, and was the fairest
man in all the kingdom.

When Theo was away he had made love to Una in
Theo's bed, on Theo's bedroom rug. Like servants.
Loathing himself, but more and more addicted to the
infernal relationship, he told Una things about Theo,
coloring them so as to put himself in the best of lights
and Theo in the most selfish and venal. Every day at the
Russian River he awoke ashamed, and vowed he would
stop this vicious betrayal of Theo. By the time noon
came, he would have done it again. Like an alcoholic
taking the first drink of the day and thus determining
the downward spiral of the rest of it. Impossible to turn
over the promised new leaf until tomorrow. Which
meant never.

Una came quickly to worship the ground he walked
on. They became a cabal of two behind Theo's generous back. Barrett craved sex with Una as intermittent
relief from Theo's expectations of him, of everyone.
With Una he could do anything he wanted. Anything.

The result of his treachery was that on that horrific
day Theo had had to die. His eyes filled with tears of

rage and self-pity. He continued to weep silently. Una would not find him here.

Toward dawn he fell asleep. When he awoke an hour later to a blunt invitation from the body next to him, he realized in the moment that he touched his mouth to the new place that he had been interrupted in the middle of a dream. A woman dressed in white linen, radiant with sunshine behind her, had come into the room. She had come to the edge of his bed, gently stroked his forehead. "You can come home now, Barrett," she had said. He thought it had been Jane.

But now his brain was swollen with his sex and his own astonishing glory, and the woman in white passed into memory. He entered the body beside him. He could exist as long as he could have this. This. This.

19

Senator White and Hal waited. Jacklin had not checked in for several days. Meanwhile someone in the press had got wind of the private investigation. The particular journalist had always been friendly to the senator, so when he made his inquiry, Hal called him.

"Give us a break, will you?" He sent around a case of good wine.

Barrett had become a needle in a haystack, and Jacklin didn't have the manpower to trace him, but more than that, he was intrigued by the growing number of people he'd met who were reluctant to believe Barrett was capable of murder. He decided he should go back over his course to reassure himself, and in the process look for what he might have missed.

His half-hour with Jerry had shaken him. Had it been his imagination, or did Father Donovan condemn him because he was hunting a man for money, possibly an innocent man, a man who Jane Donovan thought was good enough to take into her house, her bed, her life? Did Father Donovan think less of him because he supposedly came from the dark, corrupt world of shadowy people who put cash prices on others' heads? Jacklin had marked the priest's intelligence and humanity and had been set back by his cool if polite dismissiveness.

Of course, if you were a Jesuit and also a Donovan, it gave you certain inalienable rights. Like judging, from on high, mortals of a lesser sensibility. No class system in America, my ass. And that was okay, Jacklin had no particular beef against that; society had always partitioned itself that way. But how had Barrett got to all these people? The priest, whether he was hiding Barrett or not, clearly wanted to protect him.

Protect a parasite who was not much better than a gigolo, but look down in contempt at a detective?

And what about the moment that had hurt? Jacklin had seen the flash of "Oh, now I get it" in the priest's eyes when Jacklin had—foolishly—indicated his own dislike of Barrett, a man he had never met.

The uncomfortable truth was that Jacklin did indeed dislike Barrett. Barrett represented dangerous, underdeveloped emotions—sloth, perfidy, contempt. Barrett represented everything he himself might have become, perhaps any man might have become in that same society, in that same time. Jacklin and Barrett had been born within a few years of each other. They had grown up in the decade of assassinations, sexual revolution, napalm, the victory of television over daily life, and the decline of the family. Jacklin's father had also had a drinking problem, first as an Agency man, then as a private investigator, then as a total failure as a private investigator, and last as a certified loser who ran certain errands for the police. Jacklin's young life had been almost as transient and humiliating as Barrett's. His mother had left his father, simply disappeared. It had been, well, like that.

The personal sticking point for Jacklin in having to walk down Barrett's past had been the constant evidence of cupidity and promiscuity going back to when the other man had been a young teenager. "You'd think," an attractive grandmother from one of Barrett's many hometowns told one of Jacklin's stringers, "that cute dingus of his would have fallen off by now."

Behind the flash of Rossignol's conquests there was a spiritlessness that offended, but had he, Jacklin, the grieving, celibate widower of the girl with the long swinging hair, he with the limp that had erased forever his manly grace—had he come to despise Barrett Rossignol on the basis of what was perhaps an excessively finicky and unforgiving set of standards?

And had he allowed this to get in the way of his professional judgment?

Donovan had said something Jacklin would not forget. "The facts of anyone's life are not always reliable information."

Jacklin watched the fish in his tank. Back and forth. Back and forth. It *had* to be Barrett. Unless. Unless—

He decided to go to see Marly again. He walked the twenty-three blocks to her apartment. And began to count his own sins.

He was not in reality the celibate widower he called himself to himself, except in his heart. During the period in which he had been Iskan's bodyguard she had said to him very casually one night, taking off her gloves, looking in the mirror, touching her beautiful throat, "Feel free, Ciaran. Why not, now and then? I belong to an old man. You, they tell me, lost your wife two years ago and still have no friend. You look so sad to me. And I am sad too sometimes."

She had walked across the living room of the Bombay hotel suite and into her bedroom, leaving the door open. She often did this, she had lived for years with so much staff around her, never alone, but that night he followed her through the door and locked it behind him.

Walking down Fifth Avenue to Marly's apartment, he remembered he had gone down on his knees in front of his wise, gracious, bejeweled lady and wrapped his arms around her body, filled with the anguish of his loss, his loneliness, his terrible anger, his despair, his wild hope that she might heal him.

Maybe Rossignol felt like that all the time, had felt like that all his days. Maybe that hope was the daily linchpin to his existence, to his survival. Maybe for Barrett that was all there was, ever had been.

At Marly's apartment he asked her, "Why didn't Barrett continue with his impersonation act?"

She was evidently not happy to see him. "I can't really remember."

He played a hunch. "Have you talked to him recently?"

She shook her head. "I told you. He went out of my life and that was that."

"But if he was so good at it, how come he didn't go on with it?"

"Listen, I don't know. And I really have to go. I have tables to wait."

He talked to the manager of The Touch Me Club. "It was quite a while ago," the man said, "but as I recall, he just didn't show up one night. Never even called to get his pay. We wouldn't have kept him anyway. He was good, but he had just that one impersonation. When he tried out I told him he had to have more and he said he'd work some up, but he never did."

Jacklin called Una in California, left a message on her answering machine, but did not hear back from her.

Despite the advice of her brothers to move back to the city, Jane remained in the country. Hal was worried about her, and every other day he found an excuse to call. Jerry also suggested that the options and distractions of city life were indicated at this point.

"I don't need to be distracted," Jane said. "I have my next book to plan, and really, I'm better off alone."

Every time she heard a car passing she thought, *That's Barrett coming home.* Every time the phone rang she thought, *That will be Hal telling me that the detective has solved his case and it was all a terrible mistake for Barrett ever to have been considered as a suspect.*

She fantasized that Barrett had left her because though innocent, he was frightened he would not be able to prove it. That he was not so innocent of other transgressions was something that could be taken care of when they were back together and he had regained his confidence. They loved each other, that was the main thing.

Logic was abandoned.

But there was no further sign. Waking one morning, she realized it had been a month since the iris had been left on the bedside table.

She no longer cared for night. She liked day. She relied on day to keep her going with some semblance of normality. During the day she could say to herself, "It will all be explained." During the long nights she was plagued with what she knew was the truth. Wherever Barrett was, he had cut her off.

Her sleep was so troubled now that when late one

night she heard the flapping of a screen, she remained for a moment in the minuscule clouded space between dreams and waking, between eyeball and eyelid.

A floorboard creaked. Her eyes flew open.

She heard footsteps in the dark hallway outside her bedroom. Her entire scalp went numb, and she actually felt the hair on her head stand up. She tried to move her hand, her arm, to the lamp, to the telephone. She could not. Her muddled brain flashed a message she could not comprehend: *Not Barrett! Not Barrett!*

The footsteps came closer. Whoever, whatever it was had now paused at the threshold of the bedroom. Jane could now make out the shape.

Holy Mother of God. Not Barrett, a woman. The figure stood very still in the doorway for a moment, then slowly glided across the carpet. She was coming toward the bed.

Inside Jane's brain another message suddenly began to flash: *I refuse to die like this!*

She threw off the covers, and as she jumped out of bed her hand shot out for the big flashlight she kept under the little bedside table in case of power failure. Miscalculating everything, she fell against the table, crashing to the floor with it as it overturned, but her hand was firmly holding the flashlight and she switched it on, aiming it at the figure, who for a split second remained frozen, blinded in the powerful beam.

Jane saw a slender woman with masses of red hair, grotesquely made up, wearing a shirt and loose trousers. In one hand she was holding a pair of red high-heeled shoes, in the other what looked like a lead pipe.

Jane heard herself screaming. The woman, disoriented by the flashlight, threw an arm up in front of her eyes, took a side step. Jane picked up the little bedside table, heaved it at the woman's chest. It hit her squarely. The woman grunted and staggered. She dropped the pipe in order to clutch quickly at her head. Also in the process, Jane had dropped the flashlight, but the woman had turned and was running toward the door. Jane picked up the little table again and went in a stumbling fashion after her. She heard herself screaming again. "Murderer!"

Jane ran into the hallway. Suddenly there was no sign of the woman. She heard a noise in the bathroom. A screen window banged. She retraced her steps, stepped into the bathroom, turned on the light just in time to see the last of the intruder slipping out of the window. Jane ran for the window and never got there. She felt the blood draining from her face, her neck, her shoulders. As she crumpled to the floor, she heard the sound of a car starting up, the motor being gunned, and then there was blackness.

When she opened her eyes it was dawn. She was relieved the nightmare was over. Slowly she raised herself from the cool tile of the bathroom floor. She felt a slight bump on her head. Her right elbow was very painful, but she got to her feet fairly easily. She walked toward the bedroom. She would find everything normal. She had had a nightmare and then walked in her sleep.

In the bedroom she saw first the splintered table on its side, then the overturned lamp and the books and the telephone that had fallen to the floor.

Nearby lay a pair of high-heeled red shoes. She looked around for the tire iron. She thought she remembered it thumping to the carpet, but she couldn't see it. She got down on her hands and knees, looked under the bed. The tire iron had rolled under it.

The local police, which consisted of one village patrolman who had a tiny office in the town hall and an answering machine, was ruffled and even suspicious at the delay in the reporting of the break-in at the Donovan residence. He had taken the details over the telephone and had interrupted sharply. "You say this happened twelve hours ago?"

He was somewhat reassured by the sight of the man in the priest's collar who opened the door and led him into a pretty living room to meet Jane Donovan. He now remembered having seen her around the village. She rose from the sofa and offered him her hand.

"I was muddled," she said. "Then I called my brother and he said he'd drive up from the city."

The patrolman looked her over. Attractive. Had had the house for about a year. There had been a good-looking man with her until recently.

"You said the assailant was a woman."

"Yes."

"Would you show me where it took place?"

Jane led the patrolman to the bedroom. He looked around carefully.

"I haven't touched anything," Jane said. She had put the high heeled red shoes away in the closet. She didn't know why. She wondered if she was going mad.

The patrolman stayed another twenty minutes, asked the remaining expected questions, then offered, "Ever since that fellow over in Taylor City started putting on those Sunday rock concerts, we've been having disturbances. Kids from far and wide come up here for the day with liquor and drugs, and after the concert they're all het up and they drive around these roads at ninety miles an hour and make trouble. You got a security alarm?"

When Jane nodded he said, "I'd keep it on nights. This was probably a one-time-only deal. Still, you'll feel safer."

He went off, carrying the tire iron. After saying good-bye, Jane returned to the living room.

Jerry was staring at the empty easel by the fireplace which had once held the watercolor he had painted of Jane and Barrett.

"I put it away this morning," Jane said dully, and sank into a chair. "Hal was right about Barrett. You and I, we believe in the tooth fairy, but Hal sees things the way they are."

"You really think it was Barrett?"

"What else can I think?"

"You didn't mention that to the policeman."

"Hal told me not to. He was going to call the detective and have his ass, he said, if he didn't find Barrett within the next forty-eight hours. He wants to—and I quote—'get a confession out of Barrett and hand the whole thing over to the police on a platter without either White or ourselves being involved except on the periphery.' "

"Posse mentality." Jerry was frowning. "It's been like a kangaroo court from the beginning. The fact is, nobody has a shred of proof."

"What would you consider last night?"

Jerry gave her a stubborn look. "Why would Barrett want to hurt you? And dress up as Theo to do it?"

"Possibly," Jane replied unsteadily, "because he's warped. Maybe he was in a similar rage at Theo Buckley."

"You're describing a monster. The fact is, I think he's a victim."

She looked coolly at him. "Someone who dresses up as a dead woman to murder another—would you call that sane?" She walked to the window and looked out. "I loved Barrett. When I began to realize there were serious problems, I thought I could make the difference. Make the bad angel into a good angel. But his genius for deflection is the most debilitating experience I've gone through. I mean, a lot of the time I was sure everything was my fault. I still catch myself doing it."

"And you still love him?"

After a moment she said, "If I ever stop believing in love, I'll never write another word, hope another hope, take another breath."

A few hours earlier Jacklin had decided—late in the game, he had to admit—that Una was more of a key figure than he had first thought. Should he go to California again? First he had better determine if she was there. She had not answered the several messages he had left. He placed a call to an operative in Los Angeles, told him to check out Una's place, and if she was out of town to find out where she had gone and when. He hung up the receiver and immediately the phone rang. It was Hal.

Jacklin listened, asked Hal several questions, then said, "I'll leave right now. Tell her she has to talk to me. Tell her she has to let me into the house."

"She's going away this afternoon. I want her out of there in case the crazy bastard comes back."

Jacklin fed the fish, picked his jacket off a chair, and left the apartment.

"I don't have much time," Jane said when she opened the door to Jacklin. "I'm packing, I'm closing the house, and really, I've gone over everything with Hal and the police—"

"Just a few questions. And if I could get a general lay of things."

She took him through the house, showing him the window in the bathroom, taking him into the bedroom last.

He noted the four windows in the bedroom, the

thick carpeting. The rest of the house had wide board floors. "You heard footsteps in the hallway?"

"Yes."

"Loud? That's what woke you?"

"No. First the screen window."

"At what point did he drop the tire iron?"

"I don't remember."

"Try."

"I think it was when I shone the flashlight into his face."

"You've had training in self-defense?"

"No."

"He had a tire iron. He had a surprised, defenseless woman. But he ran."

"Well, yes."

"You think it's possible he was just trying to scare you? That he never intended to hurt you?"

"Scare me? Why? He must have known that after something like that I'd call the police. Name him."

"But you haven't."

"Hal told me not to. He's explained all that to you, I'm sure."

"You were on the floor with only a flashlight in your hand. He had a weapon. Why would he give you time to shove that table into him?"

"I told you. He was disoriented." She paused. "Blinded."

"Think before you answer, please. Was there anything between you that would warrant him wanting to kill you? Do you know anything about him you haven't told anyone? That would warrant him trying to kill you for fear that you would?"

She turned away. "Relationships are more complicated than questions like that." After a moment she turned back. "We were lovers. We were friends." There came a long pause. "Maybe not friends. Look, I just can't." Her look begged him to go.

"I'm sorry." And he was. But he stood there, waiting.

She made an effort. "It's possible he thought I doubted his innocence."

"Do you?"

She hesitated. "It would be provocative to say yes, a lie to say no."

"Did he speak? Say anything?"

"No."

"Was he wearing gloves?"

"It was all so quick and I never saw him very well."

"Had he been back before? Since the separation?"

She hesitated. "Once I came home and found an iris on the nightstand. I keep a flower there usually, but I didn't remember having put one there that morning." She hesitated again. "That probably sounds fanciful, I know, wishing something to be so and then believing it."

"And why should you not?" he asked quietly, regarding her. She wore her passion for Rossignol as coolly as she could manage. As a player in what would soon be the shattering of her final illusions, the least he could do was to respect her rites of mourning and hope. "How might he have got in?"

"I don't know." She stared at him. "I didn't even think of it at the time. This had been his home."

"He kept his keys?"

"He left his set on his desk when he went away. There were other sets. I haven't looked to see if they're all there."

"Why not?"

"I left it to the gods. Because I'm a child and a fool."

He looked her over, saw she was spent, and said, "I'll get out of your hair."

Something made him stand there another moment. "You're not a child, not a fool," he said. "You're a player in a mystery. It looks to me like you're practiced at protecting yourself at levels that to others might seem merely magical."

This odd turn of phrase, along with its low-key compliment, its suggestive prescience, seemed to hold them as one. A few seconds went by.

"You understand things like that?" she asked. "That sometimes we just have to throw the dice in God's face?"

"You must have been very scared all this time."

"I thought, that is, until last night"—she tried to smile it away—"that if he came back, it would be to love me."

"You mean part of you thought."

"Yes." Curiously, she looked him over. "Part of me."

He watched her considering something.

"Mr. Jacklin." Jane went to the closet, opened it, took out the pair of red shoes. She handed them to him. "These were left on the carpet there, near the bed."

She waited for him to ask her why she hadn't told the police, but he didn't.

He was looking at the shoes. "Do you recall what Mr. Rossignol's shoe size was?"

"Nine and a half." She looked at him. "What size are those?"

"I'll have to find out what they're equivalent to in a man's size."

He drove into the village, found the only pay phone, and made several quick phone calls.

20

In Los Angeles that evening, Una sat on her white sofa, wrapped in the hair shirt of her hatred for Barrett. Over the years that had passed since the Russian River, she had gradually—and it had not been without pain and confusion—come to the decision that it would be best to let sleeping dogs lie. Theo could not be brought back from the dead. Barrett could not be regained.

It had seemed the only course, just to go on.

The appearance of Detective Jacklin had stirred everything up again. Seven years had gone by, but it was as if it had all happened yesterday. The greeny, lascivious smell of the breeze on the river was in her nostrils, tearing open her heart again.

She leaned forward to take a handful of peanuts from the Lucite bowl. She was damned if she'd answer any of Jacklin's messages on the answering machine. And Barrett be fucked. Since Theo's death, or, rather, since she had been forced to accept the reality of Barrett's having tricked her, she had gradually made a new life for herself, and really, it hadn't been so bad. It was certainly comfortable. Robert had given her a very handsome severance payment, which had allowed her to buy this apartment, and the retainer he paid her monthly was a security she had come to count on. Having been Theo's assistant for so long gave her a cachet that continued to bring her intermittent, highly lucrative jobs. And Emma had not bothered her except for her initial outrage and threats over the script. That fucking script. Her own generous gift of it to Barrett. She had slipped it into his duffel bag at the last moment, so he would have a surprise. Something to remember her by while he was back east. He'd told her he wanted to be a writer. You and me, babe, he'd said.

When a few years ago Robert had mentioned he'd seen an impersonator and had described the act, she had flown to New York in a white heat and gone to The Touch Me Club. She had stood in the back, watching, then she had gone backstage. When he saw her he went white. She hissed, "I'm going to the manager. I'm going to tell him you stole this material from the estate of Theo Buckley. I'm going to tell Robert, and he'll sue you. I'm going to tell Emma."

Why had she cared what he did with his life now? Why had she gone there?

She knew, of course. To turn, once again, the screw in her heart. To make him hurt. To frighten him, which she knew she still could. His mouth had turned ugly, and he had reviled her, but she knew the minute she left he would turn tail and run. It wasn't until she was on the plane coming back that she remembered that with Barrett one never really won. He was a closer of invisible doors.

At the Russian River, with Theo freshly dead, her red hair entangled in the great tree's roots, Barrett had looked right through Una. She could still feel the icy chill of it, the horror. He had used her, tricked her. And now he was going to ditch her.

He had told her his friendship with Theo was an effort, a burden, a duty. She remembered him explaining, on the morning after their first night together. "Theo needs me," he said. "I can't deny her."

"What about last night? What about me?" she had asked in her blunt way. His gaze had traveled slowly around her mouth, as if he were outlining it. She thought she would die. They exchanged a look suffused with the fresh heat of the night before. Una had not, somehow, expected from someone so poetic and sensitive-looking a carnal menu of such demanding proportions.

In the days that followed their seduction of each other, surprise would quickly give way to addiction. She would be his. He would be hers. The lustful, fiercely exacting Barrett would belong to her. She, who had never had anything of value to speak of, only a shitty growing-up marked with illness and disappointment. Plus that breakdown when she was sixteen and that place she'd had to live at for a year where they'd given her a lot of tests and the custodian had regularly abused her—it all seemed so unreal now. Surviving that —it was survive or die—she had crawled hand over hand across the country, through day jobs, night jobs, in constant anxiety and humiliation and tedium.

She had had no fun. None at all. She had learned to type and to scheme, but neither seemed of much avail until one day she had been sent out to do some extra typing for Theo Buckley's personal assistant. A month later she had been called back for three days. During the course of this she had had to drive Theo here and there and Theo had inquired about her life and Una had more or less told her. She didn't like Theo feeling sorry for her; she didn't like anyone feeling sorry for her, but she knew having the ear of someone who merely had to wave a wand would benefit her, and it did. Within six months she had replaced the assistant. Soon she was wearing nice clothes and didn't have to ride the bus anymore—she had her own car.

And now she'd been given the shimmering reward. Barrett.

He was in charge of every move, every second. She would have died for him. He convinced her they should keep their affair secret for a time. And in the beginning it had heightened the excitement. Coming around the corner of the deck one morning, carrying a sheaf of papers in one hand, she ran into him coming the other way. He made her stop and stood there examining her up and down in that way he had. He took her free hand, placed it on his crotch. He asked with a low, caressing laugh, "Want to be a dirty girl? A filthy girl?"

She felt the wetness between her legs, and her desire was great. Then there were footsteps on the deck. Theo. A snowy white towel wrapped around her head in a turban. Large black sunglasses. A vodka and tonic. Ten o'clock in the frigging morning.

"Barrett," Theo said, "let Una get on with her work and come and talk to me. I have to blow-dry my hair and you can help me with the back bits. I'm so exhausted I could die." She turned and stalked off.

As soon as she had turned her back, Barrett continued quietly to Una. "Touch it. Take it out. No one will see."

But Una was now displeased. "Why do you have to do everything she says?"

"If I don't, she'll send me away." He stroked her arm. Up and down. Up and down. "Then you and I wouldn't be able to be together."

His logic was irrefutable. At least for now. But Una

had already begun to dream of a future in which they would leave Theo and be together always.

Thinking of those days now, Una felt again the terrible panic and rage that sometimes engulfed her and left her helpless and out of control. Last summer she had hit a woman in a restaurant. Slapped her in the face, she didn't even want to remember why, she only remembered how angry she had been. She got out of it without charges, with the right lawyer one could always do that, but it had cost.

She took another sip of vodka. In a minute she would have some more cocaine. But was there anything that would stop the pain? Even if by some lucky chance Barrett would die and release her, she would still have to carry around for the rest of her life the infernal burden of what he had done to her.

Just before midnight her buzzer rang. She got up unsteadily from the sofa and went to the intercom.

"Who is it?" It had to be a mistake. It was late and she wasn't expecting anyone. She had no friends anyway. She spent her days shopping for silk blouses in different colors or lying in the sun on the blazing roof-deck of her building.

A man's voice crackled through the speaker. "Una? It's Robert. Sorry, but it's important."

What the hell did he want? What was he doing in Los Angeles? If she'd been sober, she might have asked him, might have understood it had to be trouble. Instead, she pushed the button that would open the gates and went to the kitchen for more ice, leaving the door ajar so he could come in. A few minutes later she heard it open. She called out from the kitchen. "Want a drink?"

"No thanks" came the voice. Something was wrong. It wasn't Robert. She ran into the living room.

It was the detective, Jacklin. He smiled apologetically. "You didn't answer my messages."

He was looking down at her suitcase, which was propped up in the entry, ready to go down to the storage locker in the morning. "You've been away. Have a nice trip?" He himself was holding a small bag. Not that green canvas one he'd come with the first time. This one was cheap black vinyl.

The surprise had sobered up Una. "As you see"—she indicated her short beige silk robe—"I'm ready for bed. Call me tomorrow."

"As you wish." He indicated the black vinyl bag. "Can I leave this with you?"

She eyed it. "What's in it?"

He placed it on her coffee table, unzipped it. "These," he said. He took out a pair of red high-heeled shoes. He dangled them from his fingers for a moment and then let them drop to the thick beige carpeting at her feet.

Una stared down at the shoes. They had found Barrett and believed his story.

She glanced at Jacklin. "I gather this is some kind of joke. You're waiting for a reaction." She crossed to the sofa, picked up her drink, lit a cigarette. "Sorry to disappoint you. Now, get the hell out of here real quick or I'll call the police."

"They're already here," Jacklin said. "There are two officers outside your front door."

Una sat down, looked up at Jacklin. She was frowning slightly, but not, as far as Jacklin could see, afraid.

"The shoes mean nothing to me, but obviously you think they should. So I guess I know what this is about. I thought about coming clean with you the first time you were here, but I was afraid you wouldn't believe me. It's obvious you've talked to Barrett and he's done what he always threatened to do, pin Theo's murder on me. I'm the only one who knows he did it. I kept it to myself because Barrett told me if I said anything, he'd make sure I was the one who'd end up in the electric chair. I didn't need to think that one over too long. I mean, look how far he's got in life just by wagging his tail. I'd fry and he'd go free. I knew that."

She stubbed out her cigarette, took some peanuts. Those golden days she'd had with Barrett were the only real happiness she'd ever had. Her throat contracted. *Don't think about that, save yourself. Give it one more try.* Might as well go down fighting. What else had she ever done but fight?

"I guess you can get me for concealing knowledge of a crime, but—and naturally I already looked into this— I can claim threat and intimidation on the part of Barrett, can't I?"

Jacklin continued to regard her gravely. He had to get a confession. There were no policemen outside.

"Una," he said quietly. "I'm going to show you a copy of the sales slip for those shoes. I'm going to show you a copy of your American Express receipt for your quick trip east, from which you returned only this afternoon. I'm going to show you a receipt for the car you rented. I'm going to show you a warrant to search this apartment." He had none of these. "And I'm going to tell you why you dressed up to look like Barrett impersonating Theo and broke into Jane Donovan's house to make her—and everyone—think he was a killer, that he had murdered Theo and that now he was after Jane." He paused. "Or maybe you'd like to tell me in your own words."

Una stared down at the shoes, but she wasn't seeing them, she was seeing the long way she had come to this moment. To this. For what?

For Barrett. Why? Why? The answer had been so clear. But now there was no sound anywhere in the world. She floated through an empty universe. Alone, always alone. Sometime later she would go to jail, perhaps die. For what?

For Barrett.

"You jest." Theo, a big white flower tucked behind her ear, sat in the little rowboat facing Una. One tanned, ringless hand trailed in the sun-dappled water. She gave Una a good-humored look. "*You* and Barrett?"

Una, cock-proud, nodded. "Summer's over. He's going back east. I'm going with him. Thanks for everything."

Those were the words she had rehearsed, but she sensed something was wrong, terribly wrong. It was in the way Theo was looking at her. She had expected, relished the idea of the older woman's jealousy and rage, but not this, not this contemplative, searching gaze.

It was deadly quiet on the river. It often happened at this time of day. Not a splash, not a shout, just the silent, moving weight of the water. Una, never loved in her life until Barrett, Una, punished, abused, reviled, incarcerated, and rejected, had at last come into her own. Wanted. *Wanted* by Barrett. So why was Theo looking at her like that?

"Apparently you haven't discussed this with him."

Una stared across at the goddess. The bare bronzed shoulders, the tiny string of pearls, the rich shine of those eyes. Una began to feel the beat of the pulse in her own neck.

With one hand Theo shaded her eyes from the sun. She examined the girl with concern. "If he's led you on, I'm sorry, Una."

"*You're* sorry? Who the fuck are *you*? You don't want to believe that I got him, do you? That I drive him out of his mind, do you?"

Theo sighed. "Barrett doesn't love you."

Una's young life, dark and shameful, always hidden from the light, had come crawling up her spine. *Barrett not love her?*

"Una, honey, I'll try to explain." The goddess went on talking and looking at her in that terrible way, but black rage had flooded Una. She was standing up now, one oar grasped in both hands. She swung it in a deliberate, murderous arc toward Theo's head.

Theo ducked and it missed. She jumped up, lunged at Una, trying to wrest the oar from her. They both lost their footing and went over into the water.

Theo hit the river broadly, face down, and disappeared instantly beneath the surface. Una, a confident swimmer, treaded water and waited. It wasn't very deep there, she knew, but probably deep enough. She looked up- and downriver so she could keep an eye on whether there was anyone around. No one was.

Suddenly she felt something grasp her ankle, but it could have been a floating clump of river grass. She yanked her foot away and swam a few feet to a fresh spot. The midday sun filtered through the great trees and thousands of sparkly little lights danced on the river.

It wasn't her fault. She hadn't even meant to do it, it had just happened, and why should she care? It was too late now, anyway.

She saw the boat had drifted into a curve in the bank. She waited another few minutes and then swam to the bank and walked out of the water. She noticed there were scratches on her right ankle that looked like fingernails. Behind her the river rippled smoothly by.

Jacklin watched her. It had been quick work after all. The rest of it might take the night, but he had his answer in her face. She had taken off the red shoes as soon as she had entered Jane's house, in order not to make too much noise on the bare, wide floorboards before she found her way to Jane's bedroom. Her plan had been to wake and frighten Jane and then run; she had not anticipated the fight Jane would put up, or that the shoes would be left behind.

"I'm sorry, Una," he said.

No way out. Well, fuck it. Dry-eyed, she faced him. "People like Barrett should have to pay. But they don't, do they? They never do." She stood up, hurled her glass into the fake fireplace. "Bloodsucker!" she said under her breath. She began to tremble. She couldn't stop. And she began to rock herself.

She stood there rocking, hugging herself, and Jacklin remembered reading somewhere that in a study they had done of orphans at a Paris institution, ninety-five percent of the children, when left on their own, rocked.

Jacklin crossed to her, put an arm around her shoulder, sat her on the sofa. *I am patting the hand of a murderess. In a moment she'll have her head on my shoulder and will weep for a long time, but what the fuck else am I supposed to do at a moment like this— take notes? Put on handcuffs? Pretend I don't know what it's like to be in hell and have nobody? I don't have to like her to be sorry for her.*

She had begun to cry. He held her against his shoulder and thought about what was ahead. The call to Hal Donovan and Senator White. He had telephoned them from the airport before leaving New York and they were awaiting confirmation of Una's admission of guilt. White had given him the private number of a highly placed and discreet officer in the Los Angeles police force who was also expecting his call and could be counted on to take over the official handing over of the situation to yet another discreet official at homicide. The idea was not to have White's name or the Donovans' show up in the newspapers in connection with the situation any sooner than necessary, and even then at the barest minimum that was possible. Given the traditional exchange of favors between people in power and those in the press, and given the fact that although the woman Una had murdered was famous, she herself was a nobody, the prognosis, White felt, was favorable. The press would be invited to concentrate yet again on Theo herself and the deranged assistant who all these years later had confessed to her murder.

Jacklin listened to the terrible sound of Una's sobs. He continued to hold her hand. Restraints would not be necessary. At twenty-eight, Una was at the end of the line.

21

Jane went to the Ganges, to the Danube, to the Tagus. She did not come home for several months. Possibly she was waiting for a sign. None came. She felt much of the time as if the inner linings of her body were still dripping with blood. *Did he love me?* she asked herself in taxis, on foreign streets, in her bed at night.

Who was he? Who was he really?

She began to understand she had two choices. To continue to impale herself indefinitely on this point of anguish or to—as the world put it—"get over it." She considered the latter. *In order to get over it,* she said to herself in some puzzlement, *evidently one has first to believe that what it was is no longer worthy of being passionate about. How can I turn my back on feelings that were so powerful?*

In Madrid she ran into Jacklin. She was coming out of the Palace Hotel and he was just entering. She didn't, in fact, see him; it was he who touched her wrist and in a somewhat constrained manner said hello.

She was very surprised and thought he looked quite different, younger, or at least more relaxed, though perhaps the only difference was the pair of black sunglasses. Or the slightly longer hair. No tie. Dressed for vacation.

"I'm only here until tomorrow afternoon," he told her. "Do you know people? I mean, could we do something together, something you haven't seen? I know my way around fairly well."

Knowing he would be gone in less than twenty-four hours made it possible for her to agree to meet him the next morning. "I haven't been to the big Sunday morning market," she said.

"The Rastro."

"Yes. And I should take a look at the Plaza de Oriente."

"Pick you up at eight sharp." He looked at her for another moment, then lightly touched her wrist again and went inside the hotel.

In the slate-gray morning they walked through the deserted, stately, and derelict streets to the plaza.

"How is it you know Madrid?" she asked.

"I spent a moment of my childhood here. My father, in one of his last spurts of sobriety, was posted to the embassy, which is where they often stash Agency people."

"The Agency is the CIA? So one could say you followed in the direction of the family profession. Did you learn a lot from him?"

"I learned a lot from inhabiting his world." He took her arm and they crossed a street. "Worlds, I should say. There was a rapid progression downward, first some years of intermittent private jobs, and then the inevitable disintegration. After Spain I must have lived in fifteen American cities before I was seventeen."

"You still speak some Spanish, I imagine?"

"I know five crucial sentences in just about every language there is. Someone once convinced me that it was the responsibility of all of us today to be able to do that."

"Who?"

"A woman I worked for. I was her bodyguard for a year and we went everywhere in the world. We became friends and she taught me a lot."

"Tell me." The agate sky, the prideful, soot-veined buildings enclosed them as they walked the damp, early streets, the only two people as far as the eye could see.

Tell her about Iskan? How? He couldn't possibly. He would have to explain about Kathleen, and his terrible sorrow. Why had she asked? He glanced at her and got his simple answer. She had asked out of impersonal interest. She was a writer, after all. She had just-wanted-to-know.

He ran one hand through his hair, gave her an uncertain look. "A lot of it's classified, actually."

They had reached the Plaza de Oriente. It was a small square of city park in the French style: meticulously symmetrical; crushed, creamy pink gravel; a statue in the middle; shrubs in strict formation; a few upright green benches; and faced on two sides with some handsome several-story mansions converted—Jane guessed—into privileged apartments, some with graceful balconies enclosed by paneled glass framed in original iron trim. Across a wide boulevard on the far side was the massive frontage of the National Palace.

They entered the square. No one was around. They sat on a bench.

"What happened to your leg?" Jane asked.

Jacklin caught his breath. No one ever asked. No

one was ever caught looking. Did he himself sometimes pretend it didn't exist?

But he met her gaze. "I was twenty. I was working on a case with my father. His life was about finished and he was doing odd jobs for the police. The case involved one of the undersides of our society that the people who gave us *The Godfather* affectionately refer to as 'the family.' I only saw the first movie and I walked out, and I didn't see the sequel. I don't believe in expensive homages to thugs; I don't find it entertaining. I find it ill advised to cast glamorous role models in criminal parts and distort the truth and then send our youngsters to sit in the darkness to be seduced by the thrills of blood and money. It gets all tangled up in the fabric of whatever values kids are allowed to have left by the time they're ten. It permeates their minds with the same mentality that spews out of our television sets. I call it setting a seriously shaky course for the future. The results are already showing up, though most people don't get it yet. They call it other things, like 'I just don't understand my children.' Like 'I don't really like going out after dark.' "

He stopped, astonished at himself. He had never spoken of this to anyone.

She was sitting there quietly. He would answer her question and be done with it, change the subject. "What happened to this leg was the result of that job I was on with my father. I was lucky. I was in good shape and I'd had about two seconds of warning they hadn't counted on." He looked down at his legs. "They'd come to get both of them, I guess." He gave a short laugh. "Like some shitty movie."

Across the street the high wooden doors of the palace opened and two sentries emerged, looking sleepy and rumpled. They leaned up against the doors, resting

their machine guns against their hips. On the boulevard, almost deserted until now, traffic was picking up.

Jacklin looked at his watch. "You said you wanted
to take some photographs? We should get to the Rastro
by nine."

She stood up, took a few shots. "It looks so pretty.
The early hour, everything fresh, nothing disturbed
yet." She didn't know what to say about his leg or what
he had expressed to her. She had felt so much in her
heart when he was speaking, but now she was shy
about responding. He seemed to have found a quicker
way into her—of course, it was his profession—than
she had into him.

She decided to cross the park to get some pictures
from the other side. At a distance, she would think of
what to say.

Jacklin remained sitting on the bench, his face tilted
to the sun rising over the city.

As in a film, the Gypsies dissolved out of the air, into
the scene—seemingly from nowhere. There were seven
of them, three buxom, dirty women in aprons and slip-
pers, two youths about sixteen in yellowed white dress
shirts, and two small, ragged children who began emit-
ting strident cries. The women, flapping their aprons
with both hands, ran toward Jane with high, gurgling
cries, and the youths followed, humming and chanting
in what appeared to be hysterical distress. They looked
poor and hungry and Jane thought, *Those pitiful children, I should give them something.*

One of the women threw her apron over Jane's face
and the other got behind her and they both seemed to
be trying to put their hands inside Jane's clothes. The
chanting and trilling continued while Jane fought off
suffocation.

Because she had first thought they were begging and
only then understood she was being assaulted and

robbed, she had got a late start. Within seconds her purse was halfway across the park in the hands of one of the little children.

Jane could not budge the women from her nor the apron from her face, and it was beginning to choke her. Blindly she elbowed and kicked. She felt her watch go. Next went the gold chain around her neck, which had belonged to her mother.

She assumed, though she couldn't see, that Jacklin had the other five Gypsies on him, and she knew that the two sentries across the road would run to assist them because what was happening was in plain view of the palace, so it was just a question of holding out another few seconds.

Jacklin had one child hanging off his neck who was apparently trying to put his eyes out, so Jacklin couldn't see either. The two youths had hold of his arms, one each, while the third woman with an apron was tearing his shirt open. Where, the Gypsies wondered, was his wallet? They had done the usual frisking and had come up with nothing, nor had he any jewelry on except his watch, which seemed to be nailed to his wrist. They couldn't get it off.

It was their anger and frustration that gave Jacklin his chance. He picked the moment of their maximum distraction, which was when he heard the youths instructing the woman to check whether he was wearing a security sock. She bent down to look, and their avid eyes followed her, whereupon Jacklin, who still couldn't see, kicked viciously in the direction of where he hoped the woman's face was, suddenly yanked the two youths to their knees with all the strength in his arms, and finally tore the child from around his neck and flung him into the bushes.

He ran the few yards to Jane, pulled both women off her, and roughly threw them to the ground. He had a

split second to look up and see that all around the
square, on the pretty old balconies and in the beautifully proportioned windows, those citizens who had got
up early had been lured by the sounds of distress and
were silently and raptly watching. As were the President's two sentries across the street.

And then the two youths and the third woman were
almost upon him again, so to warn them of his seriousness he gave each of the two women he had felled a
quick, hard kick. Jane, no longer blinded or buffeted,
now stood blinking, trying to regain her balance and
staring in horror and disbelief.

The two youths jumped Jacklin while the third
woman came from behind, climbed up on Jane's shoulders, and they both went down. Jacklin swerved his
body, socked one of the youths in the stomach, and
decked him, but the other was tougher, stronger, more
tenacious. Jacklin wrapped two hands around the boy's
throat, said, "Fuck you and your golden earrings,"
placed two fingers in the place where he had been
taught, and the youth's eyes turned toward heaven and
he slipped to the ground. Next Jacklin dealt again with
the first youth, who was on his feet again and crawling
up his back. He flipped him over so that the youth's
back and head hit some pretty old paving stones.

All three women were up again. They were trilling
and chanting and converging on Jacklin and Jane, and
Jane saw that the child who had been flung into the
bushes was crawling toward them, and in that moment,
which she never forgot, she understood that short of
killing the Gypsies, there could be no victory.

Jacklin, who knew there was a knife somewhere—
possibly two—had been banking on the fact that the
Gypsies would not use them in front of the sentries.
Methodically, he decked all three women and flung the
child away a good five feet into a patch of grass. Then

he picked up Jane in his arms and stepped out into the wide boulevard, despite the fact that there were four lanes of traffic. Everything came to a halt, as he knew it would at the sight of a man carrying a woman across a street.

Two of the Gypsy women, who had dragged themselves up and started to run after them, halted at the curb, hissing and chanting, but Jacklin knew that they would not step into the traffic to continue their pursuit.

Reaching the other side, he carried Jane to where the sentries were lolling, holding their nifty weapons and smoking cigarettes. He set her down directly in front of them.

"I'll stand at the curb and flag a taxi. You stay here and look into their eyes. Don't say anything, just look into their eyes. Promise me you'll do that."

The sentries stiffened and held their guns more tightly, and for a moment Jane thought they were going to do harm to Jacklin, his contempt was so palpable, his wrath so terrible.

He stood on the curb, waiting to spot a taxi, and she stood very still and very straight and stared into the eyes of the sentries, and she thought she understood why he had told her to do that even though it was impossible to explain in words.

The sentries began by returning her look boldly and even insolently and then they looked away and then they tried to ignore her and then, because she was still standing there, one of them made as if to use the butt of his automatic weapon to shove her back, but she did not move a muscle, she held her ground.

Behind her Jacklin waited at the curb for a taxi to show up and stared pointedly back at the faces on the gracious balconies and at the well-proportioned windows. Within ten seconds there was no one left on the balconies or in the windows.

In the taxi he wrapped himself in silence. Jane asked, "Did you kill that boy? The one who stayed on the ground?"

"His condition is temporary."

For the next few blocks neither spoke.

After a time he said to Jane, "Why did you show me the red shoes?"

"I don't know," she replied, also after a long time.

The taxi stopped for a light and he saw Jane start to stare out her window in distress, looking at something on the sidewalk she didn't understand. He saw her trying to make sense of it. He had seen such a thing before, and he knew how they trained the animals for it and he prayed she would not ask.

What Jane was staring at was a pitifully ravaged, mangy little goat balancing without moving any part of himself on an elevated, crude pedestal, his four little feet forced together in a knot on a space no larger than the tiny saucer that supported him.

Jane did not know, as Jacklin did, that the goat had been trained to do this by having his feet burned over and over on hot charcoal until he understood he must do the owner's bidding. The owner, a large, untidy man, listened to fado music from a Lisbon station on his portable radio, and banged at a little drum, inviting the few passersby to contribute coins in homage to this informal Sunday morning entertainment.

The animal himself was very still, almost lifeless. His eyes were downcast, averted from all around him.

Jane could not take her eyes from the little goat. She had seen that physical language, that particular expression before. Where had she seen it, felt it? What was the word for the look on that animal's face? That heart-stopping meekness. Not modesty; it was infinity. It was abject, ultimate surrender.

And then she understood it was shame.

She became conscious that Jacklin was watching her. She tried to speak but could not.

The taxi moved away.

She swallowed a few times, tried again. "I can't explain," she tried to say in an even voice, "but that is the most terrible thing I have ever seen." She paused, then was driven to go on. "Terrible to my heart."

She wasn't looking at him, she was staring straight ahead, trying to hold herself together, but she didn't think she was going to be able to manage that.

"What," she asked him—as if conversationally, because she had either to continue talking or to permit herself to scream—"is the most terrible thing you've ever seen?"

She turned to look at him. He had not, she now realized, taken his eyes from her once. His expression was suffused with compassion. But he did not seem to have a reply.

Café bars were rolling up their shutters for the day. Several blocks ahead through the narrow canyons between the buildings, the homely banners and awnings of the Rastro could be seen. The taxi carried them through the streets.

"Why do you think," Jane asked, still finding it difficult to bring any sound from her throat, "all this is happening to us today?"

After a long time he spoke. "It's why I asked about the red shoes."

22

Jane returned to America. She surprised everyone by taking up her life again in the country. She was said to keep mostly to herself, but then, she had a book to do.

On the last day of the year, expecting guests from the city, she spent the morning looking in the tiny surrounding hamlets for what she would need over the holiday weekend, and this took her farther than she usually went. She found herself driving home through Rigby Creek.

Halfway down the beautiful, ruined main street, she suddenly turned on her left-hand-turn indicator because it looked as if that dry cleaner was still there. Hadn't Barrett said, at the end, that it had closed? She would find out if it was still in operation, and if so, open. There was a ladder against the house—and the sign in the window had been temporarily turned so she couldn't see it.

She parked in the driveway and quickly ran up the porch steps. She opened the door and went in. In a corner there was a small child sitting in a high chair, watching a portable television set on the counter.

Why didn't I like this place? And then she remembered the young woman with all the makeup and Barrett showing off. Just then someone came around the corner of the curtain. It was the same young woman, though she seemed to have gained weight and didn't look so lacquered together. In the same moment Jane heard a door open at the back and the sound of a toilet flushing.

The young woman seemed so surprised at seeing Jane she couldn't get her breath.

"Honey?" A man's voice came from behind the curtain. And then he appeared.

Barrett.

His face went white. So, Jane knew, had hers. Her heart was pounding so hard, she could feel it beating on the outside of her back. She waited for Barrett to say something.

He cast an expressionless glance at the young woman, who now leaned over the counter and said to Jane, "You think you still own him? I know all about you. I'm surprised you have the nerve to show your face here."

Jane looked at Barrett, but he looked eyeless, and so slight and so transparent that a strong light might have shone through him.

"He was in your power," the young woman continued. "Now he's free. Tell her you're free, Barrett."

Wistfully, Barrett smiled into the corner of the room —as if at an invisible cat—then disappeared behind the curtain.

The child in the high chair began to sniffle. The young woman went over to him, picked him up. She said to Jane over her shoulder, "Don't bother us again," and also went behind the curtain.

Jane went out, stumbled on the steps, fell. Banged her elbow and scraped her knee. She got up, went to her car, got inside, and backed out of the driveway. She did not remember getting home.

She called Jerry. He was out. She called Hal. "They discovered, in the course of things, where he was," he told her, and added in his blunt way, "Damned if I knew how to tell you, or if you still cared."

At dawn Barrett awoke. He lit a cigarette and lay there smoking in the dark. Beside him, Dora slept. She sure had spunk, the way she had talked to Jane. It was practically the only thing he had liked about her in the beginning, that spunk of hers.

If it hadn't been for Dora taking him in, where would he have gone, what would he have done? In many ways she was a lot smarter than Jane. Jane had seduced him with her intellectualism and her artistic talk, but as Dora said after she had forced him to tell her all about Jane, "Life's not about mind-fucking, it's about building toward happiness. It's about the American dream. Like us." She had really said that and she had squeezed his hand and with his other hand he had squeezed one of her breasts and it had been more or less like that ever since.

In those days he still felt himself superior to Dora, but life with her had taught him about the things that really mattered. Getting value for a buck. Not letting anyone put something over on you. Observing the traditions and national holidays. Not laughing at them and being blasé but honoring them. A brand-new outfit for Dora on Easter was a must, and dinner out at a strictly grown-up restaurant on Mother's Day. Dora was solid ground under his feet. A new car every three years, she said. Building toward happiness. She had now requested an engagement ring.

He had not been pleased when she had found out about his thirty-five thousand dollars. He had been obliged to put it all toward a down payment on her dream of buying the dry-cleaning business from the present owners, and the house it occupied as well. Her ex-husband paid child support, which took care of the grocery bills for the three of them. And the cleaning business was doing okay, though not great. They lived upstairs.

The disappointing thing about having been forced to spend all his money on a house was that there was no land. There they were in the country, but the place was right on the street and it was noisy and full of fumes from the traffic. But it was just, Dora said, an interim step. Building toward happiness meant that you bought and traded up, bought and traded up. They'd been taken aback by the stock market crash that fall, but one of Dora's friends who worked as a secretary at the local savings and loan told them not to worry, real estate in America always went up, never down.

Barrett got up and went to the window. Standing there, looking into the darkness, he thought about putting his head through the glass.

He had suspected for some time there might be something terrible going on inside him, so during the day he concentrated in an obsessive way on his daily routine. Except when he was sick (and this was frequently), Dora's little boy, Eddie, had to be taken to the day care center every morning and picked up every afternoon. Their dry-cleaning business opened at eight-thirty and there were always piles of clothes to be pressed. He was proud of having learned the knack of ironing so fast. And it was pleasant work. He stayed behind the curtain, kept the TV on, and drank beer.

Dora stayed out front, dealt with the customers, and did all the paperwork.

Weekends were also very busy. Dora wanted a nice home. New wallpaper, laminated countertops, cup hooks, a cabinet for the television. Dora planned every-thing and he did all the work, nights and weekends. Neither of them had any cash now except what was coming in from the business. They had strapped them-selves in order to buy the place. They were locked, bound to each other. This was the thing that gave him the most satisfaction; in fact, he had never felt so secure in his life. No matter what happened, financially it was impossible for them to split up.

It had not been his fault that he had had to make a life with Dora. It was Jane's fault. Lunch on the terrace at Torcello had been heady, but he had never known from one minute to the next whether he would make a false move and lose her. Or had it been Sara he'd been there with? He remembered the little boat with striped blue cushions and lace curtains heading into the rushes. It had been Sara. She had read to him from Ruskin and Byron. He had watched a golden butterfly with black stripes and smoked a long, thin cigar.

At least while Dora built for happiness he would be spared the agony and torment of the masquerades of his former days. Dora was a little grinding on the ear and the sensibilities, but she wasn't as hard work as Jane and Sara had been.

Or Theo. Theo, dead in the river. In that first split second when he'd looked over the deck and seen her, he'd thought she was playing a trick on him, that she would spring up shrieking "Surprise!" He'd looked down and seen her upturned face just under the surface of the pale green water near the bank, her hair fanning out, caught, entangled in the roots of the great tree. She look drowned. But it couldn't be. She and Una had been out in the boat, Theo dictating, Una taking notes, as they often did, Theo with a vodka and a cigarette, talking a mile a minute and laughing, and Una taking down everything she said.

But now where was the boat, the oars, Una? He continued to grip the railing and look down at the submerged face, the hair fanning out. He was having a hallucination.

Standing at the railing, he continued to pretend to himself that Theo must be playing with him, but of course he knew underneath that she wasn't, that she couldn't be in water by herself, he'd known it always. She'd asked him never to tell anyone. Made him swear.

And he hadn't told anyone, ever, until the night when he had—venally, tragically—told Una. He had told her merely to gain ascendance, and out of mild sadism, to impress her with how much closer he was to Theo than anyone, and how much he knew about her that no one else did.

He'd had no idea that something was terribly wrong with Una, that she was sick, terribly sick, sick enough to have not only told but boasted to Theo about her own conquest of him, sick enough to have overturned the boat or pushed Theo out of it, he didn't know, he didn't want to know.

And then Una had come to him and told him in an excited way that Theo was dead and that now they could be together always. He had turned to ice. His brain had never commanded him with such precision. He had looked at his watch, then gone and put on Theo's wig and Theo's clothes and driven her car to the little filling station down the road where all the members of Theo's household were known. He filled up her car and told the attendant that he (Theo) had to drive into the city and hoped he (Theo) would be back by ten because there was a movie on television that he (Theo) wanted to catch. Then he had turned around and gone back to the house, divested himself of the disguise, packed it into his duffel bag, and because Una refused to drive him to the bus station, he walked.

It was still only four o'clock in the afternoon, so he would be well on his way to the East Coast—with an alibi—before such time as the coroner, faced with the evidence from the gas station attendant, would eventually establish as the hour of death.

Thus Barrett, in his desperation to place himself in the clear, had unwittingly given Una the possibility of an alibi as well.

At first, while he was getting himself up as Theo to go to the filling station, she thought he was doing this fantastically clever thing in order to help her establish her own innocence. While he was gone she took out her suitcase and packed in preparation to go with him to New York, but when he came back from his impersonation, she began to understand that his intention was to leave without her.

Barrett, suddenly afraid she might try to kill him too, had lied a little to give her hope, just enough so that she would let him leave without her. He had told her it was only fair if he went back east to tell his girlfriend himself that he was breaking off with her. He had managed, when she wasn't looking, to get his address and phone number card out of the Rolodex she kept for Theo, then he wrote out his telephone number for Una with one digit wrong. Even if she asked Information she wouldn't get him; the number was listed in Marly's name, which Una did not know.

Over the long, dead hours of the trip between the two coasts in a bus that smelled of overripe apples and latrine deodorant, he had gone over and over his decision at the river not to report Una to the police. There had been only the two of them there with Theo on the last day. Emma Grace and the housekeeper were well aware of his sexual forays into Una's room, and he knew from somewhere inside his gut he might have been charged as an accessory. And Una being so crazy, she might have put the whole blame on him, whereas no matter how mad Una got at him now, she knew well enough that the best course for her was also silence. The only thing he had to fear was that someone at the police would figure out what had really happened. Or that someone else besides himself—and Una—was still alive who knew about Theo's fear of water.

Just once on that bus trip had he allowed himself to remember that last morning at the river. It had dawned hot and lazy, with bees buzzing and a soft drifty sky like down south, and he had been up early and out of the house, smelling the heat, wishing there were horses to groom, fields to fly through, princesses to court. Strolling toward the bank, he picked one of the last flowers of the season, tucked it behind his ear.

Then he had spied Theo high up in the great tree, sitting on a massive branch, her back against the trunk.

"Beau?" she called. "Come on up."

He was flooded with the sweetness of memory, transported to the fields of home. The frightened skinny boy astride the golden girl. The beginning of time. He swung himself up into the tree and plopped himself beside her. He took the flower from behind his ear, placed it behind one of hers.

She ruffled his hair, smiled at him. "Remember the willow we planted for Daisy? You want to go home with me, Beau? I think I'm going to go home for a while and come clean. I really need to do that. You need to come clean?" She laughed, then. "As if I didn't know the answer to *that*."

He scratched his head, looked as old and wizened as

he could, and said in a wavery voice, "Don't know how I fucked up my life so much, Miss Lily."

"You mean so soon, jerkeroo. Come here." She gave him a long kiss. "Yum."

"Am I the best?" he asked, already busy with her. "Am I still the best? Have we ever done it in a tree?" He looked down. "You understand, one false move and we fucking kill ourselves."

"Take your hands off me, Mr. Rhett!" she shrieked. "Wait'll Miss Scarlett catch you!" She pretended to fall out of the tree.

How could she do that? It made his heart stop. And he knew she knew he would catch her.

"That is positively not in the book," he said, dragging her up to the branch again. She gave him a veiled look which he saw was admiring and which inflamed him and he asked again, feeling tears in his throat, "Am I the best?"

"Don't be so vain. You coming with me or not?"

"I guess."

"Who'll you have to extricate yourself from? You still with that girl from up north, what's her name? Marly?"

"Never you mind." He touched her hair.

"You understand we're not starting an affair or anything. That's not the purpose."

"I understand. We'll just discuss Dostoevsky and all." He peeked up her shorts.

"Pure thoughts, Brother Beau, pure thoughts. We're going home to cleanse ourselves of our sins. Examine our consciences."

"It's supposed to work in reverse order."

"We'll help each other. Figure out why we keep picking the wrong people."

"How do you know I do?"

"I know you keep picking the wrong something.

What else could be keeping you back?" She ruffled his hair again. "Didn't anyone ever tell you that it's a sin against God not to use the gifts he gave you?"

"I'm using them, honey." He looked away because he thought the pain in his eyes would show.

"To his greater glory. You're supposed to use them to his greater glory." She sighed. "Listen, it'll be super. We'll ride, we'll eat fried chicken and deviled eggs and drink real Coke, and we'll lie on the grass and look up at that sky. It's always summer there. Beau?"

"What, hon?"

"It's going to be great." She leaned her head back, closed her eyes against the filtered sunlight coming through the branches. She tucked the white flower more firmly behind her ear.

He heard sniffling coming from Eddie's room. He got up, went into the tiny bedroom. The boy was asleep, coughing slightly. He covered him up, put his plump little arms under the blankets. Sometimes when he made love to Dora he pretended to himself he was Eddie. Not often, but sometimes he needed it badly. It helped to shut out the memory of everything since he'd grown up. It was a way to come clean with himself in the most fantastical of contexts. It had also come in handy after that terrible day he'd had to give a deposition in connection with the murder. It had been arranged so he could do it locally, down at the town hall. He had told Dora he was going to the dentist. He had stopped at a bar on the way home and become very drunk very fast and even then he had had sex with her for hours trying to blot out the horror. Still, at least there *had* been two lucky strokes—apparently Una had confessed to everything, that was one, and Hal Donovan, in doing everything to protect Jane from the media, had obviously had to insure that Barrett's role be obscured as well. Not a single reporter had been waiting for him outside the room where he had given the deposition. Of course, once it became a case and went to court, everything might be different. It could turn into a circus. But that was a long way off. And while he didn't understand how these things worked, maybe there wouldn't even be a court case, maybe there'd just be a hearing.

He went back to bed, lit another cigarette. The alarm clock would ring in another four minutes. Then he would fuck Dora and then they would get up and turn on the television and start another day.

He had known finer places, finer times. Yes. Yes. But never a haven as safe as this.

When spring came it was a wet one and there was snow as well. Barrett, standing at the counter, looked out at the thick flakes falling outside the picture window he had installed. He had wanted a real window with wooden mullions that would go with the period of the house, but Dora didn't see things that way. She wanted a picture window, one of those aluminum jobs, and she didn't want to hear any more about his impractical ideas.

Barrett, always made moody by the weather, was particularly moody today. He looked down at the plastic counter and the plastic pot with its plastic flowers and at the box of safety pins. Dora was upstairs in her plaid flannel robe with the crest in gold thread on the breast pocket which he hated so much, doing the paperwork for their tax returns, and had only just found out that he didn't exactly recall ever having done one on his own. She was in a very bad temper, not helped by the fact that the guy on the news last night had said the country was definitely going into a recession.

The door opened and in a gust of wind and blowing snow a man in a great-looking outdoorsy jacket and a great-looking navy-and-red sweater came in, shaking the snowflakes from his hair. He stamped his feet and took off his gloves.

"How may I help you?" Barrett recited dutifully. Dora took the position that the phrase was the dernier cri in commercial politesse and would not be argued out of it, even when Barrett pointed out to her that everyone who came through the door knew fucking well how they could be helped.

"I'm lost," the man said with a smile. "Even if I could see through the windshield, I started off without a map and the gas station doesn't have one. The doughnut shop is closed, so I thought I'd come in here to ask for directions. I'm looking for a road that should be somewhere around here." He pulled a piece of paper out of his pocket and looked at it. "Sanford Lane."

He was about Barrett's age, maybe a little older, and from his clothes and his manner Barrett knew he wasn't from around there. He had an attractive, kind of educated voice, and Barrett wished he would stay talking to him for a while. He had always been more confident with women than with men, but there was something about this fellow that made Barrett's heart ache with nostalgia for he knew not what.

"Golly," Barrett said. "I never heard of that street. But I have a county map in the back. Let me get it." He raced around the curtain, raced back, and spread the map on the counter so that the two of them could look at it. Leaning over it together, he caught the man eyeing him.

"You have the face of an actor," the man said, not

evidently to flatter, merely with an acknowledging nod
of his head.

Barrett's heart leapt. "I've done a little off-Broadway," he said modestly, but by the time he spoke his
next line, he was a good inch taller and his diction had
altered to the clear, precise tones he remembered using
in the past but that Dora had now decreed made him
sound like a sissy. "Actually," he improvised, "I don't
know a drying cycle from a box of starch. My sister and
her husband run this business. I just come up from the
city when I'm in a dry period, and of course I help out."
He produced a winning smile. "Where are you from?"

"I'm also from the city," the man said. He stood
back on his heels, the way a man should, Barrett noticed. "Maybe I've seen you in something."

"Not just lately." Barrett took a cigarette from his
pack and tapped it elegantly on the counter, keeping the
flick of his wrist as graceful as possible, wishing he had
that beautiful sterling cigarette case Jane—or was it
Sara—had given him, but Dora liked it and used it to
keep her false fingernails in. "My agent died a few
months ago. I've been dragging my feet about taking on
new representation. I had such regard for him and"—
he paused emotionally—"it's hard to get used to the
idea of trusting someone new to guide my career."

"I guess," the man said sympathetically. He looked
down at the map, squinted, and pointed. "That must be
it, there."

Barrett looked. "Yes. You take a left when you leave
here, go to the first set of lights, about a mile, then pick
up Route Twenty-one." By now he knew his voice had
hit a rich, mellifluous note. It excited him to hear himself. And the man had given him several interested
looks by now.

"I gather you're visiting up here?" Barrett asked.

"Pretty country." The man folded the map, handed

it to Barrett. He looked at his watch. "Better get going. Thanks."

Barrett had not lost his gifts. He sensed the man didn't want to leave. The knowing of that excited him. He rose slightly on the balls of his feet, then rocked back down again and then up. "Let me present you with a little something to take to your hosts. I happen to have a long-stemmed red rose back there in the refrigerator. It's my sister's birthday, and I was going to give it to her later, but I'll have time to get another." Actually, he had the rose in readiness to give to Dora the instant she came downstairs from doing the taxes. But he wanted to give this man something, something to remember him by. He was fairly sure by now that the man was going to come into his life and that he was a theatrical producer or in television.

"Good of you," the man said politely, "but I really can't take your sister's rose."

Barrett turned on the ball of one foot, ballet style. "I insist." He disappeared behind the curtain and came back with a red rose wrapped in plastic with a large red and gold bow.

"First we'll take off this tacky bow," Barrett said with a conspiratorial smile. He removed it, tossed it aside, and held out the rose. "For your hostess." He wished he dared ask who it was. He was sure the man was visiting one of the many big properties in the area used as country places by important people in the entertainment world.

The man took the rose. "Let me pay you, at least." He reached into his pocket.

Barrett held up his hand. "Please. I grew up in the South, where we know about hospitality to strangers." He felt new blood coursing through his veins. He was wildly happy.

"You've lost your accent." The man paused. "You sound authentically Yankee to me."

"I have many accents. My training, of course."

"Of course."

Barrett reached for a little pile of cards on the counter.

"Next time you're in the area, stop by." He saw the man looking at the card and added with a dismissive smile, "Sorry about the cutesy artwork on it. My sister chose it." The main thing was, the telephone number was on it.

The man put the card in his pocket. "Thanks very much. Well, good-bye."

Barrett was sorry there was no way to put off the moment. Wistfully he said, "Fare thee well."

As the man, buttoning up his great jacket again, walked to the door, Barrett noticed for the first time that he had a slight limp.

Jacklin got into the car, turned on the motor, the windshield wipers, the defogger, and backed out of the driveway. He headed down the road and made a right turn. After a few miles he turned onto a road he knew.

Jacklin liked to draw tidy lines under things. It had been important for him to draw a tidy line under Rossignol. His own involvement had been over since the night he had confronted Una and turned everything over to the police, but there had been this one last thing he'd needed to do.

Barrett had now been seen, looked over, noted. It was time to put him away.

But how, now that he understood, did one do that? They'd been right about him, Barrett's women. All of them. Caught in the haunted light (filled with what lush secrets?) behind the gray eyes, the slow smile that swore purity and redemption, the voice tuned by God, the sweetness, he, Jacklin, had not wanted to walk out on the man; he had been shaken, horrified by his own arrogance at not once—ever—having given Barrett his due, at not once—ever—having forgiven him one moment of his existence. Could something possibly be done to help him out of his present situation? Otherwise, spiritually, he would die there in that place, in that life—

Jacklin brought the car to a full stop. He rolled down the window and threw Barrett's rose as far as he could. Noiselessly, it landed at the edge of a snowy field where three cows lay dreamily under the thick, falling flakes. Then he rolled up the window and continued carefully on his way through the white silence.

And accepted the final lesson in the affair.

By the time he got to the house the snow had almost stopped and the landscape had crystallized. The branches on the great trees sparkled. As far as the eye could see, everything was white and silver. There was a great hush over the land. He drove carefully down the long driveway, softly skidding this way, that way, and parked by the front door.

Jane came around the corner of the house. There were snowflakes glinting in her hair.

He got out of the car and kissed her for a long time, then reached into the backseat and pulled out his green canvas bookbag, some clothes on a hanger, and a fresh, dewy bunch of spring flowers he had bought in the city.

She put one arm around his waist and they walked to the house together. They were still new at this. It showed in their glad, exploratory conversation, in their glad, exploratory looks. She told him about her week, he told her about his, leaving out the last bit—his having stopped in Rigby Creek. Would he ever tell her? That he, too, had been beguiled by the angel?

There was still an hour before dark, so they went out to skate on the frozen brook. She'd been shoveling it before he came. Jacklin, despite the leg, had come on

well during the winter. He was now able to whiz
around quite expertly for long minutes at a time without falling. "It's because I'm a guy," he'd laughed and
boasted, grabbing her fists and holding them when
she'd tried to punch him out. Jane still used a kitchen
chair for psychological support—pushing it ahead of
her on the ice—even though he had tried to convince
her she no longer needed it, and teased her about it.

So the cold winter woods often rang with their
laughter. Jacklin, who in the end had not been able to
contain the curiosity in his heart and had traveled to
Madrid and waited outside the Palace Hotel for seven
hours that day in order to make their meeting look like
mere chance, now looked across the ice at Jane. He
loved her with all his soul.

And she, skating toward him, pushing the chair
ahead of her, looked up at the stars just beginning to
come out in the navy blue sky, and said a prayer to
them, that she and Ciaran might be allowed to keep
their love.

Over in Rigby Creek that night Dora was so excited she
could hardly get to sleep, because after all, the main
attraction about Barrett from the beginning had been
his aura of glamour. When he'd started dropping in on
her she hadn't been able to believe her luck. Not in her
life had she ever expected to meet someone who had
been in the movies and on TV, who had played polo
and known famous people and entertained them in his
home, and who spoke so classy. Barrett had been a god.
Shining. Beautiful. Once he had moved in with her, he
had completely changed.

That afternoon she had come downstairs from doing
the taxes, frankly real pissed at Barrett—why did she
always have to do the important stuff, the difficult stuff,

while he just watched television and ironed? Her mood had shown in her expression. She was ready to pick a fight.

Upon seeing her, Barrett swooped her up in his arms and whirled her around and told her about the producer who had stopped by and had been wowed and would surely cast him in a show. After that, who knows, it might be Hollywood.

They had had steaks for dinner. And champagne. Barrett taught her how to pronounce the name of it.

Now he was asleep beside her.

So it had been worth it after all, the trouble he had caused her. Now she would get the things he had led her to expect from the beginning.

The truth was—though she hated to admit it—he had been, well, kind of disappointing. She had waited for his famous friends to call, but he seemed to have no friends at all. He explained that Jane had turned them all against him and that his code of honor as a gentleman prevented him from setting those people straight. He also explained that he'd been spiritually broken by the relationship and that he was adrift and needed Dora—a real woman—to help him get on his feet again.

Well, she'd certainly tried to do that, in spades. And to be fair to him, he was the most loving man she had ever known. He would do anything for her. It was just that without her ever being able to put her finger on exactly how it had happened, he had become, well, kind of a burden. She felt disloyal saying this to herself. Just to look at him, the classy way he did everything, the things he knew about, her friends had been simply bowled over. She had never been so proud. Mine, she had said to herself, *mine*. And Barrett's lovemaking, she'd never known the likes of that either, the riches were almost embarrassing. She would have been satisfied with far less.

The weird thing was that there was this kind of sissy side to him. He spent more time in front of the mirror than she did. He used cream on his face, on his neck, on his chest, like a woman. He plucked his eyebrows. Well, none of that really bothered her. He was a man, all right, she could tell the world that. Wow and double wow.

The real problem was something else. The thing she had no name for. You couldn't exactly call it "lazy." After all, look at the stuff he took care of. But he had to be told to do it. He had to be reminded, encouraged, sometimes shouted at. He would sometimes say in the stagy voice she had loved so much in the beginning, "My dear, you'll have to be more tolerant. I've never been part of the working classes."

Not even sure how much of it was a joke, she didn't really understand what he was saying, but she sensed the meaning and it had hurt. A lot of things had hurt. She'd suspected at the beginning he didn't think she was good enough. She suspected at times he was comparing her with Jane, with other women he had known. She'd come downstairs and he'd look at her and then glance into a corner, smiling wistfully.

Not good enough? She, who had taken in a distraught, weeping man, supported him, taught him the dry-cleaning business, orchestrated the purchase of their home, their business, taught him the practical rules of life, how to build for happiness? She, who now literally ran the business as well as their lives?

He refused to go out, except to nearby places. And he was sick a lot. He spent days lying in bed, watching TV. Dora liked TV—didn't everyone? But Barrett wanted it on day and night. He liked to sit with little Eddie on his lap, watching dumb cartoons with him. He would watch anything as long as Eddie was happy. Anything.

But at the end of the day, at the end of every hurt, every confusion, he got to her. Tears rolled down her face. Strange, bewildering, beautiful man. He had fallen out of the sky, appeared to Dora, deprived daughter of the gods. She didn't understand him, not really, but she knew with her heart he was her ticket to happiness.

And now their sparkling future was practically assured. He would change, make her really proud, make her glad she had been so lucky and so smart as to give him everything—from the first moment—that he had required of her. She knew, with her shrewdness, that he would have gone—that day he'd left Jane—to anyone. She knew that it hadn't been her looks or even her personality but her on-the-spot availability that had drawn him. That hurt too, but only a little now. She had been there. She had caught him. And held him, and now she would reap her reward.

They would marry. They would have a house, not on the highway but a house like Jane's, with a garden and servants and acres of privacy. She had stopped taking the pill that very night. She would have Barrett's child. They would be happy. And he would always be grateful to her for having seen him through his bad time, for having been so patient and loving.

She looked over at him and her heart filled. She, Dora, had saved him. She, Dora, would from now on have the best life ever. They had only to wait for that producer to call.

She nudged Barrett. He woke from his dream mumbling, "What is it, honey?"

Dora giggled. Lust in her limbs. She whispered something in his ear.

———•———

And in Los Angeles, where the fall of evening is brief, the small, boxy space of colorless twilight framed by the barred window high over Una's motionless, brooding, seated young figure became—in the blink of an eye —black, almost as the night.